A Sinner No More

THE SINS & SCANDALS SERIES

KELLY BOYCE

The Sins & Scandals Series

While there are those who spend their time in modest pursuits, upholding propriety befitting the lords and ladies of the ton, it would seem that for others scandal is just a sin away...

AN INVITATION TO SCANDAL
A SCANDALOUS PASSION
A SINFUL TEMPTATION
THE LADY'S SINFUL SECRET
SURRENDER TO SCANDAL
A SINNER NO MORE
THE SWEETEST SIN
A MOST SCANDALOUS CHRISTMAS
A HINT OF SCANDAL

For Georgina Haines, one of the loveliest ladies I have ever had the pleasure to know.

Chapter One

There were a few things he knew for sure. To start, he had an unwavering awareness of the pain in his head that refused to relent and give him even a modicum of peace. Following that, was the fact that when he attempted to rise up out of the bed he'd been laying in for days on end, his head swam as if caught in a whirlwind, forcing him back down into a prone position. He also knew his name was Lord Hawksmoor, as that was how the servants referred to him when they came to fluff his pillows, change his sheets, feed him, and assist him to the privy, ensuring he did not fall into the pot when his legs gave out. He did not care to think about that rather humiliating event as it ruffled his pride, which he apparently possessed in abundance.

But beyond these few, rather limited truths, the wealth of his knowledge dropped into a rather embarrassing deficit when compared to what he did not know.

Such as, where he was. Or why. Or how and when the wound to his head had occurred, or who had inflicted it. The rather serious-minded gentleman who checked in on him periodically was of little assistance in any of these matters. The man said little and gave away even less. Mostly he asked questions to which Hawksmoor had no answers. Not that he admitted to such. Acknowledging his mind had become a sieve through which all the things he had once known had leaked out served no purpose that he could ascertain.

What did one do with someone who had lost his mind? Send him off to Bedlam to be forgotten? And how was it he could remember that a place like Bedlam even existed and yet not recall his given name? Or who had given it to him?

Not a stellar commentary on his sanity.

He reached up and touched the bandage wrapped around his head, careful to avoid the area along his temple and beyond as that gave him the most pain. He must look a fine picture.

Ah, there was that pride again.

He had requested a looking glass from one of the servants, but they had shuffled off without promising anything. He should have asked the pretty young woman with the blonde hair. She seemed a nicer sort than the others. At least she looked at him instead of averting her gaze, though he doubted she was aware of his scrutiny. She only came late in the evenings and he always pretended to be asleep, watching her through his lashes.

Awaiting her arrival became a game of sorts, albeit a rather one-sided amusement. He'd pretend to be fast asleep, and then attempt to guess what she was doing based on the sounds she made. Some were easy. The pouring of fresh water into the ewer on the bureau. Straightening the blankets around him. That was a particular favorite. She smelled of wild roses freshly bloomed on the vine, which led him to discover that wild roses were his most favorite flower. At least they were now. Other movements were more difficult to ascertain. One time, the chair in the far corner out of his line of sight creaked only to be followed by a long silence. Had she sat there? If so, why?

He'd longed to open his eyes and inquire, but feared if he

did, she might slip away like a wraith and not return. A horrible thought, as her arrival provided the highlight of his day. There was something about her. More than her obvious beauty, which was indeed remarkable. But her appeal went beyond that. Something in him wanted to reach out to her. To keep her safe. Which was rather ridiculous given he did not know her any more than he knew himself.

He had, however, given her a name. Rose, naturally. It seemed fitting. He hadn't done that with any of the other servants, but she was special. He wasn't sure why, but there it was.

The door to his bedroom opened slowly and he immediately shut his eyes. The delicate scent of wild roses drifted in to greet him as she quietly moved about the room like a whisper. She conducted her duties, pouring fresh water into the ewer, straightening the blankets at the end of the bed. As she drew closer, he shut his eyes completely so as not to give himself away.

She hovered over him like a little hummingbird. He held his breath. Waited.

He stilled as the tips of her fingers pressed lightly against his chest, just above his heart that beat a little faster at her touch. Such an intimacy had not occurred before and he did not know what to make of it. No one had touched him in such a way in—well, he did not know how long.

"Thomas? Are you awake?"

Her words—the use of a given name—rattled him. *Thomas?* She knew him? Well enough to call him by his given name? He'd been about to open his eyes when she leaned in suddenly, her lips brushing his in the merest hint of a kiss.

His eyes snapped open and the breath he'd held rushed from his lungs.

She straightened immediately, but he managed to catch her hand where it rested upon his chest.

"Do you know me?" She snatched her hand away and took a swift step back, color blossoming in her cheeks. He instantly regretted his actions. He held his hand out to stop her retreat. "No, please. Don't go."

Too late. She'd moved beyond his reach and quickly turned away, hurrying through the door before he could call her back.

She knew him. She'd *kissed* him! The realization rocked him. How could that be? Who was she? Who was he to her? Question upon question tumbled through his aching head.

She was a servant. He was a lord. Yet Rose had addressed him by his given name without hesitation, indicating a level of familiarity well beyond lord and servant.

He had grown certain the place in which he currently resided belonged to the serious gentleman who went by the name of Mr. Bowen. Had he—that is to say, had *they*—but no. Surely, he had not compromised his host's servant. Had he? Did that have something to do with the wound to the side of his head? No. He couldn't have. He had better sense and scruples than that. Didn't he?

Doubt crept in and a sick feeling pooled in his stomach. How else would Rose know him well enough to call him Thomas?

He twisted the sheets in his fist and let out a guttural growl. Curse his damnable memory! While its loss was enough to send anyone to Bedlam, he suspected the questions left behind from his memory's disappearance would be what finally sent him over the edge.

Madalene splashed cold water on her burning cheeks after retreating to the small office below stairs allocated to the housekeeper. Fear and shock burned through her. What had she been thinking? She'd never touched him before, or deigned to call him by his given name. She'd only thought—

Heat flared again, mixed with a healthy dose of reproach. She'd *kissed* him!

She hadn't been thinking. Not logically. Not with forethought or prudence. Did she truly believe if Lord Hawksmoor heard her voice, if she spoke his given name, he would awaken, collect himself, and return to his scandalous lifestyle none the wiser that she had been so near?

Perhaps, if only she hadn't behaved like a prize idiot and kissed him. It was just that he looked so helpless laying there, his head bandaged and those thick lashes casting crescent shadows beneath his eyes in the dim lamplight.

She groaned. Stupid, foolish girl! Already Mr. Bowen had questioned her connection to the viscount when weeks earlier, before he'd been viciously attacked and nearly killed, Lord Hawksmoor had requested Mr. Bowen provide him with a proper introduction to her. Why had he done such a thing? It was the height of lunacy! To begin with, they were already acquainted making an introduction unnecessary. To end with, he was a Peer of the Realm and she but a servant. A proper introduction was hardly required, as they should not associate with one another based on this fact alone. Yet they had, hadn't they? But that was five years ago.

Five years, four months and twelve days, to be exact.

She dropped into one of the two straight back chairs set around the small table where she took her tea and closed her eyes, groaning yet again.

Lord Hawksmoor's brazenness at making such an odd

request should not have surprised her. He had long ago stopped being the man she had once known. He had changed since the last time she'd seen him, under circumstances best forgotten.

She stood and looked at her reflection in the warped looking glass. Once upon a time, he had been a perfectly lovely young man. Everything one could expect in a gentleman. Kind and handsome, generous and sweet. Had she mention handsome?

"Stop it!" She splashed her face once more, hoping the cold water would jolt some sense into her. The man she had known no longer existed. Lord Hawksmoor had buried him deep, smothered him under the darker, more menacing version of himself that London had come to know as The Hawk.

It was that version that resided only three floors above her. And yet...

Yet when he looked at her just now, it was the young man she remembered whose eyes implored her. The voice of an old friend that called her to come back.

Instead, she'd run away. Embarrassed, fearful.

For the first week after his arrival, Madalene had worried he would not survive his wounds. He'd been bruised and battered until the handsome face she remembered was barely recognizable. For days on end he'd languished, drifting in and out of consciousness. Dr. Bartlett had cautioned Lord Hawksmoor might never regain full use of his senses, if he survived at all, and despite the length of time since she'd last seen him, she'd realized she could not imagine a world where he did not exist.

"Miss Cosgrove?" Mr. Bowen's head poked through the door of her small office after a brief knock. She straightened quickly and reached for a small cloth, dabbing at the water on her skin. "Forgive me, am I disturbing you?"

"No, not at all." She forced a smile and set the cloth down onto the table next to the ewer of water, conscious of a droplet she had missed sliding down from her temple, past her ear. She resisted the urge to swipe it away. "Might I help you with something, sir?"

Many of the servants in the Bowen household had trouble getting used to the fact their employer felt as comfortable below stairs as he did above, but Madalene found his ease in dealing with people regardless of their station rather refreshing. Given his background, his behavior was hardly surprising. Mr. Bowen had been raised as a ward of Lord and Lady Ellesmere, but he was not a member of the ton, though he had recently married Lady Rebecca, and called Lords Blackbourne, Huntsleigh and Glenmor amongst his closest friends.

And now he had taken in Lord Hawksmoor.

Mr. Bowen stepped more fully into the office, his lean frame filling the small space. "As a matter of fact, I believe it is I who can help you."

"Me?" Did she require help? Oh heavens, had Lord Hawksmoor said something? Had he spoken to Mr. Bowen of their past association? That she had kissed him? Fear cut into her belly. She had taken such a foolish, foolish risk! Would Mr. Bowen sack both her and her father over this? She and Father had scrabbled too long in destitution to lose the best thing that had happened to them in years. They were happy at Northill. Safe from the vagaries of the world. Father had returned to a job he loved as Mr. Bowen's land steward and she had taken over as the Bowens' temporary housekeeper until they found a more permanent replacement. If Lord Hawksmoor revealed her past, and her most recent foible, might Mr. Bowen cast them both out?

"Are you familiar with Miss Rosalind Caldwell?"

Madalene blinked. What did Miss Caldwell have to do with Lord Hawksmoor? "Y-yes. She is middle daughter to

Lord and Lady Caldwell." It was difficult *not* to know of her. Miss Caldwell had a habit of championing causes she believed in with a fervor that went far beyond what society deemed acceptable in a young woman. Madalene secretly admired her.

"Well, it appears Miss Caldwell has approached my lovely wife for her assistance in creating a school for children raised under less fortunate circumstances, in the hopes of giving them a better future than they might otherwise have."

"That's very admirable, sir." Though what it had to do with her or Lord Hawksmoor remained a mystery.

"Do you know me?" Thomas's question as she bolted from the room hastened back to her. Was it possible he had not recognized her? Five years had passed since he'd last seen her, and she'd been but a girl of sixteen at the time. Or was it that the wound to his head had affected him in ways she was not aware? The possibility left her unsettled.

"Yes, I agree," Mr. Bowen said, diverting her attention back to the conversation at hand. "Lady Rebecca is eager to help Miss Caldwell. However, given her current condition, her abilities will be somewhat limited."

Mr. Bowen's dark eyes brightened at the mention of Lady Rebecca's condition—a condition that would see the Bowen family increase by one. Possibly two, given how quickly the lady appeared to be increasing.

"Given this," Mr. Bowen continued, "we both thought you might be interested in assisting Miss Caldwell and possibly becoming headmistress of the school when the time comes."

"Headmistress? Of a school?" Her head swirled. This conversation had not gone at all in the direction she'd been expecting.

"Indeed. You are educated and extraordinarily organized. As well, you possess a sensible and kind nature. We all agree the children could not be in better hands with you at the helm."

"But…but what of my position here?"

Mr. Bowen gave her an understanding smile, as if he could hear in her voice the fear she tried so hard to hide.

"I promised your father your position as housekeeper would only be temporary. As much as we hate to lose someone of your capabilities, it does not suit to have a young, unmarried lady in such a position. You have your whole life ahead of you. It doesn't seem fair to hide you away at Northill and rob you of a better opportunity."

Except that she wanted to hide. She was safe here. Her father was here, and she had already missed too many years with him during the war. She had known her position as housekeeper was only meant to be a temporary one, but she had secretly hoped they would eventually agree to keep her here permanently. Now that hope withered on the vine.

"Of course." The words mumbled out of her. Trepidation bled through her. She'd spent too many years living in uncertainty. Now that she'd finally found a safe haven, the thought of giving it up filled her with dread.

"You do not sound pleased."

"No, I am. Quite. Truly. It is kind of you to think of me." She swallowed and forced a smile, but it wobbled on her lips and refused to take.

Mr. Bowen's expression softened. "It will be fine, Miss Cosgrove. I believe you will take to being headmistress like a duck to water. And if you do not love the job, you are always free to return to Northill. We do not wish to see you unhappy. Only to give you an opportunity to spread your wings."

"It is only that Father—"

Mr. Bowen held up a hand. "I spoke with your father. He is quite thrilled with the idea. We both know he has always wanted more for you, as well he should. Lord and Lady

Ellesmere have donated a portion of their lands to build the school upon, so you will not be more than a short ride away and free to visit as often as you wish. You will always be welcomed here, Miss Cosgrove. I am not fond of casting people out and robbing them of their home."

Heat rushed up her neck and bloomed in her cheeks. Her employer had once been one of those unfortunate children he and his wife planned on giving a brighter future, and as such, was one of the few of her acquaintance that understood how tenuous security could be. Or how much she valued it. Of course, he would never cast her out.

"Forgive me." She took a deep breath. "It is a wonderful opportunity. And I appreciate your faith in me."

It had been a long time since someone other than Father had seen potential in her. Not since Lord Hawksmoor had found her reading in his family's library. But that had been in another lifetime, hadn't it?

"Very good." Mr. Bowen offered a rare smile. "Miss Cald-well should arrive in a couple of days. She will be most pleased to hear you are amenable to the prospect."

Chapter Two

Thomas. How very generic. Plain. Uninspired, really. He much preferred the sound of Hawksmoor. Now that was a good name. It made him sound rather rakish, if he did say so himself. And given that there was no one about to contradict his opinion, it stood firm.

Granted, Hawksmoor wasn't necessarily his true name, but it was a title and that was good enough. Though, it did beg the question, as a titled gentleman, why was he not convalescing within the walls of his own estate? Good Lord, was he impoverished? How positively ghastly! He didn't feel impoverished. Then again, he was laid out in a room that, while clean and well appointed, did lack a certain opulence.

Did he like opulence?

An aggravated breath huffed out of him. It was anyone's guess, wasn't it? Perhaps he did. Perhaps his own estates—wherever they may be—were draped in rich velvets and gilded in gold. Maybe diamonds dangled from the chandeliers and exotic fruits filled the orangery.

Maybe. Speculation was all he had. Whenever he searched

for something more concrete, the drafty corners of his mind gave up nothing. He had hoped Rose would return, so he might ask how she knew him. Why she had kissed him and then run off.

He touched his fingertips to his lips. It had been an innocent kiss. Inexperienced, yet soft and sweet, touching a place deep inside of him that he had been unable to access before. *How* did she know him? Or he, her? And what was this pull he felt whenever she was near?

His questions remained unanswered, festering the frustration building inside him. He banged his head once against the mahogany headboard, instantly regretting his action as pain throbbed from his wound.

He closed his eyes and groaned. The damnable headache had finally started to ease and now he'd brought it back with a vengeance.

"Bugger it," he muttered.

"No, thank you."

Hawksmoor opened his eyes to find Mr. Bowen standing at the foot of the bed, a letter held between his index and middle finger. The man moved with the silence of a shadow. It was rather disconcerting.

"And how are we feeling this morning?"

We. As if this gentleman suffered along with him. More irritating than that, however, was the fact this man likely knew more about him than he did. An imbalance Hawksmoor did not much care for.

He scowled. "*I* am feeling perfectly well. I see no reason to extend my stay much longer. It is high time I return to my own estates; wouldn't you agree?"

"Indeed. And to which estate do you wish to be conveyed?"

His jaw tensed. Was he being tested? Mr. Bowen had a habit of asking cryptic questions, probing without being direct. A tactic Hawksmoor found annoying as hell. Well, two could play that game.

"Which do you think would be best, given my current condition?"

It occurred to Hawksmoor he didn't even know which county he was in. Or if he still resided on British soil, although given the dismal mix of rain and snow and overall dreariness on the other side of the window, he considered such an assumption a rather safe bet.

Mr. Bowen gave a non-committal shrug and crossed the room to peer out the window. The letter he held twitched between his fingers. "The closest one, I suppose."

If there had been something large and heavy within reach, Hawksmoor would have thrown it at his host. They'd danced around this pretense for a fortnight now and he grew weary. They both knew he had no memory. Why his pride insisted he pretend otherwise, or why Mr. Bowen continued on as if his mind had not turned into a sieve, he could not say. Nor did he care.

Hearing his name spoken, the sweetness in Rose's voice as it whispered off her tongue, had created a deep longing within him. Though what, in particular, he longed for remained as mysterious as the woman herself. Regardless, he was done playing games. He wanted answers.

"Why don't *you* tell *me* as we both know I haven't a bloody clue," he said, failing to keep the bitterness out of his voice. This entire situation was an odd predicament to be in. To require that someone else tell you who you were, where you came from, what your life was. Hell, he was a lord, and yet had no idea of his rank. Was he a lowly baron? A duke? A duke would be nice. He'd make a rather good duke. But surely a duke would not need to be given shelter by a gentleman of no rank whatsoever.

Mr. Bowen turned to face him, lowering himself to the

windowsill whereupon he stretched out his legs and crossed his arms over his chest, in no hurry to relay the information Hawksmoor requested. If Mr. Bowen was surprised by the admission that he required assistance in this regard, it did not register on his expression. The man was an enigma.

"Have we finally tired of the ruse, then?" Mr. Bowen asked. "Truth be told, I'm amazed it took this long."

"I'm not interested in your amazement. I'm interested in answers. Where am I and, more importantly, who am I?" His fingers twisted into the blankets as he braced for the answers. He was in no mood for bad news.

"Your name is Thomas Fitzgerald."

He sighed. "Thomas. How positively ordinary."

Mr. Bowen almost smiled. "Your title is Viscount Hawksmoor."

"Only a viscount?" That was a bit disappointing. He'd really been hoping for a duke.

"It is a courtesy title. You will become Earl of Ravenwood upon your father's passing."

Ah, well, that was somewhat better. Not his father's passing, obviously, but that he had just been elevated in the ranks.

Mr. Bowen continued. "The few who know you well often refer to you as Hawk."

"Hawk." He liked it. It sounded positively dangerous.

"Those who fear you, often refer to you as *The* Hawk." Feared him? That was rather ominous, but he did not have the opportunity to inquire further, as Mr. Bowen kept talking. "As to where you are, you are at my estate, Northill Hall."

"Why here and not at my own estates?" Good Lord, was he impoverished after all? Had his estates fallen into ruin?

Mr. Bowen unfolded one arm and pointed at Hawk's head wound. "You required care."

"Would it not have made more sense to return me to my family and have them care for me, rather than bring me here?"

"Such an option was not available."

"And why not?" If he was not yet earl, his father was obviously still alive.

"They refused to take you."

"Refused?" His stomach burned as if he'd swallowed hot coals. "Why would they refuse?"

"They did not say. You have been estranged from them for many years, to the best of my knowledge."

Estranged. The word had a hollow feel to it. "I see."

Except that he didn't. What had occurred to cause such strife within his family? Strife that went so deep that even as he hovered on the precipice of death, his family had refused to care for him. Such did not bode well.

Would Rose know of the estrangement? She'd known his given name, after all. And where was she? It had been two days since he'd seen her. Since she'd said his name, then run off. Truth be told, he missed her. Which was silly. Beyond silly. It was the height of absurdity. He did not know her, not really. Yet with one small touch and a whispered name—even a plain one such as Thomas—she had made him feel human again. Connected.

But to what? To have Mr. Bowen tell it, he had little in the way of connections. His family had all but disowned him, for heaven's sake.

He cleared his throat and pushed away the growing unease building inside of him. "Are we friends then, you and I?"

"I suppose. As much as you consider anyone friend, that is."

Lovely. What a prize Mr. Bowen's description made him out to be. "Then why did you take me in?"

"I was with you when you were shot."

"Shot?" He straightened, at least as much as the feathered mattress and plush pillows would allow. When he first awoke, he had believed—hoped—the wound had come about by accident. To discover someone had intentionally tried to end his life by putting a bullet through his brain left him cold.

"Yes."

Had he been in a duel? Was it over a woman? Had he been protecting her honor against some rogue who thought to disparage her?

"Who would have wanted to shoot me?"

The corner of Mr. Bowen's mouth quirked to one side, and he tapped the letter against his square chin. "Any number of people, I would assume."

So much for the heroic image of protecting a damsel in distress. "Wonderful."

Perhaps he should stop asking questions. He had yet to hear a single answer that made him feel happy he had asked.

"But in this particular situation, it was Lord Pengrin who shot at you." Mr. Bowen continued. "The bullet grazed your skull, rather deeply, and you lost a great deal of blood. I kept you at my townhouse until the worst of the danger had passed, then brought you here."

"After my family refused to take me in."

"Yes."

Hearing of his family's refusal a second time did not make the situation sit any better. What had happened between them to bring their relationship to such a state? He did not care for how all of Mr. Bowen's answers only led to more questions.

"Where is this Lord Pengrin now?" He would make it his first order of business to ensure the man hanged for this. Lord or not, he could not be allowed to get away with—

"Dead."

"I see. By my hand?"

"No. You were busy bleeding on the floor of The Devil's Lair."

"The Devil's Lair?"

"It's a gaming hell. Your gaming hell, to be more specific."

"I own a gaming hell?" What kind of lord owned a gaming hell? It was hardly the type of thing an upstanding gentleman of quality would possess. Then again, how many men of upstanding quality had a list of people wishing to put a bullet in them?

Hawk fell back into the soft pillows. His head throbbed mercilessly. He rubbed the spot between his brows. "I think I've heard enough for now."

"Very well. The doctor indicated it would be best if you recovered your memories on your own. If they are recoverable, that is. I should warn you, it's possible they may not be."

Hawk gritted his teeth. Mr. Bowen really needed to stop talking.

His host pushed away from the windowsill and strode toward the door, stopping at the side of the bed on his way. "Shall I send supper up, then?"

Hawk waved a hand in the air. "Sure. Why not?" He had little appetite left, but perhaps he would get lucky and choke on a succulent piece of meat, thereby putting an ignoble end to what appeared to be a rather miserable existence.

"Very well, then. And here, this came for you." Mr. Bowen held out the letter he'd been holding. Hawk reached out and took it.

"Who else knows I'm here?"

"Any number of people, I suppose. It wasn't a well-kept secret. Perhaps the letter is from someone wishing you a speedy recovery."

He doubted it. "Given what you have told me, I suspect it is more likely someone wishing I had bled to death on the floor of The Demon's Lair."

"*Devil's* Lair," Mr. Bowen corrected.

Like it mattered. Hawk waited until his host left the room

before breaking the non-descript seal on the letter. He unfolded the vellum paper. The handwriting did not look familiar. Then again, why would it? He skimmed the short note.

L ord H—
        I was dismayed to hear of your recent injuries. How unfortunate it would be if you were unable to see the final outcome of the game, to see what true victory looks like. I look forward to your return to London with great anticipation.
        ~ *T.*

W hat the hell did any of that mean? Hawk re-read the letter a few more times, waiting for something in his memory to jump out and reveal the meaning of the words written on the page. Nothing came.

He crumpled the note in his hand and let it fall onto the mattress next to him. The mystery of who he was, the life he had led, remained lost somewhere in the darkness of his mind.

"M iss Cosgrove, there you are."
        Madalene turned to see Lady Rebecca's approach. Winter brought early nights and while the wall sconces burned brightly, they could not chase away all the shadows that lurked in the hallway. The display of light and dark cascaded across her employer's royal blue gown as she made her way down the hall.

"Good evening, my lady. Is there something you need?"

Madalene had developed a true affection for the lady of the house. They were of a similar age, though the daughter of the late Lord and former Lady Blackbourne had an energy and boldness about her that commanded one's respect. Only now that she found herself with child had a little bit of uncertainty crept in. Madalene had no doubts Lady Rebecca would dispatch such in short order, however, once the initial worry wore off.

"It is not so much for me, as it is for Lord Hawksmoor."

"L-Lord Hawksmoor?" She stumbled over his name.

Lady Rebecca smiled and her face brightened with energy, bringing a sparkle to her silvery eyes. "Indeed, it appears as if my dear husband may have upset our guest somewhat."

"Upset him?" Heavens, when had she become a parrot? Not to mention, she found it difficult to imagine Mr. Bowen upsetting anyone. He was the kindest of men and had been especially generous to her and Father.

"It appears Lord Hawksmoor inquired about his current situation and did not care for the answers he received. I'm afraid our fears have been confirmed—the poor man has no memory of who he is."

The words sank in, slowly. One by one. No memory. Which meant—

She closed her eyes. Which meant he did not know who she was or how they were acquainted. Or he wouldn't have, if she had not seen fit to awaken him by saying his given name and kissing him.

"Miss Cosgrove? Are you quite all right?"

She snapped her eyes opened. "Yes. Yes, of course. Forgive me. I simply...well, his condition is quite distressing news, isn't it, my lady? Losing one's memory and all that is familiar." She couldn't imagine it. Couldn't fathom waking up and not recognizing her face, or her name. Or Father.

Her employer smiled gratefully. "Yes, exactly. And given that Lord Hawksmoor has already had a rather difficult day, I wondered if we might take extra care with him this evening. Perhaps Cook could make some of her delicious butter biscuits to send up? And some of that warm chocolate you claim is comfort in a cup?"

"I see no difficulty in doing so. Of course."

"Lovely." Lady Rebecca smiled gratefully and rested a hand upon her belly, a reminder of the life growing inside. A strange hollowness filled Madalene. As a small child, she'd often imagined having a home filled with children and a loving husband. But such dreams fell to the wayside as real life intruded. She soon realized not everyone received a happy ending such as Mr. Bowen and Lady Rebecca.

So caught up in her own disappointment, she almost missed her employer's next request. "I beg your pardon?"

"My goodness, Miss Cosgrove, your mind is somewhere else today, isn't it? You haven't found a gentleman you fancy and not told me about, have you? Is it Mr. Greene from town? I think he was quite sweet on you when we went to the market last week."

Madalene's cheeks burned. How she loathed her pale complexion and its inability to disguise her feelings! "No, my lady. I...I suppose I am simply excited about meeting with Miss Caldwell tomorrow."

The lie staggered off her tongue. As significant as the opportunity being offered her may be, she feared leaving the first place in years that had made her feel safe. To step back out into the world, a world she knew to be cruel and unforgiving. And dangerous.

Lady Rebecca reached out and touched her arm. "You will be a wonderful addition to our enterprise, Miss Cosgrove. You have nothing to worry about at all. And if the position is not to your liking, you are welcome back here at any time. Do not worry yourself over it. Think of the position as a new adventure."

The thought did not inspire her. Experience told her that not all adventures were worth having. "I will do my best, my lady."

"I have no doubt. Now, as I was saying, I thought it might be helpful if you delivered Lord Hawksmoor's meal to him."

"M-me?" Oh no. She definitely did not want to do that.

She had purposely avoided his lordship's room since blurting out his given name as if they were well acquainted. They were not. Not anymore. She owed him a great debt, without question, but what his family had done afterward erased that debt to some degree in her mind and she was willing to call things even and try to forget that horrid period of her life.

"Yes. Dr. Bartlett has indicated we should not disclose too much about his past to him, but that anything familiar might help him rediscover the information on his own. I understand you were once employed by his family, were you not?"

She swallowed. She did not want to think about that time. She definitely did not want to speak of it. "Yes. Briefly."

"Then perhaps laying eyes on a recognizable face might help. Seeing Marcus and me has done little, I'm afraid. My brother, Lord Blackbourne, has promised to visit upon his return from London to see if he might be of assistance, as well as Lord Huntsleigh, but in the interim, I think we should bombard him with as much familiarity as we can. I fear if we do not, his memory may fade to such a degree he will never be able to retrieve it, and I cannot think of a more horrible thing than that. Can you?"

Madalene shook her head, though given the chance there were some things she would prefer to forget completely.

"I knew you would understand. Thank you for doing this, Miss Cosgrove."

Lady Rebecca reached out and squeezed her arm once more, a friendly gesture that reached beyond the bounds of their relationship, yet offered a sense of comfort nonetheless. But all too soon, she found herself alone, left in the hallway to watch the shadows taunt the light.

Chapter Three

For a fleeting moment, Hawk thought her an apparition brought on by his stressed mind. She walked toward him with complete grace and set his dinner tray across his lap, enveloping him in the sweet scent of roses. Surely apparitions did not smell of flowers. Or possess such beauty and refinement. Or blush quite so prettily.

She did not speak a single word. He refused to tear his gaze from her. If he did, she might disappear once more. This was the closest she'd come to him since kissing him. Seeing her now, with his eyes wide opened rather than peeking through slits—well, she quite took his breath away.

God help him, she was utter perfection. How was such a thing possible? Her eyes, the color of a robin's egg, nestled softly in a thick nest of long lashes that turned pale at the tips. Her heart-shaped face was flawless and her lips—oh those lips —were plump and perfect, begging to be kissed again. Softly. Ravenously.

She released the tray and stood abruptly, as if reading his thoughts.

"Your dinner, my lord. If you require anything further,

you have but to ring." Even her voice held a musical quality to it. Not the put-upon kind one had to suffer through at musicales and the like, but akin to quiet birdsong on an early morning. And she knew him. Enough to kiss him. It seemed almost impossible.

She made to leave and a sudden desperation gripped at him to make her stay. He reached out a hand to stop her but she was already too far away and the tray across his lap prevented him from following.

"Wait! Don't go."

She stopped and turned back to face him, the blush in her cheeks growing to encompass her throat and beyond, disappearing beneath the lace of her bodice. "Do you need something?"

Yes, you. But no. That would not do. "I need...that is, I would like some company. I find I am tiring greatly of my own."

"I shall see if Mr. Bowen is available—"

"In truth, I find I enjoy gazing upon your beauty far more than Mr. Bowen's stern features." Flattery. Yes, that was the way to a lady's heart, was it not?

Her eyes rounded and she took a step back, his attempt at playing the gallant a dismal failure.

Bloody hell. "My apologies. That was very forward of me. It appears along with my memory I have also lost my manners. Forgive me?"

She did not appear convinced, but at least she had stopped edging her way toward the door.

"Please, allow me to properly introduce myself. I am Thomas Fitzgerald, Viscount Hawksmoor, at your service." She remained silent, so he prompted further. "But you knew that already, didn't you?"

She gave nothing away as she stood there, her arms hugged around her middle as if...protecting herself? From what? Was she afraid of him? A sick feeling invaded his gut. Did she have reason to be?

"Have I..." He did not want to even say the words, because if they were true...if they were true, what? He swallowed. "Have I hurt you in any way? Previously, I mean?"

Her eyes widened further, something he'd not thought possible. "No, my lord."

He breathed a deep sigh of relief and relaxed back into the pillows. "Thank God." Mr. Bowen's revelations had not painted the prettiest picture of the type of man he'd been, but at least he'd held some standards when it came to compromising lovely young ladies.

"Please." He waved a hand toward the chair near his bedside. "Will you stay?"

She stood motionless. Was she debating his request? He had no way of knowing. Her impassive expression gave nothing away. It was not until her shoulders relaxed a fraction, he had cause to silently celebrate the small victory.

"Very well. For a few moments." She strode with purposeful steps to the straight back chair he'd indicated, pushing it back from the bed, keeping more than a proper distance between them.

Hawk bit his tongue to refrain from suggesting she could not get farther away if she sat on the other side of the room. Likely she'd take him up on that idea, as it was clear she did not wish to be in his company. But why? *She* had kissed *him* after all. And if he had not compromised or hurt her, what reason did she have for such reticence? Was it simply the difference in their stations? No. There was something else lurking behind the beautiful blue of her eyes. He did not hold his breath thinking he would experience a repeat performance of the other night's kiss.

Pity.

"I am afraid I am at a bit of a disadvantage," he began. "It seems you know my name, but I do not know what to call you?"

"Miss Cosgrove," she said.

"Ah. And your given name? Since you know mine."

She hesitated. "Madalene."

"Not Rose, then?"

Her small nose wrinkled and the motion brought a smile to his lips. It was perfectly adorable. "No."

"You smelled of roses, you see. So, I named you Rose in my mind." His cheeks warmed at the confession. Well done. He'd just admitted he thought of her. So much for keeping things close to the chest. Was he always this green around beautiful women? What an appalling thought.

He hurried on, hopeful the depth of his interest in her was not so readily apparent. "And how is it that we are acquainted?"

She sat quietly; her gaze steady but mysterious. When had she learned to do that, keep her emotions locked tightly away so that no one might read her thoughts? Likely appearing impassive was a handy skill for a servant, especially one as lovely as she. While beauty was valued amongst the ton, it could be a dangerous quality to possess for those in the lower ranks, leaving them open to inappropriate attentions. Thankfully, Miss Cosgrove was under the protection of Mr. Bowen. The man was too busy being madly in love with his beautiful wife to take part in such reprehensible behavior.

Why did he just sneer when he thought that? Did he—

He swallowed. Was *he* the sort?

The sick feeling from earlier returned with a vengeance, almost making him forget she had not answered his inquiry. Almost. Perhaps he should appeal to her sympathies.

"Miss Cosgrove, as you may have heard, it appears my memories have taken something of a holiday. I do not mean to pry into your personal life, or request inappropriate information. I am merely attempting to piece together who I am, what I should know. Please, will you assist me in this regard?"

Her mouth tightened, a nearly imperceptible movement. "Dr. Bartlett has indicated it best if you retrieve your memories on your own."

"Is that not what I am doing? Trying to retrieve them by having you tell me something that might prompt their full remembrance?"

A small muscle where her jaw connected jumped. A-ha. She was not so unreadable after all. He simply had to know where to look. Hardly a taxing endeavor. He was quite certain he could gaze upon her for hours on end without growing weary. And practice did make perfect.

"Very well. I was employed by your family years ago."

Success! "And why are you not employed there still?" One would think a position with the Earl of Ravenwood would be a loftier post than working for an untitled gentleman such as Mr. Bowen. Unless he *had* behaved inappropriately and she had determined she no longer cared to stay. Except that she had kissed him, and that alone would indicate any affection must have been mutual. Didn't it?

"I was dismissed."

His brow furrowed. That didn't seem right. From everything he had witnessed, Miss Cosgrove had proven herself more than efficient and capable. And Mr. Bowen did not strike Hawk as someone who would employ anyone who did not fit that bill. "Why?"

A long silence followed.

"You will not tell me?"

"It is irrelevant."

"Was I there at the time of your dismissal?" He couldn't imagine allowing such a thing to happen if the reasoning was unsupported. At the very least, he'd like to think he would have found her another suitable position. Something inside of him shifted and a deep affection for this young woman stirred, though he could find no context to fit the feeling around. It was apparent she did not share the sentiment save for the kiss she now seemed to regret.

Silence filled the room. Good heavens, he would never have to worry about her talking his ear off, would he?

After a long moment, she finally answered his question. "No, you were not there. You had recently left the family home."

"Never to return, I hear." *They refused to take you.*

"I cannot speak to that. I do not trouble myself with things that do not concern me." There was a slight edge to her voice.

And why wouldn't there be? His family had dismissed her. Still, he could not shake the sense that she lied to him in some regard.

"But you obviously landed on your feet, I see, having procured a good position as housekeeper in Mr. Bowen's household." Although, she was a bit young for such a high-placed position. All the housekeepers he had known had been much older and far less attractive.

His brows shot upward. "I remember something!"

Her body stiffened and her hands, where they lay clasped in her lap, gripped each other tightly. "What do you remember?"

His chest deflated. It was hardly earth shattering. "Just that..." He stopped and chuckled. "It's silly, really. Just that other housekeepers I have known were never as lovely to look upon as you."

What had his life come to that this is what qualified as good news?

Miss Cosgrove stood abruptly. "Lord Hawksmoor, I do not—"

Oh, blast it! She was like a frightened deer, ready to bolt at the slightest provocation. Had she never been given a compliment before?

"Please, don't get yourself in a dither. I am not attempting to woo you. I merely mean to state the obvious." She remained standing and he released a frustrated breath. "Very well then. You are hideous."

"I beg your—"

"Ghastly, really."

"—pardon?"

"I can barely stand to look upon you."

"I do not think—"

"Gives me nightmares, truth be told."

Her lips pursed.

"Positively horrid."

She sat down in the chair and shot him a hard glare. "You have made your point, my lord."

He smiled. "Have I? You don't look happy about it." In truth, she looked ready to smother him with his pillow. Likely she could, too. He had a long way to go to regain the strength he'd lost while languishing in this bed. Regardless, he had to admit seeing that spark in her only made him more besotted.

Besotted? Good grief. He was pathetic.

"My lord—"

Oh-oh. She had moved to the edge of her seat, ready to leave once more. Did she find him tiresome? He was so certain he was entertaining. Why, he'd made a number of very witty observations in an attempt to pass the hours. Then again, he'd hardly had an audience to bounce said observations off. Perhaps he was the only one who found himself amusing. A rather dismal thought, that.

He rushed on before she could finish whatever she'd been about to say.

"Did you know they called me *The Hawk*?" Surely that would capture her attention and make him appear a proper rogue. Ladies liked rogues. He wasn't sure how he knew that, but he was certain he was correct in that assumption. And Hawk was a far more roguish moniker than Thomas. Tom. Tommy. Oh, good Lord, had anyone ever called him Tommy?

His admission did not appear to leave the desired impression. "My lord, if there is nothing else you need, I'm afraid I have other duties I must attend to."

Why was it that in asking his permission to leave, she'd made him feel he was the one who'd been dismissed? Disappointment flooded through him, but what could he do? She was not under his employ. He could hardly order her to stay and even if he did, he was not entirely certain she would obey. "Yes. Of course."

"If you have need of anything, you have only to pull the bell. Someone will see to your needs."

"You do not care to be in my company, do you?"

Between her reaction to him and Mr. Bowen's vague references, Hawk was left with the sense he was a far different sort of man than the one he felt like. Had the loss of his memory stripped away the layers of who he used to be, leaving nothing but a blank slate? And as his memories were restored, would those layers return one by one until they smothered the person he was now?

"It is not that, my lord."

"Then what is it? What is it about me that have men attempting to kill me, my family disowning me in my time of need, and you kissing me one moment and then wanting to bolt from the room the next as if I had grown horns and a tail?"

"I cannot speak to what others wish for or think of you, my lord."

"But you can speak toward your own feelings, can you not? Please, sit with me. *Talk* to me. You knew me before, well enough to kiss me and call me by my given name. I need to know who I was. What I was like. I have tried to remember, but the best I can retrieve are vague snippets that make no sense and hold no value. Surely you can tell me something of import that might allow me to recall one proper memory."

She shook her head and desperation filled him.

"Please." How he hated to beg.

But it worked. Something in her softened. "Very well. For a few more moments only."

Relief swept through him. He had not lost her. "Tell me about my family. Is it a large family?"

"No, my lord. There are your parents, Lord and Lady Ravenwood." She stopped for a breath then added, "And you had a brother."

Hawk blinked. "I have a brother?" But no, that is not what she said. She'd said he *had* a brother. Past tense. "He is dead then?"

"Yes, my lord," she whispered.

Something tapped the edges of his mind, but when he tried to grab hold of it, the memory dissipated like smoke caught in a breeze. "What was my brother's name?"

She shifted in her chair. "Phillip."

Phillip. The name echoed inside of him until it faded completely, leaving a black void in its wake. His heartbeat strengthened until it pounded hard within his chest. Why? He looked around the room, as if he would find the answer painted upon the walls. It wasn't and he swung his gaze back to Miss Cosgrove. "What happened to him?"

She evaded his gaze, staring down at her hands where she had folded them in her lap. He'd started to sweat. Why? "They said it was a hunting accident."

No. The word came swift and determined, deeply rooted in that part of him that held his memories in its uncompromising grip. But how could that be so? Not two minutes ago he hadn't even known he'd had a brother. And why would she lie to him?

"Was he older?"

"Yes. He was heir to the earldom."

"And now I am," he whispered. What sort of man stood to inherit the title and property, yet whose family refused to take him in and nurse him back to health? Something flashed in his mind's eye. Darkness and fear, but the harder he tried to grab it, the more elusive the image proved.

"Dammit!"

Miss Cosgrove shot to her feet. "I must go. I've said too much and I've upset you. Forgive me."

"No!" He reached out for her, his knees bumping against the tray she had placed across his lap. "Ow! Bloody hell. Come back!"

She ignored his plea and swift as a hummingbird, she was gone.

Hawk bolted upright; fear rushed through him. He scrambled from the bed, trying to get away, but the blankets snared his legs and he tumbled forward. Pain radiated from his shoulder as he hit the hard floor. He pulled himself free and tried to stand. His heart pounded and blood rushed in his veins. His legs refused to cooperate. He tried to call out, but his throat closed in on him as if hands had tightened around his neck and squeezed. He clawed at his skin, but there was nothing there. His voice wouldn't work; his body lacked the strength to get away.

"Lord Hawksmoor!"

Miss Cosgrove! Where had she come from?

He reached for her, but as his hand wrapped around her

slim wrist the dark vision that had sent him reeling cleared, chased away by her calming presence. The air he desperately needed sucked into his lungs as shock kicked through him and left him gasping.

He was vaguely aware of her trying to pull away. He held tighter. He shouldn't, but he needed her. Needed the anchor she provided. She was what was real. Not this horrid scene flashing through his mind. His brother. He *knew* it was Phillip.

"Lord Hawksmoor, let me go!"

The fear in Miss Cosgrove's voice cut through everything else, echoing in his mind until he couldn't decipher where her terror originated. In his dream? In reality? Still, he hung on, refusing to relinquish his grip, afraid if he did, he would spiral so far down into the dark, he'd never return.

"Help me," he pleaded.

What he remembered couldn't be true. It couldn't!

Her attempts to pull away stopped and her body shifted, her arms closing around him as best they could. He glanced down at her. Fear filled her eyes, illuminated by the moonlight where it cut across her lovely face. Her expression shook him to the core, solidifying what the horrible memory that had crept back to torment him had revealed. He closed his eyes but there was no avoiding the truth.

"I killed him." His voice rasped out as if the hands in his dream still pressed against his throat, choking him. "I killed my brother."

Chapter Four

Madalene released Lord Hawksmoor and pulled her arm from his grip. His memory of that night dragged her back down into its darkness. She struggled to regain her footing on the hardwood floor, but her toes caught in the hem of her dress, tripping her up. She should have never come back to his room. The admonishment repeated in her head, over and over.

She should have left. Returned to the cottage she shared with Father.

But she couldn't help herself. Lord Hawksmoor drew her to him. He always had. But even as she questioned her actions and insisted returning was nothing short of foolhardy, she came anyway. Why? That part of her life, the part that he'd had in it, was over. Done with. She had buried her feelings for the new Lord Hawksmoor on the same day they had buried his brother. But she had kept the secret his parents told, insisting that their eldest had been trampled after falling from his horse.

Better that, than to admit the new heir to the earldom had killed him.

Murdered him with his own hands.

Because of her.

Madalene gave up trying to stand and instead scrambled with hands and feet until she reached the wall and pressed her back against it. Not because she feared Lord Hawksmoor, but because she feared what she might do for him. The need to offer him comfort, to ease the pain that shone so brilliantly in his eyes, overwhelmed her. Despite what he had done. Or perhaps because of it.

For the longest time, she had told herself the death had been an accident. That he hadn't really meant to go that far. The situation had gotten away from them and in the temporary frenzy, the worst had happened. But that, too, would have been a lie. Because Lord Hawksmoor had reached for her after knocking his brother down. He'd been about to take her from the larder where Phillip had cornered her. Freedom was within her grasp. Then Phillip had spoken, madness wrapped around his hateful words.

But Lord Hawksmoor had heard everything. Madalene had never seen such fury in the young lord. He released her, attacked his brother and then—

And then Phillip was dead.

Lord Hawksmoor left his family's home that night, never to return. And she had been dismissed only days afterward. Madalene had worked diligently over the years to put the events of that night behind her. To push the tormenting memory from her mind, the guilt she carried for her part in it. She'd almost succeeded too, until Lord Hawksmoor had arrived at Northill, wounded and near death, all memory of who he was and what he'd done erased from his mind.

Until now.

She should never have spoken his brother's name.

She nestled in next to the bureau, pulling her skirts from about her legs. The open door was but ten feet away. Madalene glanced at Lord Hawksmoor. He remained on the floor, having pushed himself into a sitting position. The moon shone its light through the window leaving the outline of his body evident through his linen nightshirt. He'd lost weight over the past few weeks, the proof of such in the sharp angles of his bones that had once been covered in lean muscle. Still, his grip on her had been strong, fueled by the fear of what he remembered.

"You know, don't you," he whispered, his gaze riveted to the floor. "You know what I did."

What did she say? What *could* she say? "Yes."

His brow furrowed, as if his mind worked to recreate the full memory from pieces newly discovered. "You were there."

She swallowed and glanced at the door again. Should she run? But what was the point? Where would she go that he could not find her? Shortly before the attack that left him in this state, he'd asked Mr. Bowen to provide a proper introduction to her, knowing she had been in the man's employ. After all these years, he had discovered her whereabouts. But how? And why?

His appeal had raised any number of questions with Mr. Bowen, who had summarily declined Lord Hawksmoor's request. What lord requested a proper introduction to a servant? It was imprudent. Mr. Bowen had broached the question with her but she feigned ignorance, telling him the only connection she had to Lord Hawksmoor was that she had once been employed by his family years earlier. Whether Mr. Bowen believed her or not, she could not say. But he had not inquired further and, thankfully, had refrained from mentioning the request to her father.

"Answer me." Lord Hawksmoor's words shot out, harsh and demanding.

Madalene pressed her back against the wall. This was not the man she had known. *This* was the man she had seen awakened that night five years ago, filled with rage and desperation. She should fear him, but she didn't. Instead, she feared herself. Feared the feelings he evoked within her.

"Yes. I was there."

Is that why he had asked Mr. Bowen for an introduction? Had he tracked her down, anxious she may someday reveal the truth of what she had witnessed that night? She had sworn to him she wouldn't. Promised him her silence as she tried to calm him, to erase the hint of madness from his eyes. Eyes that had up until that night, held nothing but warmth and kindness.

"This is why my family has turned their back on me, isn't it?"

She didn't answer. What could she say? His family had turned their backs on him well before that, always giving preference to his older brother and treating him as a burden, a necessity as a spare but good for nothing else. What purpose would it serve him to know that now?

"Should I call for Mr. Bowen?" She was unsure of what else to do. Leaving him alone like this, the realization of what he'd done, so newly discovered, didn't feel right. Not after everything he had once done for her.

"No!" He pushed himself backward against the bed frame, retreating into the shadows. "Please. Can we keep it between us? Just until—"

He stopped; helplessness entwined around his words. His gaze traveled around the dark room as if searching for something.

"Until what?"

"I don't remember why I did it." He looked at her, his breathing labored. The distress in his voice clawed at her heart. How did he still have the ability to do this to her? Why could she not turn away?

Because he did not turn away when you needed him, a voice

whispered from deep inside her. She pushed it away, silencing it. But the words lingered within the silence.

She stared at him, at the play of shadows cast against his angular features. Features made more prominent during his convalescence. He had always been striking, though many had considered his brother, Phillip, with his gregarious personality and crystal blue eyes, the more handsome of the two. She hadn't, though. She'd preferred Lord Hawksmoor's quiet kindness, his sweet smiles, his quick wit. Perhaps that is why she came back here this evening. During Lord Hawksmoor's time at Northill, the hardness and severity of whom he had become after Phillip's death often slipped away, revealing the man she remembered. The man she had grown so very fond of.

Even now, with the worst of his memories retrieved, at least in part, she could still see the shadow of who he had once been. It gave her hope.

But hope was not something she'd had the best experience with.

"I need to go."

Fear flickered in his eyes before a curtain fell over them, shuttering his emotions. He nodded.

She stood, gingerly testing her shaking legs. Still, she hesitated, looking down at where he sat upon the floor, alone and abandoned by both his family and his memories. "Do you need assistance getting back into bed?"

"No," he whispered, then with more force, "Go."

She did not ask again. She turned and hurried from the room, down the staircase until she reached the servants' entrance. She hastily pulled on her coat and ran the short distance through the snow-packed pathway that led from the main house to the small cottage she and Father called home.

Trepidation nipped at her heels with each step. Something

deep and elemental had shifted this night. She could feel it. And it frightened her.

Sleep remained elusive as Hawk picked through the shadows of his mind in an effort to bring forth anything else he could remember about the night his brother died. The night he'd killed him. But the details remained lost in the murk. They had fought, of that he was certain. His brother was bigger than he, heavier. He could remember the feeling of Phillip's weight pressing him into the ground.

No. The floor. They had been inside. And he remembered the fear. The belief that everything hinged on this one moment. On his ability to stop his brother. That if he failed, the consequences would be dire.

Had he simply been defending himself? But if so, why? Why would his own brother try to kill him? He had nothing to gain from it. Phillip was the heir. He had everything. And why would Hawk, in turn, go so far as to then kill Phillip, as if it was the only option available to him. Because surely, if they had been inside one of the Ravenwood properties there would have been any number of servants or family members there who could put a stop to the altercation.

Miss Cosgrove had been there to bear witness. Not that he expected she would be the one to step in. She was a tiny thing, and would have been but fifteen or sixteen at the time.

Yet she had watched him kill his brother, helpless to stop him. Was that why she'd been dismissed? Because she knew the truth? His family had obviously gone to great lengths to cover up what had happened with their cockamamie story, yet they had still banished him from their lives, despite the fact he was now heir to the title and lands.

The answers refused to come and by the time the sun rose in the sky, he was no farther ahead than when Miss Cosgrove had left him. He closed his eyes and recollected the feeling of her arms around him, comforting him. The scent of her sneaking past the hideous scenes playing out in his mind, wrapping around him like a blanket. Her sweet voice whispering nonsensical words of comfort he could no longer recall. Then she had let go of him, pulled away, and all the horror swept back in to fill the void.

"You look like hell," Mr. Bowen said as he walked into the room after a cursory knock.

Hawk glared at his host. "Thank you."

"My pleasure." Mr. Bowen crossed the room with even strides and threw the curtains open the remainder of the way. Brilliant sunshine bolted through the window and spilled across the floor.

Hawk winced. The brightness shone in stark contrast to his current mood and he did not appreciate the intrusion of the sunlight, or his host.

"You will be pleased to learn I will be taking my leave of your humble abode." It was time to go, to return to his old life. The answers he sought were out there and he needed to find them.

"And how do you plan on doing that? You can barely stand. You've easily lost a stone in weight while you've been recuperating. If you want to return to your life in London, I might suggest you ensure you have both your wits and your strength about you, in the event someone else decides to have a go at you."

Hardly an enthusiastic endorsement of the life he'd led before arriving here. "Do you mind enlightening me as to why I was attacked by Lord Pengrin in the first place?"

Mr. Bowen leaned a shoulder against the bedpost. "Pengrin was a gambler, and not a very good one. He owed you a substantial amount of money and you'd called in your markers, cutting him off at the tables and banning him from The Devil's Lair until he made good on his debts."

"I assume he was displeased by this."

"You might say that. But Pengrin was also involved in some rather unsavory dealings. One of which threatened to financially destroy a good friend of mine, Lord Glenmor. We believed you might have information that could help us in this regard—"

"Why?"

"Because you were a collector of information. You kept files on practically everyone of consequence in London. Details on their habits and vices, business dealings, money owed and to whom and for how much. Information was the true commodity you traded in. You knew enough to destroy any number of people at any given time."

"And did I?"

"Sometimes."

"I sound like a charming fellow." Mr. Bowen didn't answer, but his confirmation echoed loudly within the silence. "I assume Pengrin got to me before you arrived?"

"Yes, though not by much. Pengrin had you backed against your desk with a pistol pressed under your chin. You looked somewhat the worse for wear. He'd brought two unpleasant gentlemen with him and there had obviously been a tussle, though both of Pengrin's henchmen, as well as two of your own men, were dead on the floor by the time we arrived."

More death. More blood on his hands.

Mr. Bowen continued, "We attempted to distract Pengrin, but things went a bit awry and as a result, you just missed getting a bullet to the brain."

"You paint such a lovely picture. I take it Pengrin was not a good shot."

"I have no idea. Lord Glenmor was the one who thwarted

his attempt, throwing off his aim. Regardless, if you wish to leave, do so. But I vigorously suggest you regain your strength first, if not your mind."

"And how do you suggest I do that?"

"Eat more and move more."

"Move more?"

"A little manual labor might help as well. I'll send up my steward, Mr. Cosgrove. Perhaps he can be of service in that regard."

The name came like a punch to the gut. "Mr. Cosgrove? A relation to Miss Cosgrove?"

"Her father."

Dear lord. Would she have told the man what had transpired between them last night? Or worse, with his brother? But no, she couldn't have. Had she, any self-respecting father would have marched into the room, pistol in hand, and demanded recompense. Still, he wasn't sure he wanted to take the chance Mr. Cosgrove was merely biding his time waiting for the perfect moment. He'd had enough people shooting at him in recent history and held little interest in a repeat performance.

"I hardly think I need—"

"Nonsense." Mr. Bowen pushed away from the bedpost and waved off Hawk's attempted refusal. "Fresh air will do you good."

"Fresh air? It is the middle of bloody January!" Hawk motioned toward the window but the blue sky and sunshine lessened the impact of his claim.

"Good for the lungs. I'll send Cosgrove up when he has a spare minute. You'll like him. Good man."

Hawk sputtered as he tried to find words to stop this madness. He did not need to go outside with the father of the woman he'd been having inappropriate thoughts about since the moment she walked into his bedchamber. And he *most* certainly did not need to spend time alone outside with that man where no one was around to witness what he might do.

Even if Cosgrove didn't plan to kill him outright for past or current offenses, he could certainly work him to death. Which begged the question—what exactly was entailed in regaining his strength? Was he to toss bales of hay about? Muck out stables? He was a bloody viscount, for crying out loud! Almost an earl! He didn't do...manual labor.

But by the time this reasoning hit him, his most irritating host had slipped from the room like an evil specter, leaving Hawk to stare at the door and wonder what the hell else could go wrong in his life.

"There you are, Maddie, my dear."

Madalene jumped at the sound of her father's voice, her nerves stretched to a thin, taut line. She had not slept in two nights. How could she? Each time she closed her eyes, she saw Lord Hawksmoor's face, an upsetting mixture of remembrance and horror as the truth of what he had done cut into him like a hundred knives finding their mark.

Of all the memories he had to recall, why did it have to be that one?

She turned to find her father standing in the door of their kitchen. The steward's cottage on Northill Hall's estates was smaller than the one she had been borne to over twenty years ago on Lord Walkerton's estate, yet this one felt more like home to her than that one ever had. Perhaps because they were secure here. Treated as if they belonged. Valued. It was a new feeling and one she was afraid to get too used to.

"Good evening, Father. How was your day?" She stirred the pot in front of her, the aroma of stew and spices wafting up until her stomach gurgled in response. After her run-in with Lord Hawksmoor three days ago, she had lost her appetite, but today her body had let it be known it would not stand for such mistreatment much longer.

"Quite well." Her father leaned over her shoulder and breathed in the scents. "That smells wonderful, my dear."

"It is one of Mother's old recipes."

Her father gave a small smile and the lines around his light blue eyes crinkled in the corners. The memory of her mother was a difficult one, her final years with her father mixed with anger and resentment, smothering the love they had once shared. Father blamed himself, for the years he'd been away at war, a situation he'd had no control over thanks to Lord Walkerton. The man's death several months earlier had done little to heal the wound his actions created, both emotional and physical. The only positive to the situation had been the roundabout way it led them here, to Mr. Bowen's employ.

"You look tired, Maddie. Are you feeling quite well?"

She turned her attention back to the stew. "Yes, of course. Everything is fine, Papa. Just a bit of a restless night, I suppose. Nothing to concern yourself with."

She hated to give him cause to worry. He had spent enough time berating himself for not being able to properly provide for them upon his return from the war. People had overlooked his abilities and seen only the empty sleeve where his arm had once been. But to her, her father had always been a great man. A man who had never given up. Not on himself, not on her, and not on life, no matter how dire or dark their circumstances became.

"Very well, then." He gave her a quick peck on the cheek. "I have had an interesting request from our Mr. Bowen."

"You have?" She often found Mr. Bowen and her father with their heads bent over plans in the study, determining the best use of the fields and improvements they wished to make to the estate. It was a collaborative effort and Father relished the freedom and respect Mr. Bowen gave him in his role as steward at Northill.

"Yes. It appears Lord Hawksmoor has indicated he wishes to return to London."

Madalene's stomach dropped. Foolish. She should be happy over such news. The sooner he left, the sooner she could get on with her life without the constant reminder of that fateful night haunting her dreams.

She ladled the stew into two bowls and fought to keep her voice light. "When does he leave?"

"Ah, well, that is where the interesting request comes in. You see, Mr. Bowen has suggested to our injured lord that if he wishes to return to his life beyond Northill, he would be wise to regain his strength first. To ward off any further disgruntled customers, I assume." Father smiled and walked back to the table and took a seat.

"And how does he propose to do that?" He hadn't even been able to keep his feet under him when she came upon him the other night. His legs had given out beneath him and he'd grabbed her for support, taking them both down to the floor in the process.

"With my assistance. It seems I am to put the future Earl of Ravenwood to work."

Madalene nearly dropped the bowls in her hand as she delivered them to the table. "You are to what?"

"Put him to work. Mr. Bowen believes the physical labor will go a long way to improving the state of his health."

"And what does Lord Hawksmoor think of this?" In his younger days, she'd often found him out of doors, and riding had been a favorite past time, but neither of these came close to partaking in manual labor. As a lord, such things were far beneath him.

Father chuckled, the sound rumbling deep in his chest. "I

imagine he is most displeased with the notion, though Mr. Bowen is quite determined his lordship return to London hale and hearty."

To resume his old lifestyle. To return to the man he had become in the wake of his brother's death. Disappointment weighed heavy upon her heart. She had hoped he wouldn't go back to that life. That he would, instead, return to the man she had once known. Another foolish hope and, like so many others she had nursed over the years, it would end in disenchantment.

"Then I wish you every success, Father."

Let him go. Let him return to his old life and leave her to hers. His return to London meant nothing to her. *He* meant nothing to her.

Perhaps if she told herself this enough, she would eventually come to believe it.

Chapter Five

"I can hardly believe you have the nefarious Lord Hawksmoor only two floors above us! Why London has been completely abuzz with rumors over what occurred that night and here you have the source of it right under your own roof!"

Miss Marianne Caldwell, the youngest of Lord Caldwell's daughters, leaned forward until she practically hovered on the edge of her seat, her cup of tea precariously balanced on one knee. As far as the Caldwell sisters went, each one appeared to be cut from a different cloth as if they shared no blood relation between them. Madalene found it most odd that three young women could grow up together in the same household yet all turn out so differently. Despite such, she could not help but feel a pinch of envy. As a child, she'd often been quite lonely, especially with Father off to war. How lovely it would have been to be surrounded by siblings.

"Marianne," Eugenie Caldwell's clear voice cut off her sister's musings. "We did not come here to partake in gossip."

As far as the Caldwell sisters went, Eugenie, the eldest, was the most serious of the three and appeared the least comfortable sitting in the drawing room of Northill. Then again, given her history with Lord Blackbourne, Lady Rebecca's older brother, it was to be expected. Broken engagements could be rather awkward.

"Indeed, she is right," Rosalind Caldwell spoke up. Rosalind, the middle sister, was the instigator of this meeting that had Madalene sitting here instead of tending to her duties. "Although, heavens, Lady Rebecca, you might have given some indication he was here. I would have left Marianne at home. There is no telling what mischief she'll get up to, now that her curiosity is piqued."

Eugenie closed her eyes and sighed, leaving Madalene with the impression the eldest Miss Caldwell spent much time corralling the youngest Miss Caldwell's exuberant nature, while the middle Miss Caldwell simply went her own way.

Rosalind—as she insisted on being called to cut down on the confusion of having three sisters answer instead of one—was well known in society for taking up the charge of whatever causes she felt needed her attention. It had caused all kinds of gossip, most of which centered around the fact that such behavior would likely render her a spinster. What proper gentleman would offer for such an outspoken lady who made a spectacle of herself on behalf of the poor and downtrodden? Though such gossip did not appear to deter Rosalind in the least.

"Miss Cosgrove, I understand Lady Rebecca has spoken to you about the opportunity we wish to extend?"

"Yes, she has." The opportunity to become headmistress of a school was definitely flattering, and she knew Father wished her to be in a more suitable position that put her out in the world. Madalene forced herself not to grimace at the thought. As far as she was concerned, the world outside of Northill Hall was dark and dreary and fraught with unseen peril. She had no wish to return to it.

Rosalind smiled, causing her eyes to sparkle. The expression animated her features and made her quite pretty. "Are you amenable to becoming headmistress?"

"I will confess I have some reservations. Such a position is a rather daunting endeavor and would require that I leave Northill, and Father."

"But it is not so far away, Miss Cosgrove." Lady Rebecca gifted her with a warm, encouraging smile. "You will be but a few hours carriage ride away. You may visit whenever time allows. We would welcome you with open arms, please don't think otherwise."

"Thank you." Perhaps it wasn't so much the formidable new endeavor that made her sad to leave, but the welcome and comfort she had found here. Between Father and Mr. Bowen, she had no fear any harm would come her way. That had not always been so and she was reluctant to give such safety up without serious consideration.

Eugenie tilted her head to one side and studied her intently; the effect somewhat disconcerting as Madalene could not fathom what went on behind the other woman's dark eyes. "You do have an affection for children, do you not?"

"Yes, of course," she answered. She had always dreamed of having a big family one day. "Though in truth, I have not had much exposure to them. In one of the apartments Father and I briefly lived in, there were often many children running about and from time to time I looked after them." It had always saddened her to see the state of many of these children, often hungry and grubby and neglected. Rosalind and Lady Rebecca's proposed school would give such children an opportunity to rise above their meager beginnings. How could she not want to assist with that?

"Miss Cosgrove is far more capable than she gives herself credit for," Lady Rebecca said. "She has all of the qualities a great headmistress requires. She is organized and exudes a quiet confidence and warmth that I am certain the children will gravitate toward."

Madalene wasn't sure Lady Rebecca's praise was warranted. She did not feel particularly confident these days. Having Lord Hawksmoor in close proximity, churned up too many memories, unearthing feelings she had long repressed. The whole thing left her unsettled. How she envied him his lack of memory in this regard. Though, as it turned out, not even he could fully forget that horrid night.

"Is Lord Hawksmoor doing well?" Marianne asked, as if the conversation surrounding the viscount had not been interrupted by the actual matter they had come to Northill to discuss. "I heard he has been horribly scarred by the attack! Such a tragedy. He had such a fine and handsome face."

Despite her sisters' obvious frustration at their youngest sibling's inability to move away from the subject, Lady Rebecca smiled, her amusement evident. "You will be happy to hear that he fares well enough and that his face is as handsome as it ever was. Is it not, Miss Cosgrove?"

Lady Rebecca's inclusion of her in the discussion of Lord Hawksmoor's state of handsomeness came as a surprise and for a moment, she was unsure how to answer. Because yes, he was indeed every bit as handsome as he once was. More so, as it had been some years since she'd seen him and, in that time, he'd only grown more appealing. The recently acquired scar just above his brow added a rather alluring rakishness. But she feared addressing the matter aloud; afraid her unwanted attraction to him would be evident.

She clasped her hands together. "It is as Lady Rebecca says. He is doing well."

"And is he still handsome, as she claims?"

Madalene cleared her throat. "His appearance has been unaltered by his ordeal."

For some reason her answer appeared to amuse Lady

Rebecca. "You will have to forgive Miss Cosgrove's lack of enthusiasm over Lord Hawksmoor. I'm afraid she has had the chore of dealing with our reluctant guest on a daily basis and despite his handsomeness, he has not been the most amenable patient."

Marianne's hand fluttered to her chest. "You have nursed him back to health? Oh, how romantic!"

"Oh, good heavens, Mari!" Rosalind's practical nature flared and her eyes rolled upward in their sockets. "I am certain it was nothing of the sort. I've nursed enough soldiers to know men, when made infirm, are absolute bears to deal with. All that pride warring against their injuries. Now, if you are quite finished interrogating Lady Rebecca and Miss Cosgrove about their guest, might we return to discussing the matter of whether Miss Cosgrove is willing to accept the position of headmistress?"

Every gaze in the room swung back to Madalene. Was this what it would be like if she took the position? All of those eager little faces looking to her for answers and guidance? The import of what they asked her to embark upon struck her. She wanted to help, but she also wanted...what? More? Something else? The firm footing she'd experienced upon arriving at Northill had become unsteady, shaken by Lord Hawksmoor's unexpected presence.

A presence that had caused the embers of all the things she had once wanted to burn anew.

"Might I have a little more time to decide?"

Rosalind's shoulders drooped, but Lady Rebecca quickly stepped in. "Of course, you may. We have not yet finished refurbishing the buildings to be used for the school and dormitories, and won't until the winter passes. There is still time for you to make up your mind."

Madalene nodded. Why did she hesitate? When would such an opportunity come her way again? The Bowens had every intention of replacing her as housekeeper. She had only taken the position to help out until they found a suitable and permanent replacement.

Yet, she could not shake the sense that fate had something else in store for her than running a school. A calling of a different sort.

But whatever that something else was, it remained infuriatingly silent.

Hawk stared at the tall, older gentleman who had entered his bedchamber. It was difficult to judge how old he was. His wild hair and trim beard were snow white, a stark contrast to his eyes that sparkled with vitality and strength. In one of his hands, he held his hat. The other hand, however, was gone and the sleeve that held the arm had been neatly folded and pinned above where his elbow should have been.

"You've lost an arm."

A smile twitched at the corners of the man's mouth. "On the contrary, my lord. I know exactly where I left it."

"And where might that be?"

"The battlefields of Waterloo."

"Ah. Well, I unfortunately have no idea where I left my memory. It seems to have ambled off somewhere without notice, leaving me with both my arms but no recollection of a whole host of things such as how old I am, my preferred drink, or who you are. Do we know each other, Mr.—?" Hawk raised his eyebrows.

"Cosgrove, my lord. And I believe you to be in your thirtieth year or there about, likely you prefer a well-aged brandy and no, we have not met before, though my daughter was once in service to your family." At this announcement, the man's countenance changed, turning stern. Unyielding.

"I see." Hawk swallowed. Had she said something to him about the other night? Or was it simply that his family had sacked her that brought a sudden tension into the room? "Well, what is it that has brought you here to interrupt my day? As you can see—" He raised one eyebrow and swept his arm wide, taking in the neatly appointed room that possessed nothing more than the required furniture. No books, no newspapers, no visitors vying for the two available chairs. "—I have much going on and very little time to entertain."

"Mr. Bowen has indicated you wished to regain your strength and return to London. He has charged me with ensuring you achieve this. A task I'm more than pleased to attend to. As I am sure you can imagine, your presence here has my daughter rather discomfited. I believe the sooner you leave, the sooner she will feel more at ease."

Fear fizzled in his belly. Did Cosgrove know what had happened with Phillip? That Hawk was a murderer? Had she told him? He took a breath to steady the rapid beating of his heart.

"I see." Hawk sat up straight and did his best to look lordly and imposing. Difficult to do when one was laid up in bed wearing nothing but a nightshirt. "You'll have to forgive me, but my memory on the subject is somewhat...gone, for lack of a better word. Please, enlighten me as to the cause of your daughter's discomfiture. And feel free to speak openly." Though he had the sense the man did not require his permission on that account. From what he'd witnessed thus far, Mr. Bowen maintained a rather open relationship with his servants, speaking to them as if they were on the same level as he.

"I'm afraid I cannot give you a reason for why your presence distresses her, only that as a father, I can tell when my daughter is distracted and out of sorts. As she has been since your arrival."

"I assure you Mr. Cosgrove, I mean your daughter no harm."

The older man slipped his hat under what remained of his missing arm in one fluid motion. "Nor do I accuse you of such. Besides, you are hardly in any position to do harm to anyone."

"Yes, thank you for that reminder." Perhaps regaining his strength and rehabilitating his flagging pride might not be such a bad idea after all.

Cosgrove gave a curt nod. "I understand it is not my place to suggest you hasten your departure from Northill, my lord, but my daughter's welfare and state of mind is of utmost importance to me."

"Of course. As it should be." Or so he assumed, not having children of his own. His heart lurched. Did he? Good heavens, how could he not have asked this question sooner? He was quite certain he had no wife, but had he had one at one point? She could have died. People did that. Look at his brother. Granted, his brother had some assistance in that regard. Another lurch. Dear sweet Lord! Had he killed his wife? Was he some kind of deranged killer who went about murdering those closest to him? Perhaps Miss Cosgrove was right to be agitated in his presence.

"Are you quite well, my lord?"

Hawk glanced up at Cosgrove. "Yes. Of course. Why?"

"You've suddenly gone quite pale. Should I call for someone?"

He shook his head, which did very little to clear the unsettling questions. "Miss Cosgrove relayed to me that my family dismissed her from Raven Manor."

"Indeed."

"I don't suppose she happened to express to you the reason or circumstances of her dismissal?"

"She did, though I believe her story to be little more than hogwash. For whatever reason, she does not wish me to know the particulars."

"And this does not concern you?"

"It concerns me greatly, my lord. But my daughter, when she decides not to speak on a matter, cannot be moved in this conviction. I suspect it had something to do with your brother's death, though what exactly, I cannot fathom."

"Yes...I suppose that would do it." He forced a rather weak smile. "A dreadful riding accident, or so I've been told."

"As I understand." If Cosgrove believed this explanation, or thought it as much hogwash as his daughter's explanation of her dismissal, Hawk could not ascertain.

"Well, then." He could think of nothing else to say to add to the conversation. "When shall we begin the process of regaining my strength so I might return to my life and leave your daughter to hers?"

"Tomorrow should be soon enough. I would counsel you to eat well and get a good night's sleep. We can begin in the morning, bright and early."

"Bright and early. And what exactly constitutes bright and early in your world?"

"Sunrise."

Hawk winced. "How positively ghastly."

"I shall make the arrangements with Mr. Bowen." With a short nod, Mr. Cosgrove walked to the door then stopped. "I did not mean to give the wrong impression, my lord. If it is of any comfort, during her time at Raven Manor, Maddie had described you as a thoughtful young man who had treated her with every kindness."

Maddie.

The name tugged at his heart. Sweet and innocent. Had what she witnessed destroyed that part of her? An overwhelming urge to make things right, to give her back what he may have taken, raged through him. But the other part, the part that hissed from the shadows of his mind, told him he did not own that right.

Some things were better left to the darkness.

Chapter Six

‿ɔɔ◌

The damp air bit at his skin, seeping deep into his bones as Hawk lifted the shovel of foul-smelling mixture of manure, hay and, God only knew what else, then tossed it into the cart. He had taken off the heavy coat he'd worn and hung it on a nearby peg. Cold sweat soaked his borrowed shirt and he had lost the feeling in his arms.

No, that wasn't exactly true. He could feel them. And they hurt like hell. How much shit must he remove from the stables before Cosgrove returned and saved him from this fresh new hell he'd been thrust into?

For the love of all that was holy, was there another lord in all of England to be found in such lowered circumstances? He had attempted to bribe one of the stable boys to assist him, but the lad only laughed and waved him off. Apparently incurring the wrath of a Peer of the Realm ranked far below displeasing Northill's esteemed steward.

Oh, how the mighty had fallen.

For the past week he'd been subjected to one ridiculous chore after another. Cosgrove had started him off slow with lighter work that left him shamefully exhausted. So much so that, despite his best attempt to stay awake for Miss Cosgrove's evening arrival, he had failed. It had been a full seven days since he had laid eyes on her lovely face, yet when he awoke the subtle hint of wild roses lingered in the air around him like her own personal calling card. The effect proved most disconcerting, awakening parts of him and creating an intense longing that went far beyond what was proper.

As each day passed, the chores became more labor intensive and bit-by-bit his strength and stamina returned, bringing with it a rather voracious appetite that Mr. Bowen's cook was only too happy to feed. Hawk wondered what it would take to steal the woman away when he left. Given the loyalty the servants displayed to their employer, likely he would have to pay a king's ransom.

Did his own servants display the same type of loyalty toward him? Mr. Bowen had mentioned two of his men had died protecting him from Pengrin's attack. He supposed that was encouraging. He stopped mid-shovel. Well, except for the part where they had died, for that he felt a rather immeasurable amount of guilt. He was not entirely certain, from everything he had heard, that he was worth giving one's life for.

He tossed the stench-filled muck into the cart and leaned on the handle. Once he had cleared the disgusting layer of hay and manure, he swept out the stalls then lay down fresh hay as Cosgrove had instructed, before trundling outside to dump the contents of the cart. The only chore that remained before he could return to his room and soak his sore, tired muscles in a hot bath was to retrieve the horses from where they were corralled and return them to their stables.

Mr. Bowen had a relatively large stable of horses, each one more beautiful than the next and all in possession of very pleasing natures. Re-stabling them proved an easy enough task until he reached the last one. A large chestnut stallion with black socks and a matching mane. The beast nipped at him every chance he got and snorted and pawed the ground when-ever Hawk drew near. How the hell was he was to catch the beast and put him in his stable? The stallion had made it clear with his snorting and pawing that he had no interest in returning to his stall. Attempting to lead him there against his will would not be a pretty sight.

As it turned out, his estimation in that regard had landed on the conservative side.

Twenty minutes later, Hawk wiped a splatter of muck from his chin with the sleeve of his shirt. His head pounded and his arse fared no better as the damnable beast kept knocking him onto it whenever Hawk managed to grab its halter.

"Bloody hell!"

He stared up at the darkening sky. The cold snow beneath him seeped through his shirt and underclothes. Cook promised to have a hearty stew waiting for him when he returned and the thought of it made him salivate. But Cosgrove had given strict instructions that he was not to return to the main house until his assigned tasks had been completed. The steward had not indicated what would happen if he disobeyed this dictate. Likely he would be sent to his room without supper or some such horrific fate.

Hawk could not shake the feeling that Cosgrove took plea-sure in seeing him brought so low. Not that he was an unkind man or even an unjust one. In fact, he struck Hawk as unusu-ally fair. He explained the work he wished done in clear terms and gave praise upon its completion. At the end of the day, Hawk received a firm pat on the shoulder that he discovered pleased him immensely.

Which was ridiculous. The man was a steward and he, almost an earl. What did he care for Cosgrove's good opinion?

And yet he did.

"Are you hurt, my lord?"

The urgency in the voice behind him, and the instant recognition that jolted through him upon hearing it, made him jump to his feet. A miracle in itself as every muscle screamed in protest with the sudden movement.

"Miss Cosgrove!" Cripes, he must look like a lowly stable boy. He straightened, a vain attempt to project a lordlier appearance. Difficult to do when a mix of snow and dead grass and dirt clung to a shirt made of paltry quality. He brushed at the offensive debris.

"You are fine then?" She took a step toward the wooden fence that separated them.

"Yes. Yes, I was just—" He glanced back at the horse behind him, a little surprised the beast hadn't taken the opportunity to trample him while he lay prone on the cold ground. Was it smirking? He scowled at it then turned back to face Miss Cosgrove. "I am to stable the horses. I have one left."

"He's being rather obstinate, is he?"

"An understatement," Hawk said, offering the horse another glare. The animal remained wholly unaffected.

"Shame on you, Ares," she scolded and the horse actually lowered its head like a repentant child. What the deuce?

"Ares? He's named after the god of war and bloodshed? How appropriate," he muttered, his observation coaxing a smile from Miss Cosgrove that robbed him of breath. Sweet heaven, but he could not see that smile enough. How was it such a small expression could awaken everything inside of him?

"Ares can be rather temperamental at times, I'm afraid, but in truth he's a big baby. Here, hold this." She handed Hawk the basket draped over her arm and gathered her skirts to slip between the rails, putting her on his side of the fence.

"Madalene, no!" He reached out a hand to stop her as she stepped closer to the horse.

She turned toward him, surprised. "You called me Madalene."

He could not tell if there was censure in her voice or not. "Forgive me. I did not mean to." Hawk hesitated. "Have I done so before?"

She sent another small smile his way and it touched his heart like a gentle kiss. He pulled back the hand he'd held out to stop her and placed it over his chest, as if he could hold the feeling there, for safekeeping. "Once or twice," she said, but he'd forgotten the question and his mind was filled with the vision of reaching out and pulling her into his arms, tasting her mouth and losing himself in the moment.

Ares snorted and pawed the ground as if the beast could sense his inappropriate thoughts, quickly reminding him they were not alone and the middle of a Northill's stable yard was no place to share a kiss. Not that any place was fit to share a kiss with Miss Cosgrove, given he had no business kissing her at all. No matter how much he wanted to or how many times he had thought of such a kiss over the past few weeks.

"You should stay away from that animal. I do not wish to see you hurt."

She tossed a glance over her shoulder, the moonlight skimming across her skin. "It will be fine. He is more bluster than beast, I assure you."

As if to prove him wrong, Ares walked over to her, stopping short by several feet then stretching its long neck outward to accept the nose rubbing and sweet words she offered as if they were manna from heaven. If the deuced animal had been a cat, it likely would have purred.

Not that Hawk blamed the beast. Had she offered such sweet words to him and touched him with a gentle hand, he would have done the same thing. He added jealousy to his list of grievances against the stallion.

Miss Cosgrove offered a quiet laugh that filled Hawk with

a ridiculous amount of joy. "He's like most men. All puffed up for show when there's another gentleman about, but perfectly sane and amenable underneath."

Was that directed at him? Had he once been puffed up for show? Full of bluster? How utterly embarrassing to think he'd behaved in such a manner. He would have liked to think he'd been more dashing than that.

Miss Cosgrove made a clicking sound and headed toward the stable. Ares followed along behind her like a faithful hound. Further proof the horse was kin to the Devil. Hawk glared after the animal, determined to short change the beast on its oats the next morning. He followed along behind them, keeping well out of range of the horse's back legs. Miss Cosgrove's basket swung from his arm and he glared at that too.

"There you go, my handsome boy," she said. Normally her sweet voice would have been a balm to Hawk's wounded pride. Unfortunately, the compliment was paid to the horse and not to him. Another strike against the beast. "Now stop being such a vexation to Lord Hawksmoor." She gave the horse one last pat on its rump and swung the stall door closed. She turned to him and held out her hands for the basket.

Hawk did not immediately relinquish it. "Where is it you are going?"

It was usually much later in the evening, well after he had turned in for the night, before Miss Cosgrove left the main house. Did she plan on going into the village? He had heard one of the maids whisper to another when they thought him asleep that a Mr. Greene from town was sweet on her. Was she going to visit him? He glanced out the open stable door to the sky. The winter sun had already sunk to the edge of the horizon. Soon it would be gone, leaving the landscape pitched into darkness, with only a half moon available to light her way. Surely, she had better sense than to travel to town at this hour.

"I am returning home."

Hawk breathed a sigh of relief. Though whether the feeling was due to the fact she had no intention of traipsing around in the dark or that she was not meeting Mr. Greene, he did not dwell on.

The steward's house was visible in the far distance through a small grove of trees, connected to the main house by a well-beaten path. Her leaving now meant he would not see her this night and the realization hit him that he was not yet ready to say good-bye.

"You cannot walk about in the dark."

She gave him a surprised look. "I'm quite certain I can, as I do it every day."

Right. Of course, she did. Still, he continued to grasp at straws. "It cannot be safe."

"I assure you I am perfectly safe here at Northill."

Something in her tone caught him. An underlying insinuation? She was safe here. She had not been safe while under his family's employ at Raven Manor. There, she had lived with a madman and a murderer in her midst. And now, that same murderer stood not two feet away from her.

Except that he did not feel like a murderer. And he could not imagine any circumstance in which he would ever do her harm. If anything, he possessed an overwhelming need to protect her. A need he could neither explain nor deny.

He reached for his borrowed coat where it hung on a peg in the stable and shrugged into it. "I shall see you home."

He offered her his arm. She raised an eyebrow, her gaze steady upon him. She did not shy away from confrontations, he'd noticed. Many servants dipped their gaze in deference to their supposed betters, but Miss Cosgrove did not. She looked you squarely in the eye, shoulders back and expression held in check. He could no more read her thoughts than he could his own memories. Her bravado both fascinated and irked him.

She made no move to take his proffered arm.

He raised his own eyebrow to match hers. "You realize I will hold my arm thusly until you take it."

"You will not," she stated simply. "You have yet to regain your full strength and you have been working all day. Your arm will tire shortly and you will be forced to lower it."

He hated that she knew this about him. His weaknesses. His foibles. His darkest secret. Yet, intuition told him all of those things could not be in safer hands.

She had witnessed him murder his own brother. Yet she did not cower from him. She did not run away. Even when, in the throes of a nightmare, he'd grabbed her wrist and brought the two of them tumbling to the floor, she had stayed with him. Held him and comforted him. Was it possible he was not as heinous as he believed? Could the context surrounding his brother's murder alter the gravity of what had happened?

Likely she would know.

Perhaps soon he would find the courage to ask her. But today was not that day. Today, he only wished to see her home safely without disturbing any unwanted remembrances of things neither of them could change. As for disturbing feelings he could not control, that was something else altogether. A smart man would take her reticence as a chance to excuse himself and let her be.

But he could not remember if he was a smart man, and so he didn't.

"Please, Miss Cosgrove, will you allow me to escort you home? I promise to behave the consummate gentleman. Besides, your father has indicated regular exercise will hasten my recovery."

Her shoulders lifted in a sigh and she gave a small shake of her head. "Very well, then. Far be it for me to subvert Father's plans. But I do not require an escort."

She turned toward the steward's house, without taking his

arm. He watched her back, the way her skirts swished about her ankles where they poked out from beneath the wool coat she wore encased in sensible boots. She dressed simply given her position, lacking the adornment ladies in his world draped themselves in. Yet, if anything, the lack of such only drew more attention to her staggering beauty and in his humble opinion, no jewel or frippery would have been able to compete with her either way.

Hawk grinned, then hurried to catch up with her.

M adalene had hoped Lord Hawksmoor would soon realize the walk uphill to her home would be too taxing. Unfortunately, the man was stubborn as a mule in this regard. Worse still, the narrow pathway forced them to walk closely together with little room left over. His nearness proved most vexing.

For the past week, she had made a habit of checking in on him before she left to return home for the night. Unlike the past evenings when he'd spent the day abed, he'd been fast asleep. The effect had a startling effect on her. A fierce protectiveness had filled her, making her incapable of leaving. She'd sat on the edge of the bed, watching the rise and fall of his chest through the soft linen of his nightshirt, staring at the scar near his temple now that the bandage had been removed. She had almost lost him. The thought seemed inconceivable.

More than once, his sleep had become agitated as if his mind wrestled with its demons. When that happened, she would reach out and place a hand lightly over his heart, mesmerized as her touch calmed the beast within. Much like it had all those years ago when his family would attack him with their unfair censure and harsh words. His anger had been barely contained afterward, with nowhere to release itself, leaving it writhing inside of him. It was then he would seek her out, ask her to read to him, claiming the sound of her voice quieted the rage inside of him.

That she could do such for him had given her purpose and filled her with a need to do more, much as it did now. She walked a dangerous edge back then, and even more so now, for now she was no longer an innocent girl with silly dreams. Now, she was a woman, with a woman's needs, and somehow Lord Hawksmoor's presence had awakened every one of them.

"Might I ask you a question, Miss Cosgrove?"

His voice startled her from her thoughts and she hesitated. His arrival at Northill had her emotions teetering on that dangerous edge and she feared one misstep would send her falling over. She could not risk it. Nothing could ever come of this thing between them, whatever it was, save for heartbreak and regret.

"I see no reason for it."

Her answer appeared to surprise him if the expression she caught out of the corner of her eye was any indication. She preferred not to look at him directly. Doing so caused her to waver in her convictions. It made her wish for things she could not have.

Once again, silence descended but Lord Hawksmoor's curiosity did not allow it to prevail for long. "Your father mentioned to me that when you worked for my family you considered me a kind man."

Madalene gritted her back teeth. What in heaven's name would have possessed Father to tell his lordship such a thing? Heat flushed her face despite the winter chill that filled the evening air.

"Did he?"

"He did, and I wondered—what made you think so?"

The question took her off guard, even more so than the admission that her father had shared her opinion of him all those years ago. But how did she respond? Her feelings now were tangled up in how things had ended, twisted and imbued with all that had happened, making it difficult to discern where her original feelings had begun.

"Please, Miss Cosgrove." He reached out and rested his hand on her forearm, the layers of clothing no barrier to the flash of heat that swept through her at his touch. But before she could pull her arm away, he lifted his hand, as if he too had surprised himself with the contact. "It is just that everything I have heard about who I was before Lord Pengrin tried to end my life has been less than impressive. That you once thought me kind gives me hope that perhaps I was not all bad. Was I?"

She sneaked a quick peek at him then wished she hadn't. The desperation in his clear green eyes was too much to bear and she answered before she could think better of it, wanting nothing more than to erase his torment.

"No, you were not all bad."

"And how did you come to this conclusion?"

Where to start? There had been so much about him that spoke to the goodness that lived beneath the handsome face and charming manners. A goodness he did not always project, as his family did everything in their power to beat it down. They had made him their scapegoat for everything that was wrong in their lives, yet heaped praised on their heir, who deserved none of it. They had continuously turned a blind eye to the true monster in their midst, refusing to acknowledge the madness Lord Hawksmoor tried to warn them of. His parents had refused to listen, berating him for even suggesting such horrible things. Did they think if they ignored their eldest son's predilections that they would go away? They had been fools in that regard and she and Lord Hawksmoor had paid the price.

"Miss Cosgrove?"

"Yes, forgive me." Her memories had a way of crowding her mind when he was near. He wanted to know what good she had seen in him. There was a long list, but she decided to begin at the beginning. "My mother was the daughter of a baronet and, as such, she received a proper education that she then passed on to me, even though by then her father had died and her circumstances were somewhat reduced from those she'd been raised in."

"Your grandfather was a baronet?"

She nodded. "Yes. And while I never met the man, I was always thankful for the education he gave Mother and that she shared it with me before she died. Her encouragement created in me a voracious appetite for learning and when my family's situation changed for the worse, it was this education that I missed the most."

She paused and took a breath. It had been a dark time for her family. Mother had become ill while Father had been away at war, after she had passed away, Madalene's aunt had helped out, though she too had since died. After the war ended, Father had been let go from Lord Walkerton's employ after standing up for a maid he felt had been wrongfully accused of theft. Given her father's war injury, finding work had been difficult and sporadic, and their once comfortable lifestyle had diminished, leaving them in near squalor. Once Madalene was old enough, she was determined to do her part to help Father, but it meant leaving her education behind. Or so she had thought.

"While employed by Lord and Lady Ravenwood, I discovered your family's extensive library. When everyone else had turned in for the night, I would sneak in and read the books."

She smiled. Being away from her father had made her miserable and the hours spent in the library had been the only time of the day she'd been happy, as if a light shone in the distance and with each page she read, she grew closer to its brilliance.

Lord Hawksmoor glanced down at her. "That was rather

risky of you. Had you been caught you would have been sacked. Likely without reference."

"I was caught," she said, meeting his gaze. She refrained from raising the fact that she was sacked without reference regardless, but for reasons that had nothing to do with her sneaking off to the library. "*You* caught me. You came stumbling in early one morning and found me huddled behind the desk."

"What did I do?"

She couldn't help the small laugh that escaped at the memory. "You scolded me for taking such a risk and made me promise not to do it again. Then you sent me off to my room."

His shoulders slumped and he let out a rather despondent sigh. "That hardly makes me sound like a kind man."

"That is what I thought, as well. But when I returned to my room the following night, the book I had been reading was hidden beneath my pillow. When I finished reading it, I returned it to the library. The next day, another book arrived. For as long as I remained employed with your family, you ensured I had books to read and by doing so, my education continued to flourish."

The memory warmed her. It had been a long time since she had allowed herself to think of her time at Raven Manor. A long time since she had been able to separate the goodness found there from the horrible events that eventually followed.

"Only a kind man would have done such a thing," she said.

Lord Hawksmoor stopped walking. Part of Madalene was tempted to continue on without him. The path they had wandered onto was precarious and fraught with danger. His questions invoked too many emotions she had worked hard to hold at bay. But as she watched his sharp profile while he digested her remembrance, the tension about his eyes eased and when his gaze met hers, the thought of continuing on without him vanished.

"I had a fondness for you, didn't I?" He quickly waved a hand before she could answer. Not that she had an answer, not one she was willing to admit aloud. "No, forgive me. I should not have asked such a thing. It's just that—"

"Just what?" She should let the matter drop, but suddenly she longed to know.

He set the basket on the ground next to him. "Since the first time I awoke and sensed your presence you felt...familiar. As if whatever existed between us had been there for some time. The feelings I experienced had roots. Roots that reached far deeper than that of employer and servant. Were we friends, then?"

She hesitated. To admit such would be folly. They'd had no business being friends. But to deny it would be a lie and she did not want to lie to him. She did not want to leave him feeling alone in a world that he had turned his back on.

"Yes. In time, we became friends."

After he'd found her in the library, he had made a habit of speaking to her whenever he saw her. He would go out of his way to make her smile, ask her about the books she'd read. After a time, he would show up in the rooms she'd been tasked to clean and simply sit there reading a book and making comment on it, or writing in his journal, which he did often.

It did not take long before she grew quite fond of those moments and looked forward to the next, which never seemed to come soon enough for her liking. In short, she had become sweet on Lord Thomas, though she had recognized the fool-ishness of it. He was seven years her senior, a man in every sense of the word, while in his eyes she was just a young girl he was kind to. He was a lord, and she but a servant in his home. Nothing would ever come of it.

Lord Hawksmoor interrupted her memories and when

she glanced at him once again, his hand clutched his chest and a look of horror filled his handsome features.

"I did not...that is to say... Please tell me I did not do anything inappropriate."

She shook her head. Not that she hadn't dreamed he would in her foolish girlhood fantasies. "You were ever the consummate gentleman."

But her answer brought him no peace. Without thinking, he reached out and took her hands in his. "Then what changed? The man you describe hardly seems evil enough to have killed his own brother."

"You were not evil!" She squeezed his hands, hoping the pressure of her fingers could convey the truth of that statement.

"Then I had a reason for what I did? Please tell me this is so, that I am not a monster! Since awakening, I have not been able to shake the need to protect you. Was that it? Was that what I was doing?"

He wanted to hear her say the words, to absolve him. Perhaps protecting her had been his only motivation for killing Phillip. It certainly had been the impetus that night. Though a part of her believed that the two men had been on that tragic course well before she'd arrived at Raven Manor. Phillip had been forever baiting his younger brother, putting him down, reminding him of his place as the second son. Lord Hawksmoor had always walked away, but there was something in his eyes after each encounter. She'd seen it. An erosion of sorts, made worse by his parents' belief that the things Phillip said were true. And the warnings from their youngest son nothing but the false ravings of a jealous brother.

"Madalene, please!"

The use of her given name again pulled at her. He'd used it on that fateful night, too, the shock and horror of what he had come upon in the larder laced through the word, yet, to her, the sound of his arrival had sounded like a benediction. A reprieve.

Despite the doctor's insistence that he would be better off remembering the events on his own, Madalene could no longer stand by and watch him struggle to stitch together the torn pieces of his memories. Memories that left more questions than they did answers.

"The altercation between the two of you was the result of your protecting me from your brother's advances. I believe you meant to take me from the room. You reached for me, but then your brother said something—" She stopped. How she hated reliving that horrid night, even in words. The shadowy evil reached forward from that small room and bled through her like the worst kind of poison.

"What did he say?"

She pursed her lips and shook her head. No amount of begging would make her repeat it. Phillip was dead. Buried deep in the ground where he could no longer hurt her. "It matters not. Leave it be."

Lord Hawksmoor ignored her plea. His breathing grew labored and he pulled her closer, his hands moving to her upper arms as he searched for the elusive memory. "He said..." he closed his eyes and muscles twitched near his jaw, in his throat as he swallowed. "I can hear him. It's like a whisper."

He released her and pressed his hands against the sides of his head. She should stop him, chase the memory away. It was better left forgotten.

"You can't save her; it is all a game." The words strangled out of Lord Hawksmoor, filling her with cold dread.

"Lord Hawksmoor." She said his name in the hopes he would stop, but it was too late. He was lost in the past, the awfulness of that night washing over him like an old nightmare that had come to visit one last time. Madalene placed her hands upon his face, attempting to wrestle him away from its shadowy tentacles.

He covered her hands with his, holding them there. "He said I wouldn't always be there to protect you. That you were part of the game and if he did not get to you, Lord T would." He made a bitter sound. "What game? Who is Lord T?"

"I don't know." Madalene pulled his forehead to hers, wishing she could steal the memory away before he remembered the rest of his brother's vile proclamation.

But it was too late. The memory had returned and grown roots and she was helpless to stop it. All she could do was stand with him, and pray the rest of that horrid night would fade into oblivion forever.

"He said—" He choked, as if the vile words she knew were to come had lodged in his throat, resolute in their purpose.

"Please stop," she begged. "This serves no good."

But he was lost somewhere inside his mind. "He said if I was lucky, maybe there would be something left over for me."

Chapter Seven

Had he remembered correctly?

But, yes. He must have. Because when he opened his eyes, he could see it in the clear, pale blue of hers. The truth reflected there; its damage imprinted into each lovely feature.

Hawk remembered now. They had been in the larder. The space dark, the only light from a lamp resting on the floor and tilted against the wall at an odd angle. Carcasses of freshly killed game hung from the rafters waiting for Cook to determine they had aged the appropriate amount of time before being served in some delectable dish.

Strange, the things you notice, the odd thoughts that go through your head when you are faced with such horror. And it had been a horror to see her like that, her hand clutching the bodice of her dress where it had been torn, the predatory expression on his brother's face as she cowered in the corner, all avenues of escape blocked by Phillip's ox-like frame.

Terror stabbed through him. Had Phillip dragged her in there or had she been there already, going about her duties when he found her? Hawk tried to force the memory but it would not come. Nor could he remember what had brought him there. Had she screamed for help? For him? Yes! She had called for him by his given name.

Thomas!

Even now, the panic in her voice shook him to his core and he pulled her against him, wrapping his arms around her, needing to keep her safe even though the danger had long passed.

The rest of the memory came in disjointed flashes. Yanking Phillip away from her. A brief scuffle had left his brother lying on the floor near the table. Madalene was right—he *had* reached for her. He'd meant to take her away, to keep her safe.

But then Phillip had spoken. Threatened. Promised she would never be safe. That she was some part of a game. That Lord T would get her if his brother failed to.

Lord T.

The letter Mr. Bowen had given him! What had he done with it? He could not recall, not now. His mind sped onward, past his questions to the memory of his hands on his brother's neck. Fury had poured out of him through his fingers as he squeezed, determined no harm would come to Madalene. To save her. And then...then...what? Nothing.

As the images in his mind faded back into the darkness, he was left with sweat dampening his shirt beneath the coat he wore. His hands shook, as if they still held his brother's life within them.

"Lord Hawksmoor?"

The whisper of his name brushed against his bare throat and anchored him to the present. A present where he held Madalene in his arms, safe and solid and lovely. He shivered, though it had little to do with the cold air and everything to do with the effect having her close wrested upon him.

How long had they been there, standing like this? Why

had she not run from him? He could have taken her from the room that night, to safety. Instead, he had let her go and murdered his brother in a rage fueled by the fear Phillip would make good on his threat. That he would hurt this beautiful girl who had captivated him with her curious mind and sweet nature. The horror that if he did not stop his brother, Phillip would find a way to snuff out the only light and goodness that had come into Hawk's life.

"I remember," he said, taking a deep breath. Her hair smelled of sweet honey and wild roses, a balm to his rattled nerves.

It had been Madalene who had made his days at Raven Manor bearable. When he had let her go from the library that first night when he'd found her reading, she'd gazed upon him with gratitude. And when he began delivering books to her room, that gratitude turned into something else. He'd become a hero to her. It was the first time in his life anyone had made him feel that way. Useful. Worthy. He recognized her feelings had turned tender and that he should not allow such a thing, but in his selfishness, he could not let it go. He could not let her go. Her friendship had come to mean too much to him.

And then it had all come to a crashing end in a blaze of violence he could not take back.

He pulled away, hating how the cold rushed in to fill the space where her body had been. The loss was too much, too soon and he grasped her hands before they slid away. She did not pull back and Hawk found himself stunned by the small miracle.

"What happened? After..." He didn't want to say the words, not now that he had the full mental image to wed it with. But he couldn't avoid it. He must know. "After my brother was dead. Then what?"

"You carried me to my room and told me to stay there. You promised that everything would be fine, that you would ensure I was safe. You locked the door to my room as you left and then I suspect you went to tell Lord and Lady Ravenwood what had transpired, but I cannot say for certain. When you left my room, it was the last time I saw you until Mr. Bowen brought you to Northill."

"Then I broke my promise, didn't I?" He had vowed to keep her safe. What had he done instead? Run off like a coward? Left her alone without his protection? His family had cast her out and covered up what he had done. What Phillip had done. They told the world his brother had died in a hunting accident. Trampled by his horse. The lies sickened him. The truth even more so.

"You were not responsible for my safety," she said and he hated how easily she let him off. He did not deserve it. Did not deserve her. Yet he remembered her. When he awoke, with no memory, not even his name, she was the one that instinct pulled him toward. Somewhere, deep in his bones, he had remembered the importance of her. The importance of what he should have done for her yet failed to do.

It was the memory of her that drew him in, held him fast, and gave him somewhere to go when the road back to his memories became too dark to navigate on his own.

"How much time passed after my family dismissed you before you found suitable employment?"

She held silent a moment. A slight breeze rattled the brittle branches of the nearby trees that blocked the view of the main house. "Before my father and I came to Northill last year, we found work wherever we could. I worked as a shop assistant for a seamstress, took in sewing and laundry." Her voice drifted off but she didn't need to say more. The picture she painted was dismal enough. They had struggled, likely often going hungry. This lovely woman, the granddaughter of a baronet, toiling in poverty for five long years.

How did she not hate him for that?

"Why did you not come to me? Surely you would have known where to find me. I would have helped. I would have made things right." *Wouldn't he have?*

Her hands slid from his grasp. He was losing her. "You had changed. You were no longer the man I had known."

Her claim squeezed his heart in a painful grip. "In what way?" When she hesitated, he urged her on. "Please, I need to know."

She let out a slow breath. "Once upon a time, you were a man of character and great promise. Even if your parents never saw it, I did. But you changed after that night. Though I did not witness it first hand, I heard the rumors. Your reputation made you rather infamous in London. It seemed you were determined to embrace every horrible thing your parents believed about you, and make it truth."

"My parents said horrible things about me?" But of course, they had. These people who did not even see fit to inquire upon whether he would survive his injuries. These people who had tossed out the victim of Phillip's evil and cast Hawk out of their lives as if he meant nothing. *Was* nothing. It didn't seem to matter to them that he was now heir to the earldom upon his father's death. But perhaps that was the crux of it. It wasn't supposed to be him. It was never supposed to be him. He had stolen Phillip's life and his place in the world and is parents were determined to punish him for this.

"Did they not see the type of man Phillip was?"

"They thought the sun rose and set on your brother." She tempered her words as if to soften the part left unsaid. That they did not feel the same way about him. They hadn't covered up Phillip's murder to save Hawk. They had done it to preserve Phillip's reputation. And their own.

It filtered back, slowly. Not so much specific events, but feelings. Of being left out. Ignored. Barely tolerated. Often despised. What was it about him that had turned his family away from him? Had he known of Phillip's predilections? That he preyed on women? Surely Miss Cosgrove could not have been the first. How many others had suffered at his hands?

"She's part of the game now... She'll never be safe."

But his brother had been wrong. She *had* been safe. Whoever this *Lord T* was that had penned him the short letter had not come after her. Had Phillip been wrong about the man's devotion to whatever game they played? Or had her departure from Raven Manor saved her in the end, making it more difficult for *Lord T* to find her? And what about now? The letter he'd received made it clear his whereabouts were known. Did the author of the letter also know of Madalene's whereabouts?

Had he brought danger to her doorstep once more?

The question swirled in his head, refusing to be ignored. He didn't have the answer, but he sure as hell would not rest until he did.

"I have done you a great disservice." His words were beyond inadequate.

"You did no such thing," she said, stepping closer and taking his hand.

He stared at her for a long time, far longer than was appropriate, but he could not look away. Everything about her called to something deep inside of him and, in that moment, he wanted her with a sudden wildness he did not have the strength to tame.

He lifted his hand and touched her face, then lowered his mouth to hers, hesitantly at first, waiting for her to deny him, to bring them both to their senses. But she did not. God help him, she did not and he fell into her silence with the desperation of a dying man grasping his last chance at salvation. He slid his arm around her small waist and held her tightly, intoxicated by the closeness and the feel of her molded against him.

He cursed the cold and the barrier of their clothing and everything that kept them where they were instead of somewhere else, where this could be more than a kiss and become everything it deserved to be.

A sudden noise in the trees startled them both, enough to break the kiss, but not enough to pull her out of his arms. From the corner of his eye, he watched a rabbit hop across a fallen branch before it skipped over the path they stood upon and disappeared in the distance, its fur a proper concealment against the snow-covered ground.

"I should go home," she said, avoiding his gaze when he returned it to her.

He nodded, unsure of what to say. He should apologize, but the words would not come. He was not sorry. He would kiss her a hundred times over, if she would allow it.

"Yes, of course. You must be growing cold. I will walk with you."

"No." She offered him a small smile, though it trembled at its edges and he feared he had caused more damage than good this night by failing to hold himself in check. What she must think of him. Did she now consider him as vile as his brother?

"I did not mean to take advantage," he said, bringing her hand to rest against his chest. "That was not my intention. I just—" He tried to find the words to explain but they escaped him. Perhaps no words existed to describe what he had felt.

"I know. I...I do not hold it against you. It was...we were simply caught up in a moment. I meant to offer comfort and I should not have let it go so far—"

He gave his head a sharp shake. "No!" The word came out harshly and he took a breath, tempering it. "No, do not put the blame on yourself. The kiss was my doing and mine alone."

"I kissed you back." A fact he had been sorely aware of and

forever grateful for. For in that moment, when she responded to him with the same fervor, he no longer felt alone.

"Then we are likely both fools, are we not?" He meant to make light but she did not return his half-hearted smile.

"You should return to the main house," she said, pulling her hand from his chest. "You will need your rest if you are to tackle the tasks Father has set out for you on the morrow."

She did not want his company any longer this evening. His heart squeezed but he nodded. He would give her this. "Very well then. But I shall wait here until you are safely inside."

She offered him no argument. It would have been a fruitless endeavor if she had and perhaps, knowing him as she did, she understood.

Hawk escorted her to the edge of the trees then stood there in the cold, watching her walk away, each step a painful pressure against his heart. He continued to wait until she was safely inside and a light appeared in the window. Only then did he reluctantly turn away and make his way back to the main house. But his brother's last words dogged him and the memory brought with it the sick sensation that whatever game Phillip had referred to had not ended with his death.

If that was true, then Hawk had no other choice but to return to London and discover how to put a stop to the madness. He owed Madalene that much at least. And even without the full extent of his memories, this much he knew to be true and irrefutable—he would give his own life if it meant the safety of hers.

He may have failed her once, but he would not do so again.

"It is wonderful to see you again, Miss Cosgrove," the Countess of Glenmor said, as Madalene entered the salon where the former Miss Judith Sutherland and Lady Rebecca were having a visit. Lady Glenmor had married the Earl of Glenmor a few weeks previous in a small ceremony over the Yuletide. Both Lord and Lady Glenmor had been present when Lord Hawksmoor was attacked and nearly killed and Madalene would be forever grateful for their part in saving his life.

However, surely that had nothing to do with why she had been summoned to meet with Lady Rebecca and the new countess. She did not have a close association with Lady Glenmor beyond a passing acquaintance when she had altered several gowns during her time in London. Though she did feel a certain kinship with the countess, since, as the grand-daughter of a knight, they came from similar backgrounds in a sense.

Madalene curtsied. "Thank you, my lady. I hope the day finds you well."

"It does, thank you. Lord Glenmor and I thought we might pay a visit and see how Lord Hawksmoor fares. I am pleased to see he is doing well." Lady Glenmor smiled and the effect changed her ordinary appearance into something quite extraordinary. "I understand you have been instrumental in his care and that pieces of his memory are beginning to return."

Heat crept up her neck and the apple of her cheeks burned. The events of the night before rushed back to her. She had never meant for their conversation to go so far, to prod such memories to resurface. To end in a kiss that still had the ability to reduce her to a puddle. That the snow had not melted all around them from the heat of their embrace was a bona fide miracle. Regardless, she should have stopped the kiss instantly, but the moment his lips touched hers a hunger overtook her that went beyond her need to give him some peace. She had wanted him, pure and simple and in every sense of the word. He had held her close, but it wasn't close enough, he had kissed her long, but not long enough. And when their mouths parted, she wanted nothing more but to experience that heady sensation once again.

Had the copse of trees not protected them from view of the main house, perhaps the summons she had received to come to the salon would have been made under different circumstances. Thankfully, no one had witnessed their unintended tryst and the secrets shared between them remained theirs alone. Yet something between them had changed. Not just in the physical acknowledgement that an attraction existed between them. Something in Lord Hawksmoor had changed. The essence of the transformation had lingered in the air. There was a determination to the set of his jaw. It was the same look she'd seen when he'd taken her from the larder all those years ago and left her in her room, telling her she was safe, promising her he would return.

He hadn't, of course. She'd waited, but hours had passed and the sun had risen. Eventually she'd been forced to face the fact that he was not coming. And why would he? She was but a servant and he was a lord who had just killed his brother. What possible help could he offer her? He'd be lucky to save himself.

"Miss Cosgrove?"

She straightened. Dear heavens, they had been speaking to her. "I beg your pardon, my lady. I did not sleep well last night." Not a lie. She'd tossed and turned, the passion awakened by their kiss refusing to allow her to sleep.

Lady Glenmor offered a look of understanding, as if she too was familiar with such things. "Think nothing of it. I was simply saying that Lord Glenmor and I are returning to London to take care of several business matters. I understand you will soon be moving on from your position as house-keeper and need to hire a suitable replacement. Lady Rebecca suggested it might be worthwhile if you visited a few of the employment agencies in London to find someone."

Lady Rebecca leaned forward. "I would do it myself, Miss Cosgrove, but in my condition," Her hand dropped to rest upon the growing bump at her belly. "I'm afraid Mr. Bowen worries about me traveling and the doctor has seen fit to take his side in the matter. But I have the utmost faith in your ability to select a suitable candidate if you are amenable to going in my place. Lord and Lady Glenmor will see you there safely and Lady Dalridge has offered to provide you a place to stay and proper chaperone during your stay."

"We would do it ourselves," Lady Glenmor said, "but we shall be traveling on from London after a proper night's rest to see what progress has been made to the renovations at Maple Glen."

London.

Returning to the city struck a small sliver of fear in her heart. While Lord Hawksmoor only remembered his brother's words the night before, she had lived with them for nearly six years. His threat that she would never be safe had forced her to live constantly looking over her shoulder. After a bit, when no one came after her, she grew complacent and began to believe no such man as Lord T existed, that his claims had been the rantings of a madman. But that complacency was more easily accessed while safely ensconced in the country under the protection of both Father and Mr. Bowen. Even on the few occasions when she had accompanied the Bowens into the city, she'd stayed mostly inside, not venturing out unless absolutely necessary.

Now she was being requested to return once again. "Yes. Of course, I...I would be pleased to help in that regard."

"Wonderful," Lady Rebecca said with a clap of her hand.

"It is settled then. Lady Glenmor will send word once she knows of their departure date and we will have a carriage at your disposal for when you are ready to return to Northill with your replacement. Please do not rush, take your time and enjoy the sites and spectacles of London while you are there."

Madalene forced a smile. London held no sights or spectacles she cared to see, but perhaps being away from Lord Hawksmoor would allow her the time to put her feelings for him back under lock and key. Nothing could come of the kiss they had shared. He was far above her station and well out of reach. Unless he meant to make her his mistress, a position that held no interest for her at all. No, it was best if she found the Bowens a suitable replacement as housekeeper and then moved on, whether as headmistress of Miss Caldwell's school, or somewhere else. If she did not, she would find herself haunting Northill like a specter, mooning over something that could never be.

"I look forward to finding a proper replacement for my position."

Chapter Eight

"What do you think you're doing?"

Hawk turned from the window to face Marcus Bowen who had entered the room with a man he didn't recognize trailing behind him. The second man, light where Mr. Bowen was dark, held a familiarity about him, but try as he might, Hawk couldn't place him.

He pulled his gaze away from the second man and put it back on his host. "You may need to be more specific. Do you mean at this very moment, or—"

"My valet has informed me you requested he procure you a suit for your departure. From my closet no less."

Hawk appreciated how, when Mr. Bowen deemed to speak, he did not waste time mincing words but cut straight to the heart of the matter. He admired that and suspected, in his previous life, they had held a mutual appreciation for each other. Perhaps that was why his host had brought him here, despite Hawk's rather despicable reputation.

"Well, you do have a somewhat understated sense of style that appeals to me. And we are of a similar build now that you've fattened me up over the past weeks. Why your taskmaster of a steward has me working like a veritable field hand." Much as he did not care to be mucking stables or baling hay or whatever other onerous chore Mr. Cosgrove set out for him, he had attacked each with fervor, and day by day his strength had returned.

Unfortunately, the hard work and newly returned strength had done little to keep his brain from making addled choices, such as kissing a beautiful woman he had no ability to resist. He had compromised her. By rights, he should propose. Yet, he hadn't. Not that the idea of waking up next to her each and every day did not sound like a perfectly lovely idea, but he had other matters to attend to, and likely Madalene would not have him either way. Accepting him meant living with the memories they shared. What woman would want that sort of reminder staring her in the face each day?

The other man stepped forward and spoke, concern written across his face that Hawk found rather refreshing after weeks of Mr. Bowen's enigmatic expressions. "Then you plan on returning to London sooner rather than later? Are you certain that is wise?"

"I cannot see how it is unwise. That is where I live, is it not? And who are you exactly?"

Mr. Bowen motioned toward his companion. "This is Benedict Laytham, Earl of Glenmor. He's the one responsible for your being alive, seeing as he altered the trajectory of Pengrin's bullet with his arm so it only skimmed your head instead of imbedding itself into it."

Hawk straightened. He did not care for all of this indebtedness he appeared to have racked up since the incident with Lord Pengrin. "Ah, quite sporting of you. Well, you were about ninety percent successful in that endeavor. I hope you have recovered nicely."

"I have, thank you. My wife has taken expert care of me." The expression on Lord Glenmor's face altered perceptibly at the mention of his wife, softening and strengthening all at the same time. It was a strange thing to see. Even stranger, however, was the emptiness it left echoing inside of Hawk, and the unsettling knowledge that he would likely never have an opportunity to utter those words.

"Then you're a lucky man."

The earl tilted his head to one side. "Do you really remember none of what happened that day?"

"I'm afraid not. Your heroics appear to have slipped my mind completely."

Lord Glenmor laughed. "And yet your sarcasm has been left well intact. Amazing."

"You may be the only one who thinks so. Now, if you'll forgive me, I am in the midst of preparations to leave this humble abode for my own." Not that such preparation required much. He had no belongings to speak of with him and what he did have had been borrowed from Mr. Bowen.

"Back to The Devil's Lair, then?"

"I thought I might be more comfortable in my bachelor apartments." Mr. Bowen and Lord Glenmor shared a look and frustration boiled within him. "Oh, bloody hell. Are you to tell me I do not possess proper bachelor apartments?"

Mr. Bowen raised one eyebrow and the smallest hint of a smirk pulled at the corner of his mouth. "I suppose it depends on your definition of *proper*. You reside at The Devil's Lair."

"I live in a gaming hell? Actually, *live* there. Day to day?"

"Yes," Lord Glenmor stated in a tone that implied he found it amusing that Hawk did not recall this particular fact, or that he seemed shocked by it now. How thrilling that he could offer these gentlemen such entertainment. If only they knew the facts Hawk did remember, perhaps they would not find the situation quite so humorous.

"And what of the Earl of Ravenwood? I find it odd he would not have a home in the city."

"He does." Mr. Bowen left it at that, but it was enough to convey his meaning.

"But I am not welcomed there."

Silence. Wonderful. Just...wonderful. He sighed.

"I am leaving for London within a few days," Lord Glenmor stated. "If you are determined to return to the city, I can convey you."

"Thank you, but do not trouble yourself." Being further indebted to this man who had saved his life irked him. Worse, it was still up for debate whether the life Glenmor saved had been worth the effort.

"It's no trouble. We are escorting Miss Cosgrove as well. The more the merrier."

What the deuce? She had no business being in London, alone and unprotected! "Do you think that is wise? She is a young woman, an innocent, and London is—"

"Calm yourself, man," Mr. Bowen said, leaning his shoulder against the bedpost and crossing his legs at the ankle. "She is quite capable of taking care of herself and Lady Glenmor has procured Lady Dalridge to act as chaperone."

Lord Glenmor grinned. "It appears the viscountess is still feeling a bit contrite over having sacked my wife."

Sacked his wife? Hawk leaned forward, suddenly intrigued. "Your wife was *employed*?" Something akin to hope tingled at the back of his neck. Would he not be the first of his acquaintance to develop tender feelings for a servant? Yet, in truth, he did not see Madalene in such a way. He saw her as a person, a resilient young woman with a strength that set her apart from the others.

"Yes," Lord Glenmor replied. "Judith had been hired as companion to Lady Dalridge's great-niece, Lady Henrietta."

"Then she was not a lady before she married you?" His memory may be shot full of holes, but even he knew men of his station generally married women of the same ilk. If Lord

Glenmor had broken ranks, would it be so strange if he were to—

What the hell? Where did that come from? Why, he had no intention of marrying Madalene. Marrying anyone for that matter. He was damaged goods—a murderer. He lived in a gaming hell. Hardly fit husband material for anyone, least of all Madalene. Not that she'd have him, regardless. Although, she had returned his kiss with equal fervor. But no. No. He would not drag her into his dark world.

"No, she was a miss," Lord Glenmor answered. "Her grandfather had been knighted by the queen, as was her uncle. Though I believe her to be more of a lady than many of my acquaintance."

"Indeed." Good Lord, the man positively gushed about his countess. Was that what awaited Hawk if he continued mooning over Madalene? God help him.

He needed to quit while he was ahead. A difficult task if they were sending the poor woman into the mouth of the beast, returning her to London where she could potentially be in danger, if his brother's dying declaration was to be believed.

Which meant distancing himself from Madalene would have to wait; at least until he determined any remaining threat to her had been eliminated. He drew his hand to his chest. One of the maids had set the crumpled note he'd received from *"T"* on his nightstand and he'd stowed it in his pocket for safekeeping.

"I believe I will take you up on your offer, Lord Glenmor. I shall be ready to leave for London when you are."

The journey to London was made in a day, though the length of the trip felt more like an eternity by the time they arrived in the city well after the sun had set. Lord and Lady Glenmor provided excellent company and conversation, but watching the two of them together, happy in their newfound love and marriage, made Madalene's heart ache with a loneliness she had not expected.

It wasn't often she allowed herself to consider her own solitary state. She rarely stayed in one place long enough to form the type of attachments that would lead to a permanent change. Not that she hadn't noticed a fine-looking gentleman from time to time, but somehow, they never quite measured up to the one gentleman she had known all those years ago. The one who had been kind enough to supply her with books to read, who had spoken to her as if she were a real person and not just an anonymous servant meant to blend in with the walls. The one whose smile had the ability to bring sunshine to a dark day and comfort to a lonely heart.

The same one who sat across from her now, who had spent the duration of their trip staring silently out the window at the passing landscape as if she didn't exist. Had Lord Hawksmoor so easily forgotten the intimacies they had shared? The closeness that led to their kiss? Had he no inkling of the desire the touch of his lips had aroused within her or how desperately she wished to experience his mouth upon hers once more?

He'd contributed little to the conversation, leaving it to Lord and Lady Glenmor to carry the bulk of it, something the couple did quite easily, speaking on any number of topics from politics to social issues to plans they had for ongoing renovations of Maple Glen, the earl's countryseat. Lady Glenmor spoke knowledgeably on each subject and her husband listened with rapt attention, never once treating her as if her opinion was of little consequence. An uncommon occurrence in the houses Madalene had worked in over the years. It gave her hope that maybe someday, if she did marry, she might expect the same respect from her own husband.

Her gaze drifted to Lord Hawksmoor then just as quickly skidded away. She had no business letting her thoughts carry her down such a path. A man of his stature would never consider a woman like her. The kiss they'd shared when he escorted her home several nights ago was nothing more than an anomaly brought on by the anguish he'd experienced in remembering what his brother had done.

It had nothing to do with her, despite how it had affected her.

She let out a slow breath and turned to stare out her own window as the carriage navigated the streets of Grosvenor Park. She had never worked in this part of the city before. Her work as a servant had occurred mostly in the country houses. It wasn't until she was dismissed from Raven Manor that she and her father were forced to go to London in search of whatever work they could find.

"I will deliver the ladies to Lord Ridgemont's first," Lord Glenmor said, directing his statement to Lord Hawksmoor. "Then I shall convey you to The Devil's Lair. I would prefer the ladies not be exposed to that."

Lady Glenmor gave her husband a grateful smile. "Thank you, Ben. No offense to your establishment, Lord Hawksmoor, but I have no wish to return there any time soon."

"You were there previously?" he asked, her comment grabbing his attention.

"I was. The night you and Benedict were injured."

His brow furrowed as if he was putting the pieces of a puzzle together. "Did you know Lord Pengrin?"

Her expression darkened. "I did."

Lord Hawksmoor nodded but must have sensed, as Madalene did, that it was not a subject she wished to discuss further and he let the matter drop, returning his gaze back to the window without glancing Madalene's way.

His avoidance of her made her heart ache. Was he embarrassed about the other night? Did he resent having kissed her? There were so many things she wanted to ask him, so much he likely had locked inside of his head about his brother and whatever game he insisted involved her, but she was afraid to broach it. Afraid he would shy away from the dark memories and lose them forever.

Her breath caught. His journals! How had she not thought of them before now?

Madalene straightened sharply in her seat. Lord Hawksmoor had kept journals. How many times had she entered a room to clean or deliver tea or do whatever task had been assigned her, and there he would be, sitting in a quiet corner or at a table, writing in one of his leather-bound journals. It was rare for her to see him without one close at hand, yet he guarded them religiously, never letting anyone else so much as touch them.

Once, as their friendship grew, she had been so bold as to ask him what he wrote in them.

"Observations, my curious little pet. Thoughts I have."

She liked that he called her that—my pet. It made her feel special. Important somehow, even though she knew deep inside she was nothing more than a little mouse in a very big house. She skittered about quietly, beneath the notice of others. At least she had, until he held out a piece of cheese and enticed her out of the shadows.

"Observations about what?" She took a step closer to him, forgetting herself. Her position, or lack thereof.

"Whatever I see. You never know when such information may come in handy someday."

"What have you seen today?" How easy it was to talk with him. His warm smile and lovely green eyes exuded such warmth they drew her in against her better judgment. She did not think a more handsome man existed in all of England.

"I have seen that you need a new pair of shoes."

"Oh."

She glanced down at her feet, embarrassed. The side of one shoe had begun to give way from its sole. She had been afraid to bring the matter to the housekeeper, Mrs. Brewster. She was not a kindly sort and took a portion of Madalene's pay to cover any such expenses. Money she preferred to send to Father to ease his hardships.

"I shall see that you have a new pair straightaway."

She shook her head. "No, that is fine. I shall repair it—"

"I will not have you going about with your feet coming out of your shoes," he said, his voice about as lordly as it got. "You will have a new pair. And do not concern yourself with Mrs. Brewster. I will take care of her."

And he turned back to his writing, dipped his quill and made a notation on the page, smiling as he did so in such a way her heart expanded until it ached. Next to Father, he was the best man she had ever encountered. She hoped her employment at Raven Manor continued for years to come, for if she were to leave, she would miss him very much. Too much.

"Miss Cosgrove?" She pulled herself back to the present to find Lord Hawksmoor and Lord and Lady Glenmor staring at her. "Is something the matter?"

Lord Hawksmoor's voice sounded the same now as it had that day in the library when he'd noticed the state of her shoes. And in that moment, she wanted nothing more than to help him, to return a long overdue kindness.

"You kept journals," she told him.

"Yes," he nodded. "Mr. Bowen mentioned as such. They are at my office."

"No." The journals she had heard Mr. Bowen mention were observations, yes, but of a business nature. He had used them to further his own interests, to use against those whose influence he could manipulate. "Personal journals. Ones written before..." Before his brother's death. Before he had turned into the man referred to as *The Hawk*.

His eyebrows knitted together and he leaned forward. "Are you certain?"

"Yes. I've seen them."

"Do you know where they are now?"

She shook her head. "I assume you took them with you when you left Raven Manor. You were quite protective of them, so I do not imagine you would have left them behind."

He straightened in his seat. "Then they must be at The Devil's Lair."

Lord Glenmor shook his head. "Marcus found many journals when he went through your office after the ordeal with Lord Pengrin, but none of them were of a personal nature."

"If I was protective over them, as Miss Cosgrove indicates, likely I would have kept them well hidden," he said, the words coming slowly, like a discovery he'd only just made. Something hidden in the shadow that had suddenly drifted to the surface. He turned his attention back to Madalene. "Do you know where I kept them when I lived at Raven Manor?"

Her cheeks flamed. If she admitted the truth, it would illuminate the interest she had taken in him, the silly infatuation of a young girl with a tender heart. But she was not that young girl any longer, nor was he the man she had once known, yet her feelings for him had not faded, as an infatuation should have.

"The hearth in your bedchamber had a loose stone along the side of it."

Lord and Lady Glenmor's eyebrows lifted in tandem and the heat in her cheeks burned even hotter. Curse her pale skin!

"And how, exactly, did you know this?" Lord Hawksmoor asked.

She cleared her throat. "I was a maid of all work and was often tasked with cleaning out the hearths. One night, I noted the loose stone. When I tried to put it back in place, something prevented me from pushing it in. I pulled it out to investigate and discovered a narrow cubby. Resting inside of it were several journals."

He leaned forward. "And did you read them?"

"I did not."

He lifted one dark eyebrow. "Such admirable restraint."

He didn't sound as if he believed her and she'd be lying if she claimed not to have been tempted. She had been. But something had stopped her. What if in these journals, he spoke of a young lady he had taken a shine to? A young lady far more befitting a man in his position than she could ever be? It had stayed her hand. She did not want to give up the fantasies she had concocted in her mind. She wanted to hold them safe and keep them from being tarnished by harsh reality. She'd had enough disappointments in her life.

"They were not my thoughts to invade, my lord," she said, finally.

He remained silent for several minutes and a pregnant tension filled the interior of the carriage. "I suppose I shall have to look for loose stones then, hadn't I?"

She was spared from answering him as the carriage slowed to a stop in front of a splendid townhouse. Madalene glanced out the window, past Lord Hawksmoor's sharp profile.

"We are here," Lady Glenmor announced.

Madalene heard the smile in her voice but did not turn toward her to verify such. She was too mesmerized by Lord Hawksmoor's serious expression, filled with intent and purpose.

What did he hope to find in those journals? And would their contents help or hinder his quest to recapture his past?

———

L ady Henrietta Harrow hugged Lady Glenmor tightly, her happiness in seeing her friend obvious, though a hint of sadness still lurked in the young lady's eyes. Lady Glenmor had mentioned that she had grown close to Lady Henrietta during her brief time as the lady's companion, but had been forced to break her heart in an attempt to stop her from making a decision that would ruin her life. While their greeting today was warm and the affection between them evident, it was also obvious that they had not yet recaptured the closeness they once shared.

"So, this is the young lady that requires a chaperone, is it?" The formidable Lady Dalridge dragged her assessing gaze up and down Madalene, her ornate walking stick tapping lightly against the hardwood of the receiving room. "Well, we can hardly traipse her about London in such underwhelming apparel. That must change. Did you bring other frocks with you, my dear?"

"Yes, but—" Madalene stumbled over her words. What did the woman mean by *traipse her about London*? There must be some mistake. "I am only here to interview potential housekeepers. My current apparel is more than adequate."

"Adequate? What proper young lady wishes a wardrobe that is merely *adequate*?" Madalene glanced at Lady Glenmor for assistance but Lady Dalridge waved a hand in the air, calling her attention back to her. "Heavens, do not look to Lady Glenmor in that regard. The machinations it required to get her into anything with a frill or flounce during her time with us was Herculean. Please tell me you will not be so difficult as she."

Madalene refrained from reminding Lady Dalridge it had been she who had been summoned by Lady Glenmor's cousin, Patience, to help alter one of those dresses she now referred to. Still, she would require no such dresses for her brief trip.

"Forgive me, my lady, but I think you misunderstand the purpose of my visit—" Madalene looked once more to Lady Glenmor, but she only smiled, any hard feelings she'd had toward Lady Dalridge for dismissing her obviously smoothed over. Would Madalene ever feel such forgiveness toward Lord and Lady Ravenwood? Doubtful. Her good nature did not extend that far.

Lady Dalridge banged her walking stick to regain Madalene's attention. "Was your grandfather not a baronet, my dear?"

"Y-yes, he was, but—" She had not known the man. He had passed away shortly before she was born and his stature in society had died with him.

"There is no but about it, I'm afraid. In fact, I met your grandfather on several occasions before my marriage to Lord Dalridge. He was a lovely man and while his daughter may have married beneath her station, I see no reason that should affect you now that you are here with me. I think during your stay we shall make a bit of a project out of you."

A project? Madalene's heart plummeted. She did not care to be someone's project. "Lady Dalridge, I appreciate that you—".

"No, you don't," the viscountess said with a wave of her jeweled hand. "You think me an interfering old lady who is sticking her nose into business where it doesn't belong. But I can barely get Lady Henrietta to step foot out of the house since the whole regretful incidence with Lord Pengrin and I am quite at a loss as to what to do with my time. Now, if I am to play hostess and chaperone to you, my dear, the least you can do in return is allow me to take you somewhere more interesting than dreary employment agencies."

Lady Glenmor laughed. "Don't bother trying to fight her, Miss Cosgrove. She is determined to have her way. And it would not hurt you to have a little fun while you're here. Lady Rebecca insisted you take some time to enjoy yourself."

"And if it stops her from badgering me, all the better," Lady Henrietta added and though she said the words with the hint of a smile, there was something desperate in her gaze that spoke to Madalene and made her want to help. Lady Henrietta pulled nervously at the thick layer of golden hair that fell over her shoulder, partially concealing the burn scars on her neck. Her self-consciousness was obvious. No wonder the young woman cared little for being out in society.

"Very well then. But I do not plan on staying for long." Besides, it was the middle of winter. Surely there could not be that many entertainments going on in the city with most of its inhabitants gone to their country houses until the new Season began in April.

"Long enough to provide me with some amusement, I hope," Lady Dalridge said. "Now come, Lydia will show you to your room and get you settled. Then we shall see what we can do about this sadly lacking wardrobe. My lovely niece has any number of gowns going to waste, now that she refuses to leave the house."

Lady Dalridge cast a glance over her shoulder at Lady Henrietta, but her gaze softened when it rested on the young woman, a mix of worry and despair written in the lines of her face.

When they reached the top of the steps, Lady Dalridge looped her arm through Madalene's and lowered her voice. "Perhaps having another young lady about the house will entice her to rejoin society instead of hiding away. She had done so well while Lady Glenmor was here. I berate myself every day for being so blind and foolish as to send her away."

The elderly lady sighed and shook her head and Madalene realized the offer of chaperone extended by Lady Dalridge had not come without a price, though as far as prices went, this one was easy enough to pay. Lady Henrietta's appeared of a sweet nature. If her presence here helped the young woman in any way, she was happy to do it.

"I will be more than happy to offer her my friendship, my lady, but I do not know if that will entice her into doing anything she does not wish to do."

"I do appreciate that, Miss Cosgrove. You are a definite jewel. Lady Glenmor and Lady Rebecca were not wrong in that regard."

The thought of facing society did not make her feel like a jewel. It made her feel like a fraud. What did she know about conducting herself in society? Her only exposure to that world had been on the fringes as the daughter of a land steward or a maid in their houses. Her mother had taught her proper etiquette, but the lessons had been so long ago, they had gathered dust in her memories.

What would society do if they discovered a servant walked amongst them, pretending to be one of them? Would they run her off for the imposter she was? Her best hope was to find her replacement as soon as possible and return to her safe little world on the Northill estate. Then again, even that would come to an end once she found the new housekeeper.

A cold fear of the unknown settled in her belly and bled into her veins. Her world slowly tilted upside down and she had nothing of substance to grab hold of to keep from losing her footing.

Chapter Nine

H awk had exhausted every possibility in searching for the journals Madalene insisted he had once possessed. Every nook and cranny had been poked, prodded, yanked and eventually kicked in the hopes something would fall lose.

Nothing of import did, other than a stack of letters tied together. Though he feared he may have broken his toe, a fact that did little to improve his darkening mood. Equally as disconcerting, were the stains on the carpet that had soaked into the hardwood beneath. Not just inside the office where he now stood, angry and embittered, but outside its door as well, marking the spot where two men had died because of him.

His staff at The Devil's Lair had welcomed him back with a polite deference. And while none of them appeared overjoyed at his return, nor did they appear disappointed either. They simply seemed...indifferent.

"You did not mingle with your staff," Lord Glenmor had informed him when he'd mumbled like a spoiled child at their lack of enthusiasm. "They are simply treating you in the manner you had always wished to be treated. The fact that most stayed after two of your men were murdered trying to protect you speaks volumes, one would think."

Murdered. The word reverberated through him. Two men had traded their lives for his. The knowledge left him extremely uncomfortable. How did one repay that kind of debt? Especially when the recipients repayment was owed to were buried six feet under.

"I shall ensure their families are cared for." It was the only avenue of reimbursement left. And the least he could do.

Lord Glenmor raised his eyebrows at his suggestion, as if surprised he would do such a thing. God help him, what kind of tyrant was he? Maybe Pengrin had good cause to put a bullet through his head. How many others would be just as willing to follow in his footsteps and succeed where Pengrin had failed?

He glanced at the door Lord Glenmor had departed through several hours earlier. A new set of doors had been installed during his absence and a sturdy bolt added. Two new men recently promoted in the ranks stood guard on the opposite side of the doors, much as the previous two men had done the night he was attacked. It did not make him feel any safer. Someone had gotten past them once and he'd be a fool to think it couldn't happen again.

His gaze drifted around the room. Beyond the office there was a bedchamber, rather small and sparsely decorated, lacking any hint of the individual who occupied it. The bedchamber could have belonged to anyone. It was his, yet the room revealed nothing of a personal nature. The office had a sitting area with a small table he supposed was where he took his meals, a desk with a rather extensive library behind it, and a reading area made up of two wingback chairs set in front of a decent sized hearth. On the far side of the room was another door that led to a private billiards room.

Despite all these amenities, it did not feel like home. It felt like a prison—one of his own making. Frustrated at his lack of success finding the journals, he snatched the stack of letters from his desk and was about to untie the bundle when a brief knock at the office doors interrupted him.

He sighed and tossed the letters back on the desk. "Come in."

The door opened and Rickard, one of the men he'd hired, stepped inside, leaving the door slightly ajar. There was a well-dressed man on the opposite side. "Lord Tunsten t'see you, m'lord."

"Lord Tunsten...?" He had informed certain members of his upper staff that due to his injury, he was experiencing some brief memory lapses, though he did not go into the depth or breadth of their severity. He did not want their pity, nor have them take advantage.

"Yes, m'lord." Rickard lowered his voice. His thick cockney accent forced Hawk to strain to make him out. "Viscount. Owes a tidy sum t' the 'ouse so 'is lordship comes once a month t' make 'is payments."

Payments. Hawk glanced around the room to the pile of ledgers Mr. Bowen had left neatly stacked on his desk. He hadn't had time to review them in detail, but the name Tunsten rang a bell. He issued a curt nod. "Send him in."

Rickard opened the door and Lord Tunsten sauntered in as if he was out for a leisurely stroll. He did not immediately address Hawk, but instead looked around the room. Hawk took the opportunity to make a quick assessment. The viscount was a tall, lanky sort, though not exactly thin. His dark hair was heavily peppered with gray and his nose shot out like a hooked beak. His eyes were small and beady but he missed little. The tightness around his mouth and the way his right thumb continuously rubbed his adjacent forefinger revealed he was not happy about being here. The man had an ego and did not appreciate being indebted, nor reminded of his indebtedness. He thought himself above this. Above Hawk.

Yet it was his vices—his weakness—that led him to be here. And it was the reminder of that weakness that he despised most of all.

All of this information filled Hawk's brain during little more than the time it took to take a cursory glance, then it swam inside his head bringing on a wave of dizziness. He reached out and touched the edge of his desk with his finger-tips to anchor himself. Was this a memory of the man, or just something that Hawk did—sizing people up in an instant and taking in the information they unwittingly revealed?

"I had expected the room to look a bit worse for wear," Lord Tunsten said, turning to face Hawk for the first time. "Given your recent unfortunate incident."

Hawk said nothing.

"The ton is quite abuzz with it. Some say you are dead. Others that your brain has been addled to the point of uselessness."

"Ah, well," Hawk gave a non-committal shrug. "As you can see, both reports are false." He gave no more information than that. The less people knew about the extent of his injuries, the better.

"But you did not come out of it completely unscathed, I see." Lord Tunsten motioned toward the wound on the side of his head. It had healed well, thankfully, and appeared more as a red welt than an open wound. Yet, given its positioning, there was little hiding it.

"I survived. Lord Pengrin, on the other hand, well..." He let his voice trail off, then smiled. "Do you have something for me, Lord Tunsten, or did you simply stop by to chat?" Lord Glenmor had informed Hawk that he was more often than not a man of few words and the words he did offer were limited and to the point. He did not suffer fools lightly and had little sympathy for those who gambled away their purses and then begged for mercy.

"*Mercy was not generally something in The Hawk's repertoire.*"

Tunsten's expression hardened. He did not like being called to task. Likely he wished Pengrin's bullet had killed Hawk and, given the hate in the viscount's eyes, if it had been a slow, agonizing death, all the better. Lovely. How nice to engender such devotion in one's peers.

Tunsten reached inside his well-tailored jacket and pulled out an envelope too thick to contain a letter or bank draft. "I do not know why you insist on having me deliver this in person. Do you like rubbing my nose in it? Does it give you some kind of perverse pleasure?"

"I am not the one who risked my fortune on the turn of a card," Hawk said, motioning toward the table rather than taking the envelope from the viscount. "Nor did I force you to stand at the tables and gamble away what you could ill afford to lose."

Funny how when things went sour no one wanted to take responsibility for their part in it.

Tunsten tossed the payment on the desk behind Hawk where it landed next to the letters, but the viscount did not immediately turn away. His glare cut into Hawk like a knife to the flesh. Hawk refused to flinch or look away. Instead, he raised one dark eyebrow.

"I despise you," Tunsten said, the words hissed out of him like acid. "One day you will pay for all the misery you have brought."

"Is that so?" Hadn't he already paid? Wasn't the loss of his memory enough?

"Mark my words." Tunsten took a step back but his expression did not soften. "You are nothing like your brother. His death was a great loss to your family. How disappointing for Lord Ravenwood to know you are now his only heir."

"I suspect the latter part of that statement is quite true." Hawk took a breath, struggling with the anger roiling inside of him. "The former, however, I have my sincere doubts about."

Before Tunsten could continue, Hawk looked past his shoulder and called out to Rickard. When the burly man opened the door, Hawk turned his back on the viscount. "Show Lord Tunsten out, would you, Rickard? Our business here is concluded and I find I have grown weary of his company."

"You are nothing more than filth dressed up in a fancy suit," he seethed at the dismissal. "Title or no, that will not change."

His words sliced into Hawk, cutting deep into the fears he had tried to keep at bay as he discovered more and more about the man he had become. When his memories returned, was this who he would be? This despised creature that lived in a dark hovel and thought nothing of destroying his peers as if it was all a game? It sickened him. Perhaps he was not much different from Phillip, after all.

He waited until he heard the main door to the gaming hell close and for his men to throw the bolt across it before he turned and hurled his brandy toward the fire, watching as the flames flared, then settled once more.

He needed to find those journals. And he needed Madalene to do it. She was all he had, a thin, tethered rope between the man he once was and one he had become. It had been she who had unlocked the memory of what had happened between him and Phillip. Perhaps if she could help him find the journals as well, he would find the rest of the answers he sought. He would discover why he had changed so drastically from the man she claimed was filled with goodness. The man he wanted to be for her again.

But how in the hell was he to bring her to The Devil's Lair without ruining her completely? It was impossible. He would die a thousand deaths before exposing her to anything that would cause her pain or upset. She had suffered enough at his hands.

No, he was on his own. A state he should be all too familiar with.

Frustrated, he strode to his desk and grabbed the packet of letters, then returned to the wingback chairs by the fire and pulled at the bindings holding them together.

L ady Henrietta circled Madalene staring at the pale blue gown that drifted down her body like a cloud. "I believe this gown is far more suited to you than it ever was me, Miss Cosgrove."

"Oh, I don't know about that." Madalene was not used to such compliments and besides, she and Lady Henrietta were of similar build and coloring, with their blonde hair and blue eyes. Why, they could almost pass for sisters.

"I do," Lady Henrietta said. "And your skill with needle and thread is beyond compare. Where did you learn such a skill?"

"My mother and aunt. After Lord Walkerton relieved my father of his duties, I often took in sewing to help make ends meet and for a brief time worked in a seamstress's shop." The memory, never far from her mind, did little to calm her nerves over the upcoming dance Lady Dalridge insisted on taking her to.

"Do not worry." Lady Henrietta placed a gentle hand on Madalene's forearm, as if sensing her fear. Then again, likely she knew a thing or two about facing society while knowing she no longer fit within it. Her scars set her apart, as did Madalene's background.

"I cannot help but feel they will recognize I do not belong the moment I step foot through the door."

"You are the granddaughter of a baronet, and possess an astonishing amount of poise. You will fit in quite nicely and I suspect none of them will be the wiser. Aunt intends on introducing you as the granddaughter of a longtime friend who has since passed on. I dare say, no one will challenge the great and imposing Lady Dalridge."

The way Lady Henrietta imparted that last bit made Madalene smile. "I do wish you were coming, as well."

"Oh, well." Lady Henrietta waved off the comment, her gaze dropping away, but not before Madalene saw the sheen of tears sparking in her eyes. "I think my days in society are over, brief as they were. Between my scars and the horrible fiasco with Lord Pengrin, I have determined I would be better served keeping my own company. I cannot bear the stares and whispers, I truly can't."

Madalene reached out and took Lady Henrietta's hand. "Forgive me. I should not have suggested such a thing."

"It is of no matter." Lady Henrietta smiled, but it lacked a certain happiness one would expect from such a lovely young woman who should have held the world by the tail. "Now, come. Let us show Aunt how absolutely lovely you look! I will be surprised to hear if you are not the belle of the ball."

Madalene's heart pounded as they entered the grand home of Mr. and Mrs. Lindwell. The American couple had spared no expense. The extravagant décor stopped just short of being garish, though to see the upturned noses of several guests, she may be the only one who thought so. During the short ride over, Lady Dalridge had prepared Madalene for the fact that the Lindwells were not well thought of and only the fact that Mrs. Lindwell was a second cousin to the Duke of Franklyn even remotely allowed them to move about society as if they belonged.

"Which they don't," Lady Dalridge added.

"Then why are we attending?" Society baffled her. There were so many rules, hidden and otherwise, that made no sense at all. So much emphasis was placed on things no one had any control over, all in an effort to place importance on things that were not really important at all. Titles and wealth and propriety and manners. What did that matter if one did not possess character and goodness and a willingness to help others in their time of need?

"We are attending, my dear, because entertainments are sparse this time of the year and I thought this might be a good place to start your introduction to society, seeing as your own connection to it is rather thin."

It was skewed logic at best, but Madalene didn't bother questioning it. What good would it do her now? She was trussed up in a fancy dress, her stays so tight her bosom threatened to spill over the bodice. Her hair had been pulled up in what Lady Henrietta referred to as a Grecian style, that she would never be able to duplicate in a hundred years. Why, she even had tiny blue flowers that matched her eyes and gown poking out of her tresses as if they'd grown there naturally. It seemed a strange amount of effort to go through just to spend a few hours at a ball she did not particularly desire to attend in the first place.

"Now, remember," Lady Dalridge said, as they approached the receiving line populated by Mr. and Mrs. Lindwell and their two daughters, Temperance and Constance. "You are the granddaughter of a dear friend. If they begin to question you in detail, pay them a compliment. It will divert their attention back to their favorite subject."

"Which is?"

"Why, themselves, my dear." Lady Dalridge snapped her fan open and smiled behind it, her eyebrows lifting in amusement. "You will find most lords and ladies prefer to talk about themselves just slightly more than they like to gossip about their peers. Though not by much."

The viscountess's explanation did not prompt any confidence that Madalene would ever fit into this strange group of people. With each step she longed to do an about face and return to Northill, to the simple life she had left behind, populated with people who put character and substance far above pretty dresses and fancy balls. Yet, in fairness, the titled lords and ladies of her acquaintance were perfectly lovely people. Not once had the Bowens or their close friends looked down their noses at her or treated her as inferior because she did not possess the proper pedigree.

Perhaps it was she who was guilty of prejudice, basing her assumptions on experiences in her past and using that as a measuring stick for anyone bearing a title. With that thought in mind, she drew a deep breath and stepped in line behind Lady Dalridge to be greeted by the Lindwells and face the gauntlet of the ballroom just beyond.

"They seem like lovely young women," Madalene commented with respect to Temperance and Constance Lindwell. Both were of an age close to Madalene's own one and twenty years and, although twins with similar features, they were easily told apart by their divergent coloring. One was light, the other dark. The trouble only came when one had to remember which one was the dark one, and which the light.

"I suppose they are well behaved and polite," Lady Dalridge allowed, though it came begrudgingly. "I can only hope they do not attempt to set their caps for James. He is rather susceptible to a pretty face."

James Harrow, the Marquess of Ridgemont, was Lady

Henrietta's older brother. He had not been in residence at the time she arrived. Lady Henrietta had told her that he had traveled to visit his close friend, Lord Rothbury, who mostly kept to himself since the death of his wife years past. Would Madalene have been so quickly invited to stay with Lady Dalridge and Lady Henrietta if the marquess had been in residence? Would Lady Dalridge fear she would try to set her cap for Lord Ridgemont as well, in an effort to better herself? She needn't worry on that account. For as much as Madalene tried to deny it, her heart was otherwise occupied, tied to another gentleman far above her station who barely remembered her, or himself for that matter.

"Good heavens," Lady Dalridge muttered as they entered the ballroom. The crush of bodies surprised Madalene. For a family who inspired upturned noses from the ton, they had certainly turned out in droves to attend their party.

Lady Dalridge slipped an arm through Madalene's and used her walking stick to poke and prod people out of her way. "Stay close, my dear. We shall find our way through eventually."

And they did, though Madalene could not recall it ever taking so long to traverse the length of a room before. Once on the other side, several younger women quickly vacated their chairs upon coming in contact with Lady Dalridge's cutting glare. Once seated, the viscountess pointed her walking stick toward the lengthy table filled with sweets and drink in the nearest corner.

"My dear, might you have the fortitude to bring this old lady a glass of what is likely to be insipidly sweet punch? I find I am quite parched and all of these bodies have this room sorely overheated." She snapped open her fan and waved it in front of her face. "Why they will not crack open a door I cannot say."

"Yes, of course, my lady." Though the idea of carrying

anything through the thick grove of bodies was rather daunting.

Madalene skirted the edges of the crowd, avoiding eye contact with those she passed, though she could feel several sets of eyes upon her, burning into her exposed skin, of which there was far too much for her liking. Did they recognize her as someone who didn't belong? Did her lack of pedigree emanate outward as if she carried a painted sign over her head?

She did her best to ignore the stares as she dipped the ladle into the punch and poured a generous amount into an ornate cup with its matching saucer. The Lindwells had spared no expense in order to attract the attention of the ton and, as Lady Dalridge claimed, titled gentlemen for their daughters.

"Ah, refreshments. I feared I might never make my way through the crowd to find such an oasis."

Madalene glanced to her left unsure if the masculine voice addressed her directly or if he simply made the comment to himself. As he was looking straight at her, she assumed the former, but as they had not been properly introduced, she didn't quite know how to respond. The rules were much different in this world than the one she'd come from and though Lady Dalridge had peppered her with proper etiquette for the past two days, most of what she'd learned appeared to have been forgotten, leaving her to stare blankly at this man in regimental uniform standing next to her.

"My humblest apologies," he said. "We have not been properly introduced, have we? May I present myself then? I am Major Timothy Gibbons, at your service, my lady."

He bowed with great flourish, or perhaps it was the expert cut of his uniform that made it appear so. When he straightened, she took a closer look. He had a slim build and stood a few inches shorter than Lord Hawksmoor or her father. A hint of gray had infiltrated the hair near his temples, but his face had very few lines suggesting to her he would fall some-where in his mid-thirties.

"And might I ask your name?" he prompted.

"Oh." She glanced around, fearful for making a gaffe. She did not want to upset Lady Dalridge who seemed overly inter-ested in presenting her as above her station. But no one paid her much heed beyond an occasional, questioning glance.

"I have embarrassed you with my forward behavior, haven't I?"

"Oh, no. Miss Cosgrove. That is me. I mean, my name." She fumbled with her words, shooting them out in piecemeal. It was so much easier talking to Lord Hawksmoor. When she spoke to him, it was as if she were conversing with an old friend, which she supposed in a way she was, even if that friend had a hazy memory.

"Well, Miss Cosgrove, I have only been back in London for a few months, but I do not believe I have seen you about. Are you not from here? Or has your family been hiding you away, afraid all the other ladies will throw fits of jealousy over your superior beauty?"

As compliments went, it was a little over the top. "I—"

"I've overstepped again, haven't I?" He winced; his expres-sion instantly charming. "How have you not tossed that glass of punch in my face yet?"

"I do not want to create a scene," she said, warming to him. "I fear my chaperone would approve of that even less than she would of finding me speaking to a strange man."

"I promise I am not all that strange, most days. And who, if I might ask, is your chaperone?"

"Lady Dalridge."

"Good heavens!" The expression on his face turned comical and a small laugh escaped her. "Then I had better be on my best behavior."

"She is quite formidable."

"Might I escort you back to her?"

Madalene opened her mouth to respond, but before the words could come out a murmur went through the crowd, gentle at first, like a whisper, but quickly growing into a loud buzz. Her heart chilled. Had she been discovered? Did someone recognize her as a servant masquerading as a lady? She straightened her shoulders and turned to face them, prepared for the worst.

The horde of guests parted and the din of voices grew. Soon, she realized it was not she who had caught their attention. She sighed with relief. But as the buzz grew, she noted a distinct anger in their tone that kept her rooted. Whoever it was, it was clear they were not welcomed.

A sick feeling invaded her stomach and even before the crowd had parted to reveal the newcomer's identity, she knew.

Lord Hawksmoor.

Her breath caught in her throat. There had been several instances during her time at Raven Manor when his family held parties and she had seen him *trussed up* as he had called it. And despite the years that had passed, the effect of him in formal attire was still a sight to behold.

Her heart fluttered in her chest as her gaze greedily supped on his lean frame, broadened with hard muscle that had overtaken the lankiness of his youth. Time had filled him out, and pugilistic pursuits had honed his build, if the shop girls at Madame Belliveau's dress shop were to be believed. Though, there was no evidence of such in his features, sharp and straight. He was even more handsome now than he'd been as a young man.

Although, the man who approached her now, resplendent in unrelenting black, was not the man she'd known all those years ago. This man was darker, more dangerous. More like the man they called The Hawk.

"Perhaps I should escort you back to Lady Dalridge,"

Major Gibbons suggested, but his voice sounded far away and she paid it no heed.

Even if she had, she would not have left, as Lord Hawksmoor's expression held her rooted in place. At first glance, he appeared unreadable, but she had spent far too much time studying each plane and angle of his face until even the smallest ripple of discomfort or distress became an easy read. Tonight, was no exception. In his hypnotic green eyes, his suffering called out to her. What had happened in the days since she had seen him last? Had he remembered more of his past? All of it? Had it been too much to bear?

How badly she wanted to rush into his arms to offer the comfort his expression told her he sorely needed. Her toes curled in her slippers.

"Miss Cosgrove? Are you certain I cannot escort you—"

"No. Thank you." She should tell him she knew Lord Hawksmoor, but that would require more of an explanation than she wanted to give, revealing where she had come from, or suggesting a relationship that might call both their reputations into question. Hers more than his. Lord Hawksmoor's reputation had already been dragged about as low as one could get, not that he had appeared to care. His disdain for society had been obvious in his actions, destroying many whose finances fell to a state of disrepair within the walls of his establishment.

Perhaps Major Gibbons was right. Perhaps she should leave. Showing a friendship with Lord Hawksmoor would do her no favors in the eyes of those present, including Lady Dalridge, who had gone to great lengths to make her appear as more than she was.

But none of that convinced her to move. Instead, she remained. Waited.

What had he learned upon his return to The Devil's Lair? Was there something even darker lurking in the depths of his mind than the death of his brother? What she knew of his life after he had left Raven Manor was based on rumors and hearsay, secondhand accounts of how he had immersed himself in the seedier side of London, increasing his power by trading on the weaknesses of his peers.

Had he been happy? She doubted it. Not if the man who arrived at Northill had been any indication.

Lord Hawksmoor greeted her with an expert bow. "Miss Cosgrove," he said, his voice a whisper barely heard above the din. He cast a glance in Major Gibbons' direction, then summarily dismissed him as his attention reverted to her.

She curtsied. "My lord. I am surprised to see you here this evening."

The hint of a smirk curled one corner of his beautiful mouth. "No more than the rest of them, if my current reception is any indication. It shows how little the Lindwells know of London society that they even let me through their doors."

"You are still a Peer of the Realm, are you not?"

He shrugged. "I suppose."

Major Gibbons stepped closer to Madalene. "Why did you come here tonight if you did not expect to be welcomed?"

Lord Hawksmoor cut a cold glare in the major's direction, one that would have sent most men scurrying off to the corners in retreat. But Madalene supposed having seen battle, Major Gibbons did not scare as easily as the regular gentleman.

"And you are?" The words dragged out of Lord Hawksmoor and he arched one dark eyebrow skyward.

"Major Gibbons."

"A soldier, then?"

Major Gibbons stiffened next to her, as if Lord Hawksmoor had meant the inquiry as an insult. "I am a close advisor to our Prime Minister."

If such a claim was meant to impress Lord Hawksmoor, it did not and he returned his attention back to Madalene once again, giving her a sweet smile reminiscent of the ones from years past. Warmth pooled low in her belly.

"To answer your question, Miss Cosgrove," Lord Hawksmoor said, his voice the consistency of warm chocolate. "I came here to find you, of course."

Chapter Ten

Hawk continued to smile as Madalene's eyes opened round and wide and her mouth dropped open slightly. At least she was not completely immune to him. It was something at least, to know he had some effect on her. A pretty pink blush infused her cheeks and made her even more striking. Quite the feat, given she had never looked more beautiful than in that moment when the crowd parted and he saw her standing near the refreshment table, a vision in pale blue.

He was less than thrilled to see her talking to another gentleman who appeared far too interested in her, based on how close he was standing or the way he leaned in when she spoke. Highly inappropriate in his opinion. He imagined picking the shorter man up by the lapels and throwing him into the crowd to be trampled. It proved a most pleasing image.

Hawk should not be here. His reception made it clear he was not wanted, but after reading the letters, the need to ensure Madalene's safety overpowered any reticence he had at rejoining society.

Those damned letters. They had been sent religiously, the first one arriving three months following Phillip's death and then every three months afterwards. They possessed no return address, no distinctive seal, no proper signature other than a scrawling *T*. The letters were brief in nature, yet taunting in tone. Their contents made it clear the threat to Madalene had not ended.

The last one had arrived at Northill, following the same three-month pattern. He'd questioned his staff about the letters, but they could offer no clue as to who had sent them. They arrived without fanfare, left somewhere within The Devil's Lair where they would be easily found, collected and brought to him. No one saw who left the letters and they were never left in the same place twice.

The words still echoed in his mind and struck fear deep in his heart. Madalene remained at risk. He had to see her, to protect her.

"I understand your brother failed in his quest. Such a shame to see the mighty fall. But have no fear; I shall take up the cause. The game is still afoot."

"My quarry is an elusive little minx. Each time I think I've found her, she escapes into the mist. But I shall not give up."

And the second to last one, arriving shortly before his run-in with Pengrin. *"A little bird has told me my quarry resides within the home of a friend of yours. How safe she must think she is. How wrong she will find herself to be."*

But she was no longer at Northill. Now she was in London, flitting about as if no danger existed. It took every ounce of strength he possessed not to snatch her from this overheated ballroom and carry her off to the catacombs of The Devil's Lair where he could watch over her and ensure no harm ever came to her.

He may not be able to do the latter, but he'd be damned if he let her out of his sight whenever she stepped foot outside of

Ridgemont's townhouse. Although, he had not expected her to step out and end up at the Lindwells' overdone party.

He had originally hoped to speak with her at Lord Ridgemont's town house. To impress upon her the need for caution, without scaring her by telling her why. He did not want to fill her with the fear he now lived with. Let that be his burden to carry.

Unfortunately, the marquess's footman informed Hawk that Madalene had accompanied Lady Dalridge to this god-awful party. His first instinct was to dismiss the statement as false. Despite her grandfather being a baronet, a society party did not strike him as something Madalene would be overly keen on attending. Nor welcomed to.

But the footman had insisted and so Hawk found himself rushing back to The Devil's Lair to change into proper evening attire, before barging into the Lindwells' over-decorated abode without benefit of an invitation, as if he belonged there.

They did not bar his entry. He was still a Peer of the Realm after all, no matter how low he had fallen in their estimation. Not that his title afforded him a reprieve from the silent censure of the guests present.

Regardless, here he stood, facing the woman who had haunted his thoughts since his return to wakefulness. He could not pinpoint what disconcerted him more: that she was speaking to this dandified solider, or that he could not come up with a single, intelligent thing to say to impress her.

"It appears I am unable to find those items we spoke of earlier." A stellar beginning. Well done. Quite vague. She should have no problem at all discerning he spoke of his journals over any other item that he might have misplaced. "That is, the books." He raised his eyebrows, silently begging her to understand. Though what he thought she would do upon deciphering his meaning remained a mystery. Conjure the journals out of thin air perhaps?

That damnable mouth that he could not tear his gaze away from formed a perfect little 'O'. "I see."

"I thought perhaps I would request your assistance." A completely foolish idea. She owed him nothing. And he had already determined he could not bring her to The Devil's Lair to assist in his search.

"I'm not sure how I may be of help to you, my lord."

"Nor is it proper for you to request such a thing from her," soldier boy said, his voice clipped at the edges.

"I don't believe you are qualified to make that decision, Mister—I'm sorry, what was your name again?" Hawk lifted his eyebrows in question.

"*Major* Gibbons," soldier boy answered. The man's eyes were a cold brown color. Funny, Hawk thought brown normally a rather warm color, like chocolate. Not in the major's case however. They looked like two beady pebbles.

"Well, as it stands, *Major* Gibbons, Miss Cosgrove and I have a lengthy acquaintance and as such, I feel perfectly qualified in mentioning a matter of past discussion with her. You don't mind, do you Miss Cosgrove?"

Hawk swung his attention back to her, as she was a much prettier picture to gaze upon than the major with his cold eyes and disapproving manner.

"Not at all, my lord. And I am sorry to hear you were unsuccessful in your endeavor." Her gaze drifted away from him toward the French doors that remained firmly closed despite the stifling heat of the ballroom. Or was the heat he felt due to his close proximity to Madalene and the effect she had on him? "I promised Lady Dalridge I would bring her some punch."

The major took a step closer to her. "I will escort—"

"Nonsense," Hawk said, cutting off Gibbons' offer with

one of his own. "I'm certain you have more pressing matters to attend to."

"I'm certain I do not. And I cannot imagine it would do the lady's reputation any good to be seen with the likes of you."

A low blow, even if it did hold the ring of truth to it. Still, Hawk was not about to give up so easily. In the end, it turned out he did not have to.

"Gentlemen, please." Miss Cosgrove took the cup and saucer Major Gibbons held in his hands. "It does no one any good to have you two disagree so. Lord Hawksmoor, I would be pleased to have you escort me back to Lady Dalridge."

"Then I insist upon a dance," Major Gibbons said before Hawk could lead her away from the annoying little man. Granted, he was likely only a hand shorter than he, but regardless.

"It would be my pleasure, Major Gibbons," Madalene answered with a small nod of her head.

"Just not the waltz," Hawk cut in. "I'm afraid that one has been promised to me." The major glared at him, both of them knowing it was a boldfaced lie. He had only just arrived and could in no way have claimed any dance, let alone the coveted waltz. Thankfully, the man's manners overrode any need to contradict him. A mark against him in Hawk's estimation. He would have fought harder for her.

He had fought harder for her. Once upon a time, he had fought to the death for her.

Hawk took the punch from her and offered his arm, once again conscious of the stares that followed them as they left Major Gibbons and the refreshment table to find their way back to Lady Dalridge.

"Do you remember how to dance?" she asked him.

He stopped and lifted his eyebrows. A very good question indeed. "I have absolutely no idea. I suppose we shall soon find out. At least the waltz will make it easier to discuss matters of import if we are not constantly exchanging partners or being pulled apart."

She glanced up at him with a quick smile. "Then you do remember how to dance."

He returned her smile with a hint of surprise. "Yes, I suppose I do. Now, if only the rest of my memories would return so easily, I might not have to constantly annoy you with my pleas for assistance."

"You do not annoy me. I enjoy your company."

Her confession humbled him. He did not deserve such latitude where she was concerned. If anything, she should deliver him a proper slap and demand he never speak to her again after he'd kissed her as he did. As he wanted to, again. And again.

"I can't imagine why. I have behaved abominably where you are concerned."

Pink colored her cheeks. He had never met a lady who blushed so spontaneously and yet so prettily. At least, he didn't think he had. "We were both at fault in that regard," she said.

"No. I take full responsibility. You were simply being kind."

"It was not kindness, my lord."

Her answer surprised him and his need for her surged, stymieing any attempt to come up with a pithy quip to lead them to a safer avenue of conversation. His mind fixated on reliving the kiss they had shared and refused to stop. He swallowed. If this kept up, the effect of that kiss would be embarrassingly evident.

Thankfully for him, Madalene's mind was not as mired in lust as his; something to be expected, he supposed, yet still rather disappointing. "Did you recognize anyone when you arrived, my lord?"

"No. Although if the greeting I received upon my arrival tonight is any indication, I am not a man people care to be around or remembered by."

"Perhaps that is because they are looking at the man you became, instead of the man you were." She looked up at him again and he found himself becoming lost in her all over again. The clear blue of her eyes reminded him of endless pools and he could not help but dive into them as if salvation lurked somewhere in their depths.

"But if that is the man I became, is it not who I am?"

"Perhaps, in some ways. But when you awoke, with no memories to bind you to any particular personality, the man you revealed to me was the man I remembered. The man I—" She stopped.

"The man you what?" He whispered the question, afraid of what she might say.

Her expression softened and filled with something he had not seen in—well, he had no idea how long, but he suspected for quite some time. It struck him deep in his core and he leaned into it. Had he not been holding the drink for Lady Dalridge in one hand, he would have cupped her lovely face and—

And what? Kissed her in the middle of the Lindwells' ballroom for all to see, ruining her forever? God above, man, pull yourself together! It was one thing to steal a kiss behind a copse of trees, but to create such a spectacle in the middle of London? It would not do. She deserved far better than that.

He took a deep breath and straightened before she could answer. Best he let her answer remain silent. If she were to say anything other than what he wanted to hear, it would devastate him. Yet he could not allow her to say what he hoped for, as he could not act upon it without ruining her.

"Forgive me. I should not have asked such an impertinent

question. Come, let us deliver this drink to the parched Lady Dalridge before she sends out a search party to find you."

Not that arriving with him would likely calm the viscountess's nerves any. The faint memory of a walking stick and stern expression crossed his mind then slipped away like smoke. Still, when they reached Lady Dalridge, it pleased him that the thin remembrance had been startlingly accurate. Perhaps the darkness was finally lifting. The question remained, however, which man would he find standing behind the veil once his memories returned—the one reviled by his peers? Or the man admired by the lady whose arm looped casually through his?

"Lord Hawksmoor." Lady Dalridge's silver eyebrow rose skyward in a slow, pointed manner. "And to what do we owe this honor?" Her gaze drifted from his face, to his arm and he experienced a pang of regret as Madalene's hand slipped away.

"Is it an honor, my lady?" He smirked, the expression coming easily. "It was difficult to tell, what with all the glares of my peers cutting through the cloth of my favorite suit."

"Perhaps it has something to do with the general fleecing a great many of them have taken at your tables, Lord Hawksmoor." She returned his smirk with one of her own, her remark direct and to the point. He liked her immediately, though the sentiment did not appear to be reciprocated.

"I'm afraid I cannot be held responsible for the weaknesses of others. I simply provide the venue. Whether or not they choose to make use of it is entirely up to them."

After reading the letters, he'd spent part of the evening reviewing the business journals Mr. Bowen had left stacked on his desk in an orderly fashion. They contained great detail about the guests of The Devil's Lair—what they owed, their vices, their deepest, darkest secrets. The actions he had taken when they could not pay for their losses at his tables.

Some he had shown mercy. Others, he had destroyed. What had tipped the scales one way or the other seemed to be predicated on what information they had willingly provided in exchange for a reprieve. Yet one thing was clear—everyone who came through the doors of The Devil's Lair did so of their own volition and the choices they made once they entered had been their own. That he used such to his own advantage was left up to interpretation as to whether it was warranted or not.

Lady Dalridge tilted her head to one side. "I'm certain such logic will garner you any number of supporters."

Her sarcasm was not lost on him. "I have requested a dance from Miss Cosgrove, my lady. I hope you will not object," he said, hoping to change the subject.

"Did you now? And what answer has Miss Cosgrove given you?"

"I have said yes, my lady. If you feel you can spare me."

Lady Dalridge did not immediately answer, her gaze moving between the two of them. "I'm certain I can entertain myself for the duration."

Her answer came as the strains of the waltz hovered over the din of the crowd and couples took their places on the dance floor. Hawk offered Madalene his arm once more and bowed to Lady Dalridge before turning away.

But escape was not to be such a simple enterprise. "Lord Hawksmoor?" He turned back to face the viscountess. "I will be watching you. And there will be reprisals, should I find your actions or manners even remotely questionable."

He offered her a brief smile, though he felt none of it. "I would expect nothing less."

Holding Madalene in his arms once again proved an amazingly thrilling endeavor. He had not thought to ask if she could dance, but as it turned out, she did quite well. Better than that even. It was almost as if she glided along on a cloud.

Fanciful thinking for a man of his alleged reputation, but he could not help it. She inspired such foolishness in him.

What would his peers think of him now should they know the truth, that he was emotionally felled by a small slip of a thing who held no standing in society, no fortune to entice, and cared little for the accouterments those of his ilk deemed necessary for life?

Perhaps if he had not been so quick to leave her behind when he left Raven Manor, his life would look far different than it did now. Had he ever considered doing such? Taking her with him? Spiriting her away? Would she have gone if he had asked?

Likely not. She had far more good sense about her than he, and she had been too young for such things then. Now, however, was a far different story. Now, she was a woman, in every sense of the word.

"I am disappointed to hear you had no luck in finding the journals, my lord. I had been certain you would have taken them with you upon leaving Raven Manor."

"You should call me Hawk." He was apparently determined to continue making a fool out of himself.

"And why should I do that?"

"Because it is my name and I think our acquaintance is long and varied enough that we might refer to each other by our given names, don't you?" And also, the kiss, but he did not reference it again. It was far too dangerous a topic to bring up while he held her in his arms.

She did not answer his question directly. "Your given name is Thomas, not Hawk."

Funny how foreign that name felt to him except when she said it.

He spun her around, drawing her a little closer as he did so. "I prefer Hawk much better. Though, I might point out that when you thought me still dead to the world, you used my given name then."

"I thought it might help revive you if you heard it."

"And so, you were right." In more ways than he could have ever imagined. Her voice had given him something to hold onto, a light at the end of a very dark tunnel. "I waited each evening for you to arrive, did you know that?"

They passed a table of lit candles and the light from the flames wavered across her cheeks caressing her skin. "Lord Hawksmoor—"

"No, do not chastise me for my impertinence. I know I am completely in the wrong to tell you such things. It is just that... you are the only one I can talk to. The only one I feel knows me. *Sees* me. I realize it is wrong to put such a burden on you. Heaven knows, you do not deserve the liberties I have taken. I would not blame you if you stalked off this dance floor right this very moment and never paid me another second of attention for the remainder of your life."

He stopped talking, unsure of where to go after that. He'd talked himself into a corner, one in which he stood in alone, because he had no right to drag her in there with him and he knew it. It was just that—

"I need you." The words tumbled out of him and knocked her off balance. He pulled her closer to help her regain her footing then rushed on. "Forgive me, there I go again. Likely, I am ten times the fool to admit such, but it is true. I desperately wish it wasn't. I wish I could let you go so that you might live your life far away from the mess that is mine, but I cannot seem to convince myself to do so. But if you insist upon it, I will. I will leave this instant and never bother you again."

"Will you?"

He swallowed. He really should not make such cavalier promises when he had no intention of keeping them. He could not leave her alone. She needed his protection, even if she was unaware of the danger she was in. "Forgive me, but no."

She laughed lightly, seemingly unbothered by any foolish

claim he'd made so far this evening. How did she do that? Any other lady would be so scandalized at this point they'd likely swoon in his arms. "Then I shall keep that in mind."

He blinked, unsure of what do to. She had not turned him away despite his awkward, foolish, flat out ridiculous admission. It could mean only one thing.

She was as crazy as he was.

He pushed the notion away and attempted to return to a safer topic of conversation. "Can you think of anywhere else I may have hidden the journals?"

Madalene let out a deep breath as they made a turn around the ballroom. How perfect it was to hold her in his arms, but even the small space between their bodies was too far. He longed to pull her closer, to cradle her in his arms and kiss that delectable mouth. To peel away the enticing layers of her gown until she stood before him—

"Is it possible you left them behind?" she asked, interrupting his wayward thoughts just in time before they became embarrassingly evident. "You did leave Raven Manor quickly. Perhaps you thought them safer where they were, especially if you did not have a set destination in mind when you departed."

The notion had merit. She had indicated he did not return for her as he said he would and, knowing his feelings for her, he could not imagine he would have done so without reason. Had he been forced out of Raven Manor by his parents? Tossed out with only the clothes on his back? It seemed inconceivable they would have done such a thing to their own son, yet...yet when he lay at Death's door, they had refused to take him in.

"Perhaps you are—"

A commotion near the edge of the dancing disrupted their conversation. Hawk quickly realized the direction the noise had come from and grabbed Madalene by the hand as he pushed his way through the throng, Madalene trailing behind in his wake.

When they made their way to the front, Lady Dalridge lay on the floor as if she had slipped out of her chair and pooled on the parquet flooring in front of it.

Madalene released Hawk's hand and dropped to her knees in front of Lady Dalridge while everyone else simply hovered above and around her, as useless as statues. Did the imbeciles think whatever had felled her was catching?

Madalene turned to the onlookers, her quiet demeanor changed to such a degree he almost didn't recognize her. She addressed a gentleman to her right. "Get the footman and help me get Lady Dalridge upstairs to a room." Then she turned to the other gentleman to her left. "Have someone send for the doctor immediately."

She barked out orders like a seasoned general and the men quickly disappeared to do her bidding. No wonder she made such a commendable housekeeper. Despite her young age, she exuded an air of competence and was able to translate that into authority. Why in the world the Bowens wished to let her go astounded him. Any house in the land would be lucky to have her. Not that he particularly cared to see her in service. She deserved a better life than that. She deserved the world.

He knelt beside her. She had picked up Lady Dalridge's fan and waved it above the older lady's face to create a cool breeze. Hawk lifted his head. "Someone open the damn doors and let some air into this place."

"Thank you," Madalene whispered, but she didn't look at him. Instead, she gently tapped Lady Dalridge's face. The elderly lady in turn tried to move away from her touch, her eyelids fluttering. When they opened, they were unfocused. He could sympathize. He'd experienced something similar when he had come to and found himself in strange surroundings. Then again, any surrounding would have been strange to him at that point, given he had lost his reference as to what was and wasn't familiar.

The footman appeared, along with Mr. and Mrs. Lindwell. The latter had turned ghastly pale. Or perhaps that was simply the effect of the hideous choice of color of her pea-green gown. Madalene moved out of the way and allowed the footman to lift Lady Dalridge into his arms. The crowded ballroom parted, much as it had when he had arrived, allowing the group to pass through it. But this time, no one paid much attention to him and all eyes rested on the footman and Lady Dalridge.

"What has happened?"

Hawk threw an irritated glance at Major Gibbons. The man was like an annoying fly buzzing about one's head. No matter how often you swatted it away, it kept coming back.

"It is none of your concern."

The major puffed out his chest with obvious umbrage to Hawk's dismissal. "I beg your pardon; it is as much my concern as it is yours."

"I fail to see how."

"Gentlemen!" Madalene glared over her shoulder at both of him, a fact he did not feel was warranted where he was concerned. "Quit squabbling like children."

Major Gibbons' eyes widened. "Did she just—"

"Chastise you for your behavior? Yes, she did."

"I believe her comment was directed toward the both of us."

"I doubt it. You were the one acting like a child. I was merely suggesting you go elsewhere to do it. She is my friend after all." Granted, it was an odd friendship, and, in truth, he thought of her as more than a *friend*, but none of that mattered in the grand scheme of this conversation in his opinion.

"You, sir, are an arrogant ass," Major Gibbons hissed

under his breath. They had climbed the stairs to the bedchambers above.

"And you, *Major*, are embarrassing yourself. What assistance do you believe you can offer Miss Cosgrove or Lady Dalridge? What is your stake in any of this?"

"I have a passing acquaintance with Lady Dalridge, I will have you know and a newly formed friendship with Miss Cosgrove."

Hawk turned on the major at the entrance to the bedchamber as the footman carried Lady Dalridge inside, followed by the Lindwells and Madalene. "A newly formed friendship? You met her all of thirty minutes ago and did not know of her existence before that time."

"How do you know how long I have known her?"

How did he—? The man was an idiot. He refused to listen to logic. If he'd had a swatter, Hawk would have used it to bat him away, back down the stairwell and straight out the front door.

"Go back to the party," Hawk stated, annunciating each word carefully as it was obvious Major Gibbons had difficulty understanding simple concepts.

He turned to enter the room but stepped back quickly as the door swung closed in his face with a resounding bang.

Chapter Eleven

Their foolishness maddened her. Poor Lady Dalridge had taken ill and those two infuriating men could not stop bickering like children. Honestly! Did they not sense the true urgency of the matter at hand? What if Lady Dalridge was in a bad way? What if Madalene had to arrive back to Ridgemont House and deliver the worst possible news to Lady Henrietta?

She squeezed her way past Mrs. Lindwell who stood on the periphery of the bed wringing her hands and asking repeatedly what they should do.

"All that can be done, has," Madalene told her, when her husband refused to answer her and instead followed the footman downstairs to await the doctor's arrival.

When the footman opened the door to do his employer's bidding, Lord Hawksmoor and Major Gibbons had been ousted from their position by a gaggle of young ladies, two of whom were the Lindwells' daughters and the other two being Miss Patience Elmsley, a cousin to Lady Glenmor, and another lady with a pinched face that she did not recognize. All four ladies pushed their way in and rushed to Lady Dalridge's bedside.

"Good heavens, Mama, what has happened? Clara Chambers said Lady Dalridge fainted dead away." Temperance—or was it Constance?—gasped suddenly as she looked down upon the bed, her dark curls bouncing about her fine-boned face and lowered her voice. "Oh dear, she isn't truly dead, is she?"

"She isn't dead," Madalene said, as she seemed to be the only one answering any questions. She didn't fault the young woman for asking, however. Lady Dalridge did appear deathly pale. Madalene kept telling herself she would be fine, but worry had started to edge in the longer the viscountess remained unconscious.

The young woman gave her a relieved smile. "What good news! How awful that would have been for Lady Henrietta."

"Awful for your family even more, one would think," the pinched face woman said, stepping forward and casting a quick glance down at Lady Dalridge before dismissing her as if her current state of health was of no matter. Madalene disliked this woman instantly.

"How so?" Mrs. Lindwell finally deemed to enter the conversation, though she continued to worry her hands to the point Madalene feared she would wear the skin straight off them.

"Well, you can hardly afford to be the family who had a hand in bringing about the demise of someone as revered as Lady Dalridge."

"Lady Dalridge is not in any state of demise, thank you." Madalene's voice rose above the others and pitched them into silence. The sensible part of her brain warned caution. She trespassed in a world not her own.

Pinched Face glared at her with cold eyes. "And who might you be?"

Madalene stood and straightened her shoulders. "I am Miss Cosgrove. I accompanied Lady Dalridge this evening. And who might you be?"

"Oh!" Miss Elmsley nudged past one of the Lindwell daughters. "Miss Cosgrove, I did not recognize you. You are here with Lady Dalridge?"

The confusion in Miss Elmsley's voice was unmistakable. And why wouldn't it be? The last time she saw Madalene it was in the role of servant, altering dresses for her cousin. What possible reason could there be for her to be here now with the viscountess? And yet here she was. "Yes, I am."

Pinched Face turned on Miss Elmsley while pointing her finger in Madalene's direction. "Do you know her? I have never heard of a Miss Cosgrove and I'm quite certain I know everyone of consequence there is to know."

"Yes, of course, I know her." Miss Elmsley said, not in the least cowed by the other's abrasive manner. "She was the seamstress for Lady Blackbourne's wedding dress several months ago and also helped my cousin, Judith, with several of her gowns. You remember my cousin, Judith, don't you? Or should I say, Lady Glenmor. How is your husband hunt, coming along by the way, Lady Susan? I understand the Duke and Duchess of Franklyn are most anxious to have you married off, yet, here you are, still...not married."

Lady Susan snarled at Miss Elmsley like a viscous dog and only Mrs. Lindwell's question to Madalene stopped what might have become an unpleasant scene. Why it looked as if Lady Susan meant to leap at Miss Elmsley!

"You are a seamstress?" Mrs. Lindwell's tone made it clear the very thought she had allowed someone of such low stature into her home left her horrified.

Miss Elmsley answered for her, likely thinking she was doing her a good turn, but Madalene knew better. "No, she is housekeeper to Mr. Bowen and Lady Rebecca. But her skill with a needle is absolutely divine. Quite a talent in my estimation. Why, I can't even master a simple needlepoint."

Lady Susan forgot Miss Elmsley and turned swiftly toward Mrs. Lindwell. "Are you trying to ruin any remote chance your family has of being accepted by society? Is it not unfortunate enough that you have decorated your home like some gauche circus and prance your very loose familial association with my parents about like a banner? Now you are inviting *servants* to attend your parties? What will others think when they learn of this? I knew Mother was foolish in insisting I attend this debacle."

Mrs. Lindwell sputtered, though Madalene was quite certain her reaction was less from outrage than from the fear Lady Susan was correct in her assumptions, and would be only too pleased to deliver the information to her other guests with all due haste.

"I-I did not invite this woman!" Mrs. Lindwell pointed an accusing finger at Madalene. "Lady Dalridge brought her and as a revered lady of society I assumed—"

"Lady Dalridge is a doddering old fool—"

"She is nothing of the sort!" Madalene spoke up in defense of the still unconscious viscountess, taking umbrage to Lady Susan's unkind and untrue words. The other woman looked down her nose at her then continued speaking as if she wasn't there.

"If you cannot even tell the difference between a peer and a servant, what hope is there for you or your family? Why, I am embarrassed to be seen to know you and I am certain everyone else will feel the same way when they hear about this."

"Mother," Constance sat on the bed, sinking into the feathered mattress, "I am certain—"

Mrs. Lindwell waved her daughter off and turned to Madalene. "You must leave immediately."

"I beg your pardon? I cannot leave Lady Dalridge."

"You can and you will." Mrs. Lindwell had apparently, at some point in the past few minutes, discovered a backbone. Much to Madalene's dismay. "I cannot be seen to have you here. It is highly irregular. I do not know what Lady Dalridge was thinking, bringing you into our home as a guest. I can only assume that whatever illness felled her at our party must have addled her mind when she extended an invitation to the likes of you.

"Perhaps what felled her was the stifling heat in the ball-room and the lack of opened doors to alleviate such," Madalene countered. Heavens, she needed to calm down. Getting her dander up was not going to help matters. She took a deep breath. "Forgive me, I do not mean to speak out of turn, it is just that I do not wish to leave until I know Lady Dalridge is well."

Temperance approached her mother, her slight figure gliding across the room with a confident stride. "Mama, surely there can be no harm in that. Allow her to wait below stairs if you must, but—"

But Mrs. Lindwell refused to be swayed. "No. You must leave. I cannot take the chance that her presence here will reflect badly on you or Constance. It is a tenuous rope we walk on and I will not have it severed by a lowly servant."

Miss Elmsley gasped. "You cannot simply banish her or send her out on the street unprotected!"

"And why not," Lady Susan said, a thin smile stretched across her face. "Is that not where she belongs? It isn't as if she needs worry about her reputation. She's a *servant*."

"Come," Temperance turned her back on the others and reached a hand out to Madalene. Unsure of what else she could do, her role in this room made painfully clear, she took it and allowed the woman to lead her out of the room. She cast a quick glance back.

"I will ensure she is well cared for," Miss Elmsley said,

giving her a firm nod and taking Madalene's place at Lady Dalridge's side. It was the most serious she had ever seen the lively young woman, but the encouragement did nothing to settle her nerves over what would come of Lady Dalridge, or herself.

Temperance slipped her arm through Madalene's and leaned in close, keeping her voice low. "Forgive my mother. She has it in her head that we must marry a titled gentleman and is willing to take Lady Susan's counsel over everyone else's. She fears one word from her will ruin any chance we have."

Madalene remained unmoved. "Forgive me if your mother's fears are not high on my list of concerns at the moment, Miss Lindwell, as I must find my way back to Ridgemont House to tell Lady Henrietta what has transpired."

"And I will see that you get there safely. I am not about to send you out into the streets like Lady Susan suggested. I saw you speaking to Major Gibbons earlier, were you not?"

"Y-yes, what does that matter?"

Temperance smiled, the expression giving her face an almost serene appearance. "It matters because Major Gibbons came with his sister, Mrs. Clara Chambers. Mrs. Chambers was widowed several years ago and now lives with her brother. She can provide you with a proper chaperone and Major Gibbons can ensure you arrive at Ridgemont House safely." She came to a stop at the top of the stairs and pointed toward a bench against the far wall beneath a painting depicting a scene of an entwined couple lacking a proper amount of clothing. Madalene was embarrassed to stare at it for too long. "Wait here. I will fetch them both."

Madalene did as Temperance instructed and waited on the bench as the minutes ticked past one by one on the large clock tucked into a corner on the opposite side of the hallway.

Where had Lord Hawksmoor gone? Or Major Gibbons, for that matter?

She leaned her head back against the wall and closed her eyes. This night had not turned out at all as she had expected. When she had agreed to allow Lady Dalridge to drag her to this party—not that she had been given much of a choice in the matter—her biggest fear had been not fitting in, or making a gaffe in etiquette. She had never imagined poor Lady Dalridge would faint dead away and she would be sent off into the night with a man she had only just met to deliver the news to Lady Henrietta whom she had only a brief acquaintance with. The safe, orderly life she had built at Northill seemed a million miles away at the moment.

"Madalene!"

She looked toward the stairs to see Lord Hawksmoor climbing them two at a time. "Oh, you're here!" Relief trickled through her.

"Where else would I be?" He crouched in front of her and took her hands in his, the inappropriate gesture somehow the most comforting thing she had experienced all evening. Still, she could not afford for Miss Lindwell to return and see them exchanging such a familiar touch. She was on shaky ground as it was. With great reluctance, she pulled her hands away.

Lord Hawksmoor stood, though she recognized the hint of hurt in his eyes where the candlelight flickered over his sharp features. She offered him a smile of apology but could not hold his gaze.

"I have arranged a carriage to take you back to Lord Ridgemont's," he said, a hint of formality entering his tone. "It is outside awaiting us. It would likely be best to leave Lady Dalridge here until the doctor can ensure it is safe to move her. I will check back on her once I have delivered you safely home."

"Miss Cosgrove already has an escort home."

Madalene turned toward the familiar voice and found Major Gibbons standing at the top of the step with Temperance and another woman she assumed was his sister, Mrs. Chambers. She stood and glanced between Lord Hawksmoor and the others. She did not have the energy to put up with another battle this night.

"I am perfectly capable of escorting Miss Cosgrove home, thank you, Major. Your assistance is neither required nor wanted," Lord Hawksmoor stated, his demeanor a far cry from the one he had greeted her with only a moment earlier.

"Not without ruining her reputation, you can't," the major answered. "Or do you have someone who can offer a proper chaperone as I can? Miss Cosgrove, may I present my sister, Mrs. Chambers."

Madalene forced a smile. "It is a pleasure, Mrs. Chambers. I appreciate your willingness to help."

Lord Hawksmoor held his hands fisted at his sides. Something about the gesture called back to her, tiptoeing through her memories. She had seen it before whenever he exchanged words with his brother. Phillip had repeatedly gone out of his way to antagonize his younger brother and though Lord Hawksmoor had always managed to hold in his anger, the telltale sign of it had been displayed in the way he would clench his fists. Until the day he lost his temper.

She stepped forward, hoping to avoid an unfortunate incident. "It is fine, Lord Hawksmoor. I appreciate your desire to help, but Major Gibbons is correct. If I wish to arrive home with my reputation intact, I cannot do so by riding without a proper chaperone."

Lord Hawksmoor's hands continued to work, as if he wished to hit something. Or someone. Then, just as suddenly as it appeared, his anger vanished and an impenetrable veneer slid over his features.

"Very well," he said, then turned away from the trio to

address her. "I will wait here until the doctor determines if Lady Dalridge may leave. I shall call on you and the family tomorrow to see how she fares, if it is not an imposition."

"Not at all. I'm sure she would appreciate that." Though she had no idea whether Lady Dalridge would welcome his visit or not. She had not seemed pleased that he had asked Madalene to dance this evening, but nor had she rejected his request.

"Come then, Miss Cosgrove," Mrs. Chambers said. "Miss Lindwell has indicated we should leave with all due haste, though I have not inquired upon the why of it."

She may not have inquired, but the look she rested upon Madalene made it clear she was not at all pleased with the situation. Likely it had been Major Gibbons who had insisted they aid her in arriving home safely and quickly to impart the unfortunate news to Lady Henrietta. It was a thoughtful gesture. One she would be sure to thank him for.

"I appreciate your kindness, this night, Lord Hawksmoor. I do hope you are able to uncover the whereabouts of your books," she said, though she could not shake the fear the journals would unleash more unwanted memories. Life with his family had not been easy. He'd been treated with cold disdain or ignored completely. It had taken its toll and she loathed the idea that his memories would awaken the hurt his family had caused him. She despised even more the thought that those memories would harden his heart and bury the man she cared for, instigating the return of The Hawk, until nothing of Thomas remained.

Lord Hawksmoor gave a slight nod of his head but said nothing more and as Madalene traveled down the stairs behind Mrs. Chambers, she could not help but feel as if she was walking in the wrong direction.

Chapter Twelve

"I do not see the point in lazing about when I am perfectly fine," Lady Dalridge announced when Lord Ridgemont arrived home from his travels to hear the news his great-aunt had fainted at the Lindwells fete and spent the night at their home before being returned to her own. An experience, she indicated, that was far worse than fainting dead away in front of half of society.

"Aunt, I think it best if you listen to Dr. Mulcair's advice. He is after all—"

"An old fuss pot." Lady Dalridge settled herself even farther into her chair in the small salon kept for family. "I fainted because the Lindwells did not have the good sense to properly ventilate their home in accordance with the amount of people filling it until it became so stifling the only way to escape was to faint! Miss Cosgrove will verify such."

"Oh," Madalene had not expected to be drawn into the conversation as she sat at the small writing desk, sending a note to the employment agency that she would be available to interview potential candidates the following day. "Yes, it was quite stifling."

"See. Now stop worrying. I may be old but I'm hardly at Death's door yet. You shall be stuck with my company for quite some time yet."

Lord Ridgemont let out a loud breath and ran a hand through his dark hair. The poor man had come home after several weeks away visiting an old friend to be faced with a stranger in his home, an upset younger sister, and an irate great-aunt. It was a wonder the man didn't turn around and make all haste back to Lord Rothbury's remote estate and stay there for the duration.

"Very well then, but I want you to rest. Do not overtax yourself with visitors." He turned to Madalene then, drawing her back into the conversation though she was not sure she had any place in it. She was not a member of the family, or even a close acquaintance. Lady Glenmor had deposited her here at Lady Dalridge's request, an attempt, Madalene believed, for the older woman to make amends for the treatment the new countess had received during her stay only a couple of months prior.

"Miss Cosgrove, perhaps you and my sister might manage the visitors inquiring after my great-aunt's health? I would do it myself but I have spent the last two days traveling and I'm afraid if I do not find my bed soon, I may meet a similar fate as my aunt did last night. I'm certain the ton does not need more fodder for their grist mill where my family is concerned."

He wanted her to receive visitors on his family's behalf? If he hoped to squelch any gossip, putting her front and center in such a way was not the best plan of attack. "With all due respect, my lord, I am not sure that is a good idea. It was revealed during Lady Dalridge's, uh, temporary incapacitation, that I was a servant—"

"You are the granddaughter of a baronet," Lady Dalridge interrupted.

"And yet still a servant," Madalene countered. "If I am

seen to be receiving guests on your behalf, I do not think it will help calm any gossip last night's events have invoked."

"Nonsense." Lord Ridgemont cut his hand through the air as if to erase her suggestion. "You have been promoted by Aunt and such carries much cache. While society may think it odd, they will allow it given the source from which it comes."

"I am quite revered, my dear," Lady Dalridge said, a wily smile playing about her lips. "You will be fine, and Lady Henrietta will not do well on her own. She is still finding her feet where society is concerned and it has been a bit of a slow process thanks to Lord Pengrin's despicable actions."

Her gaze traveled to Lord Ridgemont but he did not meet it and tension throbbed quietly in the air.

"It is settled then," the marquess said. "I thank you, Miss Cosgrove, for your assistance in this matter. It means a great deal to my family."

His sincerity, and the exhaustion evident in every aspect of him, forced Madalene to smile. As much as she disliked the thought of playing hostess to people who looked down their aristocratic noses at her, she could hardly say no. The Harrows had offered her their home and treated her like a lady during her stay. Helping in this regard was the least she could do to repay their kindness and generosity.

As it turned out, half of those who had stayed in London for the winter arrived at Ridgemont House's doorstep during proper visiting hours, though despite their fervent assurances that Lady Dalridge would be fit as a fiddle after a day's rest, doubt lingered in many of their eyes. Though most disconcerting was the treacherous hopefulness in some of the older ladies and the barely disguised disappointment upon hearing she would be around for many years to come.

"Old battleaxes," Lady Henrietta whispered to Madalene as Ladies Mumford and Thwacker-Downes exited the receiving room. "They cannot wait for Auntie's demise in the hopes of taking her place, as if either of them has the ability to play the part of society's Grand Dame."

"They did seem rather mercenary in their concern. Do you think we have seen the last of the visitors for this day?" A quick glance at the clock revealed it was almost five o'clock.

"I do hope so. All of this smiling and pretending that they're not staring at me as if I am some kind of freak on display has me exhausted. Perhaps I should try falling down in a dead faint to escape it."

"And leave me to face the throng alone? Don't you dare."

Lady Henrietta smiled, this one genuine, and it transformed her completely, relaxing the tightness around her eyes. The poor thing had not had an easy time of it and Madalene's heart went out to her. What a horror it must have been to lose her parents in a fire, only to be left with scars down one side of her neck and beyond. Madalene could not say how extensive the scars were, as Lady Henrietta kept herself well covered, even wearing her hair down long and draped over one shoulder in the hopes of hiding the marks on her neck.

"Very well, we shall soldier on. Hopefully—"

Cleveland, the butler, arrived at the door, cutting Lady Henrietta off from whatever she had been about to say. "My lady, there is a Miss Rosalind Caldwell and Lord Hawksmoor requesting to see you. Shall I show them in?"

Madalene's heart pounded in her chest. Despite the uproar of last night, the moments she had spent waltzing about the ballroom in Lord Hawksmoor's arms, his claim that he needed her, continued to rise to the forefront of her mind. How she had wished she could have left the Lindwells' with him, to share a few more private moments in his company. To hear him say those words once more.

"Now there is an interesting combination of visitors," Lady Henrietta said, her smile growing. "A handsome rake and a lady rebel. Suddenly I feel re-invigorated. Please, see them in, Cleveland."

Miss Rosalind Caldwell strode into the room, her self-assurance reaching out to fill the space like a trumpet. The woman would never be called demure. Instead, she was a force of nature that, Madalene believed, was not to be trifled with. Oh, to have that kind of confidence. Did she ever doubt the path she had taken, as unorthodox as it was, championing the underdog with such fervor? If Madalene had half of Miss Caldwell's conviction, she would—

She would what? The question was not one she could answer with any clarity, other than to say there must be more to life than what she had thus far experienced. But what that something was remained as elusive as smoke caught on a breeze.

Lord Hawksmoor entered the room with much less fanfare though his presence dominated in a quiet, much stealthier way. It slid in around her feet then twisted and wound itself up her legs, hips, and arms. It seeped into her skin until it filled every part of her inside and out.

Miss Caldwell, who continued to insist upon being called Rosalind, walked directly to Lady Henrietta with her hands stretched outward. "Lady Henrietta, tell me how your great-aunt fares. I heard the upsetting news and hoped to arrive to much better."

Lady Henrietta smiled, seemingly at ease in Rosalind's presence. Not that it was difficult. The young woman had the ability to make everyone—peer or commoner—feel as if they all stood on equal footing and held her full attention. And she did all this with a warmth and sense of purpose few women of Madalene's acquaintance possessed.

"She is well and quite perturbed that my brother insists she stay abed for the day. I suspect by tomorrow she will be out paying calls and showing the world she is right as rain."

"Capital news," Lord Hawksmoor said.

Lady Henrietta became shy again and offered a brief curtsey without meeting Lord Hawksmoor's gaze. "Thank you, my lord. I will send her your good wishes."

"And Miss Cosgrove," Rosalind left Lady Henrietta and came to take Madalene's hands in welcome. "How fortunate for her that you were there, although I hear Lady Susan created quite the ruckus and practically had you ousted from the Lindwells' home. I swear, that woman becomes ever more unpleasant as each day passes. One day soon, all of her pettiness will come home to roost, mark my words."

"I hope I am there to see that day," Madalene said, not bothering to disguise her newfound animosity. While this had been her first run-in with the Duke and Duchess of Franklyn's only daughter, she had heard the stories of past escapades meant to hurt others of her acquaintance. She had been a thorn in everyone's side for too long. "It was the height of embarrassment being shuttled out of the Lindwells' house as if I were a leper. Had it not been for Major Gibbons and his sister offering me a proper escort home, I am certain I would have been made to leave by the servant's entrance."

Which is where she should have left, given she was but a housekeeper, yet—

Yet what? She furrowed her brow as the thought entered her head, strange and unexpected. The fact of the matter was, she did not *feel* like a servant. Certainly, the Bowens had never treated her as such. Yes, she had a job to do, but Mr. Bowen, having grown up as ward of Lord and Lady Ellesmere before becoming Lord Ellesmere's man of business, did not care for such division in his home. It was completely unorthodox, and likely shocking to the peers of his acquaintance, but he insisted all of his employees be treated with the same respect as anyone who walked through his front door. It was part of what made working at Northill such a pleasing affair. She would miss it terribly when she left.

"I am pleased to hear you arrived home without mishap, Miss Cosgrove."

Lord Hawksmoor offered her a brief smile and Madalene realized in praising Major Gibbons; she negated to thank the one person who had first offered her a way out. "I should extend a thank you to you as well, my lord, for offering to see me home. I am sorry I could not take you up on it. I always find your company most satisfying."

"Most kind of you to say, but I should not have made such an offer. I wasn't thinking clearly. I feared, as you did, the Lindwells would cast you out into the street and only wished to see you safe. Thankfully, one of the Miss Lindwells had the good sense to ensure both your safety and your reputation remained intact." Then one side of his mouth lifted into a crooked smile and a gleam sparked in his green eyes. "Even if it meant Major Gibbons got to do the honors instead of me."

Rosalind turned to face him. "You do not care for Major Gibbons, my lord?"

"I have only just become acquainted with him, but I can find nothing about him that brings him into my good favor."

"Does his delivery of Miss Cosgrove safely home not count in his favor?" Lady Henrietta asked, sweeping an arm toward the sitting area, indicating everyone should take a seat.

Lord Hawksmoor took the armchair that separated the two short sofas. "I believe he had ulterior motives."

"Indeed?" Rosalind leaned forward, obviously intrigued. "And what ulterior motive might the major have had?"

"To court our Miss Cosgrove."

Our Miss Cosgrove, as if she somehow belonged to them. To him. Such claim of ownership should have irritated her, but instead it filled her with unexpected warmth. A sense of inclusion she had not experienced since being befriended years earlier by the second son of an earl.

Lady Henrietta forgot her shyness for the moment and caught Madalene's gaze. "Is it true, Miss Cosgrove? Has the major expressed an interest? My heavens, Auntie will be over the moon to hear such wonderful news."

The exasperated expression on Lord Hawksmoor's handsome face, however, clearly indicated he did not view such attentions on behalf of Major Gibbons at all wonderful. The idea that Lord Hawksmoor might be even the smallest bit jealous over Major Gibbons' possible interest thrilled Madalene, but she quickly tamped the emotion down. While she had spent the past little while being treated as an equal in the Bowen household, she was not. She was a servant. And when her time at Northill came to an end, she would, at most, be a headmistress to a school, should she choose to accept the position. Future earls did not marry commoners. It simply wasn't done.

"Major Gibbons did ask me to join him and his sister two days hence at St. James Park to go skating." The invitation had taken her by surprise, coming at the end of such an eventful and upsetting night.

Lord Hawksmoor did not appear pleased. "And you said no, of course."

"On the contrary, I accepted."

The tea and biscuits arrived, giving Madalene something else to do as she offered to pour the tea. Unfortunately, it did not stop Lord Hawksmoor from expressing his views on the subject.

"But you only just met. You hardly know the man. He could be...he could be a nefarious sort, or a depraved lunatic, or—"

"Good heavens, Lord Hawksmoor!" Rosalind let out a laugh. "You would have Major Gibbons in Bedlam before you finish that sentence. I am certain if he had any inclinations toward lunacy our Prime Minister Canning would not see fit to have him on his staff, wouldn't you think?"

Lord Hawksmoor reached out and took the tea from Madalene, his gaze fixed upon her as he delivered his answer. "Lunacy is not always readily apparent."

A chill swept Madalene as the tips of their fingers brushed against each other. The reference to his brother was unmistakable and the images of that hideous night even more so. She shoved the ugly thoughts to the dark recesses of her mind and turned away from him, but the truth followed her back to her seat.

Lord Hawksmoor was right. She had not seen the depths of Phillip's madness. Not at first. In hindsight, there had been hints. The disturbing intent he displayed in tormenting his younger brother. The leering looks he had given her, sideways remarks made in her presence, though not directly to her. Whenever he entered a room, her instinct whispered she should make haste to leave. There had been something there, something sinister lurking beneath the surface. But it wasn't until the night he attacked her that she saw the true face of evil.

"Lord Hawksmoor makes a good point," Lady Henrietta said, a mix of sadness and anger twisting around her words. "I had thought Lord Pengrin the best of men, as had my brother. We were both horribly mistaken in this estimation."

"Well, this has become a rather maudlin conversation," Rosalind said. "And I cannot see what harm can come to Miss Cosgrove on a crowded skating pond. I assume Major Gibbons' sister will come along to chaperone?"

"Yes," Madalene answered, a fact that filled her with no joy. Mrs. Chambers had been less than pleased with the request, if her expression had been any indication. But Lady Henrietta had already informed her that Mrs. Chambers' late husband had mismanaged their funds and left her little in the way of inheritance upon his death. She lived on the largess of her brother and therefore was at his mercy. Not that Major Gibbons appeared to mistreat her in any way. If anything, he was most considerate toward her.

"And do you skate, Miss Cosgrove?" Lord Hawksmoor asked.

"No. I have never had the occasion to."

"Then it will be an exciting learning experience, I am certain," Rosalind said, before steering the conversation down another avenue. "And speaking of exciting experiences, I had hoped to entice you to join me next week, Miss Cosgrove, and you as well, Lady Henrietta."

"Join you?" Lady Henrietta paled considerably. Quite a feat given her porcelain skin.

Lady Dalridge had informed Madalene the young woman had not ventured out into society since the Lord Pengrin incident, as the family referred to it, though they preferred not to refer to it at all, if possible. It was an ugly occasion best left forgotten. But personal experience had proven to Madalene the uglier the incident, the more deeply entrenched it became in one's memory.

She didn't blame Lady Henrietta for her reticence in venturing beyond the safety of her home. The ton was not always kind, and as Lady Henrietta had previously stated, she did not care to be stared at as if she was an exhibit at the zoo.

"I am hosting a party at the Pavilion in an effort to raise funds for the school. My hope is that through the generosity of those who are more fortunate, we can build the school's library to a substantial degree by the time we are ready to open its doors. Unfortunately, given my—" Rosalind cleared her throat. "—unorthodox approach to things, it has been brought to my attention that I might have more success if I had a few proper young ladies to assist me in hosting the event."

"But I am hardly what society would consider a proper young lady. They see me as nothing more than a commoner." A status enhanced by Lady Susan's proclamation, one she likely shared with anyone who would listen.

"On the contrary," Lady Henrietta said. "If anything, you are the perfect example of what an education can do to help elevate a young girl from a difficult situation. Look how far you've come despite the hardships your family has suffered. Besides, if you hide away after what happened last evening, it only gives credence to Lady Susan's claims."

"True words," Rosalind said. "And you, Lady Henrietta, will add the gentile touch that I sorely lack. And, taking the words from your own mouth, hiding away doesn't do anyone any good. I know you suffered heartbreak, but do not let that hold you back from life. Do not let Lord Pengrin win."

"Oh. No. I don't...I'm afraid my..." Her hand fluttered around her neck where her hair hung over her shoulder, covering it. "I look like a—" Her voice drifted off and she kept her gaze lowered.

"You look like what?" Lord Hawksmoor asked and Madalene shot him a hard look. He lifted his hand slightly as if to prevent her from trying to silence him. His voice gentled when he spoke again, sliding across the room like silk. "Like what, my dear?"

Lady Henrietta looked up, as if his words propelled her to do so. "Like a monster."

Madalene opened her mouth to refute such a claim but Lord Hawksmoor spoke before she could.

"I am pleased to report you are most incorrect in that assumption, Lady Henrietta." Hawk added the warm smile Madalene had received more times than she could count to soften his words further. Such power it held, such mesmerizing strength. "You see, I have seen monsters in my lifetime."

"You have?"

"Indeed. Which means I can say with complete confidence that you bear no resemblance to them at all. I have every confidence that you could not be in safer hands with Miss Cosgrove and Miss Caldwell, should you agree to take part in this event. It is as Miss Caldwell says, if you hide away, you allow the true monsters to win. I believe that would be a genuine shame, as I'm certain you have much to offer that would make this world a better place."

Silence descended upon the receiving room as Madalene and the other two ladies stared at Lord Hawksmoor. While Rosalind and Lady Henrietta looked shocked at the encouraging words coming from a dastardly rake such as Lord Hawksmoor, Madalene saw only the man she remembered. The man who had encouraged her love of learning and ensured she had the tools needed to build upon it. The man who had held her heart in his hands. Whom she feared still did.

Madalene turned to Rosalind. "I would be more than pleased to assist you with your event."

Lady Henrietta pulled her gaze away from Lord Hawksmoor, her fingers self-consciously pulling at the hair looped over her shoulder. "I...I will as well." Her smile wobbled and did not quite find its footing, but Madalene admired the woman's courage. Attending the event was a first step back to the life she deserved and Madalene would do whatever she could to ensure her experience went smoothly and without incident.

"I am pleased to hear it," Lord Hawksmoor said then stood. "Now, if you ladies will forgive me. I have preparations to make."

Madalene rose to her feet. "Preparations?"

"Yes, I have decided to return to Raven Manor."

His admission startled her. "Raven Manor? Are you—" She caught herself. His loss of memory was not something widely known. A fact Mr. Bowen had claimed to be a wise decision, indicating those hoping to gain an edge over him would exploit any weakness.

Lord Hawksmoor offered his arm. "Would you see me to the door, Miss Cosgrove?"

"Yes, of course." She looped her arm through his and remained quiet until they had reached the stairwell that led down to the foyer. "Are you certain that is a wise decision?"

He glanced down at her, a self-deprecating smile playing about his lips, enticing her to lean up and kiss them, but she held herself in check. Barely.

"Because my family despises me?"

She looked away; afraid if she did not, he would see the truth in his eyes. Because it was true, horrible as it was, and she could find no reasoning for their feelings. What parent treated their own child with such aversion, as if he was not worthy of their time or love? And if they were to do so, then why choose the one who was a good man, rather than the one who had proven himself to be nothing short of the monster Lord Hawksmoor spoke of earlier?

He patted her hand where it rested on his arm. "Do not fret. I know the type of welcome I will receive. But my hope is twofold—to search for my journals and to see if the familiar surroundings of my childhood will help resurrect more memories. If it is as you said, and I left Raven Manor in haste, then perhaps I had no other alternative but to leave the journals behind."

Madalene had no argument to offer against his logic as they made their way down the staircase. If the journals were not at The Devil's Lair, then they must be at Raven Manor. There had been little time between when he took her to her room and when she had to go below stairs a few hours later to attend to her duties or risk losing her position. When she arrived in the kitchens, one of the other maids indicated he'd had a row with his parents and left some time through the night. It was a day after that when the servants learned of the death of the heir to Ravenwood, but by then, the new Lord Hawksmoor was long gone. If any of the other servants considered the two events strange or connected in any way, no one said as much to her.

Cleveland met them in the entrance hall and held out Lord Hawksmoor's coat. Once on, Lord Hawksmoor dismissed him. The servant glanced at her, and for a brief moment looked as if he might decline for the sake of propriety, but then thought better of it and turned and disappeared down the hallway, the heels of his shoes clicking against the polished marble floor.

"You will take care of yourself?" she asked. She would miss him. The thought of days stretching in front of her without the likelihood of seeing him seemed more depressing than she cared to contemplate. He had quickly become a constant in her life once again, and the idea of him suddenly not being there left an unwanted emptiness inside of her that she did not know what to do with.

"I will, have no fear. And I shan't stay long. A day or two at most. I will return in time to attend your event for the school." He reached out and took her hand, covering it with his own. She had not worn her gloves, and he had yet to put his on. The warmth of his skin seeped into hers and spread throughout.

"I will look forward to seeing you upon your return then." Her voice caught and she swallowed. How silly this reaction to his leaving. Sillier still, how badly she wanted to cling to him and beg him not to go. To admit she needed him too, even if she didn't fully understand what for.

"I promise to return," he told her, as if reading her mind. Her heart. "I will not fail you this time."

He lifted her hand and bowed over it, pressing his lips against her knuckles. A thrill shot through her and her breath caught on a gasp. He lifted his gaze and her cheeks blazed with heat and longing and a hundred other things he evoked within her.

He smiled, the effect every bit as intoxicating as the touch of his lips had been. "Loath as I am to admit it, my dear, I would kiss you on the lips right here and now but I fear it would scandalize you and make you question my honor."

She could not help but smile back even though his suggestion *had* indeed left her somewhat scandalized, though most of her shock came from her disappointment that he planned on not delivering such a kiss and how badly she wished he would change his mind.

"I would never question your honor."

He chuckled quietly. "You should. It hangs from an extremely thin thread when I am with you."

He leaned in and placed a soft kiss upon her forehead and chaste as it was, her body's reaction to it was anything but. She longed to curl into him, have him wrap her into his arms and hold her there forever, their bodies melding together into one.

"Good-bye, my dear. I will see you soon. Promise me one thing—that you will take every precaution to stay safe while I am gone?"

She glanced up at him, the fervent nature of his request taking her by surprise. "Am I in danger?"

He hesitated, the intensity of his gaze leaving her captivated. But as quickly as it appeared, it was gone, covered with the flash of a smile. "I worry about you, is all. I do not like the idea of you traipsing about London without a protector."

"And are you that protector?" She wanted him to be, the

truth of her need for him rampant through every inch of her body.

He did not answer, but instead leaned in and kissed her forehead once again. "Promise me you will take care?"

Disappointment flowed through her, but what had she expected? That he would profess his love? Sweep her up into his arms and carry her away? Now that would cause a proper scandal. Not that she would mind if it meant she would not have to part from him again.

"I promise," she whispered, pushing aside her foolish fantasies. They had no place in real life and so the words remained tangled in her throat, held back by good sense and the unabated knowledge that nothing could come of her feelings for Lord Hawksmoor save for heartbreak.

Despite any feelings they may share, they came from different worlds. Nothing could change that. Regardless of how much Lady Dalridge trumped up her lineage, it would never suit. Their worlds were never meant to collide as they had all those years ago.

And once her sojourn to London was over, they never would again.

Chapter Thirteen

The carriage ride to Raven Manor took a full two days, despite its relatively close proximity to London. Hawk cursed the fretful weather, snowing one minute and turning to sleet the next. The sun once tried to break its way through but the dark clouds overpowered it, leaving the sky an unwelcoming gray.

A rather ominous portent.

He scowled up at the sky. Anything that delayed his return to London was met with anger and trepidation. He should not have left Madalene behind, unprotected. What if Lord T discovered she was there? He cursed his stupidity at not telling Lord Ridgemont to watch out for her.

Despite his growing unease, the closer the carriage drew to Raven Manor, the more familiar the landscape became. Hawk began to guess at what might be up ahead or around the next bend and experienced a small victory when his guesses proved correct. Slowly, but surely, pieces of his missing memory trickled back. It gave him hope that his return home would be worthwhile in the end.

The carriage labored up the graveled drive, still slick with last night's sleet and snow and stopped in front of the wide arced stairway. Hawk closed his eyes and pictured what he would find on the other side of the door. The entrance would be awash in red and dark wood. There would be a small table at the far end near the staircase that served to collect the day's mail. A large oil painting—a landscape— would hang on the wall and beneath it another narrow table and a porcelain vase filled with fresh flowers from the greenhouse.

The door to the carriage swung open, interrupting his memories and the confusion that surrounded them. Why was it he could remember the unimportant aspects of his life, yet the pieces of the puzzle he needed to ensure Madalene's safety —such as what information he had collected on Lord T's identity—continued to elude him? What if he never remembered? What if his journals were never found? Or what if he did find them only to discover they contained nothing to help track down the man Phillip had played his demented *game* with?

"M'lord?"

Hawk shook off the questions and waved off his driver who offered assistance in getting down from the carriage. There was no need getting ahead of himself. If such things did come to pass, he would find another way to keep Madalene safe. For now, he needed to keep his wits about him and navigate the battlefield that was his family.

Before he reached the front door, it opened, revealing a well-dressed, older man. Hawk struggled for a name. Rodney? Randall?

"Roberts," he said, the name coming to him at the last minute and with it a rush of information. The family's house steward. He'd been with the family for as long as Hawk could recall, though the man before him appeared older than his memories allowed for. Perhaps it was the shocked expression on his face that made it so, or the snow-white hair that grew in a strip around his head, leaving the top completely bald.

"My lord...we were not expecting you."

Hawk had not sent word ahead. "I thought I might surprise them." *Them.* Mother. Father. Titles issued out of courtesy, but with no true affection attached. He stepped across the threshold into the home of his childhood. A quick scan of the entrance hall indicated his memory had been spot on, save for the painting. It was no longer that of a landscape. Instead, he discovered his brother's accusing gaze staring down at him. He turned his back to it.

"Are they at home, Roberts?"

The steward hesitated, his stoic manner showing the smallest hint of uncertainty. "Indeed, my lord. They have only just sat down to dinner."

Hawk nodded, working his memory once more. The beginnings of a headache had developed behind his eyes, accompanied by a dull throb near his temple where the scar from his misadventure with Lord Pengrin resided. He walked past Roberts, ignoring the bluster that spouted out of him as he suggested his lordship wait to be announced.

He tossed a glance over his shoulder at the older man. "Is it required that I am announced in my own home?"

Roberts hurried behind him, but his steps had become slow and he had a limp Hawk did not remember. "Of course not, my lord. However, your parents have not seen you in quite some time—"

"They could have seen me sooner than today, had they bothered to take me in after my rather unfortunate brush with death. But they did not," Hawk stopped and Roberts nearly ran into him. "Did they, Roberts?"

"I am certain Lord Ravenwood was quite concerned about your well-being, my lord."

Hawk raised his eyebrows. "I think we both know that is not the case, don't we?"

Roberts didn't reply, but in his silence, the truth resided. Hawk turned on his heel and continued down the hallway to the dining hall. He gripped the brass knobs on the door and pushed them open, standing on the threshold.

His parents glanced up in tandem and stared as if seeing a ghost. In a sense, that's what he was to them, was he not? The wavering image of the son they had cast out and forgotten, in favor of worshipping the memory of the one truly gone. As if Phillip was worth such adulation, a sick excuse of a man who preyed on those weaker than he for sport. This venerated son with a soul as black as night.

This is whom they chose to love.

His mother's expression changed from surprise to cold disregard and a rush of memories assaulted Hawk one after the other, doing little to alleviate the ache growing behind his eyes. His mother's sharp words, her constant irritation with him, questioning over and over why he could not be more like dear, sweet Phillip. He had never measured up in her eyes.

He never would. Not even now. Not even when he had laid at her feet the evidence of the evil Phillip had perpetrated —what her eldest son was capable of. Instead, she had turned her back on the truth and on Hawk and never looked back. It had been on her command that he had been banished from his own home, his father standing in the shadows mute, rendered useless from the shock of his heir's death at the hands of his second son. It had been Mother who had taken the reins, pushing her grief aside to issue the directive of what would be done, how Phillip's death and his memory would be recorded and preserved.

"What are *you* doing here?"

Something shifted inside of him at the revulsion wrapped around each word she spoke. Without warning, he changed.

His posture straightened, his face hardened, as did his heart. The blood in his veins ran cold. He became, in that instant, the man he had heard so much about but had yet to truly meet face to face.

He became The Hawk.

"Good evening to you as well, Mother. Such a warm welcome on this cold night." He gave her an emotionless smile before shifting his gaze to where the earl sat at the head of the long table. "Father, you're looking...well."

He stumbled over the lie. As it turned out, his father did not look well at all. Always a thinner man, he now appeared gaunt. Sickly. Skin hung from his bones as if the man was ready to slide away into an early grave. A chill passed through Hawk.

"Have you come to see for yourself, then?" Even his father's voice sounded frail.

"See what?"

"I am dying, that is what." The declaration was delivered with nonchalance, a quiet acceptance of the inevitable.

"I did not know." How could he, given the fact that since he'd rejoined the land of the living, his memories had not bothered to return with him? Had he been aware of his father's failing health before Lord Pengrin's attempt on his life? He could find nothing inside of him that indicated he did, though it seemed strange given information was the currency The Hawk traded in. Perhaps he had washed his hands of his family in much the same way they had of him and cared little when it came to hearing news of them.

His mother scoffed and Hawk's hands fisted at his sides. "Yet, how convenient that you have arrived. Are we to believe it a coincidence?"

"You can believe whatever you wish. I care little. But I can assure you, my being here has little to do with either of you."

"Then why are you here? Has it not been made clear you are not welcome?"

He let out a sharp laugh that neither sounded nor felt like the laughter he experienced in Madalene's presence. This laugh had nothing to do with merriment and affection. Instead, it shot out of him like a weapon and he experienced a fleeting moment of satisfaction when his mother jerked in her seat as it found its mark.

"You have made your stand on the matter perfectly clear, Mother dear. I simply have no interest in what you think or feel. I have some business to take care of. Once I have done so, I will leave. Though," he looked at his father, "I suspect I shall return in due course."

His mother rose to her feet, a piece of silverware clattering to the floor, its impact echoing in the cavernous room. "You are not welcome now and you will not be welcomed then."

Hawk grinned again, his mother's hatred fueling his response. "You forget, Mother. When Father dies, Raven Manor will no longer be your home. It will become mine, as will all other properties and incomes attached to the Ravenwood title. And when that day comes, you may rest assured it will be *you* who will no longer be welcomed within these walls."

He ignored her gasp and turned his back on them, making a slow exit from the dining hall. "Now, if you will excuse me. I have had a long trip and I believe I shall retire to my room for the evening."

Hawk left his parents behind, their collective glares cutting through his flesh like daggers. He kept walking, up the two flights of stairs to his room above, only realizing once he'd closed the door of his bedchamber behind him that he had found the room without thinking. Another memory had returned, quietly and without fanfare. Coming here had been the right thing to do; though he could not rid himself of the selfish wish he had brought Madalene with him. Her presence would have been an effective balm to soothed the hurt of his parents' hatred.

He fumbled in the dark and lit the candle next to the bed. A cold draft made the flame waver before it took hold. When had the room been used last? He ran his finger along the oak surface of the table and looked down at the dust covering his fingertip. A long time, apparently.

He picked up the candle and crossed the room to kneel before the hearth. It had been cleaned out and left empty with nothing to warm the room. He set the candle next to him, feeling about for the loose stone on the side; Madalene's directions clear in his mind. It took a few attempts before he found it, but a soft knock came at his door before he could loosen the stone and pull it free.

He straightened, bringing the candle with him. "Yes?"

The door opened slowly and a small head peeked in. "M'lord?"

"Come in." A young girl, likely no older than Madalene had been when she began working for his family, appeared, her arms laden with supplies. He resisted the urge to rush forward and help her.

"Mr. Roberts asked me to light the fire and clean the room for you." Her words came in a whisper, like a timid bird flitting about, looking for a safe place to land.

"Did he?" He supposed Roberts understood which way the wind would blow once the earl met his end. Such a strange thought. For years, his father had been dead to him, yet now that his death was imminent, it left him out of sorts, unsure of what to do with the information.

"Yes. Might I?"

He offered the girl a warm smile and The Hawk receding into the shadows. "Yes, please. It would be most appreciated."

She curtsied as best she could, given her burden.

"I shall leave you to it then." If he could not retrieve the journals at present, there was something else he could do.

Go below stairs and see the room where Phillip took his last breath and where Hawk became a murderer.

"There you go, you're well strapped in," Major Gibbons said, though the act of doing so had scandalized his sister so her cheeks had turned a proper shade of red and nothing short of disgust burned in her eyes. Her discomfort bothered Madalene. It was ill placed. She had kept her ankles covered and he'd touched nothing beyond the front of her boots, but Mrs. Chambers' reaction gave the impression he had reached under her skirts and caressed bare flesh!

Madalene turned away from her, the woman's embarrassment casting a pall over what should have been a fun excursion. She glanced down at her skates and moved them back and forth over the packed snow beneath her feet.

"I do not know if I can do this," she admitted. "I've never skated before."

Major Gibbons stood steady on his feet as if he had been born with blades poking out the bottoms of them. "Shall I give a demonstration then?"

"Would you?" Perhaps if she could see it done, study the movements, she would feel more secure about hurtling herself out onto the ice and into the path of others, for it seemed half of London had the same idea to come to St. James Park on this sunny winter's day to partake in the activity.

"It would be my pleasure." Major Gibbons executed a bow and walked easily across the snow to where the ice began a scant ten feet away. "I shall take a turn about the ice then, how will that be?"

"Perfect. I promise I shall muster up my courage by the time you return."

"Very well, then. Commence mustering." He smiled and she returned it easily. The more time she spent in the major's company, the more relaxed she became. His easy nature made him an amenable companion who caused none of the confusion she experienced when near Lord Hawksmoor.

His sister on the other hand...well that was another matter.

"Have you skated before, Mrs. Chambers?" Madalene briefly shifted her gaze to the woman next to her before returning it to the ice where Major Gibbons had begun his lap with easy strides. Mrs. Chambers had spoken little to her since she and her brother arrived at Ridgemont House to take Madalene skating and the few overtures Madalene had made were met with brief, almost curt, responses.

"Of course," Mrs. Chambers answered, affecting a rather pompous air. It was clear the woman did not favor Madalene at all, though why, she could not fathom. It wasn't as if the Gibbonses were high born and had any right to look down upon her.

"Have I done something to offend you, Mrs. Chambers? I am left with the distinct impression you are not pleased with my association with your brother."

"Indeed, I am not."

Madalene's body jerked. Mrs. Chambers' abrupt response took her aback. "I...I see." Except that she didn't, not really. "And why might that be?"

Mrs. Chambers cut her sharp gaze to Madalene and she was struck by how similar the woman's features were to her brother's, though they did not translate quite as well and where Major Gibbons could easily be described as handsome, on Mrs. Chambers it only left her looking rather...less so. Although, that could also be contributed to the fact she rarely smiled, where her brother did often. And where the major exuded a certain charm, Mrs. Chambers radiated constant disapproval.

"You are hardly of a quality I wish for my brother to court, Miss Cosgrove, which is exactly what he is doing. You are aware of that, are you not?"

That the woman deemed to speak to her as if she were an idiot stoked Madalene's ire. She may be country born, but she was educated by a baronet's daughter and learned on any number of subjects likely Mrs. Chambers had never heard of. But saying so now would hardly improve upon their relationship or the conversation.

"I am aware that your brother has treated me kindly as a friend. As to courting, he has made no overtures that would lead me to believe he has anything save friendship in mind." Which was a partial lie, perhaps. While the major had not come out and claimed a budding affection, Madalene was not a blind fool. She had seen the look in his eye when he thought her unaware of his perusal. It held a hint of hunger; the kind men would get where women were concerned. She had seen it repeatedly throughout her life from the time she was a young girl. She had seen it in Lord Hawksmoor's brother, though he had taken it too far, allowed his desire to grow into madness and violence.

She pushed the ugly memory aside. Major Gibbons had been the perfect gentleman and while he had looked at her with hunger, he had made no move to act inappropriately.

Mrs. Chambers scoffed and shook her head. "My brother is a gentleman, that is why he has not indicated an interest as yet. But he is still a man easily turned by a pretty head. Regardless, a relationship between the two of you will simply not be countenanced."

She made it sound as if Madalene carried the plague. "And why is that, exactly?" Not that she was necessarily interested in going beyond friendship with Major Gibbons. It was difficult to consider such a thing when the sensation of Lord Hawksmoor's chaste kiss still resonated deep within her and his absence made her long for him all the more.

"You are a *servant*, Miss Cosgrove, despite Lady Dalridge's attempts to elevate your status based on a distant relation to a baronet."

"I would hardly consider my grandfather a distant relation," Madalene countered, but Mrs. Chambers paid her comment no heed.

"I have decided my brother will marry one of the Miss Caldwells."

Her claim baffled. "*One* of the Miss Caldwells? Did you have a particular one in mind, or does it matter not which one?" The woman spoke as if she was picking a squash from the market and one would do just as well as the other.

Madalene received another glare for her impertinent inquiry.

"Obviously, we cannot hope to reach beyond that, but certainly when a baron has nothing more than a houseful of daughters, he will be willing to part with one to an untitled gentleman who has proven himself in battle and now has the ear of the Prime Minister and the potential of a well-placed political career."

"And have any of the Caldwell ladies indicated an interest in marrying your brother?"

"That is hardly here nor there. The eldest Miss Caldwell already has one broken engagement in her pocket, to the disreputable Lord Blackbourne at that, and the middle sister has embarrassed herself with her public displays and opinions. Either one will have a hard time finding a husband given such history. The youngest one is still salvageable, however. My brother's interest in her will likely be looked upon favorably and with gratitude."

"And how does your brother feel about the notion of marrying one of the Caldwells?" Madalene glanced out onto the ice. The major had stopped briefly on the far side of the pond to chat with an acquaintance.

Mrs. Chambers' voice turned as hard as the ice Major Gibbons skated upon. "My brother will do as I advise him. It has always been so."

Her claim proved the most surprising thing she had said thus far. Major Gibbons appeared to Madalene as a man with his own mind and while he didn't strike her as someone who would ignore his sister's counsel outright, it seemed odd that he would allow her to make his decisions for him, especially about something as important as marriage.

"Would you not prefer that your brother choose his own wife?"

"Men cannot be counted upon to make a proper choice in that regard. They are too easily sidetracked by womanly wiles, as is proven here."

"I beg your—"

"Please, Miss Cosgrove. Do not play coy with me. I am certain you are well aware of your powers to lure a man. You are a beautiful woman, of that there is no doubt, and men are simple creatures, effortlessly distracted by such. But that is all you are—just a pretty distraction. If you have any hopes beyond that with regard to my brother, you are to be sorely disappointed."

Madalene did not have a chance to respond as Major Gibbons had completed his round about the pond and came to stand in front of them once again. Not that she had a response. Mrs. Chambers' accusations and insinuations against her character had left her completely and utterly speechless. And angry.

"Are you ready, Miss Cosgrove?" Major Gibbons held out his hands to assist her onto the ice.

She rose to her feet and stomped over the snow, determined to leave Mrs. Chambers and her rude comments behind on the cold bench.

"Indeed, I am, Major." She slipped her hands into his, her legs wobbly as a newborn colt as she navigated the slippery surface. Her companion laughed heartily and pulled her arm through his, holding her firmly against his side. It was the most contact they'd had thus far and while it felt peculiar to have him so close, she allowed it for no other reason than the discomfort it would cause Mrs. Chambers.

Chapter Fourteen

H awk found the larder with ease, instinctually knowing which stairwell to go down and which hallway led to it. He knew to step outside this door, turn that way, and walk back to another door that finally brought him to the kitchens and attached at the end of that, the larder. He remembered the larder had two entrances, this narrow one from the kitchen, and the one accessible from outside. But given the weather had yet to let up, he opted for the interior one.

Even the names of a few of the surprised servants he passed on his way drifted back. Mary. Ethel. Bert. It was as if being in this house had opened the door to where his memories had stolen off to and coaxed them back to where they belonged. And they had come easily; unlike in the early days when pulling his teeth out would have been an easier venture than recalling even the simplest of memories.

He passed through the kitchens, ignoring the gasps of the staff present, acknowledging their curtsies and *m'lords* with a brief nod, yet no break in stride. He wanted this done with. The sooner the better.

He stopped at the door leading to the larder.

"Lord Hawksmoor? Is there something I might help you with?"

Hawk kept his gaze fixed on the door, his hand shaking where it rested on the cold, iron handle. Did the servants know what had happened in here despite his parents' attempts to cover it up? Were they aware of Phillip's madness? If so, they gave no indication. "Yes, Mrs. Tipley, you may. I would like the servants to vacate the kitchens, please."

"I beg your—"

"I would like them to leave. Go elsewhere."

Mrs. Tipley's hand fluttered at the base of her neck. "But, my lord, they have duties to attend to and Lady Ravenwood would not be pleased to discover they had left them undone."

"Mrs. Tipley," Hawk said, sliding a glance toward her. "As you well know, my father is gravely ill and likely not long for this world. Upon his demise, who will become your new employer?"

Mrs. Tipley was quiet a moment before answering, "You will, my lord."

"Exactly." He said no more and after a moment, Mrs. Tipley gave a short curtsey and scurried away. Behind him, he heard her usher the servants out, hushing their questions and calming their fears over not being able to finish their duties.

Silence descended around him once they had all gone, its sound deafening. Blood pounded in his head and rang in his ears. A cold sweat broke out all over, droplets of sweat finding their way down his spine. He swallowed. Every ounce of him wanted to turn and run, to leave the ugliness of that night in the past. But he could not. He needed to know the truth. All of it. Was Madalene still in danger? If he walked away now, he may never know. If anything happened to her because he had been too much of a coward to protect her, he would never be able to live with himself.

He took a deep breath and pushed the door open. He stepped inside, leading with the candle he had swiped from the table in the kitchen, much to the surprise of the servants who sat around it, scrambling to stand upon his unexpected arrival. The small, unglazed windows high up on the wall of the larder were opened slightly and a cold draft filled the room, causing the flame of his candle to dance. He sheltered it with his hand. Night had fallen hard and dark, its shadow sliding over joints of meat where they hung from hooks in the ceiling, reaching toward the cold stone thrawl that lined the far side of the wall and served to chill the room. Shelves filled the empty spaces, housing bottles of preserves and what not.

It took little time for the sound of Madalene's voice to reach out from the past and call from the depths of his mind, pulling at him. That guttural cry, laced with a fear he had never encountered in his life before or since, cut through him now, as it had then.

"Thomas!"

Years ago, her voice crying out for him in terror had propelled him forward even when a sense of self-preservation demanded he run the other way.

He'd had no idea of what he would find when he reached the larder. What awaited him was nothing his imagination could have conjured up despite his brother's threats.

The threats! Yes. Hawk ran a hand through his hair, gripping a handful as the memory shot forth from the depths. His brother had let something slip before that night. He'd been well into his cups, a state that had become more and more common before his death. Was it due to guilt? Or just another aspect of his madness? It hardly mattered now.

"Don't be so naïve, brother dear." Phillip always spoke to him in the most condescending manner, as if Hawk was an uninitiated buffoon who had no inkling how the world really worked. *"They are but playthings. Nothing more. They*

are here for our amusement. Our pleasure, to take as we see fit. If they cry or squeal, it only serves to increase the gratification."

His words had sickened Hawk then and still did to this day. But the part that had frightened him most had been the way in which his brother had said *them*. With a twisted gleam in his eye. It was in that moment that Hawk realized his brother was nothing short of a madman.

"What have you done?" He whispered the words aloud and listened as they echoed in the quiet around him, bouncing off the stone walls before landing quietly at his feet, absorbed into the mud floor. He closed his eyes and crept back into the past, to that conversation with his brother.

Phillip had laughed and waved a hand as if to dismiss the question. As if his actions bore no consequence. He had believed himself untouchable. In a sense, he had been right, as Hawk soon discovered with horrible clarity. *"What does it matter? For the most part we stick to those who are of no consequence."*

For the most part.

We.

His brother's choice of words disturbed him even now and he sifted through his mind for the rest of the memory. Had he asked his brother what he meant by *for the most part*? He squeezed his eyes shut tighter and pushed past the aching in his head.

Yes. Yes, he had.

"Sometimes a lady is so fetching, the challenge so delectable, one cannot help themselves. I found one such lady and I simply had to have her. Though, in the end, her willingness became rather tedious, despite the thrill of putting one over on that pompous Lord Rothbury."

Lord Rothbury? Hawk's heart pounded even harder. He remembered now and the name punched into him like a fist.

Alexander St. John, Lord Rothbury. The Duke of Franklyn's only son and heir.

"You cuckolded the heir to a duchy? Lord Rothbury is not a man to be trifled with. Are you mad?" But yes, he was. Hawk understood this even as the question left his mouth.

Phillip shrugged. "It is not as if he knew. Either way, his wife is dead now and the dead cannot confess their sins, can they?"

Dead. The word reached from the past and reverberated in Hawk's head. Dropped him to his knees. Filled the room and closed in around him. Dead.

Lady Rothbury had been found on her husband's estate, floating in the lake in mid-winter. Most of the details surrounding her death had been kept hushed, much as Phillip's own would be a few scant weeks later. As much as the ton loved to delve into the dirty laundry of their peers, they preferred to keep their own neatly folded and tucked away where it could not be found. Regardless, something in the way Phillip had responded to Hawk's question left him questioning what little he did know about the lady's sudden and unfortunate demise.

"Did you—?"

Phillip shrugged. "When you play the game, you must abide by the rules. When a challenge is set down, you do not balk. To do so would be to lose to the other player. To choke on your pride and stand by impotently while they finish the challenge you failed at. And I refuse to fail or to lose. My pride is well intact and shall remain so."

The words came back to haunt Hawk. Phillip had not claimed responsibility for Lady Rothbury's death outright, but he didn't need to. Hawk knew. Somewhere deep down in his bones, he knew. The lady's death had not been an accident any more than Phillip's had been. She had been murdered and Phillip had been the one who had murdered her.

"You could hang for this!"

Phillip had laughed, a deprecating sound that echoed within Hawk still, all these years later. *"Hardly. I am a peer. Besides, clearly, everyone believes it to be an accident. Some even whisper she may have done it to herself. My accomplice is quite adept at covering such things up when he has the correct incentive to do so."*

"And what incentive is that?"

Phillip smiled; a sick, twisted expression that made Hawk's blood run cold. "The aforementioned hanging you so urgently mentioned. He's quite fearful of having his precious neck stretched beyond its limits."

The candle dropped from Hawk's hand and rolled a few feet away until the flame extinguished. It hardly mattered. He was not looking at what was in front of him, but instead had delved inside, resurrecting long buried memories.

He had gone to his parents with the information; afraid of what else Phillip and his accomplice might be capable of. Fearful of who else may be in danger. He had begged them to send Phillip away, put him in a sanitarium if need be. Anything to prevent the same thing from happening to another innocent woman targeted by his brother and whoever he played this insidious *game* with him. But his pleas fell on the deaf ears of parents who refused to accept their firstborn, their heir, was anything but the perfect son. Instead, they accused Hawk of jealousy, of trying to hurt his brother's reputation for his own gain.

Their indifference, their refusal to believe the evidence he laid at their feet, left him stunned. But he was not willing to give up. Perhaps if he could find Phillip's accomplice, root him out and force him to talk, it would convince them.

But before he could, his parents turned on him. His mother informed Phillip of what Hawk had accused him of. Enraged, Phillip had burst into Hawk's bedchamber and attacked him, startling him with the ferocity of his violence. The blows had come fast and furious, leaving him no time to mount a defense. Hawk had come away from the encounter bloodied, his brother's threat ringing in his ears.

"You will pay for this, little brother. My next conquest will be someone you hold most dear. I will make you regret this day for the rest of your life. Every day you will have to live with what your disloyalty to this family—to me!—has wrought."

But whom had Hawk cared about? He was courting no one and had shown no woman a particular interest. Save for one. But he had not thought of her. His brother had no way of knowing about his friendship with Madalene. He had been discreet, fearful his attentions would be misconstrued, or cause her difficulty with the other staff.

Hawk shook his head. To this day, he did not know how Phillip had discovered their friendship. Not that it mattered. The result was the same. His brother had hunted her down and attacked her.

What if Hawk hadn't heard her scream? What if he had not been outside that night, agonizing over what to do about his brother to hear her scream, carried on the night air but a hundred feet away? But he had heard and he'd come running. He'd freed her from his brother's clutches, tearing her away and turning the attack onto Phillip, his fists propelled by fear and rage. How dare he? How dare he touch her! She was innocence and sweetness. She was his friend, his confidante. And the only one in this godforsaken house that had ever treated him as if he mattered. When he was with her, he felt whole. Accepted. Loved even.

And his brother had sought to destroy that, to take away her goodness, her innocence as retaliation against him. The more the truth of what his brother intended and why sank in, the more his rage and his guilt grew. He was vaguely conscious of Madalene behind him, screaming—for him to stop? He couldn't remember. He was lost, lost in a world that allowed Phillip to continue his evil, to hurt more innocents who lacked the ability or resources to fight back. He couldn't let it continue.

Then his brother's promise came, rasped between the breaths Hawk had not yet squeezed out of him. The name of his accomplice in this twisted game he played. *Lord T.* And the reminder—no—the guarantee, that if one player failed, the other took up the charge and completed the challenge. There would be no reprieve if Hawk killed Phillip. It would not save her, not so long as this *Lord T* was able to finish what Phillip started.

Beyond that, Hawk remembered nothing specific, just flashes. The color red blinding him. The pounding in his head. Desperation. The pressure as his hands pressed into flesh, harder and harder until nothing was left but silence. His brother's empty eyes staring up at him. Phillip was dead. He cared little. He had saved her. But only from Phillip. Not from the other player in the game.

Not from the elusive *Lord T.*

Hawk spun on his heel and strode with purpose from the larder, taking the stairs two at a time. When he reached his bedchamber, the little maid had left, her duties completed. It had all been for naught. He had no intention of spending more than one night here. He knelt once more by the hearth, the warmth from the fire pressing against him as he wrestled the loose stone free to reveal a narrow cubby. Inside, he discovered a bundle swaddled in linen and covered with the dust from the stones and mortar. He pulled the package out and laid it on the floor, unwrapping the material to reveal three separate leather-bound journals.

He carried them to the small table, flanked by two chairs near the fire and brought a lamp over to assist him. Then he sat down and began to read. The words flowed into sentences and the sentences created the story of his life over the two years that spanned the length of the journals. With each entry, his memory recovered the fine details the words left out. The sense of aloneness he had experienced living in his brother's shadow, ignored by his parents, tormented by his brother. His observations of Madalene and how he thought her out of place amongst the servants. The way she gravitated to the library as if the books on the shelves called out a siren song to her.

The entries changed after he decided to make it known to her that he had noticed. She was reticent at first, attempting to keep the distance between servant and employer. It had taken every last ounce of his charm to coax her into a friendship, but eventually, the barriers between them relaxed and a light entered his life.

He sought her out, knowing their friendship was ill thought out, that his attention could cause her difficulty if discovered. But he had been unable to stop. Her sweetness and warmth were too potent a force. Being in her presence had placed a balm over the wounds of his family's indifference. In her, he saw a sharp intelligence and, while he could not free himself from the existence he'd been shackled with, he could maybe save her. Give her the opportunity to reach for something better than servitude. He wanted to arrange for her to get further schooling. To give something back to her after all she had given to him.

Hawk rested the journal in his lap and rubbed his burning eyes. If he had only known then the depth of his brother's madness, he would have sent her away sooner. Ensured the opportunities she deserved were given her. But he had been selfish. He had not wanted to let her go so soon. The thought of Raven Manor without her was too dreary to contemplate. So, he'd put it off.

And she had paid the price.

The night wore on, and with it, the details of his brother's debauched nature unfolded. Hawk's suspicions, the things his brother said that began to add up page after page. His desperation over his failure to gain his parents' support to have Phillip removed from society. The aftermath of the beating he'd received from his brother was the final straw in bringing him to the realization that he fought a battle he could not win.

And then the last entry, written after he had admitted his culpability in Phillip's death and how it had come about. His parents had banished him from their home, his mother unable to even look at him with anything but complete revulsion, as if he was the monster and not Phillip. She'd had several footmen escort him to his room and stand outside the door as he gathered his things and made a brief, final entry in his journal.

I cannot take her with me. It would ruin her. Phillip is dead. Father promises they will keep her on, that she will suffer no ill will against her for what was done. But I must travel to London and find the mysterious Lord T Phillip referred to. I must end this madness. Until I do—until I can bring this game to an end, she will never truly be safe.

His father had lied. Or perhaps Mother had overruled him as she usually did. He'd been a fool to believe them, to think they possessed even a small scrap of honor. They had not kept Madalene on as promised. Instead, they had sacked her shortly after Phillip's funeral. And Hawk's promise to her, to ensure she was safe, had been sown in fallow ground.

He had not discovered the identity of the other player in the game. Lord T continued to remain a mystery to this day. A status he could no longer blame on lost memories. It became clear now. Everything he had done, all the research in his business journals, the notations he had made on each member of the peerage that passed through the doors of The Devil's Lair had all been a means to an end. A list of weaknesses, predilections, known associates—all of it in a search for *Lord T* with the goal to end this depraved game once and for all.

But he had failed.

And the illusive *Lord T* taunted him all the way with his letters, promising to find her. Promising to finish what Phillip could not. To win the final victory. Fear embedded itself deep in his gut, roiling through him like acid.

Hawk peered out the window. The sun had yet to rise, but the clock over the mantle announced morning was nigh. He rose from the chair, his muscles protesting the movement, and pulled the rope by the bed to signal the servants. He knew what he had to do.

He would see Madalene safe, no matter what it took. And he would find this Lord T and end him as he had Phillip.

Failure was not an option.

Chapter Fifteen

"I do believe the tea has been a great success," Madalene said, handing Lady Henrietta a freshly steeped cup before guiding her over to a set of chairs placed in a semi-circle near the fire. Most of the chairs were occupied by young girls between the ages of seven and twelve dressed in their Sunday best. Lady Henrietta visibly relaxed as she took her own seat amongst them.

The event, meant to raise funds and awareness of the importance of ensuring girls received a proper education regardless of their station in life, had changed somewhat in the planning, thanks in part to Lady Dalridge's input. It had turned from a full on ask for donations, to a Winter Tea hosted by the Lindwells, where an example of the benefits of providing such a school were on full display by the children present. Children Rosalind Caldwell had sent to other schools to receive their education before determining she would start her own.

"My dear Miss Caldwell," Lady Dalridge had said, the words drawling out of her and punctuated by one arched eyebrow. "Sometimes the subtle approach is the best one when dealing with the ton. Let them think supporting such a cause was their own brilliant idea, rather than bludgeoning them over the head with your insistence that they do so. It is less likely to bruise their collective egos and more likely to get them to part with a few coins."

"Indeed, I believe it has definitely been a success," Lady Henrietta said to Madalene, looking at the girls seated around her. "And I am certain we have these beauties to thank for it." Her smile proved contagious and one by one, the girls smiled in return, the epitome of poise and good manners.

Save for one.

"Miss," a fiery little redheaded girl said, sliding off her chair to take a few steps toward Lady Henrietta. "What are the marks on your neck?"

"Ingrid!" One of the older girls whispered harshly at the younger one who had spoken up. "A lady does not ask such things of another lady! It is the height of rudeness."

For a moment, Madalene feared little Ingrid would burst into tears when her lower lip trembled at the older girl's sharp rebuke. Or that Lady Henrietta would die a thousand deaths at having her scars remarked upon in such a pointed and public manner. Thankfully, none of that came to pass.

Lady Henrietta held up her hand, quieting the older girl with a gentle look before then holding her hand out to Ingrid. The little redhead quickly trotted over to her then effected what Madalene assumed was meant to be a curtsey but looked a bit more like a hop.

"I was caught in a fire once upon a time," Lady Henrietta said, her fingers toying with the hair pulled over her shoulder to drape down her chest. "It burned my skin and left the marks you see."

"Does it hurt?"

Lady Henrietta smiled and shook her head. "No, my sweet. Not anymore."

"Oh. That's good. Would you like a biscuit?" Ingrid held out her tiny hand, revealing the crumbled remnants of what had once been a biscuit.

Madalene marveled at Lady Henrietta's ability to exude such warmth and ease toward the children, as if somehow their innocence and honesty created a safe haven she could not find amongst her peers. She had a natural ability with the young ones and it was a shame she was not in a position to be headmistress of Rosalind's school as Lady Henrietta was far more suited to the job than Madalene. The realization hit her like a brick falling from the sky and for a moment, she stood dazed by it, unable to move.

Madalene did not wish to be the headmistress of Rosalind's school.

Yes, it was a wonderful opportunity, and yes, she would be in need of employment now that she had found her replacement for Northill. But she did not want to run a school. Which made not a lick of sense. After all, she loved books and she loved learning, and she even loved children and believed whole-heartedly in education for young girls to help improve their lot in life. She *should* want to do this.

But she didn't.

Which led to the inevitable question—what *did* she want to do?

When she was young, before her father lost his position as land steward at the late Lord Walkerton's estate, she had been happy. She had missed Father, of course, when he was forced to go off to war and leave them behind, but she had been young enough that she did not dwell on his absence, but reveled in the letters he sent, the stories he told within them, and the visits he made home.

The country life had suited her with its wide-open spaces, the animals, the extended family of servants. She had assumed that one day she would grow up, marry a wonderful man like

Father and continue to live a bucolic life in a small cottage in the country, surrounded by all the things and the people she loved.

It had been a child's dream, one brusquely snatched away when Father had stood up to Lord Walkerton for his treatment of a maid unfairly accused of stealing, but it was a dream she'd never truly been able to give up. She thought to recapture it when she was hired into service at Raven Manor, and for a little while she had, though as a housemaid, she'd not held the same stature as daughter of the land steward. Her duties left her busy from before sunrise until well after it set. Only Lord Hawksmoor's attention, the way he had treated her as if she were an equal, had buoyed her.

Until that too had been destroyed.

While she and Father struggled to survive in London, living in one ramshackle dwelling after another, it was her remembrance of life in the country, of better times, that kept her going. She drew strength from these memories and from Lord Hawksmoor's belief in her inherent intelligence and ability to do and become anything she wished.

Though hanging onto that belief while in London had been almost impossible. She'd been on the brink of giving up hope when the Bowens came into their lives and hired Father as land steward to Northill. She had taken on the job as housekeeper through necessity when several employees who had lacked the willingness to work had been let go. It was never meant to be a permanent position. Father feared it would put her on a shelf and she would miss out on experiences such as marriage and a family of her own.

But, in truth, she liked running a household, and what's more, she was good at it. She had a head for figures and figuring out solutions to problems that arose. She excelled at hiring the right person for the jobs required and bargaining with the local shopkeepers for the best cuts of meat and freshest produce. She had created a happy and warm atmosphere amongst the staff that pleased her greatly.

It was the perfect training ground for when she finally had a home of her own, should that day ever come. Unfortunately, most of the young men of her acquaintance were not interested in her for who she was on the inside, but instead commented on her comely appearance and how many offspring she could provide them. Her interest in books and learning new things were an oddity and they expected her to give it up upon marriage, seeing no value in it.

No value in learning! Imagine. She sighed. And so, with her employment prospects less than appealing and her chance of marriage to a man who valued her for whom she was non-existent, her future appeared rather bleak, indeed.

"You appear to be having quite a conversation with yourself, Miss Cosgrove, if the passing expressions on that pretty face of yours are any indication."

Lord Hawksmoor's voice to her left rushed through her with thrilling surprise and she turned toward him, unable to contain the smile that burst across her face.

"Lord Hawksmoor! I had begun to believe you would not make it home in time to join us." Was it wrong how much she wished to throw herself into his arms to ensure he was real and not simply conjured up by her imagination? Oh, how many hours had she spent dwelling on his absence? Imagining the moment of his return. Too many to count, for certain.

"And miss such a warm welcome? I would have traveled half way around the world for a glimpse of your smile upon my return."

"Only half way?" Who was this woman who teased future earls like a coquette? Her cursed cheeks warmed and she bit her lower lip.

Lord Hawksmoor laughed and took her hand, bringing it to his lips. He did not wear gloves, a glaring breach of etiquette that would likely send Lady Dalridge into a fit of outrage if she spotted him. But their absence made Madalene loathe her own, creating a barrier between his mouth and her skin. Still, the pressure of his lips tingled all the way to her toes, making a rather noticeable stop along the way at the juncture of her thighs. The heat in her cheeks burned hotter.

"All the way, then," he said and straightened, giving her hand a brief squeeze before letting go. "I have missed you to a rather embarrassing degree, I'm afraid."

His bold admission left her breathless. "Have you?"

"I have." He offered her his arm and she accepted it without hesitation, caring little as to where he intended to lead her. Somewhere more private, she hoped. Now that he was here, she did not want to share him with the masses, nor subject him to the stares of derision from those who did not appreciate his presence. She wanted to protect him from such things, from people who did not know the man she did, who had forgotten the goodness in him because of his ability to expose their own weaknesses.

"Was your trip successful then?" He appeared at first glance to be in a rather buoyant mood, however closer inspection revealed a hint of something about his eyes, a tension or unease.

"To some degree. I found the journals." He patted her hand as they strolled toward the hallway, away from the great room and the crowd that filled it. "Thank you for your assistance with that, by the way."

"You're quite welcome." Though whether finding the journals had been a good thing, she could not determine. "Were they helpful?"

"Yes. Though perhaps not in the way I had expected. I am afraid I remain in the dark as to the name of the man my brother had partnered with in the depraved game he played.

However, being at Raven Manor and reading the journals seems to have opened the door on my memories."

"Then you are fully recovered?" Why did this disappoint her? Should she not be happy for him?

"For the most part, I believe."

"I'm so pleased to hear this." And, of course, she was. Truly. It had been such a torment for him trying to navigate his world without them. Yet...now that they had returned, would he return to the man referred to as *The Hawk*, or would he remain the man she knew, the man she had once loved?"

The man she loved still.

The sudden realization rocked her and she stumbled. Lord Hawksmoor caught her. "Are you all right, my dear?"

"Yes. Yes, of course."

Loved him? She searched her heart, but it was a fruitless effort if she thought to find only friendship there. This man had changed her life, saved it, made it better without ever being aware he did so. It wasn't that friendship did not exist between them. It did, providing the roots from which love had bloomed, making it stronger and surer. A love that then blossomed into feelings she had no context or comparison for, becoming larger than life. Denying the existence of such would do little good. Now that he had returned, that she stood before him once again, her love for him rushed at her full force and demanded its due.

Lord Hawksmoor stopped. "What is it? Something is wrong. You were happy only a moment ago and now...I can see it in your face. Your brows are doing that thing."

"What thing?"

"The thing where you pull them together here—" his finger pressed lightly between her brows "—and then you purse your lips. Yes, like that." He smiled and his finger drifted down her nose, falling off the end to land upon her mouth for an all too brief heartbeat, before he dropped his hand away.

Spirals of pleasure shot through her and pooled low in her belly.

"I have missed you as well," she said, unable to reveal the depth of her feelings. The realization of them too new, and forever doomed to disappointment. He was a viscount, destined to be an earl and she was...well, she was nobody, really. Their worlds may have collided to bring them together, but reality colluded to keep them apart.

He smiled at her, desire and hope burning in his eyes until they turned an even brighter green, reminding her of a lush meadow. "Might I steal you away from this? Do you think they would miss us?"

She shook her head. In truth, she had no idea if she would be missed, but in that moment, she did not care. His absence had dragged on forever, with each day feeling as if it lasted for two. She had missed him. Horribly. Far more than she had any right to. And now that he had returned, all she wanted was to enjoy a little time in his company, alone, the way they used to all those years ago in the library at Raven Manor where she first fell under his spell. A spell time and circumstance had not broken.

He took her hand and pulled her farther down the deserted hallway. They turned left and then took a sharp right before reaching a small anti-chamber being used as a private salon. He had not hesitated in finding it.

"You've been here before?"

"Yes. Several times. Before the Lindwells rented it, the house had belonged to Lord Tunsten. Unfortunately, he was forced to let it for a rather exorbitant amount in an effort to cover his debts."

He did not say to whom the debts were owed, but given the amount of information he had on the matter, Madalene put two and two together. How closely tangled together Thomas and *The Hawk* were, like two sides of one coin. But she had little time to dwell on the thought as his body stiffened.

"What is it?"

"Tunsten."

He made no sense. "What about him?"

He pulled her into his arms and she marveled at how natural it felt to rest against his hard chest, the superfine wool of his jacket beneath her cheek. "Phillip had referred to his... associate, for lack of a better term, as *Lord T*. It could be possible that Lord Tunsten is that man."

It was difficult to concentrate on what he was saying while the warmth of his body seeped into the length of her. "I'm certain there are any number of your peers whose titles begin with the letter T, my lord—"

"Good heavens, I am holding you in my arms considering all the different ways I'd like to kiss you. Can you not now bring yourself to call me Hawk?"

"Hawk? Not Thomas?" Had he given himself over to his darker side then? Her heart sank. Was she losing him so soon after finding him again?

His lips brushed her temple and his breath tickled her skin when he spoke. "I suppose in my mind Thomas was the man who had failed to protect you. After that night, I changed. I had to. Something in me hardened. Maybe it had always been there, I don't know. Either way, it kept me focused even in the face of constant failure, as every avenue I took to find this *Lord T* became a dead end."

She wanted to look up, but she didn't want to interrupt the closeness binding them together. "You spent all these years looking for him?"

"Yes, of course. It was the sole purpose of everything I did. How could it not be? Until I find him, you remain in danger. I could not allow it. So, I collected what information I could. I bought The Devil's Lair and used people's weaknesses to extract information. You'd be surprised what people will reveal if it keeps them one step ahead of their own ruin. I traded this information for more information, or I used it to extort what I wanted to know. Along the way, I made a reputation for myself as a ruthless, heartless bastard. To my face, they referred to me as Lord Hawksmoor. Behind my back they called me *The Hawk*."

"It sounds like a rather lonely existence."

"I suppose it was. But after what I had done, I wasn't fit for much else. I immersed myself in the darkness and was quite content to remain there until I rooted out Lord T."

"Did you have no friends or allies?"

"A few. Lord Blackbourne, for one. I think we both understood what it was like to have blood on our hands, to stand on the brink of an abyss with the edge crumbling at our feet. He is the one who first referred to me simply as Hawk. He and his closest friends had a habit of giving each other nicknames, and while I never considered myself part of his close inner circle, I valued his friendship immensely. As well that of Huntsleigh and Mr. Bowen. Though I likely would have died before ever admitting it."

At this, Madalene looked up. "I have met Lord Blackbourne, he seems quite a happy and settled man. It is hard to imagine he dwelled in such a dark place."

Hawk smiled down at her but the ever-present sadness that lurked in his eyes burned deep. "He did. We both did."

"And do you dwell there still?"

His thumb caressed the curve of her cheekbone then found her mouth, tracing the edge of her bottom lip and coaxing the embers of her longing into a raging fire with one simple touch. Her heart stalled and she watched breathless as the sadness in his gaze transformed into something else. Something far more intense than she could find words for.

"Sometimes," he whispered. "And other times, someone

quite lovely and beyond compare shines a light in and chases the darkness away."

He spoke of her. Even without saying her name, she knew. Her heart swelled. How she wished to be that light for him every day. It could not be, logically she understood this, but her heart recoiled from the hateful fact.

Madalene lifted herself up onto her tiptoes and pressed her lips against his mouth, unable to resist the unfathomable need that had welled inside of her, building each day she spent in his presence, and increasing tenfold during each moment without him. He had become a secret wish that laid untilled within her since the first day he had spoken to her, befriended her, believed in her. In the years they were separated, she had tucked those feelings away, but fate had brought him back to her. And in doing so, her affection had been resurrected, the tender infatuation of a young girl growing and strengthening into something much deeper. Love.

His arms wrapped tightly around her and pulled her into him, his mouth searching hers, gentle at first then with a hunger that matched her own. Unbidden and unrestrained, she let herself go, allowed herself to be swept up into the kiss, into him. She had never experienced anything so glorious. She had been kissed before, but they were chaste pecks of courtships that never went anywhere. Hawk's kisses were something else entirely. They were everything. They were the air she breathed. The blood that flowed in her veins. The love that beat in her heart.

How had she gone this long never knowing such wonder and excitement existed? And what would she do now that she did know? Would she be able to simply let him walk out of her life again? No. She would not. Could not. The idea was inconceivable, the thought of her life without him a vast landscape of gray, void of any color or life.

One of his hands slid to her hips, lower. He pulled her

against him and through the muslin of her dress, she could feel his need. It thrilled her. Scared her. Beckoned her. She wanted to give herself to him, to let the clothing they wore slip away until she could feel his skin upon hers, feel what it was like to be filled by him, entangled in such a way there was no beginning or end.

Hawk broke the kiss and loosened his hold, then quickly released her and took a step back. The absence of him rushed up to greet her and she longed to pull him back. His chest rose and fell as he dragged a hand through his dark hair, leaving deep grooves.

"Forgive me." His breath came in ragged gasps. "I should not have—"

She cut him off with a sharp shake of her head. "No. It was I. I kissed you. I wanted to. Do you not want..." Her words trailed off.

"No! I mean yes. I do. Desperately." He shook his head and took a step toward her, shortening the gap that lay between them. "It is only that...I suppose I fear forcing myself on you...after what my brother had done."

"But you are nothing like your brother! What he did was madness. Violence. You would never hurt me or force me to do something I did not want. I know that. I trust you."

"I don't." He gave her a wry smile that stilled her heart.

"Why ever not?"

"Because I quite lose my head when I kiss you. All good sense flies straight out the window and all I can think of is—" He stopped and let out a hard breath. "Well, never mind what I think. Suffice to say, it is best if I do not make a habit out of kissing you."

His posture straightened and his shoulders pulled back, a small movement that spoke volumes. He meant to place distance between them. It broke her heart that he compared himself to his brother in such a way, but she did not know how to fix it. She did not know how to get him past the horrible memories of that night, of the blame he placed upon his shoulders or the guilt that lived in his heart. She wanted to tell him she felt safer with him than anyone else, but she sensed such a claim would only make the burden he carried heavier, the task he'd set more daunting.

She searched for something to say, something to breach the tension that had crawled between them.

"What is your plan now that you have returned to London?"

"The same as it has always been," he said, a resignation in the tone of his voice that had not been there before. "To find the man my brother referred to as *Lord T* and stop him from hurting anyone else. From hurting you."

Madalene did not know what to say. He had dedicated his life to protecting her, to protecting anyone who may become a victim to this mysterious lord bent on preying on helpless victims for the sake of a sick game. It was a noble cause, and a part of her could not help but feel awestruck by his diligence, his willingness to give up everything to succeed. But the other part of her, the part that wanted everything for him that had been denied, cried out in sorrow at what his life had become because of it. Stilted, somehow. Reduced to such a narrow focus that it hardly resembled a life at all. In a sense, it was as if his brother had won.

"But what of you? Do you not want anything for yourself?"

He looked at her for a long, quiet moment before offering her a sad smile. "Nothing I am at liberty to have, I'm afraid."

He stepped forward and took her hand, turning it to expose the sensitive skin of her wrist. He pressed his lips against her pulse point causing it to beat erratically.

"I will leave you here. I should not be seen with you. I fear it may prove detrimental to your reputation, given mine."

"Hawk—" It was the first time she had said his new name out loud. He was right. It did suit better than the name bestowed upon him by his parents, somehow blending the parts of the Thomas she had loved with aspects of The Hawk he had needed to survive.

He interrupted her before she could continue. "Are you able to find your way back to the great room?"

"Yes, but—" But what? *Say it. Tell him!* "Please don't go. I do not care what others think."

Again, the sad smile, cutting into her heart. She knew he would refuse her even before he spoke the words. "I must. It is for the best."

Hawk turned and she watched as his lean frame slipped through the door of the small salon leaving in his absence a gaping hollowness that crept in and overtook her inch by inch. Madalene closed her eyes, unable to move, afraid if she did, she would somehow increase the distance he had purposely placed between them.

"Miss Cosgrove?"

She jumped and opened her eyes. "Major Gibbons."

The major stood in the doorway a proper distance away and in full view of anyone in the hallway, so as not to give the appearance something untoward was going on. "I have been commissioned with the task of finding you."

"You have?" How much time had passed since she stole away with Hawk?

"Lady Henrietta feared you might have gotten lost in the winding hallways and requested I see if such was the case. Was she correct in her assumption?"

Madalene forced a smile. She *had* become lost, though not in the way Lady Henrietta had meant.

"I am fine," she said. "I simply needed a few moments to myself."

"Shall I leave you then?"

She was about to nod then stopped. She could not stay in this room forever wishing for a different outcome. Hawk had made his choice. He would not return. He had charted his course with the determination to see it through and while his cause was a noble one, this fact offered her no solace. He would return to his solitary existence, and she would be left to carve out a life of her own without him.

"Perhaps you might escort me back to Lady Henrietta to ease her mind that I have not become lost in the catacombs of the Lindwells' home."

"I would be most pleased. And perhaps, if I might be so bold, you would allow me to invite you to join me for a stroll through Hyde Park tomorrow? I am certain my sister would be more than pleased to provide us with a chaperone."

She doubted that, given her last conversation with Mrs. Chambers and the plans she had for her brother, but Madalene did not have the heart to tell him no. He had been kind to her, and with Hawk determined to pursue his course; she was now left to build the future she wanted.

Unfortunately, what she wanted did not include acting as headmistress for Miss Caldwell's school. What she wanted was a simple life. A cottage in the country far away from the glare and grime of London, children of her own filling the beds, and a man who loved her for all she had to offer, and not just her ability to breed or look pretty on his arm as if she were nothing more than an ornament.

Did Major Gibbons envision himself as this man? She could not say.

What she could say, however, was that when she closed her eyes and allowed herself to dream, to picture this pastoral existence in her mind, it was not Major Gibbons who held her in his arms and kissed her with such passion her toes curled inside of her shoes. Instead, the man who held her was a dark-haired, enigmatic man who walked a fine edge between light and dark until both flowed through him in equal parts.

She forced the image away. That part of her dream would never come to fruition. Hawk had made it clear where his future lay and beyond saving her from the threat of a man who had not paid her an ounce of attention and may well not even exist, she did not factor into it.

Sadness seeped through her, invading the marrow in her bones, making her limbs heavy with loneliness.

Madalene took the arm Major Gibbons offered. "I would be pleased to join you for a walk tomorrow. It is kind of you to ask."

Chapter Sixteen

He should leave. Walking about the great room of the Lindwells' home, Hawk was as conspicuous as a house on fire. Even before his brother's madness changed the trajectory of his life, he had not spent much time in the drawing rooms and balls. He'd been a young man and given to chasing the entertainments young men prefer. And once he'd purchased a controlling interest in The Devil's Lair and set about using the gaming hell to assist him in uncovering the identity of Lord T, invitations to such parties and events no longer came his way. Not that he would have attended if they had.

So, it should not surprise him now that his presence left many speechless and even more suspicious. The lords gave him a wide berth, likely because a large portion of them owed him a significant sum, while others feared he would not keep his own counsel when it came to their secrets.

The ladies, on the other hand, while they did not outwardly engage with him, did stare over the tips of their fans and whisper from behind them. With his memories now returned, he was rather embarrassed to recall several of the ladies present had warmed his bed a time or two, though no more than that. He had not been interested in anything more. He did not have time for such entanglements. Nor was his heart up for grabs.

Not much had changed in that regard, though the reasons for such had changed. Before, he had locked it away. Being ruthless and calculating was more easily accomplished if one did not involve themselves with the softer emotions. But now, much to his dismay, his heart *had* become engaged. Or rather, stolen.

No. That was incorrect. Madalene had not stolen his heart. He had given it to her. Willingly and blindly and without forethought. If he had any sense at all, he would take it back, but he did not know if such a thing was possible and, in truth, he did not want to. Likely it was far safer in her hands than in his.

"Lord Hawksmoor, how surprising to see you here."

A scowl pulled at Hawk's mouth as he turned around to find Lord Tunsten standing behind him. His first instinct was to land a cutting remark about the man returning to the home he'd been forced to let. A fortnight ago, he would have done that, but now that his memories had returned, he did not have that luxury. Lord Tunsten was on his short list of possible accomplices.

When he'd returned from Raven Manor, the first thing he had done was review the information he had accumulated on the viscount. The man's preferred game was roulette, despite his lack of skill and luck at the wheel. He also had a penchant for young ladies—the younger the better. At the time of Phillip's death, Madalene had been sixteen.

"Tunsten. I might say the same about you. Charity teas hardly seem to fit in your repertoire. Then again, given the amount of tender young girls about, perhaps I spoke too soon. Are you searching for someone in particular?"

Tunsten's cold eyes bored into him. Hawk cared little. Despite the man's hostile demeanor, they both knew Hawk could destroy him in an instant by reneging on the payment plan currently in place and insisting he pay the full amount owed immediately. Tunsten had no way of coming up with such a sum. He had already mortgaged all his properties to the hilt to fund his predilections.

"I thought it time I take another wife," he said, casting his gaze about the room. "I hear the Lindwells' are desperate to marry their daughters off to a titled gentleman and willing to pay a hefty dowry to do so."

"Aren't the Lindwell ladies a little old for your particular tastes?"

Tunsten's attention cut back to Hawk. "Keep your voice down."

"Or what?" Hawk smiled when Tunsten did not provide an answer. "You impotent fool. Do not think to order me about. I hold your fortunes in my hands, or do you forget?"

"Unless I marry one of the Lindwell twits. The dowry will be sufficient to pay off my debt and wash my hands of your threats."

Hawk leaned in; his mouth close to Tunsten's ear. "Until the whisper of the roulette wheel calls you back, as we both know it will."

Tunsten pulled away, anger turning his cheeks florid. "You can rest assured I shall never grace the door of The Devil's Lair again."

Hawk shrugged. "If not my hell, it will be someone else's. And I will hear about it. When I do, rest assured, I shall relieve them of the burden of your debt and own you once again. Do you think Lindwell will bail you out a second time? He will have already accomplished his goal. His daughter will be a viscountess. What incentive will he have to garner your good-will after that?"

"Your brother was right about you. You're a first-rate bastard."

The insinuation cut into him, as if his brother was anyone to judge. Or Tunsten for that matter. "I may be, but I have taken nothing from you that you have not lost by your own hand, unlike you. You, I have learned, prefer to take what is not rightfully yours with little care to who gets hurt in the process, or how young they may be at the time. Tell me, if Lindwell knew of this, do you think he would be so willing to hand over one of his daughters to you? I doubt even he is that desperate."

"You—"

"Save your insults," Hawk said, cutting him off. "You are nothing. I have scraped better off the bottom of my shoe. Make no mistake, I will not countenance you attempting to tie yourself to any of the young ladies of the ton, and I include the Lindwell ladies in this lot."

"My, my," Tunsten said, changing his tone. "But what is this sudden attempt at chivalry, Hawksmoor? Have you developed a tenderness for one of them? Do you fear I will get to them first? But no, it is not the Lindwell chits you have been seen in the company of recently, is it? You seem to prefer your ladies to be of a lower status than even the Americans."

Hawk refused to answer, but that did not prevent Tunsten's insinuation to send a cold chill up his spine. He had noticed the attention Hawk had paid Madalene. Had Tunsten been watching her? Watching them? Was he the *Lord T* that Hawk sought? He recalled the man had attended parties at Raven Manor. Had he been patiently biding his time since Phillip's death to strike, taunting Hawk in the meantime with his letters?

Hawk gritted his teeth. Damn his inability to find the answers he needed!

"Heed my warning, Tunsten, if you go anywhere near her,

I will gut you. And it will not be a quick affair, I assure you," Hawk said, before he turned and walked away. Even a few minutes in Tunsten's company had left him with the desperate need to immerse himself in a hot bath and scrub the encounter from his skin.

But he could not depart as yet. He could not leave Madalene unprotected with Tunsten nearby.

How he wished Madalene would return to Northill. As much as he preferred to be the one to protect her, he knew her father and Marcus Bowen would never let anything befall her.

Unlike he had.

But she was not at Northill. She was here, in London, at least for the time being. And he would be damned if he would let Tunsten get anywhere near her. He'd kill the man with his bare hands before he did.

His stomach heaved as the image of his dead brother's frozen expression staring up at him wavered in his mind's eye. He closed his eyes briefly and forced it away.

Whatever it took.

What it took, apparently, was another hour spent at the godforsaken tea until Hawk swore he would need something far stronger if he was to endure one more minute. Perhaps it would not have been quite so deplorable had he not had to watch Major Gibbons fawn incessantly over Madalene while he watched from afar. The man had no sense of finesse or subtlety. Why, if he kept this up, Hawk half expected the major to drop to one knee and propose before the tea ended.

A horrid notion and not one he would countenance. She was his. To protect, that is. Nothing more. The kiss they'd shared in the salon earlier aside. Though it had been the most enticing kiss he could ever recall receiving. So much so, he'd quite lost himself in the sweet taste of her mouth, his gentle intentions trampled by his baser needs. Bloody hell, but he had wanted her. He'd wanted to drag her to the floor and cover her with his body. He'd wanted to peel away the layers of clothing and worship the soft skin lurking beneath begging for his touch.

But the glorious image of her head thrown back in passion as he filled her quickly became juxtaposed over the fear he'd seen in her eyes the night Phillip had attacked her, and it was enough to cool his ardor. She told him she knew he would never hurt her, but he feared his passions, once let loose, would not be held in check. That if she asked him to stop, he would not comply. What if he lost his head, his restraint? What if, despite her assurances he would not, he became just like his brother?

Misery shrouded him in a dark cloud and weighed upon his heart as he stood alone in the corner of the Lindwells' great room waiting for the crowd to thin. Once both Tunsten and Major Gibbons had left, he followed suit, unsure if Madalene even noticed his departure.

Or if she would even care.

"Will you be returning to Northill soon then?"

Madalene glanced up at Major Gibbons as they slowly strolled through the pathways of Hyde Park, her arm looped through his. The day had turned mild and having the opportunity to be out of doors helped improve her mood, if only a little.

"Yes, I expect so. I have found a suitable replacement for my position and there is really no reason left for me to tarry any longer in London."

"No reason at all?" He smiled down at her and Madalene quickly looked away at the landscape blanketed in white.

Major Gibbons' interest in her, while flattering, was also

fraught with difficulty. His sister had made it clear she did not find Madalene a suitable choice for a wife. Even now, walking several paces behind them, Madalene could feel her eyes burning holes through her wool coat. The woman made her uncomfortable, as if Madalene had to be on her guard for whatever veiled barb or cutting glare came her way. Should she encourage the major's affection for her, likely these things would only increase. And what then?

Madalene redirected the conversation back to safer ground. "I have informed Miss Caldwell that I will take the position of headmistress once the school opens." It had been a difficult decision, but after the charity tea and Hawk's pronouncement that nothing could come of whatever affection laid between them, she needed to do something. She could not spend her days at Northill living with her father. She loved him dearly, but she needed something that kept her busy. To be useful. The way things stood, her future was a blank slate and she had no idea what to draw upon it. At least being headmistress of the school would keep her mind off the life she wanted but could not have. It was employment, a steady income, and a modicum of independence.

"And are you happy with this decision?"

"I suppose so." She was not necessarily unhappy.

"Is this what you want for your life?" His question was gentle, but pointed.

"It will suffice for now."

"And what if a handsome gentleman comes along and sweeps you off your feet? Would you be amenable to leaving your position as headmistress to marry him and be mother to his children?"

The major did not mince words and while it wasn't exactly a proposal, it definitely laid the foundation for one to come later, should she profess an interest. Madalene stepped lightly over a small puddle and chose her words carefully. She liked

Major Gibbons well enough, but she loved Hawk. Major Gibbons considered her as a potential wife. Hawk had made it clear he did not. If she did agree to marry Major Gibbons, would she then have the life she had always wished for? Or would it simply be a pale imitation?

"Anything is possible." It was the best she could do without offending him or making promises she may not be able to keep.

"And should I find myself near Northill, would you be amenable to a visit?"

His question startled her. She had thought his work with the Prime Minister would keep him in London. "Of course. Did you expect to be in the area?"

He glanced at her and smiled, offering a quick wink. "Anything is possible, Miss Cosgrove."

They walked on, the weight of what he had intimated settling around them like a heavy cloak. Madalene did not want to incite an interest she wasn't yet sure she could return. Her heart was engaged elsewhere and somehow it seemed wrong to encourage Major Gibbons to give his heart, if she was unable to return the favor.

Major Gibbons stopped and turned toward her, taking her hands in his. "Perhaps I overstep my bounds, Miss Cosgrove, but I feel it necessary to inform you that my interest in you goes beyond friendship."

"Oh." Oh, dear. Were they really going to have this conversation right here in the middle of Hyde Park? With his sister not twenty paces behind them, glaring with hatred at Madalene's back? "Major Gibbons, I am quite flattered, but I—"

He shook his head, interrupting her before continuing on. "I realize we have known each other less than a month, but in that time, I have discovered you to be both lovely in appearance and kind in your nature. I would very much like to advance our relationship, but I first feel I must inquire about the nature of your relationship with Lord Hawksmoor."

"Lord Hawksmoor?" Had her affection for him been so obvious? Had Major Gibbons seen him leaving the salon after their kiss? Or had the aftermath of the brief passion they'd shared been obvious to see when he came upon her but a few moments later?

"Yes. I have seen the way he gazes upon you and I worry with your soft heart you may feel you should be kind to him, which may lead him to believe something untoward may be possible."

"Untoward?" Her face flamed despite the cool February afternoon. "Major Gibbons, I assure you—"

Again, he waved her off, refusing to let her have her say. A rather annoying habit in her estimation.

"It is just that I knew his brother, briefly. We had a mutual acquaintance in Lord Rothbury. I confess I found the first Lord Hawksmoor to be a rather disturbed individual, though he hid it well in polite society. However, they say madness can run in families. Madness, I believe the new Lord Hawksmoor may have inherited, and that while some say he possesses a certain enigmatic charm, I suspect it may all be for show. A mask, if you will. I fear if you allow yourself to get too close to him, the mask will come off and you will be faced with the monster that lurks beneath it."

With each word Major Gibbons spoke, Madalene's heart beat harder and faster until it reverberated beneath her breast. How well did the major know Hawk's brother? He said they shared a mutual acquaintance in Lord Rothbury, but had they spent any time together? Would Phillip have said anything to the major that might lead Hawk to uncover the identity of *Lord T* and finally find some peace?

"I can assure you, in the many years I have known Lord Hawksmoor, and despite his current circumstances that may cause one to think otherwise, he is a good man at heart. He would never hurt me."

Before Major Gibbons could respond, Mrs. Chambers stepped forward, her stride carrying a hint of anger, her feet hitting the ground as if it had offended her greatly. "You have known Lord Hawksmoor for years? How is this possible?"

Her abrupt interruption took Madalene by surprise and she took a step back, her hand sliding out of Major Gibbons hold. "I was employed at Raven Manor."

"When?"

Madalene wasn't sure what it mattered but she took a deep breath and struggled to be polite. "Five years past now."

"And what was it you did there?"

Madalene straightened, refusing to be cowed by Mrs. Chambers' opinion of her simply because she'd had to make her way in the world. "I was a house maid."

Mrs. Chambers turned her attention to her brother, her expression hard and uncompromising. If being a housekeeper to the Bowens had been a mark against her, likely the news she had been a house maid previous to that was more than Mrs. Chambers was willing to accept in a future sister-in-law. Imagine her complete horror if she were to discover Madalene had also taken in sewing and worked as a shop girl and any number of other sundry occupations to help her father put food on the table and keep a roof over their head.

"Brother, dear, I find I am coming down with a beast of a headache. Would you be so kind as to cut your visit with Miss Cosgrove short and take me home?"

The major's gaze bounced between Madalene and his sister, his uncertainty palpable. Madalene forced a smile, making the decision for him as she wished to be away from Mrs. Chambers as much as his sister wished to leave. "Of course, you must, Major Gibbons. We may visit any time, but your sister's health at the moment is tantamount."

"Yes, of course. We shall return to the carriage, shall we?"

"I think that would be for the best." Madalene needed to return to Ridgemont House and, between making arrangements to return to Northill. She also needed to send word to Hawk that Major Gibbons may be a source of information with respect to his brother's activities and associates.

---

awk read the note from Madalene again, his gaze traveling over the perfectly formed letters, even and unwavering, much like the writer herself. Was she really suggesting he meet with Major Gibbons to see if he knew something about whom Phillip may have associated with? And how did Gibbons claim an acquaintance with either Phillip or Lord Rothbury? It wasn't as if they ran in the same social circles.

Yet, according to Madalene, Gibbons had claimed Phillip was a deeply disturbed man. What information did he hold to form the basis of this assumption? The only way for Hawk to find out would be to corner the major and get answers straight from the source. Provided Gibbons would be willing to give them. Their first meeting had not exactly gone well. Nor their second for that matter.

ajor Gibbons has asked me to join him as his guest at Mr. and Mrs. Dunhill's party this evening. After that I shall return to Northill.

. . .

She was leaving London. Leaving him. The news hit him with blunt force. Though he believed she would be safer out of the city, he had not been prepared to let her go so soon. This pathetic need he had for her, to be close to her, to protect her, refused to leave. Last night he'd practically depleted his brandy stores trying to rid himself of the longing to be near her, but all that had accomplished was to give him a beast of a headache this morning and the knowledge that his feelings for Madalene Cosgrove were not going anywhere any time soon. If ever.

He had quite fallen in love with the little beauty and there seemed little he could do about it. Her hold on his heart was absolute. He woke in the morning having dreamed of her and he went to bed at night with thoughts of her on his mind, affecting his body in ways that only tormented him further.

And now she was suggesting he attend Mr. and Mrs. Dunhill's party so that he might question another man who obviously felt the same way as he where she was concerned.

Had she kissed Major Gibbons? Had the major experienced the sweet taste of her? Likely not. At least that's what he told himself. To tell himself anything different would likely drive him straight back to the brandy.

Hawk crumpled the note from Madalene and tossed it into the fire. It was highly improper for her, a single lady, to be penning him a letter. He did not want to risk someone finding it and using it against her to get to him. Paranoid thinking, perhaps, but in the weeks since he'd returned to London, he had been inundated with desperate men begging, bargaining, and threatening in the hopes he would forgive their debts.

He watched as the vellum notepaper withered in the flames. He was done with this hellish existence. Done with living in the small, dimly lit living quarters in the catacombs of a gaming hell. Done with being *The Hawk* and making his life's work destroying others in an effort to uncover information none of them had. He had enough money to live comfortably for several lifetimes. He would soon inherit the earldom from his dying father and, with it, the properties entailed to the Ravenwood title.

He could leave London. Leave all of this behind and start a new life. The idea appealed to him, save for one small factor—Madalene. Whether he left London or stayed, if she was not with him what kind of life would he have?

An empty one.

And what if he could not find Phillip's associate, the elusive Lord T, and bring the man down or to justice, or whatever it took to ensure Madalene was safe and the madness was ended? How could he leave her unprotected, knowing this faceless madman could be lurking around the next corner, stalking her, biding his time until he could make good on a challenge accepted years ago?

He couldn't. It was as simple as that. Which left him only one alternative.

He must somehow convince Madalene to marry him.

Chapter Seventeen

Hawk leveled his most potent glare at the butler who requested to see his invitation. He continued to hold his gaze steady, saying nothing until the man began to squirm to an acceptable degree. "Do you know who I am?"

The butler's Adam's apple bobbed in his narrow throat. "Lord Hawksmoor, my lord." The words came as a whisper, as if speaking them too loudly would cause bats to fly from the rafters and demons to burst through the marble flooring demanding the souls of the innocent. Hawk had to force himself not to hiss at the man just to see if he would explode out of his perfectly starched collar.

"Then you know it is likely in the best interest of your employers that I not be left standing in the entrance hall as if I was not welcomed into their home, don't you?"

Silence littered the space between them as the butler glanced nervously toward the hallway that led to the ballroom then back to the front door where other guests continued to arrive.

"I will cause a scene, if that is what you are wondering.

And I assure you, it will be quite spectacular." Hawk smiled but the gesture lacked warmth.

The butler's eyes bulged out of their sockets and he swallowed with great effort. "May I take your coat and hat, my lord?"

Hawk unloaded both with great flourish. "Well done, my good man. Your employer will thank you for your astute decision later." As it turned out, after a brief look at his business journals, Mr. Dunhill did, in fact, owe him several hundred pounds, and while hardly a significant amount to most of his peers, the celebrated barrister with political ambitions had been slow in paying the amount off. A debt Hawk was now moved to forgive in recompense for pushing his way into a party he had not been invited to.

In fact, it appeared not many lords and ladies had been invited to the party, or if they had been, sent their regrets. Hawk crossed the threshold into the small ballroom and surveyed those present. He found several high-ranking politicians, a few more individuals with similar ambitions, and others who, though they lacked titles, were in possession of significant fortunes. Members of the peerage that were in attendance included Lord and Lady Caldwell. Neither of who owed him a single pound or had any unfortunate predilections to make them of any use to him—unless one could count having no direct heir and three daughters that required marrying off a predilection, which Hawk did not. More like an unfortunate circumstance.

He gazed about the room, searching for the blonde head that would lead him to where he needed to be. It did not take long. She drew his attention like a beacon of light standing near the refreshment table, sipping on a cup of what was likely overly sweetened punch if the way she wrinkled her nose was any indication. Next to her stood Major Gibbons, his rapt attention focused solely on Madalene as if the other women around them bore little to no significance. Why, the man was practically making cow eyes at her. Hawk had the sudden urge to drive his fist hard into the man's besotted face.

He bit down on the unexpected rush of jealously brought on by seeing them together and strode through the crowd, ignoring the gasps and whispers as he passed. Granted, this was hardly a gathering a man of his stature and reputation would normally attend, but they hardly had to behave as if he had just escaped from the bowels of hell to cast a pall upon their party. He had two objectives to dispatch and then he would be on his way and leave them to their silly little merriments.

His first order of business was to question Major Gibbons about what he knew of Phillip's madness. To determine if he had any information that would lead him to Lord T. Once that was completed, he would move onto his second order of business—proposing to Madalene.

A mixture of excitement and trepidation coursed through his veins. Surely, she would say yes—wouldn't she?

Upon reaching his destination, he still had no answer to that question though her eyes did light up upon his arrival. Unfortunately, the smile she offered was nothing more than polite, bordering on staid. Had he been wrong about her affection for him? Had she come to her senses after their brief tryst at the tea and determined he had been right to pull away from their kiss and indicate they could take their relationship no further?

The major, for his part, was far easier to read given that he practically snarled at Hawk's sudden arrival, interrupting what he was certain was a completely banal conversation. Though it didn't appear Major Gibbons shared that opinion. Had the man been in possession of his sword, likely Hawk would have found himself run through. Not the warm welcome he had hoped for, but he'd experienced worse. At least no one was pointing a gun to his head this time.

"Miss Cosgrove." Hawk reached for her hand and made a show of bending over it and kissing her knuckles. A little over the top, perhaps, but it seemed appropriate to send a message to Major Gibbons that he was out of his element. Madalene was his and he had no intentions of sharing. "It is lovely to see you, as always."

"My lord," she answered, slipping her hand out of his and offering a shallow curtsey. It struck him as odd to greet each other in such a way. They seemed so far beyond that. But they were in public, so he did not let it deter him.

Hawk shot a brief glance at the others present. "Ladies, Major Gibbons. Good evening to you all."

Major Gibbons straightened, pulling at one of the sleeves of his regimental coat. "Lord Hawksmoor. I wasn't aware you were invited to this event."

Hawk grinned. "You know, I so rarely get invited anywhere, so I simply show up. And as they always let me in, I can only assume the lack of invitation was merely an oversight."

"Or perhaps it is that you hold their secrets over their heads and they are too afraid to do otherwise for fear of retaliation."

Ah. So, the major drew first blood. "Well, if they had not had the secrets in the first place, there would be little to fear from me, wouldn't you agree? And what of you, Major? Do you have any secrets you fear me finding out?"

By now, Hawk noticed several of the ladies who had been vying for Gibbons' attention had moved away, distancing themselves from the conversation, or more likely, from Hawk, as it seemed he had that effect on people.

Well, most people. Madalene remained and in the end, she was the only person's opinion he truly cared about.

"There is nothing about you that strikes fear in my heart, Lord Hawksmoor. You may rest assured on that fact."

"That's a little short-sighted, don't you think?"

Before Major Gibbons could answer, one of the Lindwell ladies—Hawk never could determine which was which despite their vastly different coloring—joined their group, slipping her arm through Madalene's. "Miss Cosgrove, I was wondering where you had wandered off to. I just had the loveliest conversation with Sir Thornfield about Miss Caldwell's proposed school. He was much interested in speaking with you about it."

"With me?" Madalene appeared genuinely surprised at Miss Lindwell's claim though Hawk recognized it for the ploy it was. Miss Lindwell had also been the one to save Madalene from being sent out the servants' quarters at their ball, sending her off with Major Gibbons instead. Now, she had come to her rescue once more, though this time he suspected it was from him as if his reputation might reach out and taint her.

Perhaps it was for the best. Gibbons may be more amenable to tell the truth without Madalene's innocent ears hearing the details of Phillip's madness. Little did the man know that Madalene had already had a front row seat to his brother's special brand of malevolence. And Hawk was not going to be the one to tell him.

"Who better to inform Sir Thornfield, Miss Cosgrove," Gibbons said, his voice smooth and irritating. "After all, have you not decided to accept the position of headmistress?"

Shock hit Hawk like a punch to the stomach. Had she? When? And why hadn't she told him? He struggled to keep his expression neutral. He would deal with this issue later, after she accepted his proposal. She could hardly be viscountess and headmistress at the same time, after all.

"I hope I might see you later on," Hawk said. He would find her once the conversation concluded and fill her in on what he learned from Gibbons. Then he would propose and she would accept. She had to accept. Keeping her under his wing was the best chance he had of keeping her safe. Surely, she would see the sense in this.

"As do I," Major Gibbons chimed in and Hawk once again resisted the urge to plant his fist into the major's horribly ordinary face.

Hawk waited for Miss Lindwell to lead Madalene away before turning back to Gibbons. "Major, there is a particular topic I would like to discuss with you but I do not care to have it in the middle of a crowded room. Perhaps we could retire to the library where we might converse in private."

Gibbons stared at him, his expression giving little away other than suspicion. "I can't imagine anything we have to discuss."

"Then come to the library and allow me to enlighten you." Hawk turned and headed back toward the entrance of the ballroom. He had been to Dunhill's only once before many years ago, but the layout of the townhouse was like many others. He suspected if he walked farther down the hallway he would come upon the library and as it turned out, he was correct. He was also correct in his assumption that Major Gibbons would follow without further prompting.

Curiosity was a difficult mistress to ignore.

Hawk entered the library and raided Mr. Dunhill's rather impressive brandy collection, pouring a drink for himself and Major Gibbons before settling into a chair by the fireplace where a small fire burned in the hearth. A moment later, Gibbons arrived and Hawk motioned toward the drink he left sitting on the bar.

"Join me, Major."

Gibbons hesitated a moment, then took the drink though refused to join him by the fire. It hardly mattered. "What is it you feel we need to discuss, Lord Hawksmoor? I suggest you keep it brief as I can think of far more pleasing ways to spend my evening than conversing with you."

The implication of his words weighed heavy in the air. He planned on continuing his campaign to woo Madalene. Perhaps Hawk should tell him he was wasting his time, but something about the man's sureness of his pursuit created a thin fissure in Hawk's own confidence. He had shared but two kisses with Madalene. And while both kisses had been filled with passion, her demeanor this evening gave him pause. Had it only been he who had felt the life-altering desire to go farther, to entwine their bodies, their hearts, their lives? Or had she, upon reflection, determined his presence in her life only conjured up repulsive memories of his brother?

What if *he* repulsed her?

He shook the notion free. No. They were friends. More than friends. When he professed his need for her, she had not turned away or turned him down. Then again, she hadn't parroted the same feelings back to him either. Nor had she argued with him when he put an end to their kiss and suggested they could take it no further.

Bloody hell. Did the major actually stand a chance at turning Madalene's head and her heart? Would she prefer to be with a man who had no connection to the incident at Raven Manor? A sick feeling coiled inside of him.

He gave Gibbons a cursory glance where the major leaned against the mahogany bar, a study in irritation. Hawk conceded he was a relatively handsome man in an ordinary sort of way and gave off an air of competency. And yes, he cut a fine figure in his uniform. Hawk was not blind to the fact many women were wooed by such things, but was Madalene?

He waved off his doubts. It didn't matter. He would propose to her tonight and she would accept. How could she not? He was a viscount after all, and who would not want to become a viscountess? A future countess? She would never have to worry about her future ever again. And he would not have to worry about her coming to harm. She would be safe with him. He would be certain to stress that point to her.

"Tell me what you know of my brother," Hawk said, skipping past the pleasantries. It seemed redundant, in his estimation, given neither of them felt even remotely pleasant toward the other.

"I'm not certain what you mean." Gibbons took a slow draw of his drink, watching Hawk over the rim of the glass.

Hawk let out a sigh and unfolded himself from the comfort of the chair to stand before the fire. "Come now, Major. Let us not play these games, shall we? The sooner you answer my questions, the sooner we can both go about our business and be done with each other. A moment, I'm certain, we both look forward to with equal fervor. I am aware you believe my brother was a disturbed individual. As it happens, this fact may be the one and only thing we have in common."

"Aside from Miss Cosgrove."

Hawk took a sip of his brandy, wishing the drink held the ability to burn away his irritation with the major as easily as it burned the surface of his throat. It did not. "Your interest in Miss Cosgrove is a lost battle you would do well to retreat from. As a military man, I would think you'd be able to realize such."

The major swept Hawk's set down away with a wave of his hand. "I realize no such thing. It is you who holds the unfounded delusion that she would countenance an association with you if it were up to her. You embarrass her with your unwanted attentions and assumption that the two of you hold more of an acquaintance than former employer and servant."

The niggling doubt of Madalene's interest took another hit, but he shoved it aside. "Miss Cosgrove and I are indeed friends. That you cannot see as much only further strengthens my earlier claim of your blindness to the situation. But I did not come here to discuss Miss Cosgrove."

Major Gibbons stepped away from the bar bringing his drink with him, though beyond that first sip he did not seem inclined to further imbibe. Odd. Mr. Dunhill had extremely good taste in his brandy.

"Has it not occurred to you she is merely being polite? She is a sweet natured innocent, not a plaything for the upper classes."

"A plaything?" The major's words cut into Hawk, painting his likeness a little too similar to that of his brother's. "I have treated Miss Cosgrove with nothing more than the utmost propriety."

Save for insisting they refer to each other by their given names. Or looking for any opportunity to spend time alone with her. To touch her. And then there was that first kiss. And the second one...

"Regardless, when others see your attention to her, it calls into question her reputation, for what other reason would a viscount have for acting besotted with a former servant than to make her his plaything? It is not as if you plan to make her your viscountess. Imagine the scandal of that." Gibbons laughed as if the suggestion Hawk and Madalene might marry was the most ridiculous thing he had ever heard. It cut far too close to the bone for his liking.

"And what would it matter if I did make her my viscountess? I'm certain the ton would raise their collective eyebrows at any lady I deemed to marry, given my reputation. So why not Miss Cosgrove?"

Gibbons stopped his slow pace about the room and stared at Hawk, amusement written over his face. "Is that your intention? Truly?"

The man laughed again. This time much longer and harder than before. Hawk fisted his hand at his side and took a deep breath to keep from vaulting across the room and kicking the man in such a way it would ruin any hope he had of propagating an heir.

"I'm so pleased to see the idea amuses you, Major, but tell me—what option do you think would appeal to a lady more? Marrying a military man with no hope of moving beyond where he is now? Or becoming the future Countess of Ravenwood?"

Hawk had so much more to offer Madalene than this smug bastard. Surely, she would see that. Wouldn't she? Doubt continued to creep in, soiling his pristine hope with its dirty feet. He took another swallow of brandy.

"I am certain Miss Cosgrove would be more interested in marrying a man of similar background as she. What kind of life would she have, married to the likes of you? What do you have to offer her? A brother with a history of madness and a family that despises you and has all but disowned you. Not to mention the fact that your reputation makes you a pariah and will make her one as well, should she become your wife. I would hardly call that a future one would willingly embrace. Would you?"

The fire in the hearth crackled and a log shifted, sending sparks snapping in the air behind him. Hawk hated how the major's words pummeled him, each one finding his most vulnerable spots, the ones where his doubts hid. He wished to retaliate, but what ammunition did he have? That he loved her? Would that be enough to overcome all the rest? Could he make her happy? Or would being married to him only cause her a lifetime of grief?

The answer to that question tormented him with its elusiveness. He pulled his attention away from it and focused on something else Gibbons had said.

Your mad brother.

"What makes you think my brother was mad?"

Gibbons shrugged. An irksome gesture. In truth, everything about the man annoyed him and he could not fathom what it was that Madalene found even remotely charming about him. Between his smugness and his churlish sister who padded around after him like a dreary shadow, he could find absolutely nothing that would appeal.

"Your brother hid it well, for the most part, I will give him that, but there were some of us who noticed his rather... odd...preferences."

"Those preferences being?" Hawk's heart pounded in his chest as he awaited Gibbons' answer.

"Your brother liked a challenge, shall we say. He made a contest out of it, being the betting man, he was. He would choose someone to conquer, for the sheer thrill of seeing if he could do so and get away with it, and invite others to join in his game."

"And no one he approached with this wickedness thought to stop him?"

"Your brother picked his audience well. Choosing others with the same tastes as he. As for who he set his sights on, he was careful, often choosing those of little consequence."

Those of little consequence. The phrase burned through Hawk's blood like venom. Phillip had not thought Madalene of little consequence. In fact, his brother had been well aware of her consequence to Hawk. That was why he had chosen her. In that respect, Gibbons was mistaken, but Hawk held his tongue. He would not endanger Madalene's reputation for the sake of proving this arrogant bastard wrong.

"Often, but not always? Did he stray from this course then?"

Phillip's voice whispered in the back of Hawk's mind. *"Sometimes a lady is so fetching, the challenge so delectable, one cannot help themselves."*

Major Gibbons leaned against the back of one of the chairs that flanked the fireplace. When he spoke, he dropped his voice to a conspiratorial whisper, as if sharing a secret Hawk knew nothing about.

"There was a rumor that your brother had decided to up the ante of his little conquests and try for a bigger prize—the wife of a future duke, I heard."

Lady Rothbury. Hawk fought to keep his expression neutral. "And was he successful in this endeavor?"

Another shrug. It was as if the man had a tick of some sort. "I have heard that a certain duchess took a bit of a shine to the late viscount. Thought him quite charming. Of course, in the end, the poor lady wound up dead. Drowned, I believe they said. Odd, don't you think, for a lady to get it into her head that she needed to take a swim in the dead of night in the middle winter?"

"You refer to Lady Rothbury," Hawk said.

Yet another shrug. Hawk's ire rose as Major Gibbons continued. "If memory serves, your brother left for Italy only a few days after her death, did he not?"

Hawk did his best to regulate his breathing, to appear unaffected by Gibbons' claims that so closely echoed the story Phillip had admitted to him years earlier. The horror of which still haunted him.

"Why did you not take your suspicions to the authorities, then?" A question he could have asked himself as well. His parents had put a stop to his inquiries, set Phillip's anger upon him and then punished their younger son with their silence, cutting him off financially for a time, forcing him to stay put at Raven Manor.

Gibbons gave him a look that stated he thought Hawk a shortsighted imbecile. Hawk gritted his teeth. The major was a scant few seconds away from being delivered a facer of epic proportions.

"Turn in a Peer of the Realm with nothing to substantiate my claims? That would have been a quick way to terminate my burgeoning career. No, I'm afraid I am far more astute than you give me credit for. Instead, I went to the aggrieved widower, Lord Rothbury. As it turns out, the future duke had no wish for my information to reach beyond his own ears. Likely, he did not care to have the world know he'd been cuckolded to such a humiliating degree and offered to speak to the Prime Minister on my behalf in exchange for keeping silent on my suspicions."

"Yet you break it now."

Gibbons smiled, a cold, knowing smile that chilled the marrow of Hawk's bones. The major might be a supercilious prick, but he wasn't an idiot. "I don't think I am telling you anything that you don't already know, am I?"

Hawk didn't answer. What was there to say? "How is it you know so much about my brother?"

Gibbons took a slow draw on his drink, drawing out the moment on purpose. "You are not the only purveyor of information in this city, my lord. The more I know of those in your position, the more I am able to use it to my benefit. When one is not born with a title attached to their name, their options are limited. I do not care much for limits and I am not above using what information I have to surpass them."

"Do you know who my brother associated with in these sick pursuits?"

"I did not involve myself in such. My association with your brother was that of a passing acquaintance and nothing more. The things I learned were gleaned from my observations, from droplets of conversation overheard and then pieced together. I did not involve myself with your brother to any deep level. As I have said—I believe he was a sick man."

Hawk could not blame Gibbons for his assumptions on that account. Much as he loathed the man, how could he fault his inaction when Hawk, too, had refrained from going to the authorities, having no tangible proof other than hearsay which his brother could have easily refuted, with his parents' backing.

"Now, if you will excuse me, Lord Hawksmoor. I find this conversation has come to a conclusion and I have nothing left to offer you but the simple admission that I have no intention of dropping my interest in Miss Cosgrove. In truth, I do not think she wishes me to, and I know I certainly do not. It is past time I found myself a proper wife and I find her to be a most suitable candidate."

"How romantic," Hawk muttered under his breath, but if Gibbons heard him, he gave no indication.

"Good day, my lord." Gibbons gave him a brief, dismissive nod and set his glass onto the nearest table before quitting the room, closing the door behind him.

Hawk raised his arm and made to hurl his own glass against the closed door but stopped before the snifter left his hand. It would not do to bring a hoard of guests rushing to the library to discover him in a pique of anger. No, he must find Madalene, preferably before Gibbons reached her.

Find her and convince her to marry him.

Then he could quit this godforsaken city and find somewhere secluded for her to hide away while he set about finding Lord T and putting an end to this madness once and for all.

Chapter Eighteen

"There you are."

Madalene turned at the sound of Hawk's voice coming up from behind her, something about his expression taking her aback. He seemed...what? Determined? Upset? "Is something wrong, my lord?"

"I must speak with you." With barely a glance, he grabbed a discarded shawl from the back of a chair and pushed it at her, then placed his hands on her shoulders to turn her about and steer her toward the doors that led to the small, snow-dappled garden at the side of the house.

"What are you doing? People will—"

"No one is looking. They are all involved in their own foolish lives. And this is of utmost importance." He opened the door only wide enough for them to slip through. "I'm certain once you hear what I have to say, you will not regret coming with me."

The bitterness and anger in his voice surprised her and she allowed him to propel her through the narrow opening in the door. Above them, the stars sparkled and shined, causing the light covering of snow on the ground to sparkle with light. But the beauty was lost on Madalene as the cold stone floor seeped through her slippered feet.

"What is the matter with you?" She pulled the warm shawl he'd given her around her shoulders to ward off the chilly night air.

"I spoke with Major Gibbons," he said, though the process did not appear to be one he had enjoyed.

"And?"

"And he was aware of Phillip's behavior. He indicated that he had heard whispers of his sick contests. Yet instead of going to the authorities with his suppositions, he went to Lord Rothbury instead."

"Lord Rothbury? Why?"

"Because Major Gibbons believed Phillip to be responsible for the death of Lady Rothbury. He used this information to leverage a favor from Rothbury who did not care to have his wife's reputation sullied upon her death, nor have society know that he had been cuckolded."

Madalene gasped and grabbed the edge of her shawl tightly in her fist. "Did he have proof of your brother's involvement?"

"What?" Hawk shot her a look she could only read as disappointment, but what else was she to ask? "No. He simply put two and two together and figured it out. Much as I had to some degree, before Phillip filled me in on sick details."

"You knew?" Her mind whirled with the newfound information. How awful a thing! A shudder echoed down her spine. Would Phillip have killed her if Hawk had not saved her when he had?

"Yes. He had said something that led me to believe what he had done. He did not come straight out and confess, but he said enough to let me know her death had not been an accident and that Lord T assisted him in the cover up afterward to make it appear an accident."

The punch she drank earlier curdled in her stomach. "And you did not tell anyone?"

"What? Yes, of course I did. I went to my parents and begged them to stop his madness, but they refused. Instead, they told him and he burst into my room and—" He stopped and Madalene didn't press. She remembered a time shortly before Phillip had attacked her that Hawk made himself scarce, staying within the confines of his room. A heavy tension had filled the house and there were whispers below stairs of a physical altercation between the brothers.

"But you took the matter no farther than your parents?"

"No, but—"

"But what? Are you not accusing Major Gibbons of doing exactly what you had done?"

"I did not go to Lord Rothbury and use my suspicions to further my own career!"

"You do not have need of a career; you are a Peer of the Realm. Major Gibbons does not have that luxury and must make his own way in the world. Perhaps he took the information to Lord Rothbury as it would be he who had the most to suffer should Major Gibbons make his suspicions public?"

Hawk took a step away from her; betrayal written over each one of his sharply defined features. "So, you defend his actions then?"

"I defend you both. You both took the information you had and brought it to the people you thought needed it most." Madalene softened her voice. "You both did the same thing, did you not?"

Hawk sputtered. "It is not the same thing!"

"Hush! Keep your voice down." Madalene glanced toward the door, a gauzy window dressing the only thing keeping them hidden from the other guests. "I am simply saying that neither of you had actual proof. There was little you could do beyond that. You both did what you could."

"Did we?" And there it was, the guilt she had seen in his eyes since his memory had returned. The same guilt she had seen when he'd rescued her from his brother's clutches the night he had attacked her.

"If there was more you could have done, I am certain you would have."

Hawk's shoulders slumped and he dragged a hand through his dark hair. "I wish I could believe you. Had I alerted the authorities, perhaps Phillip would have been locked away in Bedlam or...somewhere. Somewhere where he would not have had access to you. If I had done more, had him removed from Raven Manor, he would not have had the opportunity to retaliate and use you to punish me."

Madalene stepped closer and placed a hand upon Hawk's chest, feeling the uneven rise and fall as anger and remorse disrupted his breathing. "You cannot change what was done. And I am certain whatever threat your brother intimated that day is no longer a factor. It has been over five years. If this Lord T meant to take up the challenge, surely he would have done so by now."

Something indefinable crossed Hawk's face and he opened his mouth as if to say something, then closed it again.

"What is it?"

He shook his head and covered her hand, warming the skin beneath the thin covering of her glove. "My parents tossed you out. For the next five years, you and your father moved about the underbelly of London, where Lord T could not find you."

Her heartbeat accelerated. "What do you mean?"

Hawk spoke as if he knew this for sure. But how could he? He did not know who this Lord T was, or if he had ever truly existed. A part of her had always wondered if Phillip had made him up, a perfect scapegoat with whom to throw the guilt upon if his actions ever came to rest at his doorstep.

Hawk closed his eyes and the confession whispered from him. "Because he sent me letters. Every three months one would arrive, letting me know his search continued. That he had taken up the challenge and had every intention of seeing it through to its conclusion."

The blood in her veins turned to ice, frozen there by the sudden fear that filled her. "He did what? Why did you never tell me?"

His grip on her hand tightened. "I feared contacting you would lead him to where you were. I could not risk it. I've spent the last five years trying to hunt him down, but the man is like a shadow, slipping in and out and disappearing whenever I think I am drawing close."

Her breath lodged in her throat and her head buzzed. Hawk had tried to protect her, to find the man who threatened her life. Who planned to end her life in such a way she couldn't even allow the thought to enter her head. She should be grateful, but she wasn't. She was angry. He'd had no right to let her live in the dark, a threat hiding around each corner she turned without her ever knowing it. Had she known, she could have taken precautions. What precautions, she didn't know, but he'd had no right to keep such information from her!

And now she had returned to London, been seen in society. Why she might as well have painted a target on herself and waved a flag in the air! Did this Lord T know she was here? Was he watching her now, at this party, biding his time before he struck?

She took a deep breath, then another, fighting back the fear. Her hand had fisted into the lapel of Hawk's coat. She loosened her grip and forced her mind to return to rational thought. "I am leaving London before week's end."

"Leaving?"

"Yes. I came here to find my replacement for Mr. Bowen

and Lady Rebecca. I have accomplished this task and now I shall return with her and make arrangements to begin my new life."

"New life? Then it's true? You have decided to take the position of headmistress?"

She shook her head. In light of what Hawk had revealed, she would now have to decline. Too many people knew of her plans. She would be too easy to find and she would not risk the lives of any of the schoolgirls, should Lord T come for her there.

"I will have to go into hiding. Obviously. Change my name even." Would she ever be able to see Father again? Or would that put him at risk? Tears pricked the corner of her eyes.

"You do not need to go to such lengths."

She let out a sharp laugh that echoed bitter in her ears. "What other choice do I have?"

"You could marry me."

Madalene blinked, certain she had heard him wrong. Marry him? Whatever was he about? Yes, they had shared a few kisses—soul-scorching kisses that had yet to fade from her memory, and yes, she loved him. But she would not have him marry her out of a misplaced sense of duty. Or guilt. Besides, did he not already say he did not contact her for fear of leading Lord T to her doorstep?

"You are not obligated to—"

"I am," he stated plainly. "I should have done more to keep you safe from my brother. He attacked you *because* of your friendship with me. It is my fault you are tied into this madness and I cannot in good conscience stand by and leave you unprotected. By marrying me, you will be a future countess. Untouchable."

"The way Lady Rothbury was?"

He looked as if she had slapped him and his hand fell away

from hers. She took a step back, needing the distance between them to grow so she might think more clearly. "It is not the same thing."

"Isn't it? She was married to a future duke, yet she could not escape your brother's madness."

"Lady Rothbury knew nothing of my brother's madness or surely she would not have engaged in an affair with him. And likely she knew nothing of Lord T. But I do and I can protect you."

Her heart broke. Under different circumstances, Madalene would have jumped at the chance to have him propose. How often had she dreamed of such a thing? To spend her life with him. To live each day wrapped in his warmth and kindness and keen observations. To pass each night enveloped in his arms. But that was not what he was proposing, was it? He said nothing of love, only responsibility. Something, in his estimation, he had failed at and now must make right. Hardly the recipe for a happy and fulfilling life, and in the end, that is all that she wanted. To be happy. To put the darkness of her past behind her and start anew.

"I am not yours to protect."

"Yes," he insisted with much force. "You are."

She shook her head and tightened the shawl around her shoulders. The damp February air had seeped through the thin material and into her heart. How she hated that this is what it came to, that this would be how it ended. How she wished she could tell him there was nothing she wanted more than to marry him, but she could not. He did not truly want to marry her; he simply wanted to assuage his own guilt. Right an imagined wrong. And one day, when the guilt faded, or Lord T was captured, he would look upon her and wish he had chosen otherwise, picked a lady more befitting his station, or perhaps return to the life he had built for himself as The Hawk.

She wanted no part in making his life something other than what it should be. Nor did she wish to spend her life indebted to him.

"I am sorry, but I cannot—I *will* not—marry you, my lord." She did not say his name. She needed to separate her feelings from the reality of the situation. She erected a barrier between her heart and the man who had stolen it away. She needed to relegate him to a memory once more.

She turned away, unable to tolerate the disbelief in his eyes. He had thought she would say yes. What lady wouldn't, after all? But she was not a lady, she was a servant, and soon she would be but a distant memory. Her destiny, her life, was in her own hands and not his. She was not his responsibility.

It was time for her to go.

She stepped inside the ballroom once again, letting the warmth created by the crush of bodies wash over her, but before she could slip the shawl from her shoulders and return it to the chair, hands grabbed her from behind and spun her around.

Then a mouth was upon hers. *His* mouth. Hot and insistent and for the most fleeting of seconds she allowed it to captivate her, to rob her of sense and time and place. Until the first gasp hit her from the side, and then another from behind. By the time she had wrenched her mouth from Hawk's, the entire room had turned to witness their kiss, the hum of what had happened moving its way through the crowd like an undulating wave.

Madalene stood frozen for several heartbeats, her hand over her mouth as the fiery burn of a roomful of stares filled with shock and disbelief, blistered her skin. How could he have done this to her?

Her hand struck out. The impact of her palm hitting his cheek seared her skin and reverberated up her arm. She used his momentary disbelief to push past him before he could stop her. She grasped her skirt, twisting the material in her hands as she ran from the room, elbowing her way through the people whose stares had turned to whispers and exclamations at what they had just witnessed, each one thrashing against her with the force of a thousand blows.

Still, she kept running.

The cold air hit her hard, robbing her of breath. After a moment, her lungs ached and her slippered feet turned to blocks of ice, skidding on the cobblestones. If she could run fast enough, or far enough, she could outrun the ruination Hawk had just brought upon her, but with each passing moment, her limbs refused to listen to her commands. Her legs turned stiff and moving them became difficult. Already she had fallen twice, her knees bruised from the brunt of it and her dress torn where she stepped upon the hem when getting up.

Why had he done this to her? What was she to do now? He had shamed her and ruined any chance she had at remaining anonymous. Soon, the town would be abuzz with what had transpired this night, making it even more difficult for her to slip away. A roomful of people had seen her horrified face and would remember it. How far would she have to go to outdistance such remembrance? To start over as someone new?

Hawk had sentenced her to this! And for what? Out of some misguided sense of guilt and responsibility?

She heard someone shout behind her, but she ignored it. Ignored them. Ignored *him*.

"Madalene!"

She stumbled again, but caught herself, pushing harder, faster. Tears froze against her cheeks, turning her lashes to icicles, but she could see Ridgemont House within sight. Candlelight burned in its windows like a beacon. She ran faster, knowing Hawk gained ground with each step.

"Madalene, stop!"

She refused, but did not waste the breath to tell him so. Anger burned through her veins, heating her from the inside out, urging her legs on. She reached the front door and rushed inside, slamming it shut behind her, startling Cleveland who came from the drawing room.

"Please, do not let him inside. Please!" Her voice shook, partly from the cold and partly from the upset of having her life turned upside down. She pushed away from the door as Hawk pounded on the other side.

"Madalene! Let me in!"

"What is the meaning of all this racket?" Lady Dalridge stood at the railing near the stairwell and looked down into the entrance from the floor above. "Miss Cosgrove? Good heavens, what has happened to you? Are you hurt? Where is your coat, child?"

The viscountess's questions peppered her as Hawk's pounding shook the door behind her back, but she had lost the ability to thread words into thoughts and explain what had happened to her.

"Help me."

Lady Dalridge motioned urgently with her hand. "Come to me, child. Hurry."

Madalene used the last of her strength to propel herself up the stairs to Lady Dalridge. The older woman grabbed her hand and pointed to a nearby doorway. "Go to my salon. Now."

Madalene obeyed, too tired, too distraught to do anything but. The salon was within earshot of the stairwell. She leaned against the doorframe and sank to the floor, her breath coming in gasps, her heart hammering hard against her breastbone until she feared it would burst through. The tears that had frozen on her face melted as new ones flowed freely over them.

What now, her brain screamed, demanding an answer she did not have to give. *What now?*

"Open the door, Cleveland." Madalene heard the door hitch followed by a brief respite of silence as the pounding stopped. "Lord Hawksmoor, what is the meaning of this?"

"I need to speak with Madalene." He was out of breath. His voice urgent. Desperate.

If any of this affected Lady Dalridge, Madalene could not tell and the viscountess did not bother to mince her words when she spoke next, her question carrying down the stairwell and into the grand entrance. "What have you done?"

Silence. Then, "I have ruined her."

Hearing the words spoken from his mouth crushed her heart. How could he have done this to her? How could he claim to have any affection for her and yet take away her future in such a definitive way?

Madalene could hear the hesitation in Lady Dalridge's voice when she spoke next. "In what way?"

"I kissed her."

The older woman scoffed. "Heavens. Young people, these days. Honestly. A kiss is hardly grounds for ruination. Simply do not speak of it again and no one will be the wiser. This seems a fair amount of drama for such a minor infraction—"

"I kissed her in front of everyone at the Dunhills' party."

The words echoed from the marble floor below and pushed against Madalene. She grew smaller, pulling her knees into her chest and burying her head into her knees. Lady Dalridge's lack of response only confirmed her worst fear. It was as bad as she believed.

When the viscountess spoke again, her voice matched the weather outside. Cold. Uncompromising. "And what, pray tell, led you to do that?"

"I need her to marry me. She refused, so I—"

"So, you took matters into your own hands, as if you had some right."

"It's for her own good."

"Ah, what every woman wants to hear in a proposal." Sarcasm saturated each word Lady Dalridge spoke. "Then, I assume, she left the party, and the humiliation you so callously wrested upon her, without even bothering with her coat. If this does not tell me she has absolutely no wish to see you, let alone marry you, I don't know what does. And where you failed to heed to her wishes, I will not. Leave this home, immediately. And do not return."

"I must see her."

"She does not wish to see you, Lord Hawksmoor."

Madalene looked up at the sound of Lady Henrietta's voice and craned her neck to see where Lady Dalridge stood addressing Hawk. Lady Henrietta had joined Lady Dalridge, her diminutive figure clad in a nightdress and wrapper, her long golden hair flowing down her back and a dueling pistol held in both hands, pointed toward the entrance hall below.

Madalene gasped. "Don't shoot him!"

"I promise, I will not. Provided he leaves our home immediately and heeds Auntie's directive to not return." Lady Henrietta's attention returned to Hawk. "I believe enough damage has been done this night. Don't you agree? If the lady does not wish to see you, then at least allow her to make that choice. It is the least you can do, seeing as it appears you have tried to rob her of all other choices with your brutish behavior."

"I did not intend—"

"Whatever you intended is immaterial," Lady Dalridge stated with finality. "What you have done was unconscionable. Miss Cosgrove needs time to process what has been done to her. Now kindly leave our home before my great-niece puts another bullet into you."

For a moment, no one spoke, but Lady Henrietta did not lower the gun in her hands. Madalene was unsure of what startled her more, seeing the timid young woman stand up for her like some warrior goddess from Greek mythology, or the fact that Hawk acquiesced to their demands.

"Very well. Madalene!" His voice called up the stairs and reached out to her, filled with the same desperation that she had seen in his eyes since the moment his memories had returned. "I will return on the morrow—"

Lady Dalridge cut him off. "You will return only when and if Miss Cosgrove requests that you do so. Not before. Now leave this house."

Hawk said no more and a cry broke in her throat. She muffled it with her hands, not wanting him to hear, afraid if he did, he would throw caution to the wind and rush up the stairs to her. She could not have that. She did not know if she had the strength to resist the despair she heard in his voice. Only when the door hitched closed did she allow herself to take in a deep breath and give over to the tears she had tried so hard to hold at bay.

Chapter Nineteen

"Where the hell is all my brandy?"

Hawk wasn't entirely sure who he meant to answer his question, or if there was even anyone nearby to hear him bellow it out. It was possible he could get up and find another bottle himself, but how strong a possibility, he was not sure. He had already emptied one bottle, perhaps two—he'd lost count somewhere in the early morning hours—and standing, or doing much of anything that required any level of coordination was slim at best. Which is likely why he found himself sprawled across the sofa in his office, his jacket and cravat long gone, his shirt undone and one boot missing.

"Don't you think you've had quite enough?"

Hawk lifted his head then wished he hadn't as the room spun around him. Though on one spin, he recognized Spencer Kingsley, Earl of Huntsleigh, future Marquess of Ellesmere. Facts rushed through his head like entries in his journals. Former rake with a penchant for having affairs with dissatisfied women of the ton. Avoider of all things marriage related. Parents dead. One of the few individuals Hawk considered friend. Recently married to Lady Caelie Laytham. Totally and humiliatingly blindsided by love.

Hawk could relate.

"What are you doing here?" He growled; his throat raw. Likely from yelling for more brandy.

"The original purpose of my trip was to look into Grand-father's shipping interests. Normally that would be Bowen's area of expertise, but with his wife in her current condition, he prefers not to be too far from home. He informed me that with my own child's safe arrival achieved, I should therefore take his place."

"You've had a child?" Hawk remembered a time where the idea of Huntsleigh or Blackbourne marrying, let alone fathering children, seemed so farfetched it was laughable.

"Yes. An absolutely beautiful daughter, which I can only assume is fate's way of getting back at me for all my past misdeeds."

"Then my felicitations and condolences in that order. However, it still does not answer my question as to what you are doing here in my apartments?"

"Ah, well that is the second component of Bowen's direc-tive. He requested that I look in on you and see how you are faring. As I find you faring not so well, I can only assume Bowen's next decree would likely be that I keep you from drinking yourself blind." Huntsleigh stretched out his legs and crossed them at the ankle, making himself at home.

"And how do you fare in that regard?"

"Dismally. You're a complete sot. But, in my defense, you were already in that state when I found you, so I take no responsibility for it."

Hawk scowled. The irritating thing about Huntsleigh was the laughter that lingered just beyond the things he said, as if everything amused him to one degree or another. Hawk recalled he did not always find it irritating, but now that it was directed at him, he reserved the right to change his mind.

"I have had some rather disappointing news and as such thought I would—"

"Drown your sorrows?"

"Perhaps. Are you planning on staying long?"

"Only long enough to convince you not to do anything foolish. Although, I may be a bit late for that, given the rumors flying about town this day. You understand Bowen will make you wish you had succumbed to the wounds Pengrin inflicted when he gets a hold of you?"

Deuce it! He hadn't even thought of what Bowen might do. He was too caught up in trying to figure out what the hell *he* was going to do.

He groaned. "Perhaps I can claim diminished capacity given my recent injuries."

"That may help you survive this, but I am not so sure such a claim will be of much help to Miss Cosgrove. From the whispers I hear, she teeters on the edge of total ruination. Lady Dalridge has made arrangements for her hasty return to Northill in the hopes retiring to the country will assist in negating the worst of the damage you have done and allow her to salvage some scrap of a reputation."

For once, Hawk heard no laughter behind Huntsleigh's words. Only censure. His stomach heaved and he pressed his hand against it in the hopes of settling it before he embarrassed himself further by vomiting over the edge of the sofa.

"I acted rashly. I wasn't thinking." It was about the weakest a defense he'd ever heard of. *So sorry I ruined your life, I simply didn't have my proper wits about me. Humblest of apologies.*

Huntsleigh echoed his thoughts. "A fat lot of good that does the girl now. What the hell were you about, behaving in such a manner?"

Hawk glared at his self-invited guest. Did the man actually think he made such a spectacular blunder without purpose? Granted, his purpose was steeped in panic and had he been given more time he might have come up with a better idea, but he hadn't had time. Or hadn't thought he did. Either way, Huntsleigh was hardly the man to be pointing fingers at someone when it came to rash actions. "I was trying to convince her to marry me."

"By ruining her? I have heard she actually ran from the party in the dead of night, no coat, no escort, nothing, in an effort to escape the humiliation."

To escape *him*. His eyes burned and he pinched the bridge of his nose. This was far, far worse than he had anticipated. He'd made so many blunders where Madalene was concerned. She had every right to never speak to him again. He had actually been fool enough to think he would kiss her and she would fall into his arms, besotted by passion and agree then and there that yes, despite his keeping Lord T's letters from her, despite the fact he was a rake of the first order, and despite the fact his brother had attacked her and his family sacked her, that they should be married.

Never, in the few all too brief seconds, between thinking of kissing her in full view of everyone and acting out his ill-conceived and horribly reckless plan, did he suspect she would reject his proposal a second time, smack him hard enough to rattle his teeth then run from the Dunhills' as if the hounds of hell nipped at her heels!

It was only as he chased after her—and where had she learned to run so fast?—that he realized his folly. What woman wanted to be trapped into a marriage, her hand forced so that she must choose between ruin and a marriage she had already indicated she did not want? Definitely not a woman such as Madalene. But by the time such realization had settled upon his addled brain, the damage had been done.

All that was left now was to try and mitigate the worst of said damage, if she would only let him.

"I tried to speak with her. I followed her to Ridgemont's but they refused to let me see her."

"I assume, given that you are not missing any limbs, that Ridgemont was not in residence when you arrived?"

"No. Lady Dalridge was, however."

"Almost as bad, though far less likely to kill you than Ridgemont."

"Lady Henrietta nearly saved him the trouble. She held me at gunpoint and threatened to end me then and there if I did not leave."

"Truly?" Huntsleigh chuckled, the sound deep and rich. "I should like to meet the reclusive Lady Henrietta. She sounds like quite an admirable woman. I take it you had no desire to find yourself shot again so soon?"

"Not particularly." Though, at the moment, with his stomach churning and his head pounding as if someone had taken a sledgehammer to it, a quick end by a bullet sounded almost blissful, save for the finality of it all.

"So, what shall you do now?"

"What do you mean?"

"Well, you have quite the mess to fix. I should think you might want to sober up and get to it."

Hawk did not particularly want to sober up. Sobriety would bring clarity and clarity would make him face the reality of what he had done. He had promised to keep her safe and instead he had ruined her.

"How am I to protect her if I cannot even see her?" The question slipped out before he could pull it back in.

"Protect her from what? Society's censure?"

Hawk shook his head then winced. Dammit. He needed to stop doing that. "No. She is in far greater danger than what society can mete out, I'm afraid."

Huntsleigh's expression hardened. He pulled his legs in and leaned forward, all hint of humor gone from his expression. "I think perhaps you need to tell me what is going on here."

"It is none of your concern."

"Miss Cosgrove is under Bowen's protection. Bowen is my family and by extension that makes Miss Cosgrove's well-being *my* concern. Given what a muck you've made of things up to this point, I suggest you tell me exactly what has been going on so we might find a way to fix it and keep her safe from whatever it is you think is threatening her—other than your abject recklessness and stupidity."

Hawk mustered up what strength he had left and lifted his head to glare at Huntsleigh. "I am beginning to regret the day I ever let you and your companions into my establishment."

"You know," Huntsleigh said, his affable smile firmly back in place. "You would be surprised by how many times we have heard that sentiment. Now get up and tell me what it is we are protecting the young lady from. If you are about to play the part of white knight, we'll need to find your shining armor."

Hawk's head fell back onto the sofa. He wasn't even sure he owned such a thing and if he did, likely it was rusted beyond repair and of little use.

"I know it seems like the worst possible thing right now, but I assure you, it will all work out in the end."

Madalene pulled her gaze away from the window and unfolded her legs from beneath her. Lady Henrietta stood near the packed trunk that awaited the footman's arrival. She was to leave. To return to Northill. In disgrace.

And with a broken heart because it seemed only fitting to add insult to injury.

"I am not sure I believe you, but I thank you for everything you have done. And for not shooting Lord Hawksmoor. No doubt that would have only made matters worse."

"To be honest, I would have been just as likely to hit Cleveland as Lord Hawksmoor. I had no idea what I was doing." Lady Henrietta crossed the room and sat next to Madalene on the window seat, taking her hand and giving it a gentle squeeze. "I know you are upset, but these things die down and are soon forgotten."

"Are they?" She glanced at Lady Henrietta, hopeful she was right. That one day Madalene would look back on this from a place of contentment, if not true happiness, and realize no one even remembered her name, let alone what had happened on the dance floor at the Dunhills' party between a disreputable rake and a servant trying to pass herself off as nobility.

"That is what Auntie tells me."

It was hardly encouraging. Poor Lady Henrietta had barely stepped foot out of the house since the incident with Lord Pengrin and when she did it was with great reluctance and took much coaxing. And to what end? So that she could bear the brunt of constant stares and whispers brought on by the scars from her childhood and then enhanced by coming far too close to marrying a complete reprobate? The fact that Pengrin had fooled most of the ton into thinking him a grand gentleman was the only part that had been quickly forgotten.

"Perhaps you will find it easier at Northill," Lady Henrietta continued. "I know I much preferred the seclusion of the country rather than being cast into the critical eye of London society. Sometimes, I long for those days when James allowed me to hide away from the world."

Hardly helpful. "What will I tell my father? He will be so disappointed. He put such faith in me."

"Your father will applaud your actions in soundly slapping

Lord Hawksmoor for his reprehensible behavior and refusing his proposal. You need not worry about that, I am certain. Although..." Lady Henrietta did not finish her sentence but merely sighed.

"Although what?"

"Well...it is just that the man did seem horribly upset over the matter. And I can't help but feel that there is a true affection there. If it is any consolation at all, I do not think he meant ill by what he did."

Madalene wanted to argue. She wanted to throw up a million reasons why she disagreed with Lady Henrietta's views on the subject. The only problem was—she didn't disagree. Which was the true crux of the matter. There was true affection between them. A friendship that had progressed into something deeper and stronger.

Had such affection not existed, perhaps the hurt over what he had done wouldn't cut quite so deep. Because in the end, it was not the ruin that upset her the most. It was that said ruin had been perpetrated by someone she loved. Someone she trusted.

Someone who had lied to her.

"Regardless," she said. "He did not have the right to take the decision out of my hands and put it into his. Even if I had been amenable to it, does he not see how ludicrous such a match is? He is a future earl. I would never be accepted into his world and he would never fit into mine."

"My dear, Miss Cosgrove," Lady Henrietta said, sounding far wiser than her one and twenty years. "Lord Hawksmoor does not seem to fit into anyone's world. He has been an outcast for years and from what Auntie tells me, his parents never gave him more than a passing thought, and none of those thoughts were of less than a critical nature. Yet, when he was with you, he seemed perfectly at ease. Perhaps, and not to excuse his behavior, but perhaps you are the only place he *does* fit."

Lady Henrietta's words settled around Madalene but did little to ease the ache in her heart. If she cut him off, what would become of him? Would he sink deeper into the dark of The Devil's Lair? The thought of such a thing, of such a loss of the goodness within him, broke what was left of her heart.

She could stop it. She could accept his proposal and offer him a safe haven. A place to call home. But how did she do that when her own feelings were so conflicted? Yes, she loved him, but he had not spoken of love or affection in his proposal. All he claimed was his need to keep her safe. To protect her. Nowhere in his proposal had he mentioned love. Or affection. Or happiness, even.

If they were ever to conquer the differences of their worlds and the censure they would receive from society for stepping outside the bounds of what was deemed acceptable, surely they would need love in abundance. Otherwise, what was the point?

"I don't even know where I fit anymore," Madalene admitted. Her position at Northill was about to be handed over to Mrs. Cleary upon their arrival. Her position as head-mistress of Miss Caldwell's school had been destroyed by the scandal. And even if it hadn't, she could never accept the position knowing that, in doing so, she might bring danger to the students with the threat of Lord T's intent still looming over her.

What did she do now? Where did she go?

A soft knock echoed from the other side of the door. The footmen had arrived to take her trunk to the carriage. Mada-lene stood, bringing Lady Henrietta with her, their hands still clasped tightly.

"I will miss you," Lady Henrietta said, turning to embrace

her in a warm hug. "Please write me and let me know how you fare."

"I will. Thank you for all your kindness toward me." Despite the bad that had happened, her new friendship with Lady Henrietta was something she would always treasure. She was a lovely, young woman with much to offer the world. Madalene hoped one day, she could find her way back out into it to share that gift.

"And who knows," Lady Henrietta said as she led Madalene from the room to follow behind the footmen and her trunk. "Perhaps your first letter to me will have good news, hm?"

Madalene forced a smile, not wanting to say good-bye on a sour note. "Perhaps."

But as she settled herself across from Mrs. Cleary in the carriage, Madalene could not imagine what course of events would need to occur in order for her to write such a letter.

T he pounding in Hawk's head had finally eased to a dull thud. He had cleaned himself up, prepared a proper speech to convince Madalene to change her mind and marry him and then made the brief carriage ride over to Ridgemont House. If his luck held, he would arrive there and not be held at gunpoint by the surprisingly fearless Lady Henrietta. Apparently, her experience with Pengrin had unearthed the young woman's bolder nature.

At least the man's existence had served some positive purpose, unintended as it might have been.

But whether Lady Henrietta and her indomitable great-aunt were present or not, Hawk's confidence grew with each turn of the wheels. Of course, he would be able to convince her to marry him. Why did he ever doubt himself in this regard? They were friends. They shared a passion for each other that could not be denied. Yes, they came from different social classes and likely the ton would raise their collective eyebrows at the match, but when in the past five years had the ton *not* raised their eyebrows at him? Her support through this ordeal had been absolute, a clear sign she cared for him as much as he did her.

Naturally, he must offer a proper and heartfelt apology for keeping the letters Lord T had taunted him with from her. But the reason he had feared contacting her was that it might put her in further danger. He'd done his best to keep an eye upon her from afar—a task made all the more difficult by the nomadic existence she and her father took up while looking for work. Should that not count for something?

Certainly, he had much to atone for in the way he went about attempting to force her to change her mind with respect to his rather blundered proposal, and he much regretted his impulsive behavior. But if she agreed to be his wife, he promised to spend a lifetime making it up to her.

Surely, once he told her all of this, she would see things his way. He leaned back in his carriage seat, feeling much better about the situation now that he had sobered up and determined a course of action.

Unfortunately, that feeling soon deteriorated when upon his approach he saw another carriage pulling away. And his confidence declined even farther when he stepped out of his carriage and questioned the butler, who scowled when he spied Hawk and haughtily informed him it was Miss Cosgrove in the carriage.

The hope Hawk had of making reparations and setting their future on a proper course plummeted deeper than the bottom of the Thames when said butler then informed him— far more smugly than any butler had a right to—that Miss

Cosgrove was leaving London for good and returning to Northill.

Any set down Hawk wished to rest upon the butler, who had made his least favorite people list, was set aside for the moment. He had more important things to deal with at the moment, such as chasing down the damnable carriage that neared the end of the street.

He shot the butler a dark look and began to run.

Chapter Twenty

Hawk skidded to a stop at the side of the carriage after the driver heeded his command and stopped. He yanked open the door, his chest heaving as he drew in deep breaths, and found himself staring at a rather strongly built, irate woman.

"Good Heavens above! What is the meaning of this?"

The older woman pressed her ample form against the plump squabs of the carriage seat and clutched her embroidered travel bag against her body as if she expected Hawk would snatch it away from her. Granted, he was somewhat disheveled from running down the street after the godforsaken carriage, and likely shouting at the top of his lungs for the driver to stop or face dire consequences that may have included disembowelment, made him appear something of a madman, but he was hardly a thief.

"It is quite all right, Mrs. Cleary," Madalene said. "I know this gentleman."

Hawk turned his head to look at Madalene. Even the sight of her was a balm to his heart. How was it simply gazing upon her could create such a warmth? A calm. A sense that everything would be fine so long as he had her by his side. Suddenly he questioned whom it was that was being saved.

"Gentleman? Hrmph!" Mrs. Cleary glared, pulling Hawk's attention away from Madalene. The older woman did not look pleased. In fact, she looked as if she might loosen her death grip on her travel bag and box him soundly about the ears. "No gentleman of my acquaintance chases down a lady's carriage in such a manner, making a pure spectacle of himself."

"Well," Hawk said, recovering his breath in great gulps and forcing his most charming smile. "I am a rather irregular gentleman."

"Obviously."

He looked at Madalene. She wore a simple travel outfit with a dark red coat that made her ivory complexion glow in the dim light of the carriage. "May I come in?"

Mrs. Cleary gasped. "You most certainly may not!"

Hawk pursed his lips. Was it not just his luck that the woman Madalene hired as her replacement at Northill would be both opinionated and equal in size to him, though he suspected she may outweigh him by at least a stone, possibly two. He had a vision of Mrs. Cleary throwing herself between them and wrestling him to the ground in the middle of Brook Street. Now wouldn't that send tongues wagging before the noon hour?

Madalene gave Mrs. Cleary a reassuring smile before returning her attention to him. Though, by then, her smile had faded. "Lord Hawksmoor, I really do not feel there is anything left to say, do you?"

Lord Hawksmoor. The proper use of his name and title saddened him. Not that he expected her to address him as Hawk in front of others, but the emphasis she had put on it indicated that, had they been alone, she would have done the same. She had erected a barrier and he was not to be invited past it.

A proper gentleman would have taken the hint and yielded to the lady's wishes. But, as he'd already told Mrs. Cleary, he was not a regular gentleman. And he certainly wasn't a proper one.

"As a matter of fact, I feel there is still quite a bit to say and given that I am underdressed for such cold weather, I thought I might come aboard and have this conversation out of the elements."

He did not wait for her invitation, unsure if it would actually come and instead, hiked a leg up and hauled himself into the carriage, taking the seat next to Madalene as Mrs. Cleary had commandeered the middle of the other set of seats.

"This is highly indecorous, Miss Cosgrove. I simply cannot allow it. Think of your reputation!"

"I'm afraid there is nothing left of my reputation, Mrs. Cleary," Madalene said and the weary sadness that wrapped itself around each word sliced through Hawk's bravado and cut him to the core.

"Her reputation is perfectly safe—Mrs. Cleary, is it?" Hawk waited for the older woman to nod begrudgingly before he continued. "We are not alone in the carriage and given you are a missus, I can only assume you to be a proper, married chaperone, are you not?"

Mrs. Cleary shifted in her seat. "Indeed, I am a widow."

"Ah. I see. Then you have my deepest condolences, madam. It must be very difficult to find yourself on your own, having lost the one person you have loved for many years?"

Mrs. Cleary appeared taken aback by his question, though if the sigh that came from Madalene was any indication, she knew exactly where this conversation was heading. Still, he pressed on. He had much work to do.

"How awful it must have been for you to wake up one

morning and discover the person you had professed your love to had suddenly left you without a word of warning, not having the common decency to even explain—"

"You did not *profess your love*," Madalene shot at him. "You *ordered* me to marry you for my own good. And when I said no, you humiliated me and ruined my reputation!"

He winced. She did have a point there. "I grant you it was not the most romantic of proposals. I should have thought it through much better. I should have offered you...what?" What had she wanted? Flowers and silly ballads and him on bended knee begging for her hand?

"You should have simply asked. Not ordered."

"I did not order you. I merely suggested. Strongly, I admit, but we both know it is for the best."

"And was kissing me in front of everyone present and ruining my reputation so that I can never show my face in London, or garner proper employment to support myself, your idea of a *strong suggestion*?"

Mrs. Cleary let out a swift gasp. "Oh, my dear!"

Hawk scowled. Any headway he may have been making getting Mrs. Cleary on his side just took a hit.

"I admit my impulsive behavior was a bit heavy-handed—"

"A bit?"

"Very." She continued to glare at him, her light blue eyes ablaze with indignation and Hawk was struck by the fact that she was even more beautiful when she was angry. How was such a thing possible? He did not know. All he knew was how much he wanted to thoroughly kiss her in that moment. Though likely, if he made the attempt, he'd find himself summarily ejected from the carriage and sitting in the middle of Brook Street looking like a complete idiot.

Hawk took a deep breath. "I have compromised you. I take full responsibility for that and I apologize profusely. I acted rashly and without forethought. But I cannot change that now. The only way to reclaim your reputation is for us to marry. But I assure you, if I did not have such strong feelings for you, I would not have made such an offer."

"An offer that I have declined. I will stay with Father at Northill. There is no reason for me to return to London ever again."

"And how long do you intend to stay at Northill? It isn't just about your reputation. Think of your safety. Lord T is out there and his letter found me at Northill. Are you prepared to stay under your father's protection forever, to possibly endanger him and the Bowens in the process?"

She pursed her lips and sat back in her seat, turning her head away from him to stare out the window. "It is none of your concern what I choose to do. I am not your responsibility and I do not wish to spend my life being such. I do not need a protector."

"Yes, you do."

She turned back to him and the lack of compromise in her expression drove the truth home. She would not budge in this regard. She was willing to take on the scorn of others and live with the scandal he'd created, live a life constantly looking over her shoulder, rather than marry him.

His heart withered and desperation rushed in to fill the space. "Madalene, I insist that you allow me to protect—"

She cut him off. "It has been over five years, my lord. If this Lord T intended me harm, surely, he would have done so by now. For all we know, he simply enjoys taunting you. Maybe his purpose is to drive you around the bend and never lay a hand on me. I appreciate your concern, but you have placed a duty upon yourself that does not belong there. I would rather you reclaim the life you should have had and leave me to mine."

"The life I should have had? And how do you suppose I

do that? Should I resurrect my brother so he might reclaim his title? Should I move back to Raven Manor to live beneath his shadow and face the derision and disappointment of my parents each morning when I wake? And when they die, shall I haunt the empty halls like a specter, alone and miserable. Is that the life you speak of?"

The sheen of tears appeared in a blink and brightened her eyes, softening the blaze that had burned in them only a moment ago. He immediately regretted his harsh words. The life he had been born into was not her fault. That he could never marry another because he loved her, also not her fault.

"I want you to be happy," she whispered.

"*You* make me happy."

"Oh! Oh my." Mrs. Cleary blurted out, drawing Hawk's attention. He'd forgotten the older lady was there. He spared her a glance and discovered she had pulled a handkerchief from her bag and now used it to dab at her eyes. "That is quite a lovely sentiment. And he is a gentleman, Miss Cosgrove. Would you not consider such a match advantageous, especially given you have been compromised and will likely be unable to find such with someone else?"

Hawk blinked. He had not expected such a turnaround from the woman who had attempted to bar him from the carriage not five minutes earlier. Who knew Mrs. Cleary would turn out to be such a blatant romantic as well as a pragmatist?

Unfortunately, Madalene was not so easily swayed by soft sentiment or honest declarations, if the shaking of her head was any indication. "It was just a kiss. If the ton wishes to make such a to do about it, that is their business, but I won't be swayed or backed into a corner by their foolish need to create something out of nothing."

Except the kiss hadn't been *nothing*. It had been something. No, it had been everything.

"Madalene, please—"

"No." Her answer came quietly but with hard purpose. "I will not spend my life feeling as if I am a burden you took on. You are not responsible for what your brother did, or for this Lord T's actions. And I will not marry you to repair my reputation. We both deserve more than that, don't you think?"

Yes. At least she did. He, on the other hand, did not. He had failed her in every respect. Knowing him, befriending him, had made her life worse. Perhaps she was right, that she would be far better off without him. God only knew, he did not deserve her. He had always known it, somewhere deep inside. She was a shining star, far beyond his reach.

But that knowledge did not change what his heart wanted. And his heart wanted her. Despite everything, they belonged together. He'd known it every day since he had awoken in Marcus Bowen's home with no more memory than a newborn babe. Even then, his heart had remembered her. It had reached for her in the dark, knowing within her lived all the things he needed.

What *he* needed. Not her. She did not need him. Nor, it seemed, did she want him.

"Lord Hawksmoor, I appreciate your proposal, but I have declined it. Repeatedly. Please, do not make this more difficult than it already is. Let me go." The last words reached him on the softest of whispers but cut him like the sharpest blade.

The strength of her conviction weighed upon him like a stone tethered to his leg, drawing him down into the dark waters. He wanted to fight against it, but what was the point? She had made her decision. She did not want to share her life with him. She did not want his protection. She simply wanted him to go away and leave her be.

Had he not been such a prideful man, perhaps he would have begged. But what good would it do? She stared straight ahead; her gaze fixed on some point beyond Mrs. Cleary's shoulder. She had already shut him out. Staying, attempting to change her mind would have just made him appear even more a fool than her solid rejection had made him feel.

"Mrs. Cleary," he said, offering the older woman a nod. "Forgive my abrupt interruption of your journey. I hope I have not caused you to suffer any undue dismay."

"Oh, no, of course," the older woman said, waving her handkerchief at him as the words tumbled out.

"Miss Cosgrove, I wish you a safe journey. Will you at least write to me when you reach Northill so I might know you arrived safely?"

"I will send word," she said.

He nodded again then lingered a moment, his body unwilling to move away from hers knowing this was the last time he would be so close. But after a moment, the silence grew tense and there was no other option for him but to leave, unless he intended them to sit on the side of the street for all eternity. He cleared his throat and reached for the door handle, swinging the door open and letting in the cold air.

He stepped outside and stood, his back to the carriage. Politeness indicated he should turn around and bid the ladies a safe journey, but he couldn't manage it. If he looked back, he would be unable to leave. He would vault himself back into that carriage, swallow his pride until he choked on it, and beg her to become his wife.

And still her answer would remain the same.

He reached back blindly and shoved the door closed. Then he forced his legs to move, one foot in front of the other, blindly walking down Brook Street with no destination in mind.

"And, so, you just left?"

Hawk did not appreciate Huntsleigh's pointed question or the way his tone conveyed that Hawk was an imbecile for having done so. Of course, he had left. It wasn't as if Madalene had given him much in the way of options on that account.

"What else would you have had me do? Abduct her and run off to Gretna Green with Mrs. Cleary in tow?"

"I would not have expected you to give up so easily and simply come back here looking like a whipped dog."

Hawk glared at his uninvited companion, wishing Huntsleigh had not chosen to come to White's at the same time as he. All he wanted was to drink his brandy in silence and mourn the loss of the woman he loved. He was in no mood to put up with his friend's jabs that he had not done all he could. It was the height of hypocrisy.

"You are hardly one to talk. Did you not do the same thing when Lady Caelie refused you?"

Huntsleigh cleared his throat and straightened in his chair. "I did no such thing."

"Are you certain? I quite remember Blackbourne indicating that you had slunk away to your bachelor apartments and stayed there until he, Bowen, and your grandfather showed up to roust you out."

"Blackbourne needs to learn to keep his mouth shut," Huntsleigh muttered. "And I would point out that his involvement in rousting me was only because he wanted to wring my neck for compromising his cousin. Regardless, my situation was completely different."

"In what way?"

Huntsleigh pressed a hand against his heart. "I was devastated. I loved her."

"Well, I love Madalene!" Bloody hell. He sank in his seat as the other patrons of White's sitting nearby turned to stare upon his declaration. Heat burned up his throat and did not stop until it reached the roots of his hair.

"Well, well, well." Huntsleigh grinned and God help him, but Hawk wanted nothing more in that moment than to smack the damn smile from the earl's smug face. "I thought as much. I've never known you to take such an interest in someone else's well-being the way you have Miss Cosgrove's. Oh, how the mighty have fallen."

"How is it that no one has killed you yet?"

"Your guess is as good as mine. But this isn't about me. If you love this woman as you claim, then you will do whatever you must to convince her of this and make her yours. Although, I would caution against kidnapping her and running off to Gretna Green. You're likely to be in enough trouble with Bowen as it is having compromised the girl. No point adding insult to injury."

"And just how do you suggest I do that? She wants nothing more to do with me. Should I rush after her and beg? Fall at her feet and pledge eternal fidelity?"

"Yes. And as it turns out, I am returning to Lakefield Abbey the day after next. That should leave you ample time to pack a bag and determine a proper course of action to convince the young lady you cannot live without her and vice versa. Although, perhaps leave off all this cloak and dagger *I need to protect you* bit. Women hate being told what to do. Trust me on this. And oftentimes, as I have discovered, they are much better at taking care of themselves than we give them credit for."

Chapter Twenty-One

The journey home to Northill proved a rather taxing affair, filled with awkward conversation that did little to alleviate the crushing ache in Madalene's chest. All she really wanted was to find a quiet moment where she might sit alone by a fire and cry until the ache eased. Unfortunately, Mrs. Cleary's presence did not allow her such a luxury. Nor was her state of mind improved by the older woman's viewpoint on the topic of Lord Hawksmoor.

"Are you certain turning down his lordship's proposal is truly the best course of action, my dear?" Mrs. Cleary had wasted no time upon Hawk's departure from the carriage before she asked the question. Perhaps she hoped Madalene would come to her senses before they were too far away to turn around and go back, should she change her mind.

"It is the only thing I can do, Mrs. Cleary. Please, do not ask me about it again. The matter is best left alone."

Hawk was not hers to have or to keep. He belonged to a level of society she had no interest in joining. Not that she would be welcomed if she did. Perhaps he did not see this as clearly as she, but eventually he would. After his father passed and he became the new Earl of Ravenwood, he would need a proper lady to be his countess, to give him heirs.

The thought twisted in her stomach until it became a tangled knot. She would have loved to be that woman. To be the mother to his children. To bask in the glow of his love and friendship, his warmth and humor. But that was not the life he had asked her to be a part of. He wanted to protect her out of a sense of misguided responsibility. He blamed himself for his brother's attack, for Phillip making her a part of his twisted game to teach Hawk a twisted lesson in family loyalty.

In the beginning, she had feared Lord T's existence. She'd spent the first couple of years after leaving Raven Manor looking into shadows for monsters that might lurk out of sight. But as time wore on nothing happened. No one came after her. No one attempted to harm her. And over time, Madalene had let down her guard, believing what Phillip had said was nothing more than one last, desperate attempt to hurt his brother.

In that, he had proven most successful. Hawk had spent the last five years trying to find a man she thought nothing more than a figment of Phillip's madness. She'd been wrong. Lord T had been out there. But she hadn't been his target. Hawk had. He'd taunted Hawk until the poor man spent his life chasing his tail trying to find Phillip's accomplice. Yet, other than the letters, Lord T had done nothing, obviously lacking Phillip's fervor for the horrific behavior.

If she married Hawk, wouldn't she be tying him to a cause that had brought him nothing but misery? If he had told her the truth about the letters earlier, she could have saved him years of torment. Released him from this ridiculous duty that imprisoned him.

No, she must not perpetuate this incessant need he had to keep her safe. As much as the idea broke her heart, it was better that she was out of his life for good. She knew of no other way to force him to let the matter go. Now he could get on with the life he deserved and leave the past where it belonged. In the past.

The trip to Northill took two days. They stopped at an inn overnight and shared a room. Throughout the journey, Mrs. Cleary kept an eye on her, as if, despite her best attempt at remaining stoic, she could sense the tears Madalene held at bay. Tears she would allow to fall once she could be alone and after she informed her father of what had happened.

That was a task she did not look forward to, though it was easier to focus on Father's disappointment than on the fact she would never see Hawk again. Such a strange sensation. Which was odd, really. She had lived the past five years without seeing him. The only information she'd had of him was from servants' gossip, snippets here and there that colored a picture of a tormented and unhappy man bent on destroying others.

The truth, as it often turned out, was a far different picture than the one painted by gossip. Yes, he was tormented and unhappy, but for far different reasons than anyone could have ever guessed. Save for someone who had been with him years ago to see the damage inflicted.

The warmth of Northill's kitchens, filled with the sumptuous aromas of freshly baked bread and roasted chicken welcomed Madalene home. She breathed in deeply of the familiar scents and prayed for strength to get through the rest of this day. If she could make it through today, then surely tomorrow would be easier and then the day after that a bit easier still. It was what she told herself, knowing it to be nothing more than a lie. Still, it was all she had.

"Oh, Miss Cosgrove!" Lady Rebecca rushed down the hallway as they emerged from the kitchens and held out her hands in greeting. "Andrews told us you had arrived. We had not expected you to return so soon, but I am so pleased to have you back. I have sent word to your father to let him know. I expect he will be along shortly. He has missed you something fierce, though he tells me he is happy you are experiencing London proper."

"Thank you, my lady." The warm greeting helped bolster her confidence that she could get through this, though she sorely hated to destroy her father's delusions over her experience in London. "May I present to you, Mrs. Dorothy Cleary. She has agreed to take on my post. I think you will be most pleased with her."

"If you recommend her, I am certain we will. It is lovely to meet you, Mrs. Cleary," Lady Rebecca said before turning back to Madalene. "Perhaps you would like to show Mrs. Cleary to her room and have her settled, then join Mr. Bowen and me in the drawing room so your father might welcome you home?"

"Of course, my lady." The sooner Madalene could reveal she returned home shrouded in scandal, the better she would feel.

Ah, more lies she told herself.

After settling Mrs. Cleary and ensuring a tray was sent up to her room before she settled in for the evening, Madalene made her way down the staircase to the second floor, her pace slowing as she neared the drawing room door. Despite repeated attempts to find the best way to break the news to Father and the Bowens on what had occurred, she'd finally come to the conclusion that, when it came to bad news, no best way existed.

"My dear girl!" Father crossed the room and embraced her with his one arm and held her close. "How I have missed seeing your smile."

She forced one now as Father let her go, not wanting to disappoint, but it faltered at the edges and all too quickly the joy in his face slipped away, his brows dipping downward. "Maddie? What is it?"

The love and concern in his voice caused her lower lip to tremble. She pulled the recalcitrant lip in and held it with her teeth, taking a deep breath before releasing it and answering her father's question.

"I'm afraid I have some unfortunate news, Father."

"Oh dear," Lady Rebecca said from her position on the sofa.

Mr. Bowen stepped forward; his face arranged in its usual serious manner. "Should we leave you alone then?"

Madalene shook her head. "No. What I must say will concern you as well, as you have the right to know and decide what you wish to do." How she loathed that what had happened might taint the Bowens' opinion of her, and by association, her father.

"Very well, then." Mr. Bowen motioned toward the short sofa opposite him and his wife. Father led her over and sat down next to her, holding her hand. They had been through much together, and they would get through this as well, of that she had no doubt. But it grieved her to cause him pain, nonetheless.

"I'm afraid I have been involved in an incident that has caused a bit of a...scandal." The last word stuck in her throat and she had to force it out.

"Maddie?" Father squeezed her hand.

She glanced down at where their hands were clasped and drew on his strength. "It is something of a long story, and I feel I should begin at the beginning so you understand what happened at the end. But it goes back several years, so please bear with me."

Madalene drew in a long breath and wound the clock back to her time at Raven Manor. She told them of the friendship that had developed between her and Hawk and the kindness he had shown her. The unkindness shown to him by his family.

"I believe our friendship benefited him as much as it did me and though I knew it was unorthodox and beyond the bounds of propriety, I did not want to take it away from him. Some days it felt as if our time together was all he had. And other days, it was all I had."

She continued on until she reached the fateful day that had changed everything. With halting words, she told the horrid tale of Phillip's attack, sensing her father's distress and wishing she could protect him from such. But she could not alter the truth, nor did she stop in the telling of it. If she did, she feared her ability to tell the tale would be forever lost.

"He saved me, you see," she said of Hawk's actions that night. "And for that, I beg you to forgive him for what he did both that night and for what came later."

"Later? Is he involved in this scandal you speak of?" Mr. Bowen asked.

Madalene took a fortifying breath. She didn't feel quite right revealing Hawk's secrets, but she needed them to understand. Though hurt that he kept the letters from her and his recklessness that left her ruined, he had saved her from Phillip, and for that she would be forever grateful.

"Yes. But first I must have your promise you will not speak of how Lord Hawksmoor's brother truly died."

"Of course not," her father said, sliding an arm around her shoulders and pulling her tight, as if he could keep her safe from something that had already happened. "If Lord Hawksmoor had not killed his brother, then, I would surely do so now. He deserved nothing more than what he got. I hope the man rots in the deepest pits of hell. Beg your pardon, my lady."

"Think nothing of it, Mr. Cosgrove. I echo those sentiments," Lady Rebecca said, her silvery eyes burning with anger. How strange to find so many champions. How comforting. "Tell us, Miss Cosgrove, how does this tie into the scandal you speak of?"

Madalene told them of Hawk's mission, to find the man Phillip claimed would come for her and finish what he had started. The guilt he carried for what his brother had done, and the need he had to protect her. Once she laid the foundation, she revealed the latest turn the story had taken: Hawk's proposal.

"He proposed?" Lady Rebecca's anger changed in a blink into wonder and...delight?

"Yes, but I declined."

Lady Rebecca frowned. "You do not share his feelings? I had been so certain there was a spark between you during his stay here."

Madalene blushed. Had it been so obvious? Had everyone seen it? "I cannot claim not to have feelings for Lord Hawksmoor, but it was not tender feelings that were the impetus behind his proposal."

"Then what was?"

It was Mr. Bowen who answered his wife's question. "He wished to protect you. He considers you to still be in danger."

"Yes. I recently discovered that Phillip's accomplice has been sending Lord Hawksmoor taunting letters, though I believe their impetus is to drive him mad and have little to do with a desire to cause me harm."

Mr. Bowen's brow dipped. "He received a letter while staying here. Was that—"

"Yes, from the mysterious Lord T," Madalene said.

"But you do not wish to marry him?" Mr. Bowen tilted his head. "Why is that?"

"Oh heavens, Marcus!" Lady Rebecca swatted her husband's arm. "Because she wishes to marry for love, not out of some misplaced sense of duty. And well she should want such." She turned her attention to Madalene. "I take it he did not speak of love when he made this proposal?"

"He did not."

"Tsk. Men." She leaned back into the sofa and shot her husband a pointed look.

"What have I done?"

"If you will recall, husband dear, your own proposal to me was steeped in duty and honor and also had nothing at all to do with love."

"I loved you dearly," he corrected her, though looked a bit sheepish as he added, "I simply forgot to mention it. And perhaps Lord Hawksmoor did as well."

Lady Rebecca straightened and looked across the narrow table between the sofas to Madalene. "Do you think this could be true? Men are not all that astute in knowing what we need to hear, after all."

Her father took her hand once more and squeezed. "She does have a point, Maddie. I made a total mash of my proposal to your mother. I was so tongue-tied I believe I ended up comparing my love for her to that which a stallion feels toward his favorite filly. It's a miracle she ever said yes."

Madalene smiled but her heart remained heavy. "Lord Hawksmoor is rather single-minded in his quest to marry me. He wishes to protect me, nothing more. He has indicated such repeatedly and mentioned nothing else in his attempts to convince me to accept."

I need you.

She shook the memory off. Need did not equal love.

"My dear," Father said, pulling her away from her memories. "I see nothing in this that leads to scandal. I assume he proposed in private?"

"Yes. He pulled me aside at a party given by Mr. and Mrs. Dunhill. When I declined him, I returned to the party thinking that was the end of it. However, he had followed and then he—"

She stopped. Her face burned and her throat constricted. Could she say the words in front of Father? The Bowens? Heavens, even the memory of it made her blush! The touch of his lips upon hers and she had responded to him instantly despite all the reasons she shouldn't have. Was it any wonder he thought there was a chance she would say yes? She loved him. That she could not deny. But she wanted his love in return, not his protection.

Mr. Bowen leaned forward; one dark eyebrow elevated. "What did Hawksmoor do?"

"He kissed me," she whispered.

"Kissed you?" Father's voice filled with anger.

Madalene nodded. "In front of everyone present."

"I will kill him," Mr. Bowen stated flatly.

"All due respect, sir," Father answered. "But you will need to stand in line behind me."

Madalene shook her head and gave both men a stern look. "Nobody is killing anyone. Please, do not hold it against him. He was desperate and his motives were honest even if his actions were somewhat reprehensible." Now who felt the need to protect whom?

"Reprehensible? That is a gross understatement, my dear." Father shook his head. "And I thought him a good man."

"He *is* a good man," she insisted. "Just misguided and reckless in his actions."

Her father gave her a dubious look. "Where is he now? I should like to have a word with this *good* man."

"London, I suppose, but Father, you must leave the matter alone. If you make a big to-do over this, it will only serve to fuel the scandal further. If left alone, I suspect the ton will soon forget and it will fade from the collective memory of society. After all, I am nobody to them. Please, I wish to put this episode behind me."

If only saying the words would make it so. It wouldn't, of course. All that had happened between them could never be boiled down to that one moment in time. Despite her claims, despite her anger at the way Hawk had kept the existence of the letters from her, had tried to force her into accepting his proposal, she could not forget that kiss. She could not forget the taste of his desperation to do whatever it took, nor her own to give whatever he needed, to see him at peace.

In the end, that was the worst of it. Loving him enough to want to give him everything, yet loving herself enough to know the cost would be too high. Neither of them would ever be truly happy with such an imbalance between them. Once she was safe and the threat of any reprisal from the elusive Lord T ended, Hawk would be strapped with the guilt of having coerced her into marriage with a man who did not truly love her, knowing he could never give her what she needed. And she would be saddled with the knowledge that he had married her out of duty, and not because he had wanted to.

Much as she wished it could be otherwise, there was no happy ending to their story.

"Lord Hawksmoor! Please, you must see me!"

Hawk glared at the closed doors leading out to the hallway and the ruckus going on just beyond them. Was he not allowed even a moment of peace to pack what few belongings he wanted to take with him to Northill? A little silence to formulate a plan that held more detail and finesse than Huntsleigh's rather vague suggestion he simply show up and profess his undying love? When the commotion did not appear to be abating, he strode to the doors and yanked them open.

"What the deuce is going on out here? Do I not pay the two of you to keep such things—" He stopped and stared at the disheveled woman being held by the burly men who guarded his door. The woman looked familiar. "Mrs. Chambers?"

Bentley loosened his hold on the squirming woman enough that her feet returned to the ground. "You know her, my lord?"

Hawk motioned toward his men to release her. "Somewhat. To what do I owe this unexpected disruption?"

Mrs. Chambers stepped forward, pulling at her wool coat to set it back to rights. "It is my brother, my lord. I fear he is about to do something foolish."

Given that Major Gibbons was her brother, Hawk did not doubt her claim in the least. Perhaps he was prejudiced against the major, but he did not put much faith into Gibbons' overall capacity to make good decisions. "I hardly see how that is my concern."

Mrs. Chambers' expression hardened and Hawk noted an uncanny resemblance between her and the major. Twins, perhaps? That would explain the unusual closeness and the way they never seemed to be without the other's company.

"It is your concern because it involves Miss Cosgrove. And unless I am mistaken, she is of particular interest to you?"

Suddenly Mrs. Chambers had his full attention.

"What do you mean? What has he done?"

"When I awoke this morning, my brother was gone. He left me this note." She shoved the sheet of cheap stationery at Hawk's chest, forcing him to take it. He flipped open the folded note, his gaze skimming over the words. Hawk's heart stilled then started up in a rush, pounding against his ribcage

much as it had done when he'd run like a demon after Madalene's carriage.

*M*y dearest sister,
I am off to make good on a long-ago wager. Do
not worry for me. I promise that I, unlike the reck-
less and long dead Lord H—, will carry out my part in our little
game well within the bounds of the law. They will not be able to
fault me and in the end, I will be the victor. I will have finally
bested the beast and proven once and for all that I am the better
man despite his lofty title. I will have proven my dominance,
that my strategy at the game was far superior to his.

I will write again once I am settled and send for you then.
All my love,
Timothy

"**Y**our brother...his given name is Timothy?"

"Yes."

A cold sweat broke out all over Hawk's body and
air constricted in his throat. Major Gibbons. Major *Timothy*
Gibbons. Could it be? He wasn't a lord, obviously, but did
that mean anything? Had his brother used the moniker as a
taunt? It would be just like Phillip to do so. Hawk stared at the
penmanship and his heart stuttered in his chest. It matched
the other letters he'd received. Still, his mind rejected the
notion. How could it be? Lord T had been right under his
nose the entire time?

"Do you know who this *Lord H* he refers to is?"

Mrs. Chambers stared at him, her dark eyes cold and
unreadable. "I believe we both know who he refers to, do we
not, my lord? Your brother lured Timothy into this sordid
contest, preying upon my brother's need to improve himself

beyond his station. The late Lord Hawksmoor made a point of humiliating him whenever he failed to meet the challenges he'd set out for him in this sick game he concocted."

Hawk shook his head. None of this made sense. "My brother referred to him as Lord T. Why? He was no lord."

"As your brother was only too fond of reminding him. Each time Timothy failed at whatever challenge had been laid down, he would be ridiculed. *Little Lord T who wants to be*, your brother would say. A reminder that Timothy would never be as good or as powerful or as wealthy. The harder Timothy tried to win, the more depraved the challenges became. If my brother thought to decline, yours would threaten to destroy his career. He even had Timothy assist him in covering up—" She stopped, but Hawk knew what she referred to. Lady Rothbury's death. "My brother had no choice but to take part in those disgusting games."

"You make him sound like the victim. But my brother has been dead for five long years. Yet I have continued to receive letters from him on a regular basis indicating his plans to carry through with the challenge. This letter," Hawk said, waving the disgusting note in her face. "Does it not indicate his willingness to continue on even when the threat of my brother's reprisals no longer exist?"

Mrs. Chambers' silence spoke volumes.

Hawk glared at her with almost as much repugnance as he held for her brother. "Not so innocent after all then."

Her mouth tightened. "He is a prideful man. Your brother's constant taunts drove him to the edge of madness with the need to prove himself the better man. I tried my best to stop his behavior, but there was little I could do. I thought when your brother died, it had come to an end, but Timothy continued to talk about one last challenge that needed to be completed. His ultimate victory."

"Did he say how he planned on completing it?"

She shook her head. "I thought as the years passed, he had let it alone. But when I noted his swift interest in Miss Cosgrove and realized her connection to Raven Manor, I feared the worst. When Timothy noted your interest in her, I believe it only spurred him on further, as if by taking her from you, it was a double victory. Still, I prayed he would come to his senses. Then I received his letter," she motioned toward the note Hawk still held in his hand. "I realized he had not and that my fears were well-founded."

Hawk's anger sparked past his fear and he stalked back into his office to grab his bag. "Why did you not seek help to stop your brother years ago? Why not come to me then?"

All this could have been put to an end. Madalene would have been safe. He could have had a life that involved something other than living in perpetual fear for Madalene.

"He is my brother! I tried to dissuade Miss Cosgrove from associating with him but she did not listen to my counsel." The anguish in her voice was real, but Hawk remained unmoved as he brushed past her and headed for the stairwell. He had no more time to pack anything. He must leave immediately if he was to reach Northill Hall before Gibbons could do any damage.

He cast Mrs. Chambers one last glance then nodded at Bentley and Rickard. "Get her out of my sight," he snarled, then took the stairs two at a time. "And contact Lord Huntsleigh to let him know I have left for Northill without him and to join me with all due haste."

If he were to go up against a madman, he would need all the reinforcements he could get.

Chapter Twenty-Two

"**M**iss Cosgrove?"

Madalene glanced up from her sewing as Northill's butler entered the salon where she sat, working on letting out several of Lady Rebecca's gowns to adjust for her growing belly.

"Yes, Mr. Andrews?"

"There is a gentleman here to see you, miss. A Major Gibbons?" The butler leaned toward her and offered her the card that rested in the center of the silver salver. She picked it up and read the name he had already said.

"Major Gibbons? Whatever is he doing here?"

"He did not indicate, miss. But he seemed rather insistent that he sees you. I told him I was uncertain if you were in but that I would check upon such and report back." The older man lifted one eyebrow as she set the card back on the tray. "Are you in, Miss Cosgrove?"

For a moment, she did not know what to say. She had hoped to avoid anyone from London who had witnessed her supreme downfall, but politeness dictated she at least see him. He had traveled all this way, after all, and surely, he had not done so to berate her for what had occurred. Given the animosity between Major Gibbons and Hawk, likely he placed the blame squarely on Hawk's shoulders.

"Yes, of course. Thank you, Mr. Andrews. I will go to him immediately."

"Very well, miss. He is in the receiving room. Shall I have Lady Rebecca join you?" His tone made the reason for his suggestion clear. Propriety required they be chaperoned. But Lady Rebecca had tired earlier and Madalene had suggested she lie down for a bit.

"No. Her ladyship is resting and I do not wish to disturb her. I will be fine."

Madalene set aside the gown she had been working on and took off the apron she wore, brushing a hand down the front of her dress to knock away any loose threads. She had chosen a deep violet dress today with blue flowers she had embroidered along the hem. Satisfied she was presentable she made her way to the receiving room. The major stood looking out the window, his hands locked behind his back. It had snowed the night before and now the grounds lay covered in a soft, fluffy expanse of winter white.

"Major Gibbons," she said, entering the room but leaving the door wide open. She had suffered enough scandal to last her a lifetime without adding more impropriety into the mix. "This is a surprise."

Major Gibbons turned at the sound of her voice, a smile upon his face that stated he was most happy to see her. She breathed a sigh of relief. He was not angry with her.

"My dear, you are a vision. How lovely to rest eyes upon you once again."

She smiled, a bit uncertainly. While Major Gibbons had always been kind with his words, this seemed a little more. "That is most kind of you to say, Major. Might I inquire what brings you to Northill Hall?"

He took in a deep breath, his smile growing. "You do."

"Me?"

"You sound startled." He took a few steps toward her.

"I suppose I am. It is a long way to travel for a visit." Her heart picked up speed and an unexpected prickling tickled the hair at the base of her neck. Something was off. They were acquaintances, yes, and he had professed his interest in her, but to come all this way...

"No distance is too far if it means at the end of the journey, I will find you."

More flattery. Oh, dear. Perhaps she should have taken Mr. Andrews up on his suggestion to fetch Lady Rebecca, for Madalene was quite out of her depth here. Major Gibbons was angling toward something, something she was not prepared for, and she was at a loss as to how to deflect it with any sense of finesse.

She steered the conversation in a different direction, hoping he would pick up on her reticence and let the matter drop before he embarrassed them both. "Are you staying nearby, Major?"

"Indeed, not too far. I have commandeered a cabin that, while somewhat rustic, is quite cozy and will suit my purposes."

Odd. "There is a perfectly comfortable inn located in the village just a short carriage ride away, Major, that you may find more comfortable."

He shrugged at her suggestion. "I find I prefer my privacy."

"I see." Silence fell between them. Madalene searched madly for something appropriate to say that was neither a pointed question as to why he was here—she did not want him to answer that as she had an inkling and did not want to encourage him—nor a comment on the weather as that conversation would be completed with one answer—cold—and lead her right back to where she was now.

"Would you care to take a walk with me, Miss Cosgrove? I know it is a bit unorthodox, perhaps, but we will be in the wide open and surely no can find fault with such. I would never think to compromise you in such a way, unlike some gentlemen who think they can take it upon themselves to ruin a lady's reputation without recourse or recompense."

Madalene gritted her teeth. His negative comments about Hawk raised her ire. While Hawk's actions were wrong, he did offer recompense.

"On the contrary, Major Gibbons. Lord Hawksmoor did, in fact, propose marriage. Both before and after the kiss."

Her words set the major aback and for a moment, he was rendered speechless. "H-he did?"

"Yes. Several times."

"And you accepted?"

She hesitated. If she said yes, it would certainly be enough to stop Major Gibbons' intent. But the lie would be found out soon enough. "No, I did not."

Major Gibbons let out a loud breath and his shoulders visibly relaxed. "Oh, that is good news, indeed! To tie yourself to such a debased scoundrel to save your reputation would have been a tragedy, my dear."

She bit down as her anger spiraled higher. "I would hardly consider Lord Hawksmoor debased." A scoundrel, perhaps, but not in an awful way. In truth, the more thought she gave the matter, the more she understood what he had done. Not that she appreciated his actions, but he had meant well and he'd had her best interests at heart. Even if his heart was not engaged in the way she had wished.

Truth be told, had it been, she would have given a resounding yes to his proposal without a moment's regret.

"Of course, you would not think so," Major Gibbons said,

taking a step toward her. "You have a very kind heart, Miss Cosgrove. I find it most endearing. But enough about Lord Hawksmoor. What say you to that walk? Will you join me while there is still some light left in the day?"

"I...I suppose that would be all right." He had, after all, come all this way. The least she could do was allow him a few moments of her time and hope that within that span she could discourage him from the course he had set. He must know that she was aware of the intent of his surprise visit. "Please, allow me a few moments to fetch my coat and I will return shortly."

She hurried from the room, her mind reeling and spinning. How was she to get them both out of this in a way that would leave their dignity intact? She did not care to hurt Major Gibbons. He had been kind to her, certainly, but she did not care for him. Not in that way. Her heart had already been given to another man. A man who was more interested in being dutiful and responsible than in loving her the way a woman wished to be.

Madalene hurried downstairs, retrieved her cloak from the closet and pulled it about her shoulders, fastening the front buttons. As she kicked off her slippers to replace them with her warm boots, Mrs. Cleary bustled down the hallway, the household ledger tucked under her arm.

"Oh, Miss Cosgrove. Are you going out?"

"Yes, Mrs. Cleary, but only for a short bit. Major Gibbons has surprised us with a visit and has asked me to take a walk with him. We will not go far."

"Oh." Mrs. Cleary straightened and her lips tightened. "Would you be needing a chaperone, my dear?"

After Hawk's commandeering of their carriage in one last attempt to convince her to marry him, Mrs. Cleary was well versed in the scandal that had caused her downfall. And despite the older woman meaning well, and she shoved her foot into her boot with a little more force than was necessary. "No, Mrs. Cleary, that is quite all right. We shall stay within sight of the house, I assure you."

"Very well then, miss," Mrs. Cleary conceded, but Madalene did not miss the raised eyebrow as the words left her mouth.

For heaven sakes. Is that what people thought of her? That she could not be trusted in the company of men simply because one of them had thought to kiss her? It wasn't as if she had wished it! Well...at least not under those circumstances. Perhaps in private, like when they were at the Lindwells' tea. That kiss was quite lovely. More than lovely, really. It had been utter perfection.

She sighed and Mrs. Cleary's eyebrows arched a little higher. Oh, bother!

Madalene turned and left Mrs. Cleary in the hallway, marching back to the entrance hall where Major Gibbons awaited her, having donned his own coat, hat and gloves to ward off the chill.

As the footman opened the door, Major Gibbons offered her his arm. "So that you do not slip in the snow, Miss Cosgrove."

With reluctance she took it, though she would have preferred to keep a bit of distance between them.

The cold winter air bit into her skin despite the bright sun that shone in the afternoon sky. They walked in silence, making their way along the path that led to the steward's house she shared with Father. Was he there now? She hoped so. Something didn't feel right, though what exactly, she could not pinpoint. Was it her trepidation over the proposal she suspected was forthcoming? No. No, it was Major Gibbons, himself. His cheerfulness and flattery were too much. False, almost. Was that simply a case of nerves, given the intent of his visit? Not knowing gnawed at her. She did not care to let matters fester. She much preferred to jump on an issue right away and address it.

"Major Gibbons—"

"Miss Cosgrove—"

They looked at each other and both released a nervous chuckle. "My apologies," she said. "Please, what were you going to say?"

"Merely that I am most pleased to have found you well. I feared after your sudden departure from London, and Lord Hawksmoor's despicable actions, that I might find you more distraught. Ruination by someone of such ill repute must be a lady's worst fear. To see it perpetrated upon someone as innocent as you, well, I thought to find you in a state of much distress."

Was it her imagination, or was he disappointed that she was not? "I am not one given to wallowing in the past, Major Gibbons. Besides, it was only a kiss, nothing more. I refuse to spend my days moping over what I cannot control or change. And I did not leave London specifically due to what had transpired at the Dunhills'. I left London as my purpose for being there—to hire a new housekeeper for Northill—had been completed."

A bit of a lie, but not much of one. She *had* completed her purpose and would have left within the week to return home at any rate.

Major Gibbons patted her hand where it rested on his forearm, steering them onto an alternate path that was an offshoot from the one that would take her home. She opened her mouth to say something, but he spoke over her, cutting her off.

"Forgive me. I do not mean to imply you were in any way at fault. Of course, the fault lies with Lord Hawksmoor. The man should be flogged for what he did to you. Obviously, he and his brother are cut from the same cloth."

"Whatever do you mean?" Again, the hair prickled at the nape of her neck and she had the sudden urge to pull away from Major Gibbons. If he did not still have his hand covering hers, holding it against his arm, she would have.

"Oh, come now, Miss Cosgrove." He gave her a knowing look. "I am well aware of what the late Lord Hawksmoor was capable of, and of what he had in store for you."

"I beg your pardon?" Madalene tried to pull her arm away but he held her fast. Her heart picked up speed and fear began to edge its way in as the pathway they were on was swallowed up by a band of trees that led out to the main road. At the end, a carriage had stopped. She thought to call out to them, but the rider was not in his box.

Major Gibbons continued on, taking no apparent notice of her sudden distress. "Lord Hawksmoor—the current one—has such an affection for you, did you know?"

Madalene did not bother to answer as she searched through the trees to find the driver of the carriage. Had he stopped to answer a call of nature? Where was he? They had picked up speed. She glanced behind her. Their boots had left tracks in the newly fallen snow. Why did this bring her relief?

Major Gibbons continued on, speaking as if they were having a pleasant conversation. "That was the reason his brother chose you as our next target, you see. To teach his sanctimonious brother a lesson after he attempted to turn their parents against him over the unfortunate incident with Lady Rothbury. The late earl mocked me, knowing he would get to you first, given his close proximity and access to you. It was an unfair advantage I was less than pleased about, but he underestimated his younger brother's need to protect you and it spelled his end. I, however, will not make the same mistake."

His words filled her veins with icy fear and each beat of her heart spread the terror throughout her body. Major Gibbons was *Lord T*? How could that be?

"What are you talking about?" She managed to yank her hand free and turned to run toward the carriage, but he grabbed her by the shoulders and spun her back to face him.

"We will marry of course."

"Marriage? Are you mad?" But, of course, he was. His madness was buried a bit deeper than Phillip's had been, but it was there. She saw it now and wondered how she had ever missed it. A gleam of malevolence, the same as she had seen in Phillip's eyes the night he had attacked her.

"I will be looked upon as your savior. I will have stolen you from both Lord Hawksmoors and, once you are mine, I will do with you what I wish and no law will be able to stop me. As my wife, you will be my property. Mine for all time. You see, unlike the late Lord Hawksmoor, I do not plan on ending you, not immediately at least. I prefer to take my time. To savor my victory."

Fear overtook her and brought with it the desperate need to survive. She wrenched free from him but when she opened her mouth to scream in the hopes the driver of the carriage would come to her aid, Major Gibbons struck her hard with his fist, knocking her to the ground. Stunned, she could not move as her head spun. Then something was held over her nose and mouth. She struggled, but with each breath the world grew darker until it drifted far beyond her reach.

L ord Huntsleigh caught up with Hawk by the time he was a few hours from reaching Northill. More familiar with the area, he'd taken several shortcuts that would have served Hawk well had he waited for Huntsleigh in the beginning. But fear had made waiting an impossibility. He needed to reach Madalene before Gibbons did.

Neither he, nor Huntsleigh, had bothered with a carriage,

instead opting for the speed of horse and rider. At each opportunity, they'd exchanged horses for fresh ones, whether at inns along the way, or farms they came upon. At one such stop; he'd practically threatened to burn a man's barn down if he did not hand over a fresh horse. This is where Huntsleigh found him, nearly out of his mind with panic as he explained the situation. The earl's charm managed to smooth things over and soon they were on their way once again.

To no avail.

"What do you mean she is not here?" Hawk's words echoed throughout the entrance hall, bouncing off the marble floors and ricocheting against the paneled walls.

"What is this racket about?" Mr. Bowen appeared at the top of the stairs, his eyebrows lifting when his gaze set upon Hawk's companion. "Spence? What the devil?"

Huntsleigh did not waste time, explaining the importance of finding Madalene with all due haste. "Is she here, Bowen?"

Bowen rushed down the stairs, barking questions with each step. "Andrews, have you seen her? Where's Blackbourne?"

"Lord Blackbourne is at the stables, sir. Mr. Cosgrove offered to show him your new stallion, Ares. As for Miss Cosgrove, I saw her earlier, but—" The butler faltered and his face paled. Before he spoke, Hawk knew what he would say. Gibbons had already gotten to her.

"But what, Andrews?"

"An officer arrived; Major Gibbons was his name. He requested to see her. I let her know. She seemed surprised, but it was clear she was familiar with the man. She told me she would go to him."

"And did she?" Hawk asked. But, of course, she had. Why wouldn't she? She had no idea the monster she dealt with.

"Yes, my lord."

"Do you know where either of them is now?"

Andrews swallowed. "I...I did not care for her to be with him in the room without the benefit of a chaperone, given the damage already done to her reputation." He glared at Hawk. Under different circumstances Hawk may have responded to such an inference, but bigger matters were at hand.

"What did you do about it?"

"I may have lurked near the doorway, sir. That is when I heard Major Gibbons request that she take a walk with him outside. That there was a matter he wished to discuss with her."

Hawk pinched the bridge of his nose. This grew worse by the second. "Please tell me she took a chaperone on this walk with her."

"She did not."

Hawk opened his eyes and glanced behind the butler. Mrs. Cleary lurked near the door that led to the dining room, her hands fisted together and pressed into her stomach.

Mr. Bowen stepped forward. "What do you know, Mrs. Cleary?"

"I suggested accompanying her, sir, truly I did. But she was adamant that she did not require such. She promised they would stay in the open along the pathway where everyone could see them. I suspected he might have had a mind to declare his intentions given he had come all this way, though Miss Cosgrove did not seem happy at the prospect."

"If Major Gibbons is as deranged as his sister believes," Huntsleigh said. "He is not likely to take her rejection well."

Bile curdled Hawk's stomach. "Nor will he allow it to be an obstacle to his intentions for her."

"Did you check the steward's house? Perhaps she sent Major Gibbons on his way and simply returned home," Mrs. Cleary suggested, her voice hopeful, though the wringing of her hands brought Hawk little comfort.

Huntsleigh shook his head. "That was our first stop. The

house is empty save for the maid who indicated neither Mr. nor Miss Cosgrove have been home since the early morning hours."

Mr. Bowen issued orders like a well-seasoned general. "Andrews, send word to Cosgrove and arrange to have fresh horses saddled and brought to the front of the house. Mrs. Cleary, inform my wife what has occurred and do your best to keep her from fretting. Tell her it is under control."

Hawk wished such were true.

Mr. Bowen turned his attention to Hawk as Mrs. Cleary re-appeared briefly with her employer's heavy coat. "You know Major Gibbons better than the rest of us. What do you think his plan is?"

Hawk forced the fear to the back of his mind. He needed to keep a clear head. Madalene's life depended upon it.

"His letter indicates whatever he plans for her will be done within the parameters of the law, keeping him safe from prosecution. I can only guess his first order of business will be to marry her. As his wife, he will have carte blanche to do whatever he pleases." A factor his brother had never bothered with, considering himself above the law.

"He will not be able to force a marriage here. They will need to leave the area, perhaps he plans a run to Gretna Green," Huntsleigh suggested.

Hawk nodded. "Likely, but with nightfall so close, he'll never make it. He'll need to stop somewhere until first light."

A cold burst of air hit Hawk in the back and he turned around to see Lord Blackbourne enter the home. He looked at the three of them and stiffened immediately, his expression growing dark as if he sensed the weight of what had happened. Mr. Bowen quickly brought him up to date on events.

"An inn will be too risky," Hawk said. "It would afford Miss Cosgrove the ability to enlist assistance in breaking free. He'll look for somewhere else. Somewhere more secluded."

The butler spoke up once more. "Major Gibbons indicated he had made arrangements to stay at a nearby cabin that was rather rustic in nature."

"The hunting cabin," Blackbourne stated. "It is in the direction he'll need to head. Do you know if he has any familiarity with the area?"

"The man consults with the Prime Minister on matters of strategy." Hawk said, the reality of what they were up against —what Madalene was up against—sat like a heavy stone in his gut. "Likely he has a cleverly calculated plan to ensure his success."

Blackbourne slapped his gloves against the palm of his hand. "Well, then we must ensure his failure, hm? Let's go, men. We have a lady to save."

Hawk watched the men file out the door one by one, and brought up the rear. It appeared he was not in this fight alone. An odd yet ultimately comforting sensation. He had not expected to have men at arms ready to fight the battle with him, but he did not argue their dedication to the cause. If he meant to stop Gibbons before he did harm to Madalene, Hawk would need all the help he could get.

He only hoped they weren't already too late.

Chapter Twenty-Three

Madalene's head pounded as her brain attempted to break free of her skull. She tried to open her eyes but even that was too much. Instead, she moved to press her hands against the sides of her head, only to discover her wrists were bound together in front of her.

Surprise froze her and fear rippled through as the memory of what had happened drifted back in spurts and starts. She had been walking with Major Gibbons, certain he intended to declare his affections and possibly propose. But things changed. Major Gibbons changed. His affable manner took a dark turn. She'd tried to run, to call for help and he'd hit her.

She moved just enough to let her fingers gingerly touch her cheekbone where it throbbed. Pain lanced through her and she drew in a sharp breath, swallowing it just as quickly so as not to let Major Gibbons know she had awakened.

Where was he?

She listened for any clue. Something across the room. A fire crackling. Warmth pressed against her, pushing out the chill. The fire must have been burning for some time. How long had she been unconscious?

She opened her eyes to slits. The room was shrouded in shadows. The sun's descent from the sky almost complete. Dim light permeated the room from two lit candles set on a small table. They were in a cabin. Rustic, but obviously used recently, as it was devoid of the dust and cobwebs one would expect from somewhere abandoned by its occupants.

"Ah, I see you have awakened my dear. My apologies for the abrupt end to our conversation earlier, but I did not want to risk you causing a scene and bringing the entire household running to your aid. Such an outburst was completely unnecessary. You are in no true danger, after all."

The rope binding her wrists together said otherwise, but she refrained from arguing. She needed to gather as much information as possible so that she might devise a plan to get to safety. She swallowed back the fear rising in her throat. She couldn't allow herself to be overcome.

"Where are we?"

"A hunting cabin. Lord Blackbourne's to be exact. Perfect little place for hiding out until morning light, don't you think?"

She did not. She did not want to hide out, or do anything, with this man. She just wanted to go home. To find Hawk. To tell him she was sorry for refusing him and that yes, yes, she wanted his protection. What she would not give to have him envelop her in his arms and keep her warm and safe.

She had been so determined to have his love, not his protection. Pride had made her a blind fool. His dedication to her, his need to keep her safe—those things had come from his heart. Hawk had seen the danger lurking in broad daylight. He had sensed it where she had not. He understood the madness far better than she, and had dedicated his life to ensuring it never harmed her. Not purely out of guilt, but out of love.

Why hadn't she seen that before? She should have said yes to his proposal. Even if she was uncertain of his love, she had never been uncertain of his loyalty. His friendship. And she certainly did not doubt the passion that had sprung up between them.

She had accused him of rash behavior, but she was no less guilty. Now, her hasty refusal of his proposal meant she might never get the chance to tell him the truth. And the truth was, she could think of no greater future than to be his wife, his confidante, his lover, and his friend. To reveal to him how completely he'd captured her heart. How deeply she loved him. Needed him.

If she did not find a way out of this, Hawk would live the rest of his life steeped in the guilt of not having saved her, without ever understanding the fault was hers. She could not allow that to happen.

"What are your intentions? Why have you brought me here?"

But part of her already knew. She understood enough to know how the game played out.

"I brought you here to end the challenge the late Lord Hawksmoor set down. To become the victor." He crossed the room, which given the size of the cabin took but a few strides, and knelt in front of her. She leaned away from him, hating his nearness. "You do know about the game, do you not?"

"I have some knowledge of it, yes."

"Hm, indeed I suppose you do." Major Gibbons chuckled and Madalene forced herself not to lash out and kick him in the ribs. She had a clear shot, but the heavy quilts he'd thrown over her weighted her legs down and would have slowed her strike, giving him ample time to catch her leg and likely bind those as he had her wrists. She needed to keep her legs free. To let him think her helpless.

Major Gibbons reached out and caught a lock of her hair, twisting it lightly around his finger. The proper bun she'd crafted hours ago had come loose at some point, leaving her hair falling about her shoulders and down her back. She held her breath and kept still, afraid of what he might do if she pulled away or showed her true disgust at his touch.

"Lord Hawksmoor—the first, not the current—was rather ham-fisted in his approach to our challenges. He thought his charm was enough to coax the lady chosen, but honestly, it showed no finesse in my opinion. Once he had her in his thrall, he would simply have his way with her and toss her aside. They always protested his advances, but he claimed to like that part of the game the most. Said it made the thrill all the more potent to feel their fear as he—" He stopped. Perhaps some of her horror had escaped into her expression, she did not know. "Well, enough of that, hm?"

Fury at what the women they'd preyed upon had suffered burned in Madalene's chest. She well remembered the fear, the glee in Phillip's face when she had tried to fight him off. He had originally attempted to charm her, but his efforts had fallen flat. She wanted nothing to do with him after seeing how he treated his younger brother, the man who had won her young heart so completely. Not that Phillip had needed her to be charmed. He called her a throwaway. Said no one would care what happened to her and would likely not even notice when she was gone.

Gone.

He'd had every intention of killing her after he'd had his way. Would he have enlisted Major Gibbons to assist him in disposing of her body? In concocting the belief that she had simply walked out the door one day, never to return? He assumed no one would question her disappearance. But he had not counted on his brother. Hawk would have noticed. He would have known she would have never have left without saying good-bye. He would have looked for her until he had answers.

She knew this in her heart. Had known even then that

something stronger than she had words for bound them together and still did. When she'd called out for help, it had been his name she had yelled. The thought of him finding her lifeless body, tossed in a creek or dumped in the woods had angered her and spurred her to fight harder, but she was no match for Phillip's superior size and strength.

But Hawk was.

He had saved her life by ending his brother's, and then dedicated every day since to finding the other man his brother threatened would come for her. Even after Hawk had been banished from the family home, he'd continued his search for Lord T, the letters sent by Major Gibbons taunting him the entire time.

If this was not an expression of his love for her, his dedication, she did not know what was. Oh, why had she not seen it earlier? What she wouldn't do for one more chance. To change her answer. To tell him she understood.

Major Gibbons snapped his fingers in front of her face causing her to jerk, the curl he had wrapped around his finger pulling at her scalp.

"Are you not listening to me, Miss Cosgrove?" Anger pinched his words and she took a deep breath. She must keep him calm.

"Forgive me. I feel a bit heavy headed."

He released her curl and cupped her face, his thumb brushing over her bruised cheekbone. She winced and he smiled, but there was no apology in the expression. "Then rest, my dear. I will want you in proper form for our wedding night."

"Wedding night?" Was he serious? Did he think she would actually go through with such a thing?

He leaned in, his breath brushing against her skin causing her to recoil. "Yes, As I stated earlier, I do not have the same protections as a Peer of the Realm, so I must go about things a little differently. I have a future to protect, after all. As my wife, under the law you will belong to me."

He grinned and his eyes lit up with a sickening mixture of madness and self-importance. "Brilliant, isn't it? Oh, I am certain the late Lord Hawksmoor is positively spinning in his grave over it. He always told me my methods lacked spontaneity and panache, but I prefer the well thought out scenario. It has a certain finesse that his bullish ways always lacked."

True fear sliced through her veins as he stood and returned to the woodstove to stoke the fire. How long had he been planning this? Months? Years? She didn't realize she had asked the question aloud until he turned around to answer.

"I have known you were working at Northill for several months. I have little birds that whisper their secrets to me. When I learned Hawksmoor was brought there after that foolishness with Lord Pengrin, the serendipity of it all was almost too much to believe. It was as if fate was telling me the time had come. I journeyed from London and came here, searched out the area for the perfect hiding place, the best route to take us to Gretna Green—"

"Gretna Green?"

He looked at her and chuckled. "I cannot risk a lengthy engagement, I'm afraid. You have a habit of declining suitors and I am quite set upon seeing us wed."

Her stomach heaved. He had thought of everything.

He continued on as if his intentions were perfectly normal. "I was set to put my plan into action while Lord Hawksmoor convalesced. Imagine my excitement over the prospect of snatching you right out from under the nose of the great man known as *The Hawk*." Major Gibbons turned his hands into claws, his fingers curling into long talons. "But alas, you went off to London and I was forced to bide my time, alter my tactics somewhat. Though I am grateful for the delay as it gave me the opportunity to get to know you first. And I must admit, that has made my victory all the sweeter."

"But why me? You did not have an argument with the current Lord Hawksmoor. Why not simply let the matter go?"

He laughed and dropped his arms to his side. "Because you were the chosen quarry. And where the late earl had failed to win the contest, I will not. I will win this final challenge and claim myself the ultimate victor. I will put to bed his arrogant belief that I could never best him and I shall do so in spectacular fashion, taking his own game to a whole new level. That the current Lord Hawksmoor should suffer as a result, is simply icing upon the cake." He stalked toward her as if she were his prey and knelt at the bedside once more. "I have waited patiently for this moment, my dear. And it was a moment that was not easy to come by, I might add. You are a hard lady to keep track of, with all your moving about over the years. But I have you now and you *will* be mine."

"You cannot force me to marry you, not even at Gretna Green." At least she did not think so. She had heard stories of people running off there and being married, but both had been willing participants. Surely, whomever it was that joined the couples in matrimony would not do so if both were not amenable to the union.

Major Gibbons' smile froze on his face. She had once thought him charming, but no longer. Now, the madness had taken over, changing features that had once seemed friendly into something darker and far more sinister. He had hidden his madness much better than Hawk's older brother ever had. She'd seen no hint of it before this day. Had Hawk? Had he suspected? He'd disliked the major on sight. Had some part of him recognized the madness even if he didn't realize what he was looking at?

"You will have little choice, my dear. If you do not, you will be completely ruined in a far worse way than Lord

Hawksmoor's ill-thought-out kiss at the Dunhills'. Why, likely no one will remember that by next month. And if they do, it will be his actions they recall and not the insignificant chit that was the recipient. But they will remember you spent the night alone with me in a secluded cabin and they will know what we did while we were here."

His threat did not faze her. Utter ruination was nothing compared to being married to this lunatic. Despite his claim that he had carefully thought out his plan, it still had several gaping holes that his arrogance had not allowed him to see. Did he honestly think anyone present at this marriage ceremony would allow him to hurt her if she refused him? If she could keep a level head, make him think her too meek to fight him; she stood a chance at escaping once they reached Gretna Green.

He trailed his fingertips down her jaw and neck, not stopping until it reached the fichu tucked into her bodice. Revulsion lanced through her as he pulled lightly at the gauzy material, a sick smile playing about his lips.

"You are quite a vision, Miss Cosgrove. My adversary chose well, I will give him that much. I shall much enjoy making you mine over and over again. You quite overwhelm me and I cannot claim I will be able to control myself and make it gentle for you."

"Don't," she said, the fear that shook her voice true and real, filling her mind with horrible images of what he might do. But how did she stop him? Her hands were bound and he had at least three stone on her, maybe more. Even if she were able to break free, where would she go? She did not even know where she was and the cloak she'd worn when she left Northill's main house was not in sight. Escape would send her out into the cold. She'd freeze to death before she ever found her way back to civilization. "Please. If we are to marry, I would prefer to come to you as a maiden on our wedding night."

He lifted his hand and stared at her a moment. Madalene struggled to hide her disgust. "It would make the victory more pleasurable, wouldn't it?"

She swallowed against the knot of fear lodged in her throat, but it refused to budge.

"Very well then," Major Gibbons said, pushing to his feet. "We shall wait. The anticipation will only heighten the reward, wouldn't you agree?"

She didn't answer but waited until he turned away before she buried her face in the feather pillow, allowing it to absorb the tears filling her eyes. The thought of this man's touch was inconceivable. She belonged to another.

She belonged to Hawk.

"How much farther?" Irritation masked the fear in Hawk's voice as he asked the question for what had to be the tenth time. It seemed they had been riding through the white landscape for days instead of hours. The fact that his jaw throbbed as if he'd been hit with an iron bar did nothing to improve his mood one iota.

Though if he expected an apology from Mr. Cosgrove, he would be waiting until hell froze over. Apparently, Bowen's steward considered it well within his rights to haul a Peer of the Realm off his horse and plant his fist into said lord's face.

For a one-armed man, he had an appalling amount of strength and agility. It had been a good hour before Hawk's head cleared well enough to allow him to start questioning how much longer he would be stuck on this damnable horse before they reached their destination. Only Bowen's calm intervention, suggesting to Cosgrove that if Hawk were knocked senseless, they would be down a man, was enough to ward off a second blow. For the time being, at least.

The men had split up. Bowen and Huntsleigh had gone off in one direction toward town in case Gibbons was foolish enough to try and hide her in plain sight, while he, Blackbourne and Madalene's father made the journey to the hunting cabin situated in the hills that separated the Blackbourne property from the Ellesmere lands.

"Not too far now," Blackbourne answered, his tone grim. The words did nothing to calm the growing dread in Hawk's gut.

The sun had dipped below the horizon, the last of the day's light extinguished, leaving behind only the glow of the moon against the pristine snow to light their way. They avoided the copse of trees that dotted the area, though normally taking the pathways through them would have saved time. But Blackbourne had indicated traversing the woods was folly as they had but one lantern amongst them and risked injury should their horses falter amongst the roots and rocks that dotted the way.

The extra time gnawed at Hawk's gut and he cursed each extra moment that separated him from Madalene. He refused to even contemplate the possibility she would not be at the cabin. She had to be. It was the only solution that made sense. He doubted a man with the strategic mind of Gibbons would ride into town where anyone could recognize her, where she could call out for help. And he had not allowed himself enough daylight to escape through the woods. But what if mention of the cabin had only been a ruse? What if he had taken another direction entirely?

He had to believe the man had built his plan based on his surroundings. That he had scouted the area around Northill. Such forethought on Gibbons' part did nothing to bring

Hawk any ease. The man had been planning this for years, the taunts in his letters a clear indication of his intent to not let the challenge go unfinished.

Fear, cold and unabated, whispered on the breeze that ruffled his hair and sent a chill down his spine.

Gibbons must have been searching for her all these years, but Madalene's constant moving around made her an elusive target. At least for the major. Gibbons may have a gift for strategy, but Hawk had excelled at gathering information. He smiled at the frustration this must have filled Gibbons with, his quarry flitting about like a firefly, leaving a trail of light that would fade before he could follow it to her new destination.

Hawk had kept a close eye on her from afar, only feeling a sense of relief once she and her father had come to Northill. Bowen would not allow any harm to come to her, of that he was certain. It brought him some comfort. Allowed him to go about his business without constant worry. He had been determined not to see her, regardless of how much he longed to. He did not want to risk leading Lord T to her. But Pengrin's attempt to kill him had put an end to that. Or perhaps it had been a sign fate wished them to collide once more.

This time, however, he had no intentions of letting her go despite the debacle of his proposal. God, he had made such a muck of it. Not that he didn't want to protect her. He did. But not out of duty. He wanted to protect her—no, was *compelled* to—because he loved her. Because every minute of his life after he'd lost her had been empty and void of meaning. Because every woman he'd met after knowing her paled in comparison and was found lacking. Because he was meant to be with her.

Until Phillip's actions made that impossible. In one horrible night, he'd lost her forever. To be with her meant putting her in danger, something he could not risk. But fate had other plans it seemed, ensuring their paths intersected once more. The moment her soft lips had brushed against his mouth and she'd whispered his name his heart knew, even when every other memory eluded him, his heart somehow *knew*. She was his. And he was and would always be hers.

Blackbourne held up a hand and Hawk and Cosgrove pulled up on the reins.

"Over there." He pointed upward over the tops of the trees in the distance where the dark sky was interrupted by a curl of smoke reaching toward the stars.

Relief swept through Hawk. They had guessed correctly. Gibbons and Madalene were at the cabin. But the fear did not leave him. When they reached her, what would they find? Had he touched her? Harmed her? Killed—

Hawk stopped the thought before it finished. He would not allow it. She could not be dead. They could not have endured all of this only to lose each other now.

He turned in his saddle to face Cosgrove. "Sir, I should inform you that when we rescue your daughter, I have every intention of marrying her."

Blackbourne turned around in his seat. "Are you mad? You want to have this conversation with the lady's father now?"

"I think he should know my intentions." Hawk turned back to Cosgrove who had yet to utter a word since socking him in the jaw. "I realize I am far from worthy of her, but I love her and it can't be helped. Once she is safe, I plan on convincing her that we are meant to be together."

"I see." Cosgrove lifted one snowy white eyebrow. "And how do you plan on doing that?"

Hawk's shoulders slumped. "I have not entirely figured that part out yet."

His love's father gave a slow nod. "Then I suppose we best

make our way to the cabin, retrieve her from that bastard, and see what we might do about your plans."

Blackbourne shook his head. "You're all madmen," he muttered.

Hawk nudged his horse onward, glancing at his old friend as he rode past him. "Might I remind you, Blackbourne, the lengths you went through to secure your bride despite being affianced to another?"

Blackbourne scowled. "Suppose we stop talking and see about saving the young lady as Cosgrove suggests. Head this way," he said pointing toward the trees. "We'll hobble the horses and go the rest of way on foot so as not to alert him to our presence."

To say walking through the shin deep snow was a cold endeavor did not do the enterprise justice. His feet had lost all feeling save for an intense burning that he was certain did not bode well. But it was a small price to pay if they were able to reach the cabin and ensure Madalene's safety.

Chapter Twenty-Four

Madalene tried to keep her eyes open, but continually lost the battle despite her best efforts. Only unfamiliar sounds would catch her unaware and jerk her back to wakefulness, bringing with it a rush of terror as she was reminded of her whereabouts and the major's intentions. She could not say what the sound was that awakened her this time. She lifted her head, her pillow damp from her tears, and searched the tiny cabin. Major Gibbons snored lightly from his position near the woodstove. He'd pulled an armchair close to the fire and thrown a blanket over his torso, leaving his legs stretched outward. Was it his snoring that had disturbed her sleep?

Another sound caught her attention. The snort of their horses in the lean-to stable outside. Had they heard an animal creeping about? What would happen if the horses were attacked? She had toyed with the idea of sneaking out of the cabin and using the horse to ride to safety. But she had quickly set that idea aside once the sun had set and left the landscape shrouded in darkness. Besides, her hands remained bound, making riding impossible.

Another snort.

Major Gibbons stirred, drawing in a deep breath before shifting slightly in his chair. The candles on the table continued to burn, but would soon reach the end of their wick, smothering the last of their light. The fire in the wood-stove burned, its glow reaching out through the narrow grate in the door but going no farther than the tip of Major Gibbons' boots. If she decided to make a run for it, the chances of her reaching the door without stumbling over something and awakening her captor were slim. Slimmer still were her chances of surviving a night in the cold without benefit of a coat.

Her only hope was to wait until daylight and then—

One of the horses neighed louder this time, enough to awaken Major Gibbons. He sat upright and tossed aside the blanket that covered him, reaching beneath his chair for his pistol.

"Come here." He motioned to her, but she didn't move. She would offer him no assistance. Goosebumps shivered down her spine. Something was happening, she could sense it, though whether good or bad she could not say.

Major Gibbons crossed the room in three angry strides and grabbed her arm, hauling her to her feet. A sharp cry escaped her as the door burst open, bringing with it a cold burst of frigid air.

Major Gibbons spun her about to face the door, the muzzle of the pistol pressed harshly against her cheek. A dark silhouette filled the empty space where the door had been and though the candles did not cast enough light to reveal their sudden visitor, it wasn't necessary. Madalene would know that frame anywhere.

Hawk.

He had kept his promise. He would protect her.

"Good evening, Major. I was in the area and thought I might come by for a visit."

Major Gibbons' arm tightened around her waist. It was clear he had not expected to be found out. So sure he had been in his abilities to best Hawk and win this godforsaken challenge, it never once entered his mind that he would be discovered, let alone thwarted. The sudden change threw his well-crafted plan into chaos and his sputtering nonsensical words made it clear he did not excel at changing course without notice and forethought.

"Not another step, Hawksmoor." The muzzle pressed harder against her cheekbone and Madalene stifled a whimper that threatened to escape. She would not give him the satisfaction, nor allow her fear to temper Hawk's actions. She needed him to be *The Hawk* now. To swoop down upon her captor and dig his sharp talons in deep and without mercy.

"That's quite inhospitable of you, Gibbons. Is this the type of manners they teach you where you are from? Tsk."

Hawk ignored her captor's instructions and took another step forward, moving deeper into the cabin. He was close enough now that the candlelight's glow danced with the shadows that covered his face. The play of light and dark gave him the appearance of an avenging angel, but likely it was more of the Devil that Major Gibbons would see this night. Just as Phillip had all those years ago when he'd tried to harm her.

A strange calm entered her. When Phillip had attacked her, she'd called for Hawk, knowing he would protect her and keep her safe. A certainty that had not diminished to this day, no matter how much she had asked him to give it up. Let it go.

He hadn't. And she had never loved him more for ignoring her insistence in that regard.

The muzzle pressed against her skin moved and pointed outward, aimed at Hawk's head. "Another step and I will finish the job Pengrin failed at, and I assure you, I am a much better marksman than he."

A low chuckle rumbled across the distance separating them. "Really? Again? All of these threats to put a bullet in my head are becoming quite tedious."

The window near the stove exploded in a shatter and Major Gibbons swung his arm wide, firing a shot toward the unexpected disturbance. Madalene recognized the voice on the other side pouring forth a series of curse words—the inventive phrasing clearly belonging to her father. Hawk used the distraction to lunge forward, tackling both she and Major Gibbons to the floor. Madalene quickly rolled away as the two men regained their feet, the sound of flesh hitting flesh echoed behind her as she scurried toward the poker resting near the stove.

Father and another man—Lord Blackbourne?—rushed in as Madalene swung the poker in a wide arc and brought it down upon Major Gibbons head. For a brief second, everyone froze, then Hawk punched him and her captor staggered once before falling forward, unconscious.

Madalene dropped the poker and jumped over Major Gibbons, launching herself into Hawk's waiting arms.

"You came! Oh, thank God, you came for me!"

He cupped her face and kissed her, his lips landing on every curve and crevice before pulling her tightly against his chest, enveloping her with his strong arms. "Of course, I did. I promised, did I not? Never doubt the resolve of a man deeply in love, my dear."

His words rushed through her, straight to her heart, chasing away the fear and filling it with everything she had ever dreamed of, all she had ever wanted since the first moment she'd set eyes upon the handsome lord.

Her father interrupted their sweet reunion. "Lord Hawksmoor, if you would please release my daughter. I'll not have you taking such liberties. Lord Blackbourne, your knife please." As Lord Blackbourne complied with Father's request, the expression on Hawk's face turned from relief to trepidation.

"Sir, there is no need to resort to violence," Hawk said as Father approached. "As I stated, I have every intention of marrying your daughter if she will have me." Hawk's voice rose in emphasis the closer Father came, the knife brandished in his hand, but Madalene could only laugh, understanding her father's purpose and holding out her hands to allow him to cut her free.

"See that you do," Father told him, the sternness in his voice not enough to disguise the irrefutable fact that he was behind the union wholeheartedly. The time he had spent with Hawk while at Northill had allowed him to see the side of him Madalene had fallen in love with.

Father winked at her before embracing her tightly and placing a kiss upon the top of her head before releasing her. He returned the knife to Lord Blackbourne, taking hold of the earl's pistol and slipping it into the sheath at his side.

"No! She belongs to me!"

Madalene whipped her head around in time to see Major Gibbons launch to his feet and run toward her. Hawk grabbed her and spun her out of the way as a shot reverberated throughout the small cabin, ringing in her ears.

Gibbons dropped to the ground like a stone.

Father lowered his arm, disrupting the wisp of smoke escaping the muzzle of the pistol he held in his hand. He stared in silence at the unmoving body on the floor. Years of wartime had taught him to act from instinct. How grateful Madalene was that he had not lost such a skill.

"You killed him," Hawk said, but Madalene heard no regret in the statement, only relief.

"That is what we do when animals go mad," Father said, his voice steady and sure. "It is the humane thing."

A look passed between him and Hawk, a knowing that went beyond the moment and reached into the past, through the understanding of what it meant to take a life, to do the unthinkable when no other option existed. To do what needed to be done to protect the ones they loved.

"Yes," Hawk answered. "I suppose it is."

"If I might have my pistol back, Mr. Cosgrove," Lord Blackbourne said, reaching his hand out. "I believe it will be best if the authorities do not feel the need to question who fired it."

Hawk pulled Madalene more tightly against him and pressed his lips against her temple. For the first time in forever she felt his body relax as if his demons had finally been put to rest. She wrapped her arms around his waist, safe and secure and exactly where she belonged.

"I love you," she whispered, not caring who heard.

"And I you." Then he dipped his head and whispered in her ear, "And I plan on showing you the depth and breadth of just how much, by making you my wife, if you are agreeable to such a union."

Her heart swelled and as his lips teased the curve of her ear, she smiled. "We should hasten that along as quickly as possible, my lord."

A warm chuckle rumbled in his chest and seeped into her heart. "Indeed, we should, my love. Indeed, we should."

Epilogue

"I have to say, I was surprised it was not Lord Tunsten," Madalene said, stretching her arms above her head, relishing the feel of her bare skin moving against Hawk's. Was there anything more glorious? She did not think so.

"Were you," her husband said, the words murmuring from him. She had quite exhausted him this evening, or so he claimed. She, on the other hand, felt quite invigorated.

"Yes, I had been certain if Lord T did exist, that he would be the one, to be honest. He is a rather vile man."

They had spoken little about the events of the past month, immersing themselves in planning a quick wedding, helped along by Mr. Bowen and Lord Blackbourne who assisted in their getting a special license. Lady Rebecca along with Lady Blackbourne and Lady Huntsleigh went about the actual planning of the event, joined by Lady Glenmor once she and her husband returned from Maple Glen. Madalene had been left with little to do but to shake her head as these titled ladies busied themselves with the wedding of a servant to a viscount as if it was the most natural thing in the world.

And indeed, it had been. For being Hawk's wife could not have been more natural. She was meant for him, and he for her. It no longer mattered where she came from or where he had been. They loved each other with such completeness, all the rest simply faded away. Miss Marianne Caldwell was thrilled to relay how the members of the ton were shocked and scandalized by the union, though she suspected their reaction was more about jealousy that she had tamed the infamous *Hawk* and he had claimed her as his own.

Marianne Caldwell, Madalene learned, was a complete and utter romantic.

"Well," Hawk said, rolling over in bed and bringing her back to the present. "The sot still owes me a large sum of money which I intend to collect, if that is any consolation."

Madalene reached out a hand and traced her new husband's collarbone, stopping when she reached the hollow at the base of his throat before moving downward. "Not particularly. Do you truly plan on selling your interest in The Devil's Lair?"

"Yes." He lifted one eyebrow as her hand trailed down his chest and continued on, but he made no move to stop her. She had married a very smart man. "It has served its purpose. And I tire of living in those dark little apartments like some troll under a bridge." She would take his word for it, for he had not allowed her to enter the premises. Instead, they made use of the dower house on Lord Blackbourne's estate for the time being, as his mother now resided with her new husband at Havelock Manor.

Madalene laughed lightly, amazed at the light and love he had brought to her life, filling it until all of the darkness that lurked in its edges had been burned away. She leaned in and pressed her lips against his. "You are hardly a troll. You are far too handsome."

"Am I?"

"Yes."

"How handsome?"

She lifted herself up on her elbow. "Oh, handsome enough."

He kissed the edge of her jaw and her need for him, satiated less than an hour before, built again. "Careful, pet. You might inflate my ego to such a degree there will be no living with me."

"It is a little too late for that, now that I have committed myself to you for the duration of my life."

"Or mine. And given the way people seem to like pointing firearms at me, mine may end up being the shorter one."

She scowled down at him, her blond hair brushing against his chest. "What a horrible thought."

H awk reached up and tucked her hair behind her ear. It slid through his fingers like silk. "Isn't it, though? Perhaps I should try to erase it from your mind."

"And how do you propose to do that?" She gifted him with one of her special smiles. The one that pierced his heart and filled it with wonder. Farther down, other parts of his anatomy stirred to life once again, demanding their due as her bare skin brushed against his. He nuzzled the sweet curve of her neck and breathed her in. He would never get enough of her.

"Oh, I have my ways, pet. I have my ways."

Hawk nipped at her ear lobe, then pulled her into a deep kiss that solidified his need to have her once again. He shifted, turning and pulling her delectable little body beneath him in one swift movement. She let out a squeal, then a laugh, and he was quite certain he had never heard anything quite so enchanting. Nor had he ever experienced such jubilation as she wrapped her legs around him and he found her as ready for him as he was for her.

Still, prolonging the pleasure did have its virtues. He kissed her once more, losing himself in the softness of her lips, the hunger of her mouth, the way she pushed her hips against his hardness until he promptly forgot whatever virtues there were to be found in delaying such pleasure.

She sighed, deep and lovely, as he pressed inside of her. He remained still, holding her body against his as he breathed her in. "It is completely impossible for me to love you more than I do in this moment," he whispered.

"Is it?" The words came in gasps, one at a time. And then it was his turn as she pressed her hips against him, taking him more fully into her. "What about now?"

"Forgive me," he said. "It seems I underestimated my capacity for loving you."

She wiggled and somewhere stars exploded in his brain. "And now?"

"Sweet heaven. If you keep this up, woman, there will be nothing left of me."

"You said that the last time," his minx of a wife said, whispering the words against his mouth. "And yet it appears all of your parts remain in perfect working order."

She traced his lip with the tip of her tongue and every last bit of restraint he had gave itself over to the need burning inside of him.

"Kiss me," she commanded and he obeyed, willfully, completely until everything else ceased to exist but this room and this bed and this woman and this love that had grown and flourished over the years into everything he had ever dreamed of and more.

And then he moved inside of her and she moved with him and the sense of never belonging anywhere became a distant memory, because he did belong somewhere. He belonged here, with her, and it was the best place in the world to be for there was nothing—and no one—left to separate them.

She was his wife. His forever.

And he was hers.

A Sneak Peek

THE SWEETEST SIN

"I will ruin you."

Lady Henrietta Harrow stared into the pinched face only inches from her own. Hatred burned in Lady Susan St. John's eyes with such vitriol Hen had no response to her issued threat. How did one react to such a pledge? Inquiring further appeared her only option.

"I beg your pardon?"

This was Hen's fifth ball of the new Season and thus far, she had managed to avoid Lady Susan by hiding amongst the plants or lingering in the shadows. Not the bravest thing to do, but unlike her friend, Patience Elmsley, Hen did not have the gumption to dump sweet punch over the young lady's head. No matter how much she may have wanted to.

Instead, she took to avoiding Lady Susan and her constant belittling, a method that had thus far proven relatively successful. At least until her great-aunt insisted she was parched and sent Hen out into the vast wasteland of the ballroom to fetch a glass of punch. A ruse, of course. What Lady Dalridge truly wanted was for her great-niece to quit lingering in the shadows and go out amongst the other ladies and lords as if she belonged there.

Easy for Auntie to say. She was not the one with scars littering one side of her body. Scars that even her best efforts could not conceal completely. The flames that had left the marks had, after all, cared nothing about fashion and therefore felt well within their rights to crawl up the right side of her neck instead of staying discreetly beneath her collar. Her only recourse to cover them was to leave her hair hanging down over her shoulder. A style neither fashionable nor subtle, and a constant reminder in case their existence should happen to slip her mind.

As if such a thing were possible.

"You heard me," Lady Susan said, her voice shooting out like a hissing snake with eyes narrowed to complete the impression. "I am going to ruin you."

Each word came enunciated with harsh purpose making it impossible for Hen to hold onto the hope she may have misunderstood. A foolish hope that was. The moment Lady Susan marched toward her like a general going into battle, forcing Hen back into a corner she could not get out of, she knew she was in for it.

Her stomach sank. Lady Susan had a bee in her bonnet ever since Hen had befriended Judith Sutherland, now Lady Glenmor. Judith had been a previous recipient of Lady Susan's special brand of venom and when Hen had stood by her friend's side, well, that had put her, too, in Lady Susan's crosshairs. Now with Judith married, it appeared she was to be this Season's prime target. Lovely.

She let out a long sigh. Perhaps she should try to get to the root of the issue in the hopes of diffusing it. "Whatever have I done to upset you, Lady Susan?"

Not that it took much to set Lady Susan off. The duke's daughter was a hateful sort on a good day and on a bad day...

"You dare to stand there as if you do not know what you've done?"

Hen had little choice as to where she stood. Lady Susan had, after all, backed her into a corner and now blocked her way. A fact that made it was impossible to escape unless she wished to knock the other woman on her bottom, hike up her skirts, and make a mad dash into the thick of the guests filling the ballroom. And while escape was the ultimate goal, she would prefer to achieve it with far less spectacle.

"I'm afraid I do not know, Lady Susan. If you would have the courtesy of informing me as to what crime you believe I have committed, perhaps we can get on with things. I'm afraid I am in the dark as to what I may have done to you that justifies such threats of ruination."

Lady Susan took a step forward, crowding Hen farther into the corner. She was a few inches taller than Hen, thin and ropey. Perhaps Hen could push past her, but she didn't care to risk it should she be wrong. An angry Lady Susan was an unpredictable entity.

"I hold you responsible for your part in Lord Pengrin's death and I will see that you pay for such."

Thoughts of escape skittered away as something cold and heavy turned over in Hen's stomach. She had done her best to push any thoughts of Lord Pengrin and his treachery into a dark hole best left untouched. Such memories were fraught with pain and humiliation. The viscount had made a fool of her, tricking her into believing he had loved her. That he had seen beyond her scars to the woman beneath. He'd made her believe she had a chance at a normal life. But the man proved nothing more than a charlatan. He had not wanted her at all.

Lady Susan's claims that Lord Pengrin was somehow the injured party left her sputtering in amazement.

"Pay? For what? For misleading me into believing he loved

me so he could use my dowry to pay his gambling debts, then toss me aside?"

"And why wouldn't he toss you aside? Do you truly think anyone else wouldn't have done the same thing? Look at you! You're a scarred little beast. What man could stand to look upon you without losing the contents of his stomach?"

Hen sucked in a shocked breath. Lady Susan had spent the past year making veiled little remarks about Hen's scars, but this was the first direct attack. The words hit hard, cutting deep into the place in her heart that knew such claims were true. She *was* a scarred little beast. A monster in a pretty dress.

Over Lady Susan's shoulder, a few heads turned in their direction. Hen took a steadying breath. She would not make a scene. Nor would she allow Lady Susan to. All she wished for was to end this night as quickly as possible and return home. Away from society's stares and whispers, away from James and Auntie's foolish hopes that she might find a suitable husband, marry and be happy. Away from the memories of what a fool she had been to once believe the same.

Also By Kelly Boyce

THE SINS & SCANDALS SERIES

Book 1: An Invitation to Scandal

Book 2: A Scandalous Passion

Book 3: A Sinful Temptation

Book 4: The Lady's Sinful Secret

Book 5: Surrender to Scandal

Book 6: A Sinner No More

Book 7: The Sweetest Sin

Book 8: A Most Scandalous Christmas

Book 9: A Hint of Scandal

THE BRIDES OF FATAL BLUFF

Book 1: The Outlaw Bride

SALVATION FALLS

Book 1: Salvation in the Rancher's Arms

Dear Readers,

Thank you so much for reading **A SINNER NO MORE**, Book 6 in *The Sins & Scandals Series*. I have been waiting to tell Hawksmoor's story since he was first introduced and I was thrilled to finally get that chance. I hope you enjoyed it!

If **A SINNER NO MORE** is the first book in The Sins & Scandals Series that you have read, I hope you will check out the other books in the series.

For the most updated booklist, check out my **website book page** or sign up for my **Newsletter** at **www.kelly boyce.com.** I send out notifications to all subscribers to let them know when a new release is on its way. Be sure not to miss it!

I love to hear and connect with my readers through social media and email and you can find all of my social media links on my website!

I hope you enjoyed **A SINNER NO MORE** and will consider leaving a review at your favorite online retailer to help others discover **The Sins & Scandals Series!**

Wishing you all the best ~ *Kelly*

Acknowledgments

While writing this book, I also made the foolish decision to also write my next novella for Harlequin Historical at the same time. Needless to say, it made for a bit of a crazy schedule and rocky ride. I will definitely not do that again! So, thanks to all my friends and family, especially to my awesome husband, John, who had the misfortune of having to live with me during that time, for sticking it out and reminding me that everything would turn out just fine. Sorry babe, still no car chase.

A special thanks to those readers who generously took some time out to email me and inquire about Lord Hawksmoor welfare. I hope **A SINNER NO MORE** was worth the wait! He was one of my favorite characters from the minute I introduced him several books back and I couldn't wait to tell his story. I hope you enjoyed reading it as much as I enjoyed writing it!

Thanks to the crew of professionals that help me put this book together: My editor, Nancy Cassidy, Kim Killion (cover designer) and Amy Atwell (formatter) – As always, you ladies rock!

A big shout out to my sister for her ongoing encouragement in the way of threatening texts to hurry up and finish the next book because she can't wait much longer, and to my dad, Garry, who reads my books while sitting in the garage waiting for his car to be fixed and talks up this new author he's discovered. Thanks, Dad!

Anne MacFarlane and Annette Gallant – you ladies are the best. Thanks for keeping me on track with our regular coffee catch ups/goals meetings! And of course, Pam Callow, Cathryn Fox and Julianne MacLean for sharing all your wisdom on the biz!

About the Author

Kelly Boyce started writing stories in Grade 2 when her favorite teacher, Mrs. Matheson, showed up with a box filled with plot ideas and she was immediately hooked. But it wasn't until she read Lisa Gregory's *Bitterleaf* that she fell in love with historical romance. Once she discovered Romance Writers of Atlantic Canada and learned how to turn those stories into books, it was full steam ahead.

A life-long Nova Scotian, Kelly lives near the Atlantic Ocean with her amazing husband and a clownish golden retriever with a stubborn streak a mile wide. She loves writing stories about relationships and creating a sense of community around the hero and heroine filled with secondary characters who take on a life of their own.

Along with *The Sins & Scandals Series*, she has also released several western historical romances with Harlequin. The first two, **The Outlaw Bride** and **Salvation in the Rancher's Arms**, AND **Salvation in the Sheriff's Kiss** will soon be re-released under her own banner; and two Christmas novellas: **The Cowboy of Christmas Past** and **Christmas in Salvation Falls** are still available through Harlequin.

Currently, she is hard at work developing a new three book series on the Lindwell Family, who were introduced in *The Sins & Scandals Series*.

Copyright